RHAPSODY IN RED

Two Novellas of
The Damned

Peter Molnar

ISBN: 978-1-945263-25-5

DEDICATION

This one's for A.J. Brown, a loyal friend, mentor, and one hell of a storyteller!

CONTENTS

THE REMAINDERS: A REVENGE FANTASY

DALLAS TELLER'S KILL LIST

THE REMAINDERS:

A REVENGE-FANTASY

*"Do I really want to be integrated into
a burning house?"*

-*The Fire Next Time*
James Baldwin

I. YOU KNOW THE DRILL

Natalie Kincaid stood in front of her grimy bathroom mirror with the drill bit dimpling a spot just below her hairline and wondered how the hell she was going to do this. In terms of preparation, this was the furthest she had gotten. She'd spread towels all over the bathroom floor. Another hung over the sink. She'd set a pile of gauze pads on top of the toilet, and a fresh roll of medical tape lay on top of that.

All within reach.

She thought of the woman in the United Kingdom who'd performed this same procedure on herself. Of course, in such a crucial moment, Natalie found herself struggling to remember the woman's name.

Amanda Fielding?

Natalie had read everything the internet had to offer about Amanda Fielding, "the woman who drilled a hole in her head to open up her mind." Natalie pored over the history of *trepanation*, both as a medieval form of medicine and, centuries later, as a strange, hip, new alternative to mescaline or peyote. A lifetime high.

Shiva, the Hindu god of altered consciousness, was trepanned.

Monks in Tibet did it to one another.

Natalie had even read about someone in Nigeria in the Sixties who said when he was thirteen years old, the "hip" kids in his village had a shaman trepan them.

"Hip" kids?

"So," she said to her reflection, "this is me being hip."

How strange she appeared, even sans the drill she held to her head. Natalie had shaved her head in preparation for the procedure. The trashcan beside the toilet overflowed with the long, straight, amber hair she'd cut away from her scalp. Her finest attribute, according to friends and acquaintances alike, relegated to the garbage bin. She had already lamented the loss of her hair and stuffed the regret down with the higher purpose for which she'd shaved her

1

head bald in the first place.

I need it back.

My gift.

I must get it back. I'm facing bankruptcy. I'm three months behind on the rent for the shop. The landlord already sent one of her enforcers *around to issue a stern warning, a Big Russian who spoke just enough broken English to scare me. "I have* no problem *putting hurt on a dyke like you!" the Big Russian told me, grinding his right hand into the palm of his left hand. "So you pay!"*

God, if this doesn't work? If this doesn't restore my "sight?"

Then that'll be ballgame.

Still.

At least I'll get to be with Danica again.

This is not to say Natalie hadn't explored other options for restoring her *sight*. She found she did not have to wander far beyond the doorstep of her apartment building in search of mind-altering substances. A meth dealer huddled in an alleyway beside the Thai fast-food joint a half block down the lane, and she bought up enough to sample. Around the corner, Natalie stumbled across a girl loitering by a UniMart dumpster in a baggy Rocawear jacket and hood that hid her acne-scarred face. Natalie had guessed at the girl's business in lingering there, and she'd guessed right. The girl set her up with a gram of heroin before slipping behind the convenience store, then it seemed, into the ether. One of the patrons to Natalie's occult shop delivered three microdots and a baggie full of shit-smelling hallucinogenic mushrooms to her apartment for practically nothing. Natalie suspected it was because the guy had somehow gotten it into his head, he'd be *the one* to convert her back to guys.

She'd let that play out in her favor, but just the one time.

The meth made Natalie manic to the point she rearranged her entire apartment, crashed, and woke up wondering how she'd ended up in *someone else's apartment.*

She chickened out with the heroin and ended up flushing it. It had taken too many of her friends' lives back in Manhattan, not to mention her *one and only* male crush, Scott Weiland.

She drew all over her bedroom walls while on the microdots, and after her pen broke in her hands, she stripped down and ran through South Philly in a bra and panties. She'd thought she was in a bathing suit racing Danica down the beach in Wildwood where they used to vacation every summer. Somehow, she escaped being arrested for disturbing the peace, even though she suspected she must have run past at least two police officers half-naked.

The shrooms were a bad trip. Under their influence, Natalie saw the Tumor Deer for the second time. She came to, hours later, crying, her cheeks wet and eyes swollen.

The first time she'd seen the Tumor Deer had been on that dark back road on the way home from Albany with Danica, her wife.

The night her life changed forever.

The Tumor Deer.

Is it real? Was it ever real, or a nightmarish hallucination now as it was then?

A haunting vision of a deer riddled with bulging cancerous growths all over its body. They looked like over ripened plums. They had grown over its eyes and around its mouth like fattened leeches. Out of all the drugs she'd tried, she wished she'd skipped the shrooms. They had opened her mind, all right.

To the horrors that roam the Earth.

That hurt the heart.

That offend the mind.

If I could go back, I would've shot the heroin and skipped the shrooms. Honest to God!

At the Market Street Mall, Natalie had stumbled across a vendor near the food court advertising for a company called NoMind Immersion Therapy, Inc. The short, middle-aged woman, who clearly worked on commission and had merely a surface knowledge of what she was selling, had shown Natalie over to what looked like a giant porcelain clam. The woman explained it was a *sensory deprivation tank*. It was filled a quarter of the way up with salt water heated to body temperature, and the interior was completely soundproof. The woman gave Natalie a brochure which explained something called REST, or "restricted environmental stimulation therapy." The brochure boasted that time spent in the tank can help with muscle relaxation, better sleep, decrease in pain, and decreased stress and anxiety. Bland reading. The woman had also mentioned she'd tried it herself. Whether or not this was the truth, she'd told Natalie how one hour in the tank had "put her into a trance-like state and opened doors in her mind she'd never thought existed."

Opened her mind.

The magic words

So, Natalie had visited the NoMind Immersion Spa in Willow Grove. She spent two hours in an immersion tank, floating freely as the salt water buoyed her upward. She shut her eyes but made sure not to sleep. She knew how to meditate and concentrated on the rise and fall of her belly amid deep breathing. The absolute silence was unsettling at first. Gradually, her body felt like it was oozing into the water. Melding with the very molecules of the liquid itself. She felt like she'd somehow become an invertebrate, gelatinous as a jellyfish. Drifting. Drifting. When the time was up and an attendant opened the tank, Natalie had thought it was Danica standing there above her. She had raised herself up out of the water, reaching gracelessly for the girl, and she'd tried to pull her into a wet embrace. "Don't ever leave me again!" Natalie had begged the confused girl. "You hear me? Never. Again!"

Mortified isn't even the word for how I felt when I left that place. I don't think there's a word for how I felt.

But there was a phrase.

Dead inside.

Natalie had nearly given up, not just on ever recovering the "sight" a car accident had stripped away, but on life itself. She had planned on chasing a bottle of Zzzquil with a bottle of Old Granddad when a thought quite literally bubbled up from out of the chasm of her unconscious mind. It had been Danica, of all people, who'd told her about an article from Buzzfeed about Amanda Fielding and her legendary "self-trepanation" experiment. The conversation had been casual enough, little more than a "would you, or wouldn't you?" And like a prompt from the grave, that conversation with Danica years ago inspired Natalie to research the procedure. With the amount of research and obsession she'd devoted to the procedure, Natalie could have delivered a dissertation on the subject in front of a panel of doctors and come out on top.

So why can't I just do it? What have I got to lose, besides a lot of blood?
She didn't fear death.
Bleeding out.
Dying alone.
So ... what then?
The drill felt like it was getting heavier in her hands. Her palms felt greased and slippery.

Natalie lowered the drill away from her head, down to her side. This was not quitting. But that's how it felt, and she'd never been known to back down from anything or anyone. It was one of the few things her parents had instilled within her from a young age, to stand your ground in the face of fear or adversity. She'd been a star athlete in high school as captain of the soccer team. Memories of the feel of the ball against the side of her Nikes thrilled then *horrified* her as she imagined that same sensation in a different scenario entirely: that of kicking off a footstool and hanging herself from the crossbeam down in the basement storage area of her apartment building—

"I need to sleep," she told her reflection. She set the drill down on the ground. Tears pricked at the corners of her eyes. She blinked them back, but they won out and skated down her cheeks. "Oh God, help me. I'm losing my mind."

That's when the light above the bathroom sink flickered.
Once.
Twice.
Then it started strobing relentlessly above Natalie's head. The lime-green tiles of the cramped bathroom suddenly appeared to be closing in. She swore she saw spiders and roaches skittering all about. Carpeting the cold tile floor. Clambering overtop of one another as they raced mindlessly all about the walls. Her skin crawled, and she checked her bare arms for the vermin, finding nothing but her own pale, skinny limbs. One wrist bore the tattoo of a dotted line across the visible veins beneath the thin skin and the words **CUT HERE** underneath in a calligraphy style. Her other arm bore a more elaborate tattoo portrait of Edgar Allan Poe from the waist up, pulling the collar of his black overcoat across half his gaunt, saggy face as if ashamed of and shying from his own greatness. The strobing light animated Poe on her arm. Tugging his coat

up across his face. Lowering it back down. So on and so on.

Nausea seized her, quick and paralyzing. It tickled the lining of her stomach until she felt vomit rise up her esophagus. Retching spasms bent her over, and Natalie splashed sick all over the floor in what felt like an endless stream.

Natalie felt her legs turn rubbery. Wobbly. They buckled. Her knees gave way, and then she hit the floor and rolled onto her side. Her eyes saw a kaleidoscope of twitchy, intersected colors that spun and spun in an endless, psychedelic rapture.

"It's all right, Nat," a voice said above her. It was a rich timber. Calming. "I'm here. As always."

Before the darkness of the epileptic seizure sent her down, down, down into the abyss, Natalie Kincaid saw him down on his haunches beside her. A handsome, dark face. Mouth in a line. Eyes big, brown. A low brow knitted in concern. "I don't want to keep doing this to you, but you won't listen. And time is not on our side the longer we wait."

She willed her hands to reach for that face, to claw at his kind eyes with her nails. To gouge at him and peel the cocoa skin of his sunken cheeks away like crinkles of confetti. But her body would not obey. Could not.

"If you can't get it done," he said, his voice drifting deeper into a vast tunnel of blackness, "we've got to try it my way."

You bastard.

II. GREGORY GAITHER

Just as the sound of it had been the last thing she heard before her blackout, Gregory Gaither's voice was also the first thing Natalie heard when she awoke.

"I don't want to do that again, Natalie," Gaither said. "But you've got to give up trying to ignore me."

Natalie had developed epilepsy when she was eight years old. One minute she was playing *Resident Evil 2* on her PlayStation in the living room, and the next moment her controller slipped out of her hands and a red aura with a yellow band bled across her vision. She felt something pop deep inside her skull, like a lone corn kernel in a microwaveable bag. The smell of burning, like a roast left in the oven for millennia. Then, she lay prone on the floor. Blackness. She woke up later in the back of an ambulance with her mother clutching her hand and her father trailing the ambulance to the emergency room in the family minivan.

The neurologist at St. Basil's diagnosed her as having photosensitive epilepsy. The horror survival game she'd been playing had frequent scenes where the lights in certain environments flickered on and off. The neurologist explained the frame rate of the game had also played a part in triggering the seizure. Natalie was an avid gamer, and this had never happened before.

But it would plague her for the rest of her life.

She learned what the *triggers* were, mostly by trial and error.

Natalie learned to shy away from nightclubs because of their flashing lights. Years ago, before things with Danica turned romantic, a girl Natalie was dating had slipped something in her drink at a bar, then led her by the hand to some underground rave a few blocks down in a South Philly warehouse. Between the colorful wristbands and neon insanity everywhere the eye could see, combined with the strobing rainbow shades spinning and splashing across the ceiling and the walls, Natalie lasted ten minutes before the dreaded *aura* pushed the rainbow craziness into the background and took the foreground. She collapsed, and if a quick and alert bouncer had not promptly scooped her up off the floor,

6

Natalie would have been trampled to death by the drugged-up party people.

She was vigilant when it came to replacing a lightbulb in her apartment the second she observed so much as twinkle. If she hadn't become so preoccupied with the present situation at hand—that of Gregory Gaither, the drill, and her own primal fear—Natalie would certainly have replaced the bar light above her bathroom sink before this.

Still, for all her cautionary measures, Gregory Gaither succeeded in sidestepping all of them.

He had been messing with every light in her apartment for the better part of a month. The first time, she couldn't sleep and had gone into the kitchen to make herself some chamomile tea. She was sitting there at the second-hand table, tracing her fingers through the scrapes and scratches cut into its rugged surface and sipping at her tea when the cheap, dangling chandelier above her head winked out and back on again. This was the pattern Gaither used. A tease. Then another. Then the strobe effect. Before long, Natalie spilled out of her seat onto the floor in the throes of a grand mal seizure. She bumped her head pretty good on the linoleum tile, and a blue and yellow bruise adorned her right temple for the better part of a week.

That was also the first time she'd seen the young, handsome black man hovering over her, the same look of concern and regret in his eyes. The first time he'd induced her seizure, he explained himself and the reason for it. "My name is Gregory Gaither. I'm sorry for this, but I need your help, and in order for you to hear me out, I needed to, well, temporarily rewire your brain so we could connect. So, you'd be able to see me and hear the sound of my voice. There's not much time. Once your brain achieves homeostasis again, I'm going to disappear, and you won't be able to hear me. I'll make this quick. First, I'm sorry about your wife. Danica? I haven't crossed paths with her over here, but this plateau—this domain—everything unfolds at random. I know your accident a year ago cost you your second sight. I'm sorry for that also.

"I was murdered thirty-nine years ago. By two men. Two strangers. Twins. I was only twenty years old. A college student at Ballantine University. You know, on Broad Street? They took me right off the street when I stepped out of a bar where I was catching a beer. They—they *drank my blood* and slung a noose around my neck. They took me away. Some place secluded. Kept me alive just long enough to do things. Bit off fingers. Toes. Then they chewed off my arms and legs. I don't know what they did to my body after that."

Lying on her back, the grand mal sending painful ripples through her body and jerking her spinal column about, Natalie had no choice but to listen. She couldn't speak. A captive audience.

"I want ... I-I *need* revenge," Gaither continued. "And I know where they can be found. I know *who* they are. It's why I need your help. I need you to do something. A few things, full disclosure. But it will help you just as much as me. Listen to me, girl. *These two men? They're not human.* Haven't been for over one hundred and fifty years. If I'm going to take them down, then I'm going to need you. Your gifts. And you'll need to recover them again. And I ..."

When Natalie found she could focus her eyes and move her lips again, the ghost of Gregory Gaither vanished, his words clipped as neatly as if they'd been struck through by some divine power's mighty red pen.

She lay there on the floor for an hour, her spiraling thoughts slowly narrowing into a stream of focus she could make sense of. There would be no trip to the ER. Natalie let her health insurance lapse months back. She'd had the gold standard, Personal Choice, back in Greenwich Village when she'd run the shop with Danica there. The money had been there back then. Lying there on the floor, Natalie had never felt so poor in her entire life. The seizure may very well have done more damage than she could detect, yet Natalie knew all she could do would be to sit up, wait for her head to stop spinning, then slowly crawl to bed.

The next time it happened, she had been standing just inside the door to her apartment, pulling on her coat. The light spazzed out the same way as before, and she had sunk like a stone. Flopped around like a fish. Before the darkness closed in once more, Gaither slipped into view beside her like before. He told her he knew she had a friend studying to be a neurosurgeon. That maybe he could be of use. That's when Gaither first mentioned the procedure called trepanning. Couldn't her doctor friend help her to "free her mind?" The very words Gaither had used, like he was quoting a popular hashtag or a verse to a pop song, like another prompt from the grave to remind her of the talk with Danica and the research she had done.

She woke up on the floor a few feet from the door, which stood open a crack. She'd nearly made it out. Natalie had felt profoundly disoriented the second time around, like an amnesia victim. She had checked her watch and discovered, much to her horror, she'd lost two hours. Her brain felt two sizes too big for her skull. She could taste the anger. It was palpable. It had shaken her almost as powerfully as the seizure itself.

Now, stretched out on her back in bed with only the residual smell of burnt roast lingering in the air of her cramped bedroom, Natalie feared for her life. The way he came and went as frequently as a roommate, stunned her to silence as she lay there beneath her sheets and quilts, frightened and wrought with an acute vulnerability. Natalie had suffered eight separate seizures after those first two epileptic episodes, all induced at will by a desperate, manipulative, and insistent spirit the likes of which she'd never known.

I am at his mercy. Completely at his fucking *mercy.*

And the worst part of it? Natalie, the sensitive and sympathetic soul she'd always been, could not shake the story Gregory Gaither had conveyed to her. The details of his murder at the hands of two men just outside a bar in Old City Philadelphia. How could it be doubted? Every bit of it had to be true, and she damned well knew it. When she'd thought him nothing more than a hallucination born of haywire synapses, Natalie had found it somewhat easier to dismiss the horrific tale of his execution.

Then, the more he'd told her during each epileptic episode (when her mind was opened enough to both perceive him and hear his words), the more the story of Gaither's murder seeped into her pores. It permeated her daily life to the point she found herself thinking about him and his proposition at least ten times a day. When her mind dared to wander, it gravitated almost immediately towards the details of the murder and the spirit who (dare she say?) had become something of a sympathetic character to her.

One more time and I could hemorrhage.

Natalie turned onto her side, maneuvering herself cautiously lest the motion force her to vomit or, worse, to black out again. She spoke into the pillow beside her head, the one that had been Danica's. She couldn't bring herself to throw it away after her wife's death.

"I let him get into my head. To the point I'm going to drill a fucking hole into my head. So I might what? Regain my gift? What if I don't want it back?"

Now you're full of shit, Nat. At least be honest with yourself.

"I know. If it worked, I'd be able to see Danica again. She could come to me. She could come through."

And honestly, dammit, *I don't know I wouldn't want the same revenge if I were Gregory Gaither …*

"If I bleed out? If it fails? I'll be with Danica again. Either way. She'll be waiting for me."

III. OUTSIDE HELP

Natalie rolled over on the bed towards the nightstand and reached for her cell phone resting there.

Chose the contact listing for **Dan McCausland**.

"Dan? Hi, it's Nat."

"Nat? Something wrong?"

"Nah ... um, I need your help."

"My *help*?"

"Yeah," Natalie said. She drew a deep breath in and out, ignoring the soreness flaring around her shoulder blades. "But ... well, how have you been? It's been a couple weeks. I know you were enrolled for some summer classes. How are they going?"

"Oh, I am *so* tired of school, Nat. It feels like I've been at Drexel for the most of my life at this point."

"You're the one who wanted to be a brain surgeon. As far as I'm concerned, it's better to be over prepared for *that* particular career than under."

"Yeah, well, no matter how many years of schooling and training I have, I'll never feel like I have any business noodling around with *somebody's* brain! None at all!"

Funny you should phrase it that way, Dan.

Dan McCausland was in his third year of medical school at Drexel University College of Medicine. He and Natalie had known one another since sophomore year at Archbishop Bevilacqua High School. He'd also known Danica through Natalie when she had brought her future-wife along to drink at an *encampment* of sorts in the woods behind the school called The Tarps. The Tarps was a gathering spot comprised of blue tarps strung along tent poles. Ever since the early eighties, students of Archbishop Bevilacqua High did their underage drinking there, concealing the illicit activities from any police or busybodies in the neighborhood. But because they declared The Tarps as solely a spot for Bevilacqua kids to drink and gather, many a turf war had been fought in Natalie and Dan's youth when teenagers from a local rival Catholic school dared try to wet their whistles at The Tarps. While Natalie had failed to keep in touch with the other handful of friends she'd made at Bevilacqua, she and Dan never lost track of one another.

There was a bond there, strong as the oldest oak and soundly cemented by an incident that took place at The Tarps years back. A couple of cheerleaders had shown up uninvited to one of the Friday night Tarps Socials. Natalie and Dan were there along with some of Dan's friends from the Drama club. The rival-school girls were already drunk when they arrived. Before long, one of them found their way into an argument with Natalie, whom she claimed was taking too long to fill her cup at the keg. Missy DePalma, the cheerleader in question, shoved Natalie aside, said, "My turn, you stupid-ass dyke!" Missy barely got her last vile word out before Natalie crammed it back into her mouth with a quick, vicious fist. Missy DePalma sat down hard in the leaves and underbrush. The other cheerleaders rushed Natalie, and while she would have been able to hold off two of them and their slashing manicured claws, Dan had put himself in between her and the other girls to even the odds a bit. He said he had access to a crude video one of their boyfriends had spread around the school. A video two of the girls had fought hard to suppress. "You thought all the copies were destroyed, but I got my hands on one," he told them. "It pays dividends when you treat the people in the AV club like actual human beings instead of how you assholes treat them. They hooked me up. I knew you'd pull your shit eventually, and I made sure to have some leverage at the ready. Consider this your one and only warning. Back. The fuck. Up." They had stood there, hands on hips, contemplating the fallout of such a video seeing the light of day once more. Then, the cheerleaders, led by Missy DePalma, with her mouth full of blood, fled The Tarps.

Thus, the bond.

Natalie wondered if what she wanted from Dan McCausland would compromise that bond. She cherished it, but there were other matters that took precedence. Ultimately, Natalie Kincaid decided she loved Danica more. Most. If this cost her the friendship with good ole reliable, loyal Dan McCausland, well, Natalie decided it was a chance she was willing to take.

She asked, "Do you remember when I asked you about trepanning? If you'd ever heard of it?"

"Yeah," Dan said, "and I did some digging into it to satisfy my own curiosity. Want to know what I found out?"

"Okay," she said, sucking the inside of her cheek, "and so have I. Looked into it, I mean. Medical journals. Statistics. The history—"

"Hold it-hold it-hold it, Nat! I looked into it like someone would check out an urban myth or something. For my own amusement. You sound like someone who's been *really* thinking about it. Dare I say, *obsessing* over it?"

"What? I'm not allowed to have a curious mind too?"

"That depends. What would be *your* motivation for researching this procedure so thoroughly? You enroll somewhere and forgot to mention it? Writing a thesis paper?"

"Oh please, like I could ever qualify for any kind of financial aid. Let alone even think about going back. That's mean, Dan."

"All right," Dan said. "I'm sorry to push. So ... I'll ask you this. And I'm only trying to understand your point of view." Hesitation. "How have you been feeling since we last spoke? Any headaches? Blurred vision? Dizziness?"

Do frequent, triggered epileptic seizures count?

No.

Natalie winced, her thoughts turning to the utter discomfort she'd experienced on the floor of her bathroom only an hour before. "No. None of the above."

"So, the double-vision? You complained to me about that when we talked before. That's stopped?"

No. But it's more important to keep on topic here.

"Yes. Listen, that's gone too. But—"

Wait! Wait-wait-wait! Slow down and let's think about this. You're going to have to backtrack a bit, and you're going to have to lie. You've got to play him. Because you can practically hear the No! *coming, and he hasn't even flat-out said it yet. But he will once you ask him. It's the* how *that matters when it comes to asking him.*

Whenever Natalie lied, her stomach lurched. Ever since childhood. Call it Catholic guilt. She spread her hand across her stomach to calm it.

"All right," she said, injecting a bit of false hesitation into her tone, "I'm lying. I just didn't want you to worry. After all, there's nothing you can do about it. There's nothing *anyone* could do to help me. I don't have any health insurance, and I'm not going to be able to pay any hospital bills the way the store's revenue is going. The books are bleeding more than a stuck pig, Dan. So just—"

"Natalie, what's wrong? You've got to tell me. I'm your friend. C'mon."

"The headaches," Natalie said, hating herself and her lie. She kept the image of Danica in her mind's eye. Held on to her for dear life. "Migraines."

"Where are they centered?"

"What?"

"What part of your head? Behind your eyes? Forehead? Crown?"

Here we go.

"Upper forehead. Near my widow's peak."

Silence.

Dan let out a long, irritated sigh. "Nat, I have only one question for you."

"Dan—"

"Why would you lie to me and tell me you're fine? And all right—I've got more than one question for you, but tough! Do you have any idea what an untreated subdural hematoma could do to you long term? I'm talking coma! Talking brain damage! Seizures!"

Natalie had to bite her lip to keep from laughing at the irony. *That's a pre-existing condition, my good man.*

"Worst case scenario? Death! You understand?"

"Yes, Dan—"

"I sure as hell hope so," he continued, on a roll. "Because if you've been putting your life at risk because you don't have health insurance, I can assure you there are ways and means to get you the treatment you need without your going bankrupt."

"*Going* bankrupt, hon? Seriously? I'm there. The wolves are at the door. They've been nipping at my heels for weeks, if not months. I'm afraid to answer my goddam cell phone for fear it's another creditor. And I can tell you, they are some of the cruelest sons-of-bitches on the face of the earth. I answered one of those calls and told them I'd be having my lawyer call them back. You know the bastard laughed at me? *He laughed at me.* Then he said he was *surprised* I could afford a lawyer, but I can't afford to pay my bills. I felt like such a piece of shit, Dan."

"I understand, Nat. I really do. But, you know, you can't put off taking care of yourself. You could've come to me. I mean, I'm your typical broke, Ramen-slurping med school student, but I'd see what I could do."

"Oh please, Dan. I couldn't. You know I couldn't go there with you. Borrowing money poisons a friendship. I would never be able to pay you back."

"Of course you would. But, Nat, I don't know I'd even be able to cover a third of what the bill would be. There are types of assistance that would—"

"I'm not a welfare case, and I don't want charity," she blurted out. "But you *could* help me, you know."

"I don't see how, I mean …"

Then, Dan McCausland most certainly *could* see how he could help.

"Oh Nat, no-no-no, c'mon. You're not seriously thinking I could take care of it myself? Tell me that's *not* what you were thinking of!"

"Well, why not? I know it sounds crazy on the surface, but I've thought about it. I've done some research, and I happened to find out more often than not, the *burr hole* procedure is conducted in the sudden event of emergency. Rarely in an ER, let alone a sterile surgery wing."

"Natalie!"

"No, seriously," Nat pressed on, breathless. "Think about it. Suppose the two of us are just chilling over in your dorm or at my apartment and I suddenly pass out or I seize, or I lose the feeling on one side of my body. Those are all signs of a subdural hematoma. And combine that with the knowledge I've just given you regarding my frequent headaches and blurred vision off and on. You're going to tell me you *wouldn't* figure out a way to perform an emergency burr-hole procedure right then and there to drain the blood on my brain?"

"*Dammit, Nat—*"

"You'd chance getting me to the hospital instead of quite possibly saving my life *right there*?"

"You going to let me talk, or should I sit back for a total filibuster?"

"Go ahead," she said. "I've made my point."

"All right, now you're going to listen, so strap in, Nat! For one thing, you're placing entirely too much faith in my skill set as of right now. I'm sure you're familiar with the Hippocratic Oath, and what you're proposing I help you to do would most certainly end up harming you in some way. And you'd be *my patient*. Best case scenario, you develop an infection and you'll end up in the ER anyway, because, otherwise, you'd bleed out in minutes. Worst case scenario (and you say you've done your research?) the burr tool creates a *stopper* effect on the hole, or it so much as nicks a portion of your temporal lobe? Brain damage. Irreparable, perhaps. Now, do you know what your temporal lobe controls? Vision. Memory. Sensory input. Language. Ah emotion. Comprehension, for God's sakes! Your temporal lobe is *everything*! And you'd be willing to have a med student—key word *student!*—drill into the part of your skull that houses the portion of your brain which basically allows for you to live a normal life? You, Nat? You're not thinking!"

"I'm thinking quite clearly—"

"I dunno if the pain is impairing your judgment to such a degree you'd even ask me to do something so dangerous. But if that's the case? If you're experiencing that level of pain and discomfort, you *must* go to the ER. In fact, I could be there in fifteen to drive you."

When Natalie started crying into the phone, it surprised her as much as it disarmed Dan. One minute, her cheeks were stinging with anger and frustration, and the next, she thought of the last time she'd seen her mother and father. Five years ago. It was ugly and still felt permanent to the point she could never actually dial through to them ever again. The things she'd said to them. The things her mother had called her while her father had stood behind her, his long and gaunt face washing out to a pastier white the more his wife berated their daughter. She missed her father. By proxy, she mourned the relationship with her mother. And all of that, the thought of her parents and how she had no idea whether they were dead or alive? It brought the tears to her eyes.

"Nat ... oh man," Dan sounded like he could read her mind. Of course, he had no idea. Nat had never told him what that parting day five years ago had been like, only it had been *hard*.

She sniffed hard, squeezed her cell phone tighter. "No, oh no, Dan. I'm not trying to guilt you. It's just …"

Don't do this, Nat! This is not you! You are not a liar.

"… just I've been living with these headaches for so long. It gets so bad sometimes I just want to—I dunno—stick a skewer in my ear! My pupils don't match sometimes when I look in the mirror. Their sizes. When the migraine's at its peak? They're different sizes. I look like a freak, Dan! Straight-up sideshow! I can't take it. I can*not* take it anymore. And I have no choice but to live the rest of my life in pain. Because the store's going under, Dan! It's only a matter of months. Then, bankruptcy. Christ, this is *all* I need, on top of everything else!"

"Nat—"

"I'll probably kill myself the day I file for fucking bankruptcy. It's fiscal death, anyway!"

"*Nat!* Don't talk like that!"

"Why, Dan?" Nat cried, and immediately regretted it as the strain arched her back. The nerves gathered around the base of her spine screamed in terrible unison. "Why *not?*"

Silence.

It was long and drawn out. It made Nat nervous.

"Nat? You there?" Dan sounded just as nervous, worried perhaps she'd already had the noose knotted and taken her death dive in those few soundless moments.

"Y-yes."

"Natalie, I-I'm sorry. I can't help you with this."

"Fine."

"Are you gonna be okay?"

Natalie hung up. She lay there with her cell against her chest, staring up at the swirly brown water stain on the ceiling, just left of where she laid her head at night. It was usually stifling in her bedroom, but right then, the stuffiness carried with it a kind of electric current that drew the hair on Natalie's arms up into fine, little, downy spikes. The feeling she was not alone in the room gnawed at her. This was not a haunting, though. Her bedroom had become a kind of *waiting room*. And she understood what the wait involved. Both she and Gaither, who lingered near enough to her bed she felt his unseen eyes and heard his muted breath beside where she lay, were waiting for Dan McCausland's second thought.

Simply put, it would be impossible for a good man like Dan to *not* have second thoughts, or some reservation, about leaving his friend Natalie to her own devices. Not after the loaded, lethal threat she'd dropped on him like a wet, dirty bag over the head. No, a friend (hell, anyone with a sense of empathy or *sympathy*, even) couldn't *not* call back. *I just told him the pain was so bad I was going to kill myself.*

Not exactly, but she'd rung that suicide bell. And you can't un-ring a bell, as the saying goes.

The sound of a bottle skidding across the sidewalk outside her bedroom window scraped her sense of hearing. Nothing left to do but let her eyes fall out of focus. It was something she did ever since she was a kid. Let the hard edges soften and the colors bleed together until her world swam in watercolor uncertainty. The unsightly hard water spot looked like it had taken to spinning. Spiraling like the eye of a hurricane on some meteorologist's map. She held back the urge to blink and clear her eyeball of the film gathering on its surface. It started to sting, but she widened her eyes and slowly turned onto her side.

"Some friend," she told herself. "I could've already done it."

Nothing.

"I could have already done it."

The thought of it started to take root. It sank its claws into her mind.

I could still do it.

"No."

Natalie switched the bedside light off.

Darkness.

It wasn't long before she slipped into a light doze.

The ringing cell phone she'd been hugging against her chest roused her around two a.m.

"Hello?" she asked, the ghost of a smile fading from her lips.

"Nat?"

"Dan. Hi."

"Did you mean what you said?"

"Er ... which part?"

"That you'd hurt yourself? Would you?"

A pang of guilt struck her in the gut. No turning back now. "Yes. The pain's too much."

"All right. Okay. I'll be over to pick you up tomorrow morning at nine sharp. I'm going to help you."

"Oh Dan, but, where are we going? I *can't* go to the ER—"

"Now, Nat, hold up a second," Dan said, a nervous laugh tittering out of him like a stitch of madness. "You have to agree to some things before I make the trip. If you won't, I really can't help you. I mean, you know I love you, kiddo. But I've got my future to think about."

"Shoot."

IV. BURR-HOLE TREPHINATION

Natalie made sure to be ready ten minutes before the time he would pick her up. An on-and-off vaper, she stood out on the stoop of her apartment building, inhaling the caramel-flavored water vapor from her mag device. She blew a thick, bilious cloud out into the dampened July air as Dan pulled up at the curb in his white Kia Optima, a Sublime song thumping at the closed windows.

Of course, the minute she climbed in and Dan pulled away from the curb, the med-student couldn't hold back. "You ever hear of *popcorn lung*, Nat?" She said she hadn't. Dan continued. "Also called Vaping Lung? Make sense now? That's what you want, on top of all the other shit?" Natalie shrugged, and Dan, only then realizing he ought to dial down his rhetoric, patted her leg and smiled at her. It was a small, sheepish smile but enough for Nat to make a note of it.

And how it betrayed his reservations about what he'd agreed to do for her.

Smiles do not always imply contentment or happiness. Sometimes, context can turn them to open threats. To outward expressions of dread or unease.

"So," he said, pulling onto the on-ramp for 95, "you're clear on what happens from here on out?"

"Yeah," Natalie said. "So, who is this friend of yours who agreed to give you access to his CT scanner? You said he's a veterinarian."

"Yes, he is. And it took some cajoling, but the guy owes me a favor."

"What'd you do? For him, I mean?"

"I introduced him to his wife. So far, so good with the two of them. If she'd turned out to be a shrew or he blew the marriage somehow, I wouldn't have been able to call in the favor. It'd be moot. So just make sure you thank Dr. Barry when we get there for being a doting, monogamous husband, because otherwise ..."

"Seriously? You want me to thank him?"

"For letting us scan your head, yes. For the other thing, c'mon, Nat. I thought *I* was gullible."

Natalie forced a chuckle. It rang out like two pennies at the bottom of a bell jar.

Dan glanced at her. "He also said the results of the scan shouldn't be used as anything more than a guideline. Or a diagnostic tool. I told him about your insurance problem and how you wanted to know what you're dealing with concerning these migraines. If there's anything going on in your attic you can't ignore, even without an HMO card. As far as he knows, that's the reason for our little field trip to his office this morning. Clear?"

"Yes. And the real reason? You want to see how thick my skull is?"

"Right, so I can calibrate the burr tool properly. If I were to drill into your temporal region blind, without a measurement, there's a good chance I could drill straight into your grey matter. I'd have no idea I even grazed the tissue until you perhaps forgot how to speak or move your arm or stand on your own. It's a good thing *you* didn't try to do this to yourself. I'd be picking out flowers for your funeral right now."

A shudder ripped up Natalie's spine, and she braced herself with one hand curled around the passenger door handle. "I couldn't. Even if I tried."

"Now, I'm not telling you this because I want you to feel guilty. It's all about full disclosure with me. I really had to stick my neck out getting my hands on an emergency burr-hole kit. I'm talking trespassing in my one professor's office. The one who actually likes me!"

"Oh come now, Daniel," Nat said, knocking him in the shoulder. "You're likeable as they come."

Dan shrugged this off. "The guy's old-school. Doesn't believe in locking his office and trusts perhaps more than he should in this day and age. I mean, his office hours are literally posted to the right of the unlocked door to his office. The poor guy's practically begging for someone to come on in and maybe have a gander at their grades or steal his laptop. I walked out bright and early with *his* kit. The one he used to teach us how to perform an emergency trephination earlier in the semester. The way I see it, he probably already covered that portion of the syllabus with all his classes, so he won't be looking for the kit in the immediate future. By that time, I will have placed it safely back up on the shelf in his office next to his book on white-guilt psychosis."

"You're trained in this?"

He nodded stiffly.

"You never told me that."

"I wasn't going to tell you."

"Why not?"

"When you mentioned it a while back, you sounded a little too eager to maybe test it out at home or something. I thought you might ask me to do ... well ... exactly what I ended up agreeing to help you with in the end."

"Dan, you don't *have* to do this. I'll be okay."

"Don't," he said, irritated. "Just remember what you agreed to. I love you, but I've got to protect myself at the same time. I hope that doesn't sound too harsh because it's not meant to. But you know ..."

"Yes, I know."

"Honestly, it makes me feel like the world's biggest shit if I were forced to do that. So, let's hope it *doesn't* come to that."

Last night, Dan had sounded like he was in physical pain while he laid out the Plan B of the procedure should it go south in any way. If Nat had offered him any further assurances that she understood the *why* of it, it would have sounded hollow. So, Natalie kept her mouth shut and moved inward, considering the elements of Dan's "cover-your-ass" plan bit by bit. Call it preparation, or quite possibly bracing oneself for the worst-case scenario.

The first thing they'd do is strip her bed, then drape it in plastic drop cloths. He'd already picked up a ten pack of them at the local Home Depot. They'd also cover the entire floor of her bedroom in the cloths. Blood is near-impossible to get out of a rug, especially a cheap polyester apartment rug. Natalie would stretch out on the bed. Dan would paint the top of her forehead with a numbing agent and then he'd drill the burr hole. As he explained it, nothing bleeds quite as profusely as a scalp wound, except maybe if someone opens an artery along the inside of their thigh. He would have copious amounts of gauze already wrapped around the crown of her skull, so once the blood started to flow, Dan would run a catheter from the hole in her skull to a receptacle. This would act as a drainage apparatus for the burr hole. The blood that had gathered there and punished Natalie with her crippling migraines would run out. Dan would then secure the catheter in place with the bandage and headwrap of gauze he'd already wound round her head to have at the ready. Dan told her he had already made arrangements and brought his textbooks and laptop so he could stay over for the next five days. He'd keep her under observation in her apartment. Natalie had tried to balk at this, but Dan wouldn't have it and threatened to pull the plug on his offer right then and there if she didn't agree to anything and everything he presented to her.

The callous part of Dan McCausland's Plan B would come into play in the event any complications arose during those five days of post-op. So many things could go wrong. Dan had made it plain to her, and he'd pulled no punches. Loss of taste. Loss of vision. Paralysis. Hemorrhaging. Grand mal seizure. Death. He'd asked her if those things sounded worth it to her as far as the risk involved. And Natalie hadn't hesitated to stand her ground. She wanted this. "All right," he'd said. "In the event any of these things were to occur, I would immediately carry you down to my car and rush you to the emergency room. But Nat, I'd have to leave you there. I couldn't even walk you inside. I mean, no one can ever know I was involved in this. That means you would take complete responsibility for all of it. The burr hole procedure. You'd have to tell them you did it to yourself. And that things went wrong."

It was Dan's future, and this was nothing in the ballpark of asking a friend to help you move or give you a ride to the airport.

This was major surgery. Performed by a friend who is an unlicensed med student. In her apartment. In her bed.

Something struck the windshield.

"HOLY SHIT!" Dan cried. His hands were a blur on the steering wheel. The whole car jerked and shuddered as he tried to force it back into their lane on the highway.

Natalie snapped out of her reverie; her hands instinctively curled around the passenger door handle. "What the hell was that?"

"A bird ... I-I think! Holy God!"

"A *bird*?"

Poor Dan looked like someone had just punched him in the gut with a hand full of brass knuckle. He was panting, bent over the steering wheel. Cars and trucks in the other lanes surged past him, beeping incessantly. A soccer mom in a minivan sailed past him on the left, flying her middle finger the whole way before cutting him off and surging forward.

The inside of the car slipped into silence. Neither one moved to turn on the radio either. They bathed in the absence of sound for their own reasons. Natalie imagined Dan was shaken up and that's what had sent him down into himself.

As for her, the swerving car had called her thoughts back to the accident on that dark road a year ago. The fluid, free feeling of forward motion as she and Danica sailed down the one-lane road, enclosed on both sides by dense forestry.

Then the deer in the middle of the road. Its starved, bony body riddled with fat, black tumors that had even grown over its eyes.

It hadn't tried to run.

But it wasn't afraid.

Almost like it had meant to be there. Right then. To fulfill its life's purpose. *Taking my wife and my life away from me?*

She sat up, swallowed a giant lump in her throat. "Are we almost there?"

"Exit's coming up."

Seven-point-one.

It had become a mantra for Natalie. An earworm, lacking music or lyrical depth. She'd asked Dan how thick her skull was *just out of curiosity*, and he'd told her—

Seven-point-one millimeters.

"Bite down on this, Nat." Dan unlooped his leather belt from around the waist of his khaki pants. "Not the cleanest thing, but it'll do. Open." She opened her mouth and thought of her dentist and how many times he'd told her to open her mouth before leaning in with his lethal little hook. His eyes wide and mouth drawn into a stern, bloodless line, Dan curled the belt into three layers and then slid a hunk of it between Natalie's teeth.

Tastes like shoe polish.

Seven-point-one.

"Last chance to change your mind, Nat. I won't be offended."

But there was no going back, and not because Gaither was no doubt lingering in the room and prepared to kick up some shit should she change her mind. Natalie saw Danica's face in her mind's eye. Her cocoa skin beaming like it generated its own light. Dancing brown eyes under tweezed, fine eyebrows with a hoop pierced into the left one. Her full, pouty lips. Luscious teeth she kept wet and glistening with constant sweeps of her tongue.

I will see you soon.

"No, don't stop," she managed to say around the belt in her mouth. "Even if I tell you to."

"All right—"

"No!" Natalie seized Dan's wrist. "I'm serious! Do. Not. Stop. No matter what I say or do!"

"If your pulse rises higher than one-seventy, I'll have to. You could have a heart attack."

Dan had wrapped her arm in a blood-pressure cuff and taken the resting BPM before even applying the numbing agent to her hairline. It was one-ten.

"Whatever, just *try* not to stop."

He stood there looking down at her, longer than she would ever have been comfortable with in any other given situation. Then, Dan opened his burr-hole kit, retrieved what looked more like a tool one would use for a car tune-up than a drilling tool for the skull. It was no shock to her, the sight of it. During her countless Google searches, she must have seen hundreds of photographs of that very same tool. She even knew its name. A *Hudson Brace*. Still, the tool's implication raised her heart rate and stole her breath. It felt like a small child was standing on her chest.

Natalie raised an eyebrow, testing the sensation, or lack thereof, in her forehead. It was a mystery to her whether they even moved. She had no idea. The muscles were dulled with powerful numbness. *Okay-all right-okay-all right-no-feeling-do-it-do-it-*

"Do it, just do it!"

When Dan McCausland leaned over her and she felt the pinprick point of the tool against her forehead, a strange and surreal calm washed over Natalie. She felt her whole body sinking into the plastic folds of the drop cloths. Falling through the mattress. The floor. Just submission.

Dan said, "Bite down now."

She did.

There came a popping sound like a cork from the mouth of a champagne bottle.

Then, Natalie fell away.

Two years ago, Natalie and Danica Kincaid had no idea how their lives would change the day Spencer Miller, an A-list actor, walked into their little occult shop in Greenwich Village and asked for a seance. He had his entourage with him: a beautiful husky with different colored, David Bowie eyes, two girls (one Spencer was dating and the other his half-sister), and two guys Spencer did not even bother to introduce to Natalie and Danica. Spencer Miller said he liked the name of their store ("Pan's Flute Spiritual Shoppe") and he "just had to pop in" on his way to the used vinyl store a couple blocks east, where he would search their stacks for Tony Bennett and MC5. None of his entourage bought anything. No candles or incense. Books. Bongs. Tapestries. And Spencer must have felt bad walking out empty-handed. Natalie and Danica had no idea actors experienced emotions such as guilt. Still, Spencer asked Natalie for a seance. "My dad died before I was born," he'd said. "Long time ago. Could you, er, put me in contact with him?" Fifty dollars changed hands, and they were off to the races, so to speak. In a back alcove, concealed by an array of sequined sheets and silken scarves arranged in a hive-like fashion, Natalie not only helped Spencer to speak to his long-dead father, Millard, but also to a high school friend who'd committed suicide and an old girlfriend who brought tears to Spencer's beautiful green eyes when she referenced the abortion she'd gotten as a Freshman at UCLA, where they'd been an item.

The young actor, touted as the next Johnny Depp, was stunned to muteness afterward. He pressed two more hundred-dollar bills into Natalie's hand and walked out, nodding his head as a "thank you." The entourage followed close behind, a few of them eyeing Natalie and Danica with a mix of suspicion and wonder.

Three weeks later, McNeezy, the world-famous rap mogul and record producer, visited Pan's Flute with his own entourage. Fifteen people in all. Every last one of them wanted Natalie to channel a loved one. Parents. Grandparents. Friends. Exes. Business associates. McNeezy covered the bill. By the time she had finished with all the rapper's people, Natalie and Danica had made more money than they'd ever seen in their lives. When asked how the rapper heard about their "out of the way shop," McNeezy told them, "My boy, Spencer Miller, recommended y'all. Highly recommended y'all!"

Next came Tina Jam, the latest bubblegum pop star from Canada.

Gordon Yang, the hottest stand-up comedian of the moment and fresh off a Netflix special.

There were too many happy dances for Natalie and Danica to count. Soon, the surrealness of the situation as it unfolded over the next four months of their lives moved the two to start talking more seriously about marriage. They'd wanted to wait until there was something of a nest egg in it for the both of them. By then, Natalie and Danica had not only garnered the nest egg, but a virtual chain of hen houses, with each bird laying a golden egg every hour.

The write-up in the Village Voice led to another in The New Yorker, which featured full-page glossies of Natalie, the most famous medium that side of the Hudson, standing proudly beside Danica, the brains of the business. Folded into this period, they received the likes of Harrison Ford, two of Howard Stern's daughters, Courtney Love, and a slew of A through B-listers in town or native to the Big Apple. Word had spread from the east coast to the west coast, or the "Best Coast," as many of the celebrities tagged it.

Right around the time Natalie and Danica started talking seriously about upsizing out of Greenwich, the call from a rep for TruthTV's program development department came through Natalie's cell. Not recognizing the number, she'd let it ring into voicemail. She didn't check the message until almost twenty-four hours later, thinking it could have been her parents on a new number trying to reach out to their estranged daughter. When she listened to it, she and Danica were getting ready to settle in for a night of binge-watching Supernatural.

Natalie had tried to rise off the sofa while listening to the rep's message, and the sensation of falling struck her all at once. Her knees went all wobbly and nearly gave out. Natalie turned to Danica, cheeks wet with tears and wearing a smile so wide it hurt the muscles of her mouth.

That night, they got to the binge-watching later than expected. The amazing news put them into an extremely randy mood. They made love with complete and uninhibited abandon; the kind born of elation that cannot be measured.

TruthTV's headquarters was in Albany, and the rep had penciled Natalie and Danica in for a meeting with their top executives a week later. Natalie and Danica decided they didn't want to wait any longer, and without Nat's parents there or Danica's military-colonel father in attendance, they said "I do" on the morning of November 12, 2018 at Beth El Non-denominational Chapel in Queens. Their neighbors, an older Filipino couple who lived in the next apartment over, stood as witnesses to the union. It was a bright, blindingly beautiful Sunday.

… a year and a month ago …

On November 18, 2018, a Friday, Natalie and Danica Kincaid signed on to film a pilot and six episodes of a show which would be shot on-location in their store, Pan's Flute. It had been given a tentative name for the sake of complete paperwork: The Ghost-Whisperer of Greenwich. Simple and to the point. The two newlyweds did not sign nor initial anything until it was added into the documents that they'd be equal partners in the enterprise and that equal camera time would be devoted to both. Danica presented herself as something of a manager to Natalie, the "talent," so to speak. Danica would be portrayed as the business-savvy partner, a role model to all young girls and women everywhere who enjoyed reading Lean In by that Facebook founder lady. The high was beyond anything they'd ever imbibed or smoked or swallowed, and they decided to stay over at a local Hilton. In the most expensive suite the hotel offered, Natalie and Danica laid awake in one another's arms until morning, talking about the future and children and healing the divide with their parents. Buying a house in the suburbs.

The distinct possibility of becoming the new reality-TV rock stars.

The next morning brought a hard, steady rain with it. Neither one of them had caught so much as a wink, but that was all right. They'd managed to plot out the course of at least the next five years of their lives together. Natalie agreed to drive so Danica could sleep, promising to wake her if her own eyelids got heavy. What Natalie had not disclosed to her wife was she was just as tired, if not more. The lack of sleep had thrown off her inner equilibrium. The road home consisted of a series of changeups between bustling highways and empty, endless byways enclosed by deep, dense forestry on either side. Natalie found herself both relieved and unnerved in equal measure at the lack of fellow motorists on a particular byway connecting an artery road to I-95. Her GPS had mapped out the quickest route for her, and often, the fastest route rarely held the driver to the same road for longer than sixteen miles or so. The clouds had bunched up into each other, creating a billowy, gunmetal grey canopy. In combination with the thick forestry bordering the roadway, Natalie felt boxed in by a building blackness as she rocketed down 173 with Danica snoring softly in the passenger seat and The Cure's Disintegration buzzing out of the car speakers.

During that drive in particular, Natalie came to understand what it means to feel completely alone when you are anything but. Her wife was there beside her, but the atmosphere seemed to press her further and further into herself, folding her once, twice, thrice into her own *mind until she was barely present. She drove with sheer muscle memory. Gas. Brake. Repeat.*

When Natalie saw the aura out the windshield, she thought it was one of those rainbow mirages shimmering above a gas patch splashed across the road ahead.

Then the fear hit her, soaking her muscles in adrenaline. She angled the car towards the breakdown lane.

The seizure took a hold of her, throttling her entire body in the driver's seat and scrambling the neural pathways of her brain.

The Tumor Deer was standing in the middle of the road, its legs bulging with what looked like black, misshapen eggplants here and there. Its legs shivered and shook, like it wasn't sure whether to break into the forest or simply to stand there regarding the out-of-control vehicle gunning its engine directly towards a fat white elm along the perimeter of the forest. The Tumor Deer stood its ground, staring through eyes blinded by two eggplant tumors bulging out of its sockets.

Natalie's foot floored the gas pedal in the throes of her seizure. The car struck the immoveable tree at sixty-two miles an hour.

She was not wearing a seatbelt. Danica was. The last thing she heard, the eggshell fracture sound of her skull penetrating the thick glass. The last thing felt, the sensation of her neck compressing as if it were spring-loaded. Natalie burst through the windshield, her last vision a harrowing one.

The Tumor Deer.

She ended up on her belly, her body half-submerged in detritus. Natalie lay face down in parchment leaves and spiky nettles. It felt like the world had turned. Revolved so many times she had become a creature out of time and space. Nothing remained for her. Still, her heartbeat and her lungs breathed. They knew something of life and its worth that she had forgotten. Natalie would have much rather died there on the forest floor, but her body had other ideas. She had slipped into a dissociative moment, pulling herself up into a sitting position. She spat out the dirt in her mouth, along her lips, and grabbed for a nearby tree to pull herself up.

Back up on feet as rickety as that of a newborn fawn, Natalie found herself face-to-face with The Tumor Deer.

Her bladder emptied down her leg at the sight of it.

Her bowels turned to water when it spoke to her, its mouth chewing cud and pronouncing nothing of the words.

(I'll take you to Danica. She's waiting)

"Is she—is she dead?"

"Yes," The Tumor Deer's voice, a drawling, gravelly delivery, concurred. "She was asleep during impact. She woke up to a heart attack. Death took her before she even awakened. A dream state, almost. I'll take you to her."

The Tumor Deer nodded its head towards a copse of trees that had grown into one another. Branches and leaves had devoured other branches and leaves, intertwining and webbing the seven or so elms until they created what looked like a massive exoskeleton growing out of the earth. The animal made for that landmark, which confused Natalie. She steadied herself against a tree, dusted off her legs. Her whole body sang with pain and stiffness. She tasted blood in her mouth and felt its tacky texture as it gummed up the muscles of her face where it had smeared.

"Wait! Isn't she still in the car? The other way? You're walking away from the road—"

"No," The Tumor Deer said, sternly. "You'd be the one walking away."

After quick deliberation, Natalie followed the Tumor Deer to the tree exoskeleton monolith in the near distance. The animal skirted the deformed tree, and Natalie did the same. Just behind the tree of nightmares, Natalie found Danica. She was lying in a shallow hole and working feverishly at scooping dirt down onto herself. She'd already managed to cover the lower half of her body in clay-like mud. Danica's head jerked towards Natalie. She opened her mouth, and a glob of bloody worms squirmed out, dropped down the sides of her face. In a water-logged voice, Danica said, "You have to bury me. Look what you did to me? I was resting in peace here in the dirt, and you just had to go and dig me up! WHY WOULD YOU?! HOW COULD YOU?! LET ME LIE—"

V. TREPANNING

A buzzing in the back of her brain.

A cacophony of voices dialed down to hisses and sighs.

All clambering to be heard, their frantic noises scrambling overtop of one another.

To be heard.

Natalie opened her eyes only to shut them up again. To squinch them. The throbbing pain in her head seemed to have woken up with her. The context of her bedridden state, the situation itself, suddenly seized her consciousness in its throttling fist. Natalie became aware of something wound tightly around the crown of her skull. She slowly fished her own hand out from under the blankets and touched the bottom hem of the gauze halfway up her forehead. Her fingers explored upward, finding a veritable beehive of the sterile bandage wound round and round into a quarter inch of covering on top of her head. *I must look like the Bride of Frankenstein if I'm to believe my fingers.*

A knuckle grazed the spot right above her widow's peak, and a bolt of lightning exploded behind the bandage. It bounced around her brain like a neuron ping-pong ball. She cried out.

"Nat!" Dan was seated at Natalie's work desk a few feet away. Textbooks lay open and spread across its surface, and he'd been balancing a fat spiral notebook across one knee when she screamed. He flung the notebook to the rug and rushed to her side. "Oh, man! Thank God! How do you feel?"

That's when the voices pushed forward like a crowd of people at a rock concert surging towards the stage at first sight of the band walking to their instruments. The stage was Natalie's prefrontal cortex. "I can hear them," she said. Her tongue felt swollen to double its normal size. "Oh, oh I hear them. They're coming, they're coming *up*."

"Hear who? I—oh. I get it. So that's been restored. I don't know how you feel about that. I would've thought you felt relieved by their absence."

He'd known about Natalie's gift ever since high school. They'd been at The

26

Tarps, and she'd been deep enough in the cups to reveal the strange truth of her reality. She'd come to hear *Them* for the first time the day she got her first period. The appearance of the bloodstain on her jeans had hardly paralleled the famous moment of truth for Carrie White in that horror movie, but the voices had tuned in to her mind that day like God suddenly spun a radio frequency dial to some station of the dead, then rigged it so the volume could be lowered but never completely muted. She'd explained it to Dan in this way, even calling God the *Great Cruel DJ in the Sky*. He'd asked her how long it took her to learn how to turn down their volume. It had taken Natalie years of trial and error before she was able to exert such control over the phenomenon as to lower its intensity inside her mind.

That's not to say she couldn't still see them. There was nothing to be done about that. It required a great deal of focus and concentration to keep them in the back of her mind, where memories remain stored away until an olfactory moment calls them out of their mental obscurity. The dead in a horde resembled shifting, shuddery shapes like actors on an old TV with a broken Vertical-hold button and bad reception. They lacked detail and looked to her mind's eye like nothing more than a noisome glob of staticky images that occasionally revealed the soft, uncertain shape of a human torso here and there among the jittery mass of dead souls in her head. It was only when Natalie called one of them forth from the staticky horde that the one in question could break from the group. Then and only then (as far as Natalie knew) could the spirit assume their bodily form once again and be heard.

"I *see* them too," Natalie said. She shut her eyes and drove them to the rear of her consciousness like a police officer working crowd control. They retreated. It was a skill she was thankful she had not lost in the year since suffering a disconnection to the spirit world. "They need taming. But ... I got it. It's all coming back."

"Good," Dan said, his voice tense. He did not want to talk about that. About them. The dead. There were more important issues at hand. "But you didn't answer my question. How do you *feel*?"

It felt like her heart had migrated north to her head. She felt a steady, terrible throbbing behind her forehead, like blood pumping into and out of a muscle. She winced, pointed at the spot where it hurt the most. The point of the burr-hole tool's entry. "Worst migraine I've ever had."

"Is it behind your eyes? How is your vision?"

"A little wonky." Dan's outline as he stood over her was soft and drippy as watercolors.

"All right. We're going to watch that. Hopefully, it's only temporary. Can you move your arms? Wiggle your toes?"

Natalie slipped her other arm out from under the blankets and lifted both left and right just enough to demonstrate their mobility. "Check." She wiggled her toes and Dan watched the movement as it bunched up the quilts at the other end of the bed. "Toes. Check."

"Good, good." He produced a pen light, and before Natalie could flinch away, he shined it in her eyes.

"Shit!" she cried. "A warning would have been nice!" She blinked rapidly and bit her bottom lip.

"That hurts your head?" he asked, switching off the light and slipping it back into his pants pocket. "Your pupils responded properly. No sign of brain damage, at least from a cursory examination."

He moved back to the desk and hunkered down to search inside his book bag. He brought out a stethoscope and returned to the side of the bed. "I need to check your vitals." Natalie pulled the blankets down, and Dan snaked the cold circle of the tool down the front of her shirt. Over her heart. Listened for a couple seconds, nodded, and then drew back. He wound the stethoscope around his neck. "Give me your hand." He took her left wrist between his thumb and forefinger, counting her pulse in his head. Nodded again. "Pulse is strong. Heart, too."

"I thought—*OW!*"

"What? What is it?"

"Feels like my head's in a vise." She licked her lips, and her tongue snagged on a spot where the flesh had split. "I thought, er, there'd be a tube. You know, a drainage tube attached to the-the hole."

"Well, you've been under for twelve hours."

"Twelve hours?"

"Yes," Dan said. "I drained a small amount of fluid. Nothing significant, which could be either a good thing or a bad thing. It all depends on whether this headache gets worse or subsides over time."

"And if it doesn't subside? What then?"

"The ER. That'll come next."

A rich, baritone voice sounded behind Dan. "That's not going to happen. There's no time for that."

Natalie jerked towards the voice, tried to prop herself up on the backs of her elbows. The bass drum in her head thudded more intensely behind her forehead at this movement. She forced herself to somehow endure or downplay the pain, but it was too much for her, and when she tried to crane her neck to see around Dan, Natalie became overwhelmed by the pain and had no choice but to lower herself back down against the low rise of her pillows.

Come forth Greg Gaither!

Gregory Gaither slipped out from behind Dan and stood over by the desk with his arms folded like an impatient man waiting in a long line. While Natalie had seen Gaither on a handful of occasions prior to this instance, it had typically happened while in the throes of a seizure. She knew he was black and quite handsome but could recall little besides those things. Now, as Gaither stood across the room from her in his fully fleshed form, she saw him more clearly. His athletic build and medium height. The close crop of his hair. Faint traces of a beard and moustache that faded to nothing the further they rode up the sides of his steam-shovel jaw. His eyes were not quite brown, not quite green, but more of an amber, like the tiger's eye stones Natalie sold for two bucks apiece at the store. He wore a red hooded sweatshirt with the Ballantine University logo emblazoned across its chest. Brown chinos with either dust or dirt at the knees like he'd just wiped off his hands there. Black and white Nike basketball sneakers.

"Nat?"

But she couldn't hear Dan. The blood pumping in her ears drowned him out. Never had she encountered an apparition so profoundly three-dimensional. Natalie could not see through him, although he did radiate a soft, ethereal glow like the rest of them when they appeared before her. Still, the glow was faint. Gaither could have passed for one among the living, so much so, she wondered if Dan would see Gaither if he were to suddenly wheel around. Gaither had let his arms drop and rested the flat of his left palm along one of Dan's textbooks while the other arm fished itself down into his chino pocket.

"*NAT?!*"

"Yeah, Dan," Natalie answered him, barely concealing the irritation in her voice. "Sorry, er, I just—"

"Where'd you go? Can you hear me all right? I need you to describe exactly what you just experienced that caused you to zone out!"

"Oh, Dan, I just—I lost my train of thought. I was just trying to trace it back."

"Does that happen to you a lot, Nat?"

"Of course it does. Just like everyone. Nothing to worry about."

"You serious? I'm not going to stop worrying until you can go a week without exhibiting any symptoms of brain damage or internal bleeding. I'm going to be on pins and needles until the moment I roll back that gauze away from your forehead and find a well-healed plug hole that's barely detectable to the naked eye. Then, I'll put my feet up and stop with all the questions concerning your well-being."

Gaither shook his head, waved his hand at Dan dismissively. "A week? Your boy Dan's a bit of a worrywart, don't you think? We don't have a *week*. We need to hit the road tonight. We've got a schedule to keep. Tight as a drum."

Natalie glanced at Gaither. "Well, you wanted him here," she blurted at him, and immediately realized the error.

Dan's brow furrowed. He followed Natalie's line of vision right before she tore her eyes away from Gaither. "What are you looking at? You wanted *who* here?"

"No one. No one. I guess I'm just thinking out loud. I dunno."

"Are you hallucinating?"

"No," Natalie said. "Not at all. Just having a hard time making sense. Putting thoughts into words."

"Well, I don't know now. Is this your regular, everyday *mental word-finding*, or are you having a hard time communicating as a whole?"

"It's just word-finding. I've always had that. I—I smoked a lot of weed when I was a teenager. This is the price I pay. Dull speech."

"Or it could be *anomic aphasia*, Natalie," Dan said, his eyes narrowing. He sat down on the edge of the bed. "I want you to do something for me. We've got to test this."

"Dan—"

He held up a hand. "No push-back. You promised. Remember?"

Gaither scoffed. "Get rid of him! So we can talk!"

Dan said, "I want you to go through the alphabet and think of a word for each letter. I don't want you to think long about each one. Just let them fly, fast as you can."

"Girl, tell him your throat's scratchy. You want a glass of iced tea. Now!"

It was exhausting. The two of them competing for her attention and allegiance. Not to mention, Dan had no idea he was even in any sort of competition. The poor guy was only trying to care for her and to cover all the bases. Natalie felt a pang of guilt over how he had been ill-used. He didn't deserve it. None of it. Her oldest and most loyal friend, and she'd done nothing but manipulate him for the past twenty-four hours. What's worse, she meant to continue with it.

For Danica. All of this is for Danica. So you'll see her again.

She hoped. Her motivation hinged exclusively on blind faith.

"I need some iced tea," she said, laying a hand across Dan's arm. "My throat's rough. Then I'll say the words."

She told him where he could find it, knowing full well it would take him longer because when he went to retrieve the iced tea pitcher, Dan would find it near-empty. Natalie told him he might need to make another batch and in which cabinet he could find the iced tea mix. He seemed to hesitate, which made Natalie's heart hurt more. There'd always been the suspicion Dan liked her more than a friend, ever since high school. They'd even gone to her Junior Prom together, and there had been a fleeting awkward moment in the limo on the way home when Natalie had felt Dan's inner turmoil hanging in the air between them. She could only assume he'd wanted to kiss her but knew full well if he so much as hinted at such a thing, their friendship would never recover. *And here I am, leading him around by the heart. Even now. This is not me.*

Gaither came away from the desk and curled his fingers around the bottom bedpost. He stared intently at her with eyes flecked in tiger's eye amber. "It's *not* you, girl. It's *me.* That's the truth of the matter, so don't feel so bad."

Dan touched Natalie's hand, nodded, and told her he'd be right back on his way out of the bedroom.

When Natalie looked towards the end of the bed and found Gaither no longer standing there, she experienced a brief respite of anxiety. Short-lived. Gaither had changed places, and he suddenly appeared at her bedside, leaning over her. It was then Natalie understood the nature of the glow coming off of

Gaither. He was not generating light, but freezing-cold air. It rose off him perhaps a quarter of an inch before evaporating into the stuffiness of Natalie's bedroom. It reminded Natalie of when she would open her freezer for a pint of Ben and Jerry's and how the cold air blew out at her, stealing her breath for a moment before she shut the door again. The question was out before she could think better of it. "Are you cold?"

"I don't know what it means to be cold anymore," Gaither said. "You should know better."

The ping-pong neuron inside her head glanced off the right side of her skull and struck the tender bone of her forehead. Natalie saw a white light, like an atom bomb just exploded inside her bedroom. She clenched her teeth, nearly cleaving off the tip of her tongue. "Talk. Fast."

"The pain's really bad?"

"No, you idiot! It's an orgasm! What do you think?"

"You're not gonna have to worry about that for much longer."

"Worry about what?" Natalie said, through gritted teeth. "The pain? What can you do? It's done, and so far, I haven't seen or heard anything from Danica. She would have pushed to the front of the pack and made her presence known by now."

"Up until this moment, there hasn't been any unfinished business for her to tend to."

Forgetting her condition, Natalie pushed off the mattress to bring herself up into a sitting position. The pain was immediate and sent her back down to the pillows, the mattress, like the finger of God. The drumbeat behind her eyes delivered two quick, disarming pulses that felt like knives stabbing from the inside out. Her tongue lolling, she managed a few words, unaware of whether they would make any damned sense or not. "How dare—"

"I didn't mean for it to come out that way," Gaither reasoned. Natalie saw him take a seat on the edge of the bed. The mattress did not carry the motion, and it was as if Gaither hovered there instead. "I only meant to convey she could be at peace. Peaceful rest. Wouldn't you want that for her more than anything else?"

"Don't you fuck with me now. You know the only reason I agreed to do this to myself … hinged on the possibility I'd be able to-to communicate with her again." A cold sweat burst from her pores, gluing the thin fabric of her concert t-shirt to her body. The wrinkled, dampened image of Debbie Harry screaming into a microphone looked twenty years older than it was. "Danica's dead. She was only twenty-five. W-we just got married. We were gonna, we … of course there's un-*finished* business. Fuck you!"

From the kitchen, Dan called to her. "Hey, Nat? You like anything else in your iced tea besides the mix? Like honey or sugar?"

Natalie squeezed her eyes shut tight. Bit her lower lip. "No, Dan!"

"All right," he responded. "Coming right up!"

Gaither leaned in. His eyelashes were longer than any Natalie had ever seen on a man, and when he blinked, she could have sworn they blew the slightest breeze across her brow.

Wait a minute! How could I not have seen this until right this second?

It might have been the low light by the desk that concealed the dark ligature mark encircling Gregory Gaither's throat. The mark looked like a scar that had been neglected and healed badly over a long period of time. From what Gaither had told her of his murder, the killers had not hanged him. What had they done to cause the lingering circular scar? Whatever caused the marks, Natalie knew it was deeply woven into the fabric of Gaither's present motives and condition. The marks no doubt hinted at a nightmarish circumstance, and she wondered if Gaither would ever tell her everything that had happened to him.

The words rolled out of Gaither like a feverish sermon. "They've come out of hiding. I found them. They're in Gettysburg."

"Gettysburg? How do you know?"

"There have always been stories about the famous battlefield being haunted. Pale faces looking out of Spangler Woods, the forest that borders the field itself. People say they've even seen soldiers walking around during tours. They look like they're doing some kind of maneuver along the wood's perimeters, maybe the last thing they did before their death. I've seen it. It's very unsettling to watch those lost souls attempting to make sense of a world that has left them behind. Lives. Movement and motion out of time."

"And you saw them? The men who killed you?"

"I walked the woods. Or I tried. The air in there, it's different. Diffused with this terrible electrical current. If you've ever been in a field or a wide-open space right before a lightning storm, you've experienced something like it. Only, this sensation was far worse. With every step, I felt like I was being torn apart. You know how Julius Caesar's own senate murdered him in the Curia of Pompey? They all rushed in and stabbed him? That's what it felt like, a hundred hands cutting me to ribbons. I had to leave. The evil in Spangler Woods … it was palpable. And I hadn't felt that mingling of horrid sensations since the last time I saw those men and they snatched me off a Philly side street. I was too weakened to confront them, anyhow, but—"

"Why Gettysburg?"

"There's a reenactment that takes place there every third of July to commemorate the three-day confrontation. Men and women come from all over the country to dress in period clothing, carry outdated artillery around, and they try to recapture—I guess—the triumph of the battle. But what these folks don't realize is they've also caught the attention of The Remainders."

"Wait—how many of these *things* are we talking about?"

"I can't be sure because they don't travel in packs or clans. They're loners by definition. Except for The Twin Brothers, the ones that took me. They're bonded by blood. I don't know much about them. Where they came from? Who or *what* made them? I only know they walk the earth and … from what I can gather, they feed off human cruelty. The psychic energy it puts out sustains them. Sadly, that source is usually plentiful enough to sustain them. Of course, when it dries up here and there, they have no choice but to feed and inflict their own means for cruelty. Beyond that, I'm ignorant of their history, or how old they are."

"And what if they're gone by the time we make it to Gettysburg? How do you know they'll still be there?"

"I don't know," Gaither admitted. "But it's taken me almost forty years just to pin them down to Spangler Woods. I—we've got to try. I don't know what their plan is, if they even have one. I can only assume they've gone to ground within the field's vicinity because the reenactment event itself seems to taunt them, to hold some symbolic meaning for them. Or the energy of the field matches the energy they knew in life. I mean, this was the battle that turned the tide for a Union victory. The Remainders fought in the Civil War, on the Confederate side. They still wear their uniforms when they rise to hunt, which is *not all that often.*"

"Still … this could pan out as a fool's errand unless they show themselves the day of the reenactment?"

"They will. I don't know *how* I know, but why else would they have been haunting the woods there for the last ten years? They've got something in mind. Maybe they've even been participating in the reenactment without having been discovered. They'd blend right in with the actors. I don't know. I only know we've got to try, before they flee Spangler Woods for good and I lose track of them again."

"Wait, you said they murdered you in … nineteen-eighty-five was it?"

"It was."

They both turned toward the sound of a wooden spoon stirring the iced tea in a glass pitcher down the hall. Time was running out for their exchange.

Gaither's eyes flashed with a terrible knowing. "If the reenactment doesn't draw them out of the ground, I will. They can't abide the black man in their midst. Their blood and bodies run on unleaded intolerance and racism. A sign of *their* times. And, Natalie, I just can't wait any longer. Not one more year. Not another second. Because I'm tired. I need to—I only want to rest. The long rest. I've been waiting for a long time."

"You didn't answer my question," Natalie pressed. "Who are these men? Sociopathic Civil War enthusiasts or something?"

"The real thing. They're not like you or Doctor Dan."

"I don't understand—"

"They're Remainders. Psychic vampires. Death can't touch them. They're both over a hundred and seventy-five years old. The other Remainders may be even older than that, but it's human cruelty that sustains them all. My murderers, they're immortal. Just like their racism. I'm going to unearth them, and I'm going to put them down. You're going to help me."

"Look at me, for God's sake. I can barely get out of bed—"

"Through possession. Consensual possession."

Natalie's mind screamed. *FUCK! NO!*

VI. GROUT

That night, Natalie's sleep was thin and meaningless while the rest of South Philadelphia snored on and on. She could not mute her thinking, and it harassed her mind to no end. There was also the fact she had just slept for twelve hours in a post-op state of healing. Not to mention, Gaither had made his proposition to her, and before she could protest or relent, Dan had come sauntering back into the bedroom with the iced tea pitcher in one hand and a glass that was filled to the brim in the other. A straw peeked out over the edge of the glass.

Just as quickly, Gaither had slipped past the oblivious med student on his way out of the bedroom. It would have brought a smile to Natalie's face any other time to watch Dan shiver just as the ghost brushed by him, but her penchant for humor was greatly diminished.

I can't let him possess me. She had never allowed a spirit to inhabit her before. Natalie had set up a strict protocol to protect herself from such a thing. They were as much safety measures as they were procedural.

When a client finds themselves suddenly speaking with a lost loved one through Natalie, emotions run high, and if not for Natalie's rules of spirit engagement (controlling the conversation, turning away anyone visibly intoxicated or under the influence of any controlled substance, to name a few rules of conduct), the whole process could take a dangerous turn very quickly. It was always a standing rule of order never to allow a spirit to enter the physical body of the medium. As far as the mind, Natalie always had specific fail safes, safety words, and mental barriers to hold the spirit no closer than an arm's length distance of her mind. What Gaither was asking (if not demanding) flew in the face of every precautionary measure she'd put in place when Natalie had decided to parlay her skills as a medium into a money-making venture.

The migraine behind her eyes felt like it had spread out. She felt its terrible pulsations behind her cheekbones. Inside her sinuses. Natalie suspected four ibuprofen tablets would do little to ease the terrible discomfort.

Nevertheless, she took a deep breath and set about hauling herself up into a sitting position. Once her head came off the pillow, it kicked the internal ping-pong game back in gear. The little ball glanced off the inner right crown of her skull and began its dreadful ricochet once more. With her eyes squeezed shut and her upper lip clenched between her teeth, Natalie slowly, slowly, slowly turned herself to face the side of the bed. Stiffly, stiffly, slowly she eased her legs off the side of the mattress and lowered her bare feet to the rug. "Excedrin," she said to herself. "Fuck ibuprofen."

Maybe you should let Dan get it for you, huh?

One more deep breath in and out. Then Natalie rose off the bed. Midway, the pain squeezed her eyes closed again. She felt dizzy and nearly fell forward when her eyes sprang open.

Gaither was standing right in front of her, hands on his hips.

"OhmyGod—"

Natalie clapped a hand over her mouth, stifling the scream of surprise. Her other hand braced her from behind as she dropped back down onto the edge of the mattress.

"What are you doing? Do you realize how much griping and groaning you're doing just trying to get out of bed? You want to wake up Doctor Dan?"

After much deliberation, Natalie had managed about a half hour ago to convince Dan to crash on the couch. He didn't want to leave her alone, but as the apartment was so small, she could practically whisper for him and he'd hear, Dan gave in. The bags under Dan's eyes had been large enough that if he were boarding a plane, TSA would force him to check them at the gate.

"You can't do that," she hissed up at him. "Can't just sneak up on me."

"You're a medium, girl. You should've seen me coming long beforehand. Isn't that how it works?"

"Not exactly," Natalie said. "I'm a medium, not a *clairvoyant!*" The ping pong ball stopped somewhere in the middle of her brain and hung suspended there. "Listen, Gregory. You're going to have to think of some other way for us to work together on this mission of yours. I'm not letting you in."

"We barely had time to talk about it. You're being a bit preemptive, don't you think?"

"I know my limits. I've got certain parameters in place. For my own protection."

"So what? You think I'm out to hurt you? How would that benefit me, Natalie? There's so much more to this than you understand. And you *wouldn't* understand because this situation is unique to the both of us. I've never possessed another human being, but I've seen it done. From my side of things. From over here. I've seen a spirit squeeze itself into a human being's body and mind as neatly as if the living person were the hole and the soul was the nail."

"Seen it done? How'd that work?" She tasted copper on her tongue. She smelled burnt toast. And Natalie was all at once hungry and repulsed in the same instance. *This is not good. Something's wrong.*

"By accident," he said. "It's not important. You wouldn't understand the *how* either. There are just some things you living folk are not meant to understand. Just know that if you were to allow me in, to possess you for an extended period of time, it would not only take away this pain you're experiencing every five seconds. It would heal you."

Natalie frowned up at him. Shook her head. "Gregory, I—"

"You know what grout is? You know what it's used for?"

She shrugged. "Never took a shop class. Sorry."

"It's a packable material used to fill the space between two elements for bonding them or to create a water-tight seal."

"O-kay …"

"Don't you see?" Gaither said. "I bear the potential to *bond* with you for the purpose of *creating a seal.* To fill the space where there ought not be a hole or a wound. And I wouldn't *alter* you as much as I'd *augment* your essence and your capabilities. Now you've just had major surgery. Consider me the salve on the open wound just below your hairline. You can barely move without it hurting. But you put me behind the wheel, so to speak? Your ambulatory wheel. I'd fill you up with the strength to walk, to run even. To drive a car, which is essential to the matter at hand."

A glimmer of consideration shone in Natalie's eyes. She held her silence, deliberating within. After some time, her inner counsel began shouting *Nonononononono.*

"No way. Something would happen to me. I'd lose myself. I-I'd lose the part of myself that ends where you begin. It'd be fucking madness. But only for me. And how the hell could I be sure you'd vacate once I helped you?"

"What reason would I have to take you over for all time?" Gaither asked, tossing up his hands. "I told you earlier, I want peace. I need to move along. But I can't until I have my revenge on The Remainders and settle that last affair."

"So, God wouldn't let you through the pearly gates until you, what? Exacted your retribution?"

"You wouldn't understand. Again, it's not something you *could* understand. Especially someone like you. What'd you have, twelve straight years of Catholic school? Nah, not you."

"Yeah, try me."

Gaither paused, then blurted, "Let's just say the God you've come to understand is *not* entirely the God of the New Testament. In fact, *that* facet of the Creator is gone. What we've got up there beyond the stars is pure and unadulterated Old Testament. Vengeful. Disappointed as a father on the day his son gets expelled from high school. I know things you'd *never,* ever wish to know. About the future. How long you've all got? Human beings. God's greatest folly. But I *will* tell you this is not a choice I've made, to forego my entrance into a higher plane of existence. No, that vengeful Creator has kept me out, and those just like myself. The ones with unfinished business in the material world. None of us can cross over until we've … handled our affairs."

His speech wound down to nothing. "And when all of us have … tied up our loose ends? God will have the final say and bring the hammer down."

"I don't believe in a god," Natalie said. "The collateral damage of those twelve years in Catholic School you're talking about."

"Oh, girl, God couldn't care less that you're gay. That's a human hang-up, you get me? There are things that have forced God to permanently retire the ole *benevolent shepherd* approach. Just nothing so trivial as who you fall in love with or who you're attracted to."

"You're not *allowed* to pass on until you … what?"

"Handle my affairs. Plain and simple. I'm God's finger on the trigger."

"It-it doesn't jibe."

"It wouldn't. And it *won't*. Until you die. Then all will be revealed. You people? You living, breathing beings? You've gotten *so much wrong*. I mean, not even close in some instances."

"Thanks for the theo—theolo—"

"Natalie? Hey? *Hey*—"

That's when the atom bomb exploded white light and tendrils outward from the core of her brain stem. She knew only impossibly blinding rays that blotted out the world.

Natalie toppled off the edge of the bed and landed flat on her belly, face digging into the rug. Nose pushed out of shape.

Then her chest tightened.

Her lungs failed.

Her heart stopped.

All would be revealed.

VII. THE REMAINDERS

Before Anton LaVey, founder of the Church of Satan, coined the term "psychic vampire" in his book *The Satanic Bible*, such beings were called "energy vampires." There was nothing metaphorical about who they were and continue to be. The key word there being "continue," for *vampires* do *continue* until they are stopped. Even then, if they are not halted properly, they linger. They continue. They remain.

They remain when everyone else has gone to dust.

The Twin Brother Remainders had *continued* for nearly a century and a half. Lingered. Loitered in the cold, dark earth. No one ever halted The Twin Brothers, but this is not to say no one ever tried. Those who tried in the past failed in that they attempted to fight off The Twin Brothers while being attacked. They had thrown fists or fired a gun or slashed a dagger at The Twin Brothers.

None of that was going to do it.

The Twin Brothers were born John and Henry Tarvill in 1840, in the city of Macon, Georgia, a city well suited to thrive on the shipment of cotton from its many ports along the Ocmulgee River and heavily populated with a workforce of enslaved African men, women, and children. As important as the city was to Georgia as a whole, in terms of its admirable economic status, Macon tried and failed at being named the state capital. In fact, Macon came in dead last at the end of the runoff of 1855.

The Tarvill family had come to manufacture ten thousand pounds of picked, clean cotton annually by that year, and with that had come a status the Tarvill patriarch parlayed into many different favors and *exceptions* to the rule of law. When William Tarvill, patriarch of the family, decided to punish a recalcitrant male slave who worked on his plantation by hanging the man's wife and five-year-old son, the courts granted him a reprieve on his word they were plotting to murder him in his bed, the father and mother and daughter together. Sometime after, Macon County officials appointed William Tarvill *lead slave catcher* of Bibb County. William handpicked his team of men, and when they were a baker's dozen, he christened them with the name The Wranglers.

Now, lying in the cold and wet earth—prone and naked and pale as two oversized grubs—John and Henry Tarvill remembered their father and his Wranglers.

They remembered the countless times Father's seat at the dinner table sat empty because he had ridden out with The Wranglers at dawn and would be gone for days at a time. While Father was away, The Twin Brothers had run the plantation in cooperation with their mother. When Father returned, it was always easy to determine whether he'd been successful in his hunt. If he threw one or both of his boys a vicious beating in the toolshed within an hour of arriving home, that meant the slave had slipped The Wranglers and made it to a free territory. But if he shared his whiskey with his boys the night of his return, then The Wranglers had snagged their prey and seen that runaway slave returned to their owner.

So it was, The Twin Brothers came to associate good times and pleasant memories with that of a captured or executed slave. Likewise, the connection to pain at the end of their father's belt with that of a runaway slave given safe harbor in a free state.

From that had come the hatred for the slave. The non-white in general.

Years wore on from there. Father eventually gave in to John and Henry's constant requests and allowed them to join The Wranglers on a hunt. A twenty-year-old farmhand named Jacob Holycomb had disappeared from a neighbor's slave quarters in the dead of night. Holycomb had stolen the largest kitchen knife from his master's kitchen. The town officials of Bibb County labeled Holycomb armed and dangerous, and any restrictions that had been in place to guarantee the slave's safe return to his master were lifted. The Wranglers were given carte blanche to dole out their own justice so long as they returned with proof of the deed. The red bandana Holycomb wore around his neck, his "lucky kerchief," would suffice. The riders were frenzied with bloodlust when they rode out. It had been like a contagion, and the Twin Brothers contracted it from the other men to the point they lost their focus and could not help but to fantasize about the possibility of stringing up a runaway by their father's side. Of watching Jacob Holycomb twitch and kick and mess his pants while he choked out above their upturned heads.

Wrapped in this shared reverie of theirs, The Twin Brothers became separated from The Wranglers. Five miles deep into Talbot Forest, a wood choked with elms practically grown into one another, with the October blood moon sitting fat in the sky and gloating like a bloodshot eyeball, The Twin Brothers knew fear the likes of which they had not experienced since they were little boys sick with typhoid. When Henry made up his mind for the both of them which direction to take, John's horse tossed him when a falling tree branch in the distance spooked the animal. The one horse's fright sparked the same response in the other horse, and Henry just barely dismounted before his animal bolted out from under him.

Of course, this was not a flash of memory either of The Twin Brothers wished to remember while they hunkered in the ground some six feet deep from the surface. Henry shuddered ever so slightly, the compacted earth barely allowing the movement. John curled his hands into fistfuls of dirt. Talbot Forest haunted the two of them even still, one hundred and fifty-four years after the events of that night.

They did not come to find Jacob Holycomb that night. Rather, it was someone (or something) altogether inhuman who found them while they wandered, hopelessly lost, through Talbot Forest. The mountain-of-a-man burst from a drift of leaves behind them and fell upon both the young men with a violence even the Tarvill boys could not have conjured up in their twisted, eighteen-year-old minds. Without a word, The Mountain (as The Twin Brothers came to call him in the absence of a true identity) dragged the Tarvill boys down into the leaves from which he'd emerged, and it was beneath the detritus and brambles and dead rodents that The Mountain imposed his dark gift upon them. Neither John nor Henry could recall with any bit of certainty or detail what The Mountain did to them. The only lingering element of the ordeal was the pungent, suffocating smell of death and rot all around them. A world of decomposition and things falling apart by rapid degrees. Their lives and their deaths bled into one another as neatly as if the barrier between the two were porous and of no consequence.

The Twin Brothers awoke in Talbot Forest the next day very much changed and, for all intents and purposes, no longer to be counted among the living. Yet, there they had stood in the late morning of a Fall day glowering at one another. Skin pallid and puckered in some spots like cottage cheese. Their brown eyes filmed over in a mucous membrane. They felt each other, examined one another from head to toe. Pronounced one another dead. The fear and the uncertainty had been unbearable for the first few months that they wandered the countryside, carefully avoiding detection and narrowly escaping the eyes of the living. They entertained the notion of returning to Father's plantation and asking for help. But both young men knew they could never go home again. Father would not hesitate to blow both their heads off with his Winchester once he laid fearful eyes on his two missing boys.

They went to ground a mile out from the family plantation. Since they could not contact Father or return to the homestead, The Twin Brothers settled for the comfort of lingering within its vicinity. John and Henry could not make sense of what happened to them or what they'd become. To be dead, for all intents and purposes, and yet to walk the earth in spite of such a development? Whereas food and drink had been the source of their living sustenance, neither one of them experienced hunger for either. They did not fear starvation, rather, their bodies seemed to crave something they could not immediately identify. They trapped rabbits and other small game as Father had taught them. Tasted the furry flesh and vomited it out immediately. The blood of their trappings did not sicken them, and while it filled them with a newfound energy and sharpness of mind, the benefits were short-lived.

It was by accident The Twin Brothers discovered the longer-lasting source of their survival. Lying in the ground beside one another in the rugged woodland that bordered the Tarvill plantation, John and Henry were awakened from a deep sleep by a sensation they had not yet experienced.

An all-consuming vitality accompanied by a shared vision that bled across their brainpans.

They saw Father in their mind's eyes. He was shouting in his terrible, guttural voice and stalking down the center aisle of the slave quarters. He swung a lantern in one hand, splashing bands of light across the wood walls of the hut, and with the other hand, Father struck out at the slaves in their beds with a long, bloody horsewhip. "If you ain't with me, you're against me!" Father screamed at them all. "The lot of you! I got a hanging branch for every last one of you, hear?" Crack of the whip. "Our production is down!" Crack of the whip. "And I will get down to whoever one of you killed my boys!" Whip-crack! The end of the hurtful

41

instrument struck out and stung the bare feet of the slaves. Their arms. It snapped a child in the forehead and made the little girl cry long into the night against her mother's bosom. Father stalked the slave quarters up and down, threatening and cursing and spitting and flailing out at them with his whip until the hut was loud with the cries and shrieks of every man, woman, and child within. That is how Father left them. Wailing.

When it was done, John and Henry pushed themselves up and out of their shallow graves. Something had kindled a fire in their guts. It was as if they had all at once become infused by the spirit of gods.

The power.

The rejuvenation.

Thus, the source of their ultimate and lasting sustenance revealed itself to The Twin Brothers. They were psychic vampires who fed off the cruelty of the living towards one another. There was no shortage of this particular brand of nourishment, especially in the time of slavery. But the country was on the brink of war. Brother against brother. To settle once and for all the question of slavery in a free country. America.

For the Twin Brothers, it was a call to arms like no other. The very future of their existence seemed to hinge upon such a question.

If there was one thing Father drilled into their heads from a young age, they were to make themselves useful whenever possible. When the bloody unrest of the Civil War found them, John and Henry enlisted for the Confederacy just in time for the Battle of Fort McAllister. How they would have loved to somehow let Father know they were serving the South by fighting the Yank bastards to preserve the way of life and order of things they had come to cherish above all other things. The question of slavery was, for the Twin Brothers, never a question at all but a staple of American prosperity, and it was worth fighting for at any and all costs. Both brothers proved fine marksmen, not to mention immortal in comparison to the hundreds of their brothers who died beside them in the countless theaters of war. Bullets passed through them, and the wounds healed instantly as if they'd never been shot.

The Twin Brother Remainders knew they were thriving as a result of the powerful psychic tremor of racial strife and blood soaking into the grasses of battlefields across the country.

And Earth itself conducted the tremor of conflict and hate and death like a tuning fork carries a tone through its metal prongs.

It carried.

And it fed every Remainder, no matter their location. Under or above ground.

War had always been and would always be a source of great energy and sustenance for The Remainders. The Tarvill Brothers were no different.

Conflict enriched their bodies. Their souls.

More powerful than a vitamin shot or adrenaline spike to the heart of a dead man.

Wherever war broke out, it was felt and absorbed by The Remainders. It infused their bones to the point of titanium strength. Nourished their blood. Of course, wars do not continue for all time. Even strife takes a hiatus. During wartime, The Twin Brothers felt no need nor desire to rise from their holes in the ground. So it was that prolonged peace time forced them to rise and to feed. To migrate towards smaller, more concentrated altercations by which they could derive energy, albeit smaller and less potent.

Decades piled on top of one another. The Twin Brothers chased the psychic vibrations of murder and death wherever it spiked. Philadelphia. Chicago. New York. Mississippi. Los Angeles. They burrowed down into the grounds of cemeteries, fields, forests, swamplands. And they dug themselves back out again when the murder, rape, or manslaughter rates of a specific region dipped back down again.

As the years wore on, wisdom and experience culminated in a new and decidedly convenient mode of travel by which they covered vast distances in short periods of time. They needed only to raise themselves up onto tiptoes as a stiff wind kicked up around them. It lifted them as effortlessly as if they were a pair of willow wisps, and once they gained a specific altitude, the Twin Brother Remainders burned across the sky, red and bright as comets, guided by the dreadful tremors of injustice and hatred and blood spilled in vain that called to them from afar. The Twin Brothers touched down in so many cities and small towns over and over again, they developed something of a uniquely intimate connection to the United States of America.

They'd come to know America in a biblical sense.

Her every blemish.

Lovely curve.

Hidden scar. Rough spot.

The Twin Brothers quickly discovered that while the question of slavery had been answered with abolition, the abuse and reduction of the African American stood the test of time.

Racism persisted.

It continued.

It remained.

The Twin Brother Remainders reveled in this above all other injustices. Jim Crow. Institutional discrimination. Structural racism. Lynching.

The new century dawned, and the years wore on. The Twin Brothers chased racial strife to East St. Louis when the race riot of 1917 broke out, resulting in the deaths of two hundred and fifty African Americans.

The Brothers cut a bright, burning swath through the sky to Chicago, and they were filled to bursting with all the negative energy born of the city's 1919 riots. A white man had decided it would be fun to throw rocks at some black people swimming on a segregated Chicago beach, and it sparked five days of shootings and hangings that ended in twenty-three African American deaths.

The Twin Brothers knew nothing of age, and they grew stronger by the day. These large-scale events, while not quite as sustaining as the death tolls of a war sufficed, and kept them fed and nurtured for long periods. Sometimes as long as five to ten years. Time did not run them down. If anything, the Tarvill boys started to believe they would run down the clock instead. With this sense of invulnerability and a building God complex, John and Henry grew more brazen. It was suddenly not enough to merely lie in the ground and passively absorb the negative frequency the human race churned out at a seemingly endless rate.

In August of 1933, they rose from their makeshift graves and hunted people as they'd done that night so many decades before with their father and The Wranglers. John and Henry Tarvill decided to double-dip into the well of sustenance by drawing energy from the deeds of other murderers and racists and maniacs.

And from their own deeds as well.

Like the devil's prodigal sons, John and Henry Tarvill returned to Macon, Georgia in the summer of that same year. The town of their birth. They burrowed into the family plot where their mother, father, and baby sister were buried. The plot became their home base of sorts. Over the course of thirty years, they hunted black men, women, and children exclusively, extracting them from the population as deftly as grim reapers.

A "free black" called up the powerful sensation of dread and painful retribution within the minds of John and Henry, born of how Father had treated his twin sons when a runaway slave escaped the Wranglers.

A caught or murdered black called up the altogether opposite effect upon the Twin Brothers. It filled them up like the Holy Spirit had once done for them during Sunday Church so long ago.

They terrorized Georgia, the easternmost regions of Alabama, and the northernmost hotbeds of Florida. The abductions were as sporadic as they were widespread, baffling detective and FBI agent alike. They worked up profiles on the suspect only to have them unravel when The Twin Brothers changed their methods of execution. Seven men and one woman were tried and convicted of the murders. Four of the convicted sat in Old Sparky. The woman was hanged.

Thirty years of terror.

Then, The Twin Brothers went to ground for five years in the family plot and fed off the racial strife that had begun to reach a fever pitch in the mid-sixties.

It was around this time the Twin Brothers began to fully experience the effects upon them from a world that was moving on while they themselves stubbornly embraced and fully embodied a time in America long dead. Lying in their graves, mere feet from the bones of their family members in the adjoining crypts, John and Henry Tarvill experienced the stirrings of their own vulnerability for the first time. A new and different psychic tremor took hold of them from a short distance.

Atlanta.

Fifty miles north of their native Macon. A feeling of lightness and hope.

The subtle shifting of a scale to balance out more evenly for all people.

A pinprick of light just strong enough to reach deep down into the earth and penetrate the Tarvill tombs. A pinprick of light that touched the pale, wormlike Tarvill Twins where they lay in the cold, compacted earth.

A light sparked by the emergence of a black pastor turned civil rights leader.

Civil rights?

Oh, how the Twin Brothers had shuddered underground as the light of the new movement dug the shadows out of their graves and threatened their existence like nothing before.

The brothers felt it on their skin. An itching. Then a flaking as the light widened and intensified in its power and influence aboveground.

The more the influence of this black pastor ...

King? How, John, can any black bear the name of King, let alone walk the earth with pride?

the wider the band of light grew and the brighter it burned ...

and the more hurt it put upon the Twin Brothers and all other Remainders like them.

August 28, 1963. Two hundred and fifty thousand people took part in The March on Washington for jobs and freedom. This "King" delivered a speech about his "dreams" in front of the Lincoln Memorial.

Lincoln! Race-changing bastard! Henry, look what Lincoln has done to our America?!

And the light widened ever further. It burned the brothers underground with psychic pulses that carried all the way from D.C. to the Tarvill crypts.

The Twin Brothers were weakening underground. Shriveling. Shrinking. Their age would soon catch up to them with a vengeance, rendering them dust and hair and bones. What's more, they were suddenly fearful of coming up out of their graves. The world had changed, and they were terrified this brave, new, and fairer land would sap them of any life left in their bodies. Would crush them under the sheer weight of equality and a drawing-down of evil among human beings. They lay in the ground, images of their own burning and combustion haunting them into submission. Freezing them in place.

The brothers learned their brand of immortality had its limits.

A hard lesson.

Then, a bomb went off at the 16ᵗʰ Street Baptist Church in Birmingham, Alabama. September 15, 1963. The explosion killed four little girls and fueled angry protests. The brothers not only felt the blast in their graves, they absorbed the overwhelming emotions of sadness and resultant anger following the tragedy. Both reactions were as nutrients to their weakened, pruned extremities and nearly paralyzed the organs The Mountain had left in their bodies. The blood in their veins, old and sour and just about useless as if it had turned to vinegar, suddenly boiled in every extremity with a newfound infusion of energy and vitality they had not experienced so fully since that night long ago when they had lain in the ground near the Tarvill plantation and drawn such powerful energy from the abusive words and actions of Father towards a shed full of slaves.

Brother, we've got to rise again before something else happens to weaken us like before—we got to strike while our irons are hot if we aim to survive!

They rose from the Tarvill crypt and bid farewell to their underground ancestors. In the dead of night, they caught the northeasterly winds right outside Macon's city limits. It carried them to a suburban town called Whitman, ten miles outside of Manayunk, Pennsylvania. They widened the scope of their prey, and at week's end following their arrival, a Japanese street vendor, an African-American newlywed couple, and even a small group of Irish men stumbling drunk down the street during Sunday's early morning hours disappeared neat as you please. Plucked from the population. And the Twin Brothers burrowed into a small, neglected cemetery called Laurel Mount. Revitalized, they lay in the ground and drew whatever earth swells of hate crimes and racial unrest bubbled up along the eastern seaboard and touched their pale bodies.

Brother, there's something looming on the horizon. I can feel the menace in my bones. It's coming. It's in the air, and it's in the ground. Do you feel it?

A static charge. A strangeness of tragedy and loss on its way. In rapid succession.

February 21, 1965. A black religious leader named Malcolm X was assassinated during a rally by members of the Nation of Islam.

Then, someone killed the "King" man on April 4, 1968 while he was catching a cigarette on the balcony of his hotel room in Memphis, Tennessee.

Unrest. Strife. Bloodshed.

Tears. Lament. Hopelessness.

All these things went into the stew of evil that fueled the Twin Brothers, all Remainders, to the brims of their very existence. They became drunk on grief as if from a barrel of moonshine.

The deaths of X and the "King," along with the sense the tide was turning backward and the clock unwinding in the Twin Brother's minds, was enough to allow for them to lie in the dirt longer than they had ever needed to before. Of course, they still enjoyed the hunt, and every couple of years, John and Henry stole a handful of unlucky souls away from their families and friends. Away from the eyes of God when they believed God to have turned away for but a moment.

So, it was for nearly three decades.

Another King, this one with a different name, was brutally battered by a group of police officers on the side of a highway in LA County. If only this had stood up as the beginning and end of the incident, the Twin Brothers would have fed upon the evil of the happening and the tremors of unrest that had once more risen to the surface like cream in hot coffee. It might have been good for John and Henry Tarvill.

But four of the officers were caught on videotape beating the new King.

Had the officers been found guilty in a court of law for their actions on that California highway, it would not have made much difference at all for The Remainders. It would have merely lighted on their skin like some annoying mosquito only to be driven off again by the sound slap of one's hand. But on April 28, 1992, those four officers were found not guilty of the charges brought against them by the people of the Golden State. What happened that night and lasted for three days would be the first time in nearly a century and a half The Twin Brother Remainders would rise from their graves and travel to a destination to take the fight to the enemy.

The Twin Brothers clawed their way out of the dirt naked and pale as porcelain. They unearthed the box buried within the vicinity of their makeshift graves and retrieved their Confederacy uniforms inside. They dressed quickly under cover of night in the Laurel Oak Cemetery. This had been their routine whenever they rose up for the sake of feeding. Twin Brothers with dirt in their thick dark moustaches, a filmy glint in their steely eyes, their bones poking out at the worn fabric of their uniform like kite sticks. Hate driving and directing them as it always had like the Devil's compass.

Shake the dirt off, John, it is another civil war. They will need us in Los Angeles.

Now, John and Henry Tarvill opened their eyes inside the earth. Nineteen years in to yet another century. The memories of their timeline on earth, both before and after The Mountain turned them, bled across their brainpans in an endless loop of equal parts triumph and despair. The Twin Brothers cannot stop it, so they decided long, long ago to embrace it. To somehow learn from the lessons of their past.

Of how best to put things back to the way they were when they were young men.

When hearts still beat in their chests.

VIII. TO KNOW THYSELF …

Natalie woke to find herself not only behind the wheel of her friend Dan's Optima, but riding (not *driving*) down a rain slickened highway with the sun just barely having lifted above the green exit sign to her right. The sign read **NEXT EXIT PA 10-S FOR OLD LIMESTONE ROAD.** Her hands lay along the wheel, fingers curled around it. They edged left and right, back and forth ever so slightly. *But I'm not driving. I can't—ohmyGod—I—*

"I can't feel my hands!" she cried.

Wait, Natalie! Don't—

Gaither's voice exploded inside her head.

But her brain was already wrestling for control, straining to shove the presence within her aside like they were standing in the middle of a grocery aisle. The numbness in her hands as they gripped the wheel turned to that familiar sensation of blood rushing back into them. Filling her fingers. Natalie could feel the wheel again and seized it just as the Optima started to veer into the next lane over to the right. It had felt like her hands, her whole body, and mind had all gone to sleep like a leg leaned on for too long. By rapid degrees, she recovered the sense of her arms, legs. Beating heart. Growling stomach. Heartburn. Feverish thoughts.

Staticky, shuddering images laid against a black backdrop instead of disembodied spirits haranguing Natalie's frontal lobe. Clamoring to be heard.

Their buzz was no match for Gregory Gaither's loud, plaintive voice.

You're throwing off our balance! You're going to get us killed grabbing the wheel away from me like that!

She couldn't catch her breath. Her chest felt tight as a drum, the skin pulled back and cinched across the ridge of her breastbone. "Wha-what the *fuck* happened? Did I have another seizure?"

That, and a mild heart attack. Nothing to worry about.

"A what? A heart attack?"

I know how it sounds, but you've got to trust me on this! Now that I'm on board the S.S.

Natalie, you're practically a damned superhero! I saved your life by possessing you.

"Hospital. I should go to the hospital, Gaither."

The three-lane highway widened into a four-lane, and suddenly there were rows of cars carrying mostly commuters on either side. In front of her. Behind. The sensation of having become boxed in. Natalie remembered the skills she'd learned when she'd had her first panic attack at the age of sixteen. It had been in Geometry class, and Mrs. Grassley had just laid a test paper on her desk. She hadn't studied, and barely grasped the material when the teacher had lectured it out to her over the course of the last three weeks. The chest tightening. Shortness of breath. Fading vision that softened around the edges. Yes, Natalie was a pro at reining in a panic attack, having done so hundreds of times since then. Only right then, it took longer, what with the fact she had come to, barreling down a major highway in a vehicle she appeared to be driving but was not in reality.

Why don't you give me back the wheel, retreat to the back of your brain, and hang out there until you've got your bearings. You'll be able to close your eyes. I have no control over your eyes, or your mouth, as you can see by now.

And Natalie very much wanted to close her eyes. Her attention was dangerously divided between the road and her current mental state.

Not to mention the presence who had injected himself into her consciousness in the name of *saving her from a heart attack.*

"No," she said. "Forget it."

Why not? Why so stubborn?

"Because the next time I may not be able to take back control. I *don't* know *you.*"

You mean you don't know my heart? Isn't that right?

She nodded and cringed, suddenly remembering the pain in her head from the trepanning procedure. Cringed because she'd expected the nodding motion to send that dreadful ping-pong ball of extreme pain bouncing around inside her skull.

There was no pain. No ball pinging around.

It was gone.

Yeah, you might want to check your head in the rearview.

"It doesn't hurt anymore," she said, befuddled.

Go on, have a look.

Natalie checked herself in the rearview mirror. The thick layering of gauze Dan had wound around her head like a white beehive was gone.

The hole Dan McCausland had drilled into her head and plugged was gone.

There was no evidence of her ever having been trepanned.

You know my heart now? I told you I'd be your grout, Natalie. I healed your wounds, and I gotta tell you—and I mean no offense—you've never looked better than you look now. I think I probably have something to do with that.

It was true.

There was no denying it.

All her life, Natalie had been fair skinned with freckles. After Danica died, she had stopped eating healthy if she ate at all. Natalie's skin tone had told the tale of her malnutrition, and she had no interest in finding out which vitamin deficiency had caused her usually porcelain skin to adopt a bluish hue. But now Natalie saw her skin had not only recovered its former healthier shade, it appeared to glow, to emanate its own light. Had he done this by occupying her? Like protective grout, as he'd said?

Someone honked long and loud at her from the right lane. Natalie tore her eyes away from the rearview and returned them to the road.

"You did this?" she asked him.

I guess I did. I knew I'd be able to heal your wounds lickety-split, but these other changes, I had no idea. I'm guessing when I took you over and came on board, it must have produced some kind of hybrid of you and I that shows up in certain features. Part Natalie, part Gaither. And it's not such a bad thing, as you can see. Don't hate me because I'm beautiful! Looks like I complement you, don't you think?

Natalie checked the road and her periphery on both sides for cars. When a sizable enough gap developed, whereby she could safely take her eyes off the road for ten seconds, Natalie seized the moment.

Not smart, Natalie! I'm telling you, let me take the wheel! You're going to crash!

Sure enough, when she checked the rearview again, Natalie found her features had changed, adapted to reflect the physical influence of her possessor's own face. Her eyelashes were long enough she'd never have to wear lash-extender ever again. Her eyes had widened to twice their formerly squinty size. They'd also turned brown, not a trace of their former emerald green to be had. She smiled and dimples she'd never had before appeared like magic. And perhaps the strangest thing of all, at least as far as Natalie was concerned, was that her previously shaved head now sprouted thick black spikes a quarter inch long all around. She'd always been a ginger, with mousy hair that drew comparisons by many of her customer's to stars like Nicole Kidman and Emma Stone.

I'm a brunette now, Natalie thought

CAR-CAR-CARRRR!

Another car horn whined right past her left ear, its sound angrier and more menacing than any human being she'd met in a long time. Natalie snapped to, just barely avoiding soul-kissing the rear right bumper of a blue, late model Oldsmobile. The driver cut her off and gave her the finger out the window before pushing the old, ugly car to its mechanical limits and burning down the center lane. In swerving to avoid the Oldsmobile, she came within an inch of a black Mustang to her left inching in front of her. Another finger paired with an indecipherable shout.

Will you get over your trust issues and let me drive? I know where we're going! I'll tell you again, we're out of balance! That's bad for both of us!

"How long have we been driving?"

About a half hour, another six to go

Natalie had *no idea* where they were going. She seemed to remember Gaither had told her. Yet, the information eluded her like a word grasped for and just out of reach.

Gettysburg.

"What?"

That's where we're going. To the national historical site. Just in time for the Battle of Gettysburg reenactment event. They tie it into their Fourth of July festivities, so it will probably draw a lot of people. Now if you don't mind, it would be better for both of us if I kept you alive instead of letting you kill yourself in a car wreck.

"Fine, all right?" she cried, more frustrated than angry. "I don't understand why I can't drive us. All I'd need is the GPS on my cell phone."

I don't know why either, but unless I have control over your arms and legs and access to your vision, we might not be able to maintain our connection. And I don't want to find out what'll happen if we're driving along a busy highway when your mind and body reject my presence and bounce me out. It could be catastrophic!

"Do *not* make me regret this later when it comes time for you to clear out!"

There was no warning. The full-on possession took place in rapid degrees. A buzzing stirred at the spot where Natalie's brainstem docked with her spinal column. An electric shock jerked her lower legs outward as if from a myoclonic jerk in sleep. Her eyes twitched, squinched shut, and flashed open. She felt her body do a quick little dance, her butt scraping to and fro across the bucket contour of the driver's seat. The strangeness of the experience then descended, affecting her core at first, then her inner thighs. It felt like the hand of God had somehow squeezed her into a body suit two-sizes too small for her. Every internal organ and muscle seemed to push outward against her skin, like it wanted out. This was Gaither shoving himself inside of a Natalie-suit and damn the discomfort. Her extremities went numb as before—the sensation of absent limbs where there, in fact, were limbs.

A band of steel sunlight glinted off the windshield, but it did not impair Natalie's eyesight. It was more of a vague discomfort.

She could see and hear her feet pumping at the brake, then switching to the gas pedal, but it might as well have been happening on a TV or movie screen. No connection to it. Physical or otherwise. Happening apart from her experience.

Yeah, I've got this now. So just, you know, relax, and see if you can slip to the back of your brain. You're good at controlling your thoughts and the soul static, so I imagine this should be a breeze for you, no?

"Not exactly," she said, still trying to get used to being in the driver's seat with the wheel in her hands and knowing she was not driving the car. She was a passenger. "I'll try it. And you're sure you know where to go? Because I can't exactly bring up the GPS on my phone without the use of my hands."

I know. I don't know how I know. I guess you could compare it to the way a cat or a dog can find its way home if you drop it off in the middle of nowhere.

It was harder than she thought, relinquishing control of her body to Gaither.

The feeling was comparable to what she imagined it felt like for a mother and father to watch their firstborn child board a school bus for the first time. Bittersweet. The *bitter* represented by the fact she wished she'd chosen differently back at the house and avoided this clusterfuck of a situation entirely. *Sweet* because she was exhausted and all too relieved to sit back and gather her thoughts from a removed vantage point. Natalie pictured herself in her mind's eye as standing in a black, depthless area without ceiling or floor. It wasn't until The Static of Souls reared up before her seemingly from nowhere that she was certain she had, in fact, succeeded in abandoning all thought. The Static of Souls roared, excited and stimulated by her presence and how much closer she suddenly came to them. In the black, they writhed and twitched and twisted as one conglomeration of *interference*—their mournful, wailing, but insistent voices swirling about; mixing together to the point not a one of them rose above the fray with any decipherable message.

Before Natalie knew what was happening, The Static let out a loud, boisterous *scree* born of a million bodiless voices. It swelled to ten times its previous size before her, and like a tsunami wave, it rose above her. Hung there like a canopy of suffering and death. Sensing the moment by which to save herself from its assault, Natalie raised her hand palm-outward like a traffic cop. "Heel! *Hold, all of you! In time! In time, people!*"

She fully anticipated resistance or even a revolt. After all, Natalie had no idea how or when she would be able to see to all of them. If she were to hazard a guess, Natalie suspected there were easily tens of thousands of souls condensed into the warbling mass of crawling, crying static before her. But, even then, The Static of Souls obeyed Natalie's command and shriveled back down to its original size. It retreated, increasing the berth between she and them. They *heeled* as she'd told them to. She focused her attention on the volume of their cries and mentally lowered it to a level she could manage. This was a power Natalie missed, and she knew she'd be lying if she were to say otherwise.

Then, she remembered what all of this was for. Or rather, who. Why she'd agreed to any of this …

Natalie took a step toward the Static of Souls. "Danica Kincaid?" she called out to the twitchy mass of electric fuzz. "It's me, Natalie! Come forward! Please!"

No voice cut through the noise, the buzzing din. Typically, if Danica were present or keenly attuned to Natalie's summons, that is what would happen.

"Can you hear the sound of my voice?"

Nothing.

"*Danica Kincaid! This is your wife! Please answer me!*"

Natalie-girl, she's not around. Not yet. But I will find her for you. I said I would. You've got to give me time.

"NO-NO, THAT WAS *NOT* THE DEAL!"

Natalie!

"You *tricked* me! Damn you—"

Listen to me!

"No!" she cried, acutely aware now how alone the darkness surrounding her made her feel. She felt shipwrecked. Abandoned. "I'm through listening to you! *Where is Danica? You bring her to me NOW!*"

She'll be right along. She can't hear you, but she can feel your need. Just give it time.

"That's *not* how it works! I've been dealing with the likes of you since I was fourteen years old. I know how the dead function, and I know how to call them out. If she were available, she would have answered me."

Silence on Gaither's end. Then, his voice bloomed inside her mind like a flower in spring.

Are you really going to argue with a dead man about how it is to be dead? Just-just listen to me. It's simple.

"Okay, then go ahead and simplify it for me!"

Danica was at peace. She transcended into the next realm. That can only mean she was certain her affairs were settled on this plane of existence. That she'd given her loved ones closure and also gained it for herself. Now, let me ask you a question. Did you dream of her shortly after she passed?

"Yes."

How could she forget *the dream?*

Natalie had heard enough accounts of dreams involving recently deceased people from so many of her clients it made hers seem quite normal in comparison. Apparently, most if not all dreams of the dead are like this. And they are *always* bona fide visitations from a loved one, a visit the loved one has put into motion to ease the minds of those they've left behind. The deceased often will visit as many as one hundred relatives in their dreams in a single evening. The number of visits was directly proportional to the sort of impactful life the deceased person lived. How many lives had they touched in life? This made Natalie wonder why Danica had taken nearly two weeks to appear to her in a dream after the burial.

Were there other people who came before me? More important people?

Gaither cut into her line of thought.

Tell me about the dream. How'd Danica visit you?

Hesitating, Natalie began. "In the dream, we were both line cooks in a school cafeteria. Talk about random, that's gotta take the cake. Right? One minute I'm adjusting my hairnet and trying not to burn a burger on the grill. The next, someone was tapping me on the shoulder. It was Danica. Wearing this precocious grin like she possessed some delicious secret and could barely contain it. She was holding her hairnet, and pulling it apart,. She said, 'You don't have to wear yours, Nat. Toss it.' So, I tossed mine on the ground. We stood there laughing, and then we both decided to do this stomp dance on our hairnets. Real punk rock, right? My tears, they snuck up on me. Took me by surprise. The memory came to me slowly, like most memories in a lucid dream. I remembered this woman standing before me who I loved so much was dead. Gone. She told me not to cry. She put her arms around me, held me close. But

… I couldn't *feel* her. Not her body. Her arms. A little bit, around my shoulders. It was like I was only entitled to a part of my wife. Not the part of her that held her heart. It was strange. But at the same time, it was …"

Wonderful?

"Yeah," Natalie breathed. "Yeah, it really was."

That was her 'see you later,' Natalie. Not her goodbye. But she did move on to the next level. Because she made sure to visit everyone she loved. You. Her parents. Her younger brother. Even grandma over in hospice care upstate. Then, she moved on. It's what all of us crave, but few of us come to right away. There are things left unsaid, things left undone that must be dealt with. Resolved. Spoken. She handled her business *and moved along. Only now, she's been given word there is a bit of new and unfinished business that just developed down here on the ground. So, that's why it's going to take a while before you can call Danica out of the Static of Souls and she'll be there waiting to answer that call. It takes time. It takes longer when they've moved on.*

"Wait a minute … so you're telling me she *was* at peace and my calling out to her has complicated things for her again? Is that what you're saying?"

Natalie, I'm only explaining things to you as I understand them. That's all.

"I—I never would've …"

Yes, you would have. And so would anyone else. Don't fault yourself like you're the first one to call someone back out again. It happens every day. You know why? Because human beings have a stronger hold on the dead than the dead have on the living. It's easier for them to, you know, let go. For you folks, not so much.

"I don't like this arrangement," she said. "Let's tweak this arrangement before the two of us settle in." The sense she'd yielded too much power to Gaither returned to her. It overtook her, and she could not ignore it. This was her body, and she would not be relegated to a portion of it. The mind was not enough. She would not settle for acting the spectator in what happened from then on. "I'm moving back to the front row. I don't like this."

That's just what Natalie did. The most obvious way she could think of to return to her frontal lobe was to walk in the opposite direction of the Static of Souls. She turned her back on them and heard something like a deep, collective sigh from the lot, as if the action disenchanted them in some way. She started walking in the pitch black. Gaither had fallen silent, perhaps sulking. *Oh well, we're just going to have to share the* Natalie *from here on out. Tough shit!* It was strange and disorienting, walking with a complete lack of direction or landmarks in her midst by which to be guided. Only ink black. All around. And the distant buzz of the Static of Souls, which sounded more like a hornet's hive than anything else.

Without warning, the light of day washed away the darkness. Natalie was seeing with her own eyes again, although her vision was impaired somewhat. The peripheries of both the left and the right were blurred out, *fogged* almost. "Can you see all right, Gregory?"

It'll have to do. But I imagine your eyes are going to get fatigued regularly as long as the both of us are making use of them. I hope they don't strain or anything at a crucial time.)

"Yeah, well, I'll settle for my eyes."

And your mouth. Don't forget about that. I'm just a voice in your head. You're doing all the talking, *so to speak.*

"Yes," Natalie said, "and I'd say to suck it up, Greg."

Not only did Gregory Gaither's voice fall silent, but Natalie also started to suspect he might have fled her body and mind altogether. The numbness in her arms and legs remained, and the fuzziness around her field vision lingered, but she felt an emptiness within that hadn't been there before. Not since before he'd taken her over and seated her in the driver's seat of a moving vehicle. She thought of saying his name, calling him back out again, then remembered he knew her thoughts, and if he wanted to talk, then he would have by now. There was nothing. It would have to do. *He's still here. Inside. He's driving, for God's sakes.*

So, who is this Tre McKinley?

"What? Who?" She felt as if he'd suddenly crept up behind her, even though they inhabited the same body. There was no word for it, how the sudden bloom of his voice in the middle of her mind felt like what people plagued by multiple personalities must struggle with every damn day of their life. The sudden, sharp arrival of a previously dormant presence.

The name Tre McKinley *crossed your mind while you were under. You were remembering him, and I seem to remember the word* fraud *followed closely behind the name. It made you laugh in your sleep. Strange. Who was he?*

"Why do you wanna know?"

Humor me, Nat. I'm doing the driving, and I like stories. Always have.

"Well," Natalie began, "it would be more interesting if you knew *who* Tre McKinley is. He wrote an award-winning screenplay in, like, two thousand six with his girlfriend at the time, and from there, the guy just blew up. He was everywhere. On every magazine cover from *Men's Fitness* to *Woodworker's Digest.* It also seemed like he was in *every* movie being made. He always seemed to be in the cast somewhere, and almost always ended up being linked to the starlet in that movie by TMZ. In the last few years, he started marching on Washington for things like equal pay and civil rights. And the guy always made sure he was right up front with the march organizers and behind the banner, if not right beside it. Now, those are some issues that have always been close to my heart, but whenever I see a dude like Tre McKinley disclaiming his wealth and the fact he was born white, it smacks of a con. Completely insincere. I think it's safe to say we were all more than a little Tre-McKinley-Fatigued by the time the guy made his way into my shop in Greenwich. And, in true *Tre-fashion*, he came walking in with a whole camera crew.

"Now, Tre McKinley didn't come up and talk to us right away. I mean, why lower himself, right? He just sort of hung toward the back of the store, checking out incense bins. The director was the one who came right up to us. Nice woman. Marla Check, I remember her name was. Documentary filmmaker. I'd seen some of her work on PBS and Discovery. She explained to us she was compiling several celebrity lineages for a series to air on one of those entertainment networks. Tre had told the director he wanted part of his story to be revealed through a seance. And I gotta hand it to the guy … he knows how to sensationalize *everything*. He'd heard of us from friends back on the west coast. So, there they all were. I remember Danica asked the director why Tre's *people* hadn't thought to reach out to us so we could be ready for his arrival. Make arrangements to close the store temporarily? And Marla, the director, she just looked like she'd been slapped. The chick was mortified. Turns out, Tre had lied to them and said he *had* booked our store a month back. Or his agent had.

"So, there we were, off to a bad start with *the* Tre McKinley. But, you know, I agreed to make contact on his behalf to anyone who came forward with a link to the movie star." Natalie paused, chuckled at the recollection. It would always be funny to her. And tragically ironic. "I'll tell you what, Greg? Mr. McKinley was not at all prepared for the voice who came when I called to the Static of Souls on his behalf. The soul told us his name was Reginald Whitman, and he was a farmer who ran a plantation in northern Virginia during the mid-eighteen-hundreds."

I can guess where this is going.

"The more background we gathered from Whitman, the wider Tre McKinley's eyes got. They were practically popping out of his head when I asked Whitman if he was a *slave owner.*"

You knew *the answer to that question. You just wanted to see this Tre fellow squirm, didn't you?*

"Tell me you wouldn't have done the same thing in my shoes. And *will you watch the road!*"

The nose of the Optima had crept dangerously close to the bumper of a silver Camry in front of it. Gaither pumped the brake with Natalie's foot until two car lengths opened between the two vehicles.

Never yell *at the driver, girl! I would've realized on my own!*

"What's your problem? You don't like the story?"

It's a fine story. Please. Go on. There was an annoyance in Gaither's voice Natalie couldn't quite explain.

"Before I could even relay Whitman's answer, which was a resounding 'Of course, I was a slave owner,' Tre leapt out of his seat and announced the taping was done. He even went so far as to try and wrestle the camera out of the cameraman's hands. Then Tre and the camera guy had words. Tre accused the whole crew, including the director, of tricking him. *Sabotaging him*, as if that were even possible? The idea to come and make contact was his idea, no one else's! The guy just turned into a loud, tweaked ball of paranoia right before our eyes. He demanded the segment be destroyed or he'd make sure the director and everyone on her crew never worked again. Really lost it! This … this celebrity snot who wanted so badly to gain some street cred for being *in the fight for civil rights*? The descendant of a slave owner! I mean, Hollywood couldn't have written it any better!"

Silence followed, a pregnant pause that stretched long enough for Natalie's curiosity about Gaither's change in attitude to deepen. Then, Gaither's voice bloomed between Natalie's ears.

Did he get his way? Did they edit it out?

"Not only did they keep the footage in the episode, they devoted the most minutes to the time they spent in our little shop! Tre tried to stop it with an injunction, but he lost in court. And now? The only place you'll find Tre McKinley is on any of the porn websites. Hollywood turned their hypocritical back on their Golden Boy, and that's how he pays the bills now. Good thing Tre's pretty. Otherwise, he'd be panhandling a block away from Mann's Chinese Theater, where his star on the Walk of Fame has been desecrated more times than any other celebrity."

The Optima's cab slipped into silence until a tricked-out Subaru with two spoilers and no muffler opened it up to their right, clearing its scratchy throat all the way down the fast lane until it disappeared into the horizon line.

"Okay, Greg," Natalie finally said, "what's going on?"

It bothers me how you sit in judgment of this man?

"Oh, really?" She was taken aback and felt like she'd just experienced the cold, dead sting of Gaither's opened palm across her face. "Wait … you're serious?"

Yes. The story you just told, it annoys me.

"Oh …" Natalie wanted to lash out. If Gaither had learned anything about her ever since he'd started visiting (harassing?) her, he must've gathered how sensitive she was, especially when it came to being blindsided by someone. Their words of unexpected derision. Condescension? But Natalie bit back the urge to holler at (herself?) Gaither. Instead, she paused, reflected, and said, "I honestly didn't mean to offend you. I mean, c'mon, dude. You know me."

Now I know you? When did that change? It wasn't all that long ago you reminded me how you knew little to nothing about me. That you didn't trust me. And, I never said your story offended me. I said it annoyed *me. Because you sound no better than this actor, Tre McKinley, even though you're posturing yourself that way.* As if to accentuate his point aggressively, Gaither quickly jerked the Optima into the fast lane and hit the gas so hard Natalie felt the sensation ride up her right shin.

Genuinely flummoxed, Natalie tried to measure her next words carefully. She was no stranger to insecurity, but Gaither's words, measured and sharp as tiny knives, had pierced her skin. "You think I'm *posturing*? Really? I let me tell you something, I've got my own skin in the game of discrimination. You don't think I've got my own sad stories to tell? I just choose not to. I deal with it all in my own way, and that works for me. But I don't know how you could accuse me of being no better than that Social-Justice-Twitter-Warrior, Tre McKinley! You don't know me, and I don't know you, and I guess we'll just have to leave that right where it is." She hesitated, asked, "How much longer?"

Long enough to change that.

"To change what?"

Our uncertainty about one another.

"Gaither, honestly, I dunno about that."

I do. That's why I think it's time I told you about my murder and the men who killed me. The Remainders. The men we're on our way to erase from the face of the earth once and for all.

They're twins. Their names are John and Henry Tarvill, and they're immortal. I only came to know the who and what of their existence after the fact. It was a bitter cold night in West Philly the night they took me. I was a senior at Ballantine University, majoring in Communications with a minor in Social Justice. My father, who'd run out on me and my Mama when I was seven, decided to re-enter our lives right around the time I turned sixteen. The only reason I was able to afford Ballantine was because my Daddy died a year after coming back to us. And he knew he was dying. He'd had his affairs in order before he even rang the doorbell to our fifth-floor walk-up. He'd taken out a life insurance policy on himself, and the payout funded my college. That was his plan. I had no idea until after his death he'd rung up my Mama before he came back and asked if it was okay. The only reason she even let him return to us was because he told her what he'd done with his insurance and how it would benefit my higher education. I still believe had I finished college and moved on to the internship at the local TV network, WTAF, Daddy would have considered his money well-spent and his life worth the sacrifice.

Around ten that night—a Thursday, I remember—I was cramming for one of my finals and it started to feel like my eyes were just going to drop out of my head. I had to give them a rest. I popped my head into the dorm room next door where my man, Kipsey, was busy rolling homemade cigarettes with a big tin of Drum tobacco. He was more interested in smoking than my offer to buy him a couple drinks down at the local watering hole, The Galley Pub. I made a couple other stops on the way into the city proper to see if I could gather any other takers, but you'd be surprised how many college guys will turn down a beer or four when crunch time comes around. It's all business. A pall pulls itself across the campus like a big ole spider web or a funeral shroud, and it doesn't lift until after the grades are finalized across the board. Not a fun time. Even more reason to dull my senses with a couple shots of bourbon and a few beers.

Ultimately, I had no choice but to drink alone.

The Twin Remainders were already there when I arrived. It was Thirsty Thursday, and that usually meant wall-to-wall coeds, but I'd been in college long enough to expect the day of the week wouldn't matter during finals week. The place was dead. It's not far from here. I don't know if you've ever been there, but the interior was done up like a pirate ship below deck. Instead of traditional tables, they had wooden wheels bolted to the floor and loose wooden, rickety chairs arranged around them here and there in no discernible pattern. The walls were oak paneling, and the place was lit with these old-school sconces. Electric light, but if you didn't know any better, you'd have thought they were lit wicks. The murmur, slurred and incomprehensible, buzzed like the interior of some massive hive. I can tell you I was probably one of maybe three coeds there that night in December. This was nineteen-eighty-five, and The Galley had a predominantly white clientele. The brothers and sisters had their own bar a couple blocks away, closer to Cecil B. Moore Street, and I don't even know they would have been all that happy if I walked in there to drink. They could've smelled the uppity on me, I imagine. The Galley was all right. They never made me feel unwelcome, and they knew me. Not in a Norm Peterson way, but I was one of them when I strode in and put my money down.

Nat, I'm not the paranoid type, but I felt their *eyes on me from the moment I arrived. You know how you can feel someone's stare at your back? Well, this was more of a burning sensation along my shoulder blades. I felt almost like I'd developed a rash in that area. It's strange to say. I have no other way of describing it. I decided to play it safe because I was alone. No backup, you know? I took a seat at the bar closest to the door. I had the forethought to carry a can of pepper spray on my keychain. Just in case. All things were not equal in nineteen-eighty-five, no matter what the history books have written about that time period since. I'd been jumped before on campus by a group of guys who weren't even students there. I was an amateur boxer in high school and knew how to swing and hit to hurt. I fought them off. Nothing like that ever happened again, but I will say there was a handful of times I heard guys—and these* were *Ballantine boys—mutter things under their breath when they'd pass by me on the way through the quad or the cafeteria. At a party. I'd never done anything to them, and I don't know if it was because I had … and it embarrasses me to say this even now … a kind of fan-club of girls at the college. They were good friends. Some of them wanted more, but I wasn't interested in anything serious. School was front and center for me. Hell, my father had to die to send me there, and I wasn't going to fool around with girls on his dime, you know? But they were mostly white girls. I know it burned a lot of them white boys bad to know I held such—I don't know—sway over the girls they wished they had the guts to ask out themselves. Nat, The Galley had become my escape. My refuge. I couldn't even call my dorm room a safe space, a place where I could depressurize. The bar was there for that. And it was all I needed.*

The Twins. Those motherfuckers. They just had *to fuck with that!*

And it wasn't just that they were staring at me so intently. Those two were a couple of creeps just to look *at, Nat! I never knew how much twins unnerved me. I studied Gothic Lit in high school, and I know one of the main staples of the genre is* Doubles, *because people seem to possess a primal, incarnate fear of them. It's sort of interlocked with our DNA. They were seated all the way in the back of the bar, maybe twenty feet away or so, in a booth. The torn, red leather of the booth's upholstery made their faces appear as pale as porcelain. White as a toilet tank. Their lips were thick and red, though. Eyes fogged over. I couldn't tell what color their eyes were, not until later that night when I got a closer look without wanting to. These Remainders? They were Confederate soldiers once upon a time. Before I knew what they were, I just thought they were a couple months late for Halloween dress-up. They were dressed in full Confederate Army uniforms, right down to the signature low-brimmed hats pulled down low enough to cast a shadow over the upper halves of their faces. The clothes were dirty, though. The Twins looked like they'd just come from rolling around in the dirt or an anthill or something. I was sure a smell was coming off them, but I was sitting too far away to take it in.*

Now, I was careful to steal a glance over my shoulder here and there, but it got to a point I had to ask the bartender if he knew these guys. I was getting mad. I wanted to stare right back at them, meet their gazes. Force the two fuckers to flinch away. To blink. That was the other thing, and that wasn't even the strangest thing about them. Neither of them blinked.

Not once. I asked Joey, the barkeep, if he'd ever seen those two guys in there before. "Never, Gary," he told me. "But I see what they're doing. Trying to intimidate you. Freaking out the few customers I got here tonight." He whipped the towel down off his shoulder and laid it on the bar top before me. "Hey, you ain't ordered you usual yet. That because of those two weird fuckers?" And Joey whipped the towel in their direction, making no effort to conceal his contempt for the two of them. It was his place after all, so.

I shrugged, told him I was just wondering. Joey knew I was put off by them, and we liked each other enough for the big, Greek bartender to handle the matter. Then, it occurred to me. Their costumes? The authenticity? Again, this is before I found out who they really were later. "Hey, Joey," I blurted, grabbing for the barkeep's arms as he crossed out from behind the bar with the twinkle of aggression in his eyes, "you know, they might be part of one of those reenactments they do around the holidays. Could be they just wrapped up. Didn't feel like changing into civilian clothing." Joey glowered at me, and I could feel his forearm muscle rippling in anticipation. Joey wanted to do something, to get into something, and nothing I said was going to hold him back from forcing the Twin Brothers out of The Galley. Even as he stalked past me towards the two of them, I called after him: "They're probably just actors, Joey! No big deal! I'll take that drink now! White Russian, Joey! C'mon …"

Joey the Barkeep lumbered over to them, tossed his damp, off-white towel back over his shoulder, and crossed his beefy, hairy arms across a barrel chest the guy had built up during his time in Vietnam as a younger, greener man. The way he took up his position, I couldn't see either of those ghouls from where I sat. I never once heard either of the brothers' voices, raised or otherwise. It looked like Joey was dominating the both of them, and he had a way of rolling his shoulders when he was getting wound up or readying himself to pounce. Joey was a tough guy, and he never hired a bouncer at The Galley because they would have been redundant to his being there. He'd toss both those creeps out by himself. He'd snatch them up by their scruffs, and he'd open the door with their heads if he had to.

It never came to that. In fact, their exit was so anticlimactic, I started to question whether I'd overreacted and gotten two paying patrons out for no reason other than they had staring problems. They filed past me, and I was surprised to find neither of them so much as glanced my way. They even walked the same way, the same stride. Over-long arms dangling nearly to their knees and swinging in ever-widening arcs like they were following the cadence of a sergeant's marching commands. On their way past, I caught a whiff of The Tarvill Brothers, and you know what they smelled like? Wet mulch. The freshly spread kind that still reeks of shit. Their uniforms hung on their twin emaciated frames like one would find an assembly of sticks in the shape of men, and a meager display of flesh stretched here and there underneath their clothing. Nothing more. They were walking kites dragged back down out of the sky. Earth bound. They left the bar courteously and quietly, as if nothing unsavory had forced their exit.

Joey walked back to the bar with that dirty white towel of his clamped over his nose and mouth. "Christ, I had to check the seat to make sure neither of them didn't shit themselves. I'll never get this smell out." He turned to me, asked, "All good, Greg?"

It wasn't all good. I felt like a shit. I thought I'd gotten two innocent people tossed out of the bar, and I felt like garbage. Call it Catholic guilt. Call it whatever you want. I didn't feel good about it, and the fact they were a couple of creepos dressed in clothing from the eighteen sixties was irrelevant. Who the hell was I to do that to them? I decided I was going to run out and try to catch them. Once Joey stepped back out from behind the bar to fiddle with the thermostat in the back, I broke for the door. It wasn't like I was running out on a tab. I never even ordered a drink. Never got around to that.

Had I known it would be my last night alive, I probably would have ordered a tub of liquor.

Things happened fast the moment I set foot on the sidewalk. I looked to the right and found an empty side-street, with the wide, white tail of a Septa bus disappearing behind a rundown brick building.

The noose was around my neck before I knew what was happening. They seemed to beset me from all sides, and I might've believed it if my feverish thoughts did not remind me there were only two of them. I knew it was the Twin Brothers. The Remainders from an evil age of cruelty and inequality and suffering. One of them stepped before me, and the other pulled the rope taut against my throat from behind. I gagged. I felt my eyes bulge, push out at the edges of the orbitals. I couldn't speak, but I remember the words in my head screaming to get out. Begging. Pleading. I thought of my poor father. I saw his face in my mind's eye. I don't know why I didn't picture my mother in that moment. I just don't know …)

"You don't have to finish it, Gary," Natalie said, in a small voice. "I'm with you in this. I'm with you. I'm going to help you."

She saw the sudden splattering of rain against the windshield, obscuring the view completely in an instant before Gaither moved her hand to the wiper switch and the water parted like a miracle. Natalie felt a heavy, dark sigh from deep within. It didn't belong to her. It was Gregory Gaither's noise, his lament given sound.

The one in front fell upon me. It felt like an embrace for the briefest of moments, until I felt his teeth pierce my throat just below the left line of my jaw. Then there was the rapidly building sensation of falling. At the exact same moment, my sneakers left the sidewalk. Lifted. The one brother clung to me, arms around me in a viselike embrace and his teeth caught in the soft, membranous skin of my throat. Drinking. The noose tightened. Tightened. Tightened. Wringing my blood right into his brother's mouth. Then we were flying. One at my back, strangling off my air while the other twin drank me dry.

"The Remainders can fly?"

Yes, they can fly.

With that, Gaither's rolling narrative seemed to break off sharply. Natalie could only assume he'd chosen to leave off the rest of it. When he spoke again, the voice in her head was weary and disenchanted beyond measure.

They buried me in the Meadowlands. New Jersey. That's where my body is, anyway. My head … there was nothing to bury of it when the Tarvill brothers were finished with it.

"I'm … I'm sorry for what happened to you."

It happened. But it's not over.

"I know."

Natalie?

"Yes, Greg?"

Try not to place yourself above anyone else when it comes to fighting for equal rights. It's obscene.

Natalie didn't hear Gaither's voice for a long time after that.

IX. MOCKERY

1992.

The Twin Remainders traveled to the epicenter of the Los Angeles Riots. Amid all the unrest, they were initially paralyzed by the chaos unfolding all around them like a second Civil War. Still, John and Henry Tarvill snapped into motion before long, dragging a handful of the rioters back into the shadows of an alleyway or the basement of a gutted, looted store where the brothers drank and fed on their victims. All of this while the new war raged on unchecked in the streets. The highways. It was during their time during the Los Angeles Riots the Remainder Twins experienced the unsettling realization their immortality might not protect them in the event of a similar reckoning.

This palpable fear was a siege which ultimately beat them back across California state lines as effectively as if the rioters had chased them there themselves.

They did not return to the epicenter of the conflict, suddenly far more concerned with the protection and preservation of their own necks.

This was another first, of course.

Terror. Vulnerability.

Consumed by this new fear for themselves, The Twin Remainders had returned to the schoolhouse with the collapsed, flaking red roof. Silently and sullenly, they burrowed back into the ground, and it was there they shut their eyes against this new, crippling fear. Deep underground, the brothers suffered fever dream after fever dream, each nightmare sharing the common thread of their demise at the hands of the ones they'd hunted and reviled and cursed for what seemed like ages.

They dreamt of The Free Ones hanging them high beside one another and then dancing beneath the two brothers' spasming boots.

The brothers dreamt of The Free Ones coming for them with spades and shovels, having finally tracked them to the schoolhouse. To the brothers' place of refuge. And The Free Ones turned up the dirt and the mud until a blood moon shone across the brothers' pale, shriveled bodies in the ground.

John and Henry shuddered and shook with absolute fright as they shared in another such terror, one which culminated in The Free Ones beheading them both in their graves and mashing John and Henry's heads against a rock until they were nothing more than oozing lumps of dripping flesh and splintered skull.

The brothers felt like grubs in the earth.

Out of time. Not of it.

There were rumblings of unrest and spilled blood and injustice in the forms of shootings and unjust convictions hatched in America's courts of law. Gang violence in inner cities spiked for months at a time, and The Remainder Twins absorbed the tragic energy. All the while, the pitiful humans mourned such losses of life and gnashed their teeth and pulled at their hair trying to hash out some solution. Gun control? Rehabilitation? Lower rates of incarceration?

The solution had never interested the brothers before, and the thought of humans arriving at some kind of solvent for this epidemic shook their limbs and hurt their dead brains and inspired more of the same nightmares.

Twelve feet underground, The Remainder Twins lay frozen and weakened. And all the while, the wheel of progressive thinking and problem-solving tilted and turned, tilted and turned, further and further towards lasting, far-reaching change.

So it was that John and Henry Tarvill laid in their graves, quaking with terror and lamenting the days when the world had made more sense, that Adams County, a town adjacent to Spangler Forest, the place of their concealment, started to suffer the effects of the Remainder Twin's psychic panic and trepidation. Their desperate wrath.

2012.

Twenty-six people, ranging in ages from twelve to seventy-four, all natives of Adams County, took their lives in a nine-month span. They leapt in front of cars. Blew their brains out at the breakfast table. Opened their wrists in a warm bath. Disemboweled themselves. One middle-aged steelworker even took his wife with him, strangling her while she was still asleep and then downing a Clorox Bleach cocktail—from a wine flute, no less. No warning. No history of mental disorders. Not a one of them. They all simply turned "blue" and chose the one and only way out they could conceive of.

The local newspaper called that year Adams County's Blue Period.

The Twin Remainders consoled one another as best they could, lying side by side in the filth and mud of Spangler Woods.

(When will the wheel turn back our way, John?)

(Soon, brother. Soon. We'll force it to do so. We'll grease its rusty hinges, and we'll turn the sumbitch ourselves. Through our deeds. We'll hunt, and the world'll swell with hate because hate remains, Henry. And it'll reach a critical mass. It'll go boom, brother! I've always told you this. Hate remains. And so do we, goddammit.)

In the coming years, the world proved John's point.

Trayvon Martin.

Freddie Gray.

The resurgence of White Supremacy.

Critical mass.

(Could this be our time, John? Coming back around again?)

(Wait on it some, Henry.)

The latter half of the decade loomed large before them, and The Remainder Twins found themselves needing to rise and hunt less and less. The earth conducted an endless resounding minor key of human decadence through every tectonic plate.

Still, The Free Ones pushed back, proving themselves time and again a worthy adversary.

There was Ferguson.

Baltimore.

New York City.

In turn, the tumult weakened the Remainder Twins considerably.

2018.

July.

(John, we can't go on like this. It's turning away from us. I'm damned tired.)

(Don't you hear it?)

(What? What is that?)

(Drums.)

Then came the cannon fire. The whistle-blast of muskets rippling across the land above their heads. Men shouting. Screaming in pain and agony. Curses. Frantic orders shouted above the din. Incomprehensible responses. Mayhem.

How sweet the sounds! They awakened memories in dormant, shadowy pockets of the Remainder Twin's brains.

(The Second Civil War, John!)

(It's begun, Henry!)

(It's not far!)

(Above us! My Christ, it's ABOVE US!)

They burst from the ground like well-watered buds and slithered around until the blood flooded back into their legs. They pulled themselves up, hand-over-hand up the steep, muddy slope of their resting grave, then along the splintery, flaking walls of the old schoolhouse's interior. Henry held the dirty wooden box in his arms. He'd brought it up out of their hole with him. The box containing their uniforms.

Another cannon blast shook them, and they glowered at one another with something of sentimentality and anticipation. The Twin Remainders stood there naked and so shriveled the slats of their rib cages looked like they would breach the skin at any moment. They dressed silently, relishing the sound of cannon blasts in the distance. The shouts and screams seemed to be closing in upon them, and this sped up their movements as they quickly shrugged themselves into the clothing, material that had held up well despite its age. They screwed their black kepi hats down onto their heads, the color of the headwear dusted to a softer grey.

John turned to Henry, nodded sternly.

(Into the fray, brother. Good things come to those who've waited the longest.)

Henry snapped off a rigid salute, and together, the Remainder Twins ran towards the sounds of explosions and musket fire and the frantic, babbling cries of men casting about the theater of battle.

Five kilometers south, they burst through the trees. The clearing was choked with hundreds of men in the midst of conflict. Cannons shone in the morning glare, and the mouths of the big black cylinders jumped and sighed thick drifts of smoke. John told Henry to clear the mud from his moustache. Henry snatched at the clotted tufts of facial hair. A hunk of it came off in his cold, pale hand. He tossed it to the forest floor. Men lay scattered across the battlefield. Splayed out on their backs, eyes upturned to the cloudless sky above. Facedown in the lush, green grass of the sweeping clearing. The ones still on their feet and alive with fire in their eyes rushed at one another. They fired on one another, some at point-blank range while others took more of a ranged shot at their chosen foe. Blurs of Confederate and Union soldiers mixing in with one another. Shock and confusion. Madness and bloodlust. Voices ringing above the din. They stabbed at one another with the blades of their muskets and—

John's heavy hand fell upon his brother's shoulder.

(They're playing. They're pretending. There's no blood. This is a game.)

Henry turned to his brother as they stood there just inside the tree line, his mouth a quivering black O.

(To what end?)

(It's a tribute. It's a celebration, Henry.)

(A tribute? It's a fuckin' mockery's what it is!)

All at once, cords of tendons pressed at the taut skin of Henry Tarvill's throat. His eyes darkened, crowding out the whites. (I want to kill them. All of them.)

Henry made to breach the tree line. John seized him by the elbow and stayed his motion.

(It could be a preparation of some sort. A training ground. If so, we ought not to stop their maneuvers.)

(We're weakened, John. We could feed. Here and now. On these play-actors!)

(We could …)

Just then, one of the soldiers, a Union man in a uniform too clean and well-assembled on his young, scrawny frame to have ever seen any real battle, slipped inside the tree line. The Remainder Twins fell silent, listening. They heard the steady stream of the young man pissing into the brambles.

A half-hour later, the Remainder Twins had gone back to ground, their bellies obscenely distended. Lying side by side in the dirt, John and Henry contemplated what they had gleaned from the Union boy play-actor. The young man broke the moment Henry laid him out in the dead leaves and pressed his boot to his throat, pinning him. The rest of the boy's body had writhed and twisted about as he tried to draw breath through a closed airway. And when Henry lifted his boot, the Union boy answered all their questions about the men in the clearing in a thin, reedy voice. The young man rubbed at his throat, and he wept. Filled his pants with shit when John showed him his fangs up close. Then, they had wrung him of all they wanted to know about the farce in the clearing—the men playing at their war games, mocking the South and its Cause. After breaking his windpipe with the downward arc of a heavy tree branch, they watched and waited for the life to leave the Union boy's blue eyes. Then they stripped the flesh from his bones and gulped every shredded morsel down their greedy gullets. John and Henry shared the boy's brain, and when a skeleton lay on the ground between them with spare bits of meat clinging to the bones, they brought the remains down into the earth with them inside the schoolhouse.

Satiated, the Twin Remainders looked to the future. July of the following year. The men would stage their wargame again, and on that day, John and Henry Tarvill planned to feed and ravage and terrorize them all. For the second time in over a century, the fields of Gettysburg would be saturated with blood and decked with carnage..

X. BILTMORE

Natalie never thought it possible to nod off while sitting at the wheel and careening down a busy interstate. Fatigue claimed her by slow degrees until she simply stopped *seeing* altogether. It felt like a temporary blindness, only sweet in its release and submission. The last thing she remembered was Danica's face floating before her mind's eye like a rippling mirage. She felt like she needed to cry, but that didn't happen. It was as if she'd somehow forgotten how to emote. What a cruel, constipated feeling it was! She slipped into sleep as if easing a stocking foot into a glass slipper.

Nat, wake up!

Instantly, she slid back behind her eyes and heard the grumbling of a Mack truck as it overtook their Optima, then growled past them, an impatient monster. It kicked rain across the windshield, and Gaither flicked the wipers back on, irritated.

Nat!

"Yeah," she answered, "what is it?"

What happened in Biltmore, Pennsylvania?

The mention of the city meant nothing to her at first. Then her mind's eye was suddenly awash in a tornado of free association. News reports delivered by anchors with serious, almost severe expressions. Shaky cell-phone footage of a police car set on fire and the cell's owner providing a blistering statement while filming: "Gonna be a long motherfucking night for all y'all! White folk gonna learn one way or another they ain't gonna get away with killing a black man for nothing!" Police lined up on the steps of Biltmore's police precinct, donning full riot gear. A wall of shields emblazoned with the stark white letters of a familiar acronym: SWAT. Citizens holding a vigil beneath a bruised, purple night sky, cupping votive candles in their hands that lit up their red-rimmed eyes and trembling lips.

I'm feeling something. It's taken hold of me, and I don't know what it is.

"I ... I understand—"

Nah, you don't! You couldn't possibly understand. Think of the saddest song you ever heard and multiply that feeling by a thousand. That's what this feels like. One minute I'm driving, and the next it's like a hand formed in the darkness and slapped me. Stole my breath!

"A terrible thing happened in Biltmore, Greg," Natalie said. "Some truly fucked events took place here a couple nights ago. And it's the last place you or I would want to be. This town is going to explode."

Greg saw the big green sign for the exit to Biltmore/ Pittsburgh a quarter mile down the highway. He veered across three lanes, narrowly missing the front fender of a Caprice, and eliciting a barrage of heavy-handed horn honking.

"What the hell are you doing?" she cried, realizing she was screaming at her own hands on the steering wheel as they operated entirely independent of her will. "Holy shit, Gregory! Did you hear what I just said? It's a bad time to be in Biltmore."

I'm not just here to finish my business. I'm here to bear witness. I need to be here, and I need to see it all through your eyes.

"You have no idea what's been going on the last couple days around here!"

I know something happened here and you're holding out on me! I can't seem to answer my own questions about it. I don't know why. I'm privy to most of the shit humans steep themselves in. This? Whatever it is? It's—it's squeezing me. Dividing me. I want to cry, but there's another side to it. I can taste my anger. It's bitter, like blood. Like I bit through your tongue or something, but I know I didn't because you'd be in pain. Are you in pain, Nat?

"No, I'm not in pain. I almost died in a car wreck a minute ago! I want you to trust me on this, Greg. Avoid Biltmore altogether. It's probably what's making you feel sick. It's working on you on some kind of—I don't know—psychic level. And I get how that would be. If you pull into a parking lot, I'll tell you everything. You can look at my phone, and I'll bring it up on a website. Trust me, *that's* what *this* is. I think you'll even out some as long as we steer clear of there."

There was the usual smattering of exit off-ramp stops lining both sides of the road, from gas fill-ups to eateries. A Roy Rogers appeared to be buffering an Exxon and a Sunoco, lest they stand side by side in a flagrant corporate dust-up of some kind. Greg remembered the burger joint and how much he'd *really* liked their chicken and roast beef. Stopping at Roy Rogers during a road trip, whether with his mother to visit family in Chicago or along with his college buddies to check out a music festival up north, seemed to make every trek all the more worthwhile. After all, Roy Rogers seemed to have gone almost entirely the way of the blue-suede shoe, and it was not only important, it was a required stop just as much as the Washington Monument would be for a Washington D.C. tourist. Seeing a Roy Rogers had become like spotting Bigfoot, the more Gaither considered it. The left side of the road boasted restaurants he'd never heard of, and he knew why. No point in wondering why he drew a blank on places like Jersey Mike's Sandwiches or Chipotle. A sense of loss came and went. The flutter of emotion hung around less and less the longer he hung around.

"Pull in there at the Dunkin' Donuts," she said. "I need a recharge."

Gaither nosed the Optima over into the parking lot and slipped into a spot towards the back where a fence held back a line of oak trees, their tendril branches dropping acorns across the front hood.

"Okay, I'm going to need you to walk me inside so I can order."

Stop stalling, Natalie.

"I swear I'm not stalling, Gary," she said. "Just, it sickens me to think about how it all went down here. I need something to prop me up so I can tell it right. I need my iced cappuccino stat, Greg."

What the hell is so special about Dunkin' Donuts? I don't remember them setting the world on fire years ago, but there's a line inside. A long line!

"In a nutshell, Dunkin's coffee used to be shit. I mean, tar-your-driveway-with-it shit, but then they must have had some kind of major overhaul within the company. The next thing you know, their coffee is the best in town, and they're customer base quadrupled in the last decade or so. Could be they're slipping crack rocks into the coffee grinders. Stranger things have happened."

Natalie.

When Natalie tried to send a message to her own hands to crank the driver's side door open, the reminder of just how futile such a thought command proved, knocked her back into a state of annoyance. She felt like a prisoner all over again, but quickly dismissed the notion. Natalie was certain she had gleaned enough about Gaither in the last couple of hours to understand he was a husk in the spirit world. Hollowed out and struggling to fill himself up with something of lasting substance. Revenge seemed to be his preferred method of accomplishing this.

"I'd rather you looked at my phone," she said. "People are going to think I'm a nut job if they see me sitting in my driver's seat having what looks like a tearful conversation with myself. I'll Google the story and give you my phone. Don't make me do it the embarrassing way."

You're not the least bit embarrassed and you know it. You've never really given a shit either way what opinions people hold about you. Only your father. You care what he thinks. Always have.

"Please don't mention my dad, Greg. Don't. Do. That."

He never wanted you out of the house. He never stopped loving you, not even after you sat your parents down and told them you were gay—

"FINE, THEN! FUCK THE CAPPUCCINO! ALL RIGHT? ON TO BILTMORE!"

Gaither backed out of the spot and eased the Optima back onto the roadway. A series of arrows leading, beckoning, him along to downtown Biltmore glowed a sickly green along the roadside, seemingly appearing out of nowhere. A sudden sheet of rain fell upon the Optima, obscuring his view out the windshield, and by the time he angled the vehicle onto Wistar Street, the windshield wipers were whipping back and forth at a psychopathic rate. Wistar

Street looked like the quintessential, nearly cliché, ideal of Main Street, USA. Both sides of the two-lane road were lined in dark monoliths of shuttered mom-and-pop stores. Gaither doused the Optima's headlights. The road was empty and open, leaving plenty of room for Gaither to glide down the slickened blacktop, already carrying a runoff of rain towards its gutters and storm drains.

The wipers had fallen behind the onslaught of rain splashing across the windshield. It obscured the shifting mass of people in the middle of the street three blocks down Wistar, blotting out some of their numbers.

A man appeared in front of the Optima, having peeled himself away from the shadows on either side of the vehicle. He slammed his hands down on the hood of the Optima, rattling the frame. He barked something incomprehensible at Natalie and Gaither and made a motion similar to that of an air-traffic controller on a runway brandishing their orange lights at incoming 747s.

"I think he's telling us to get out of here," Natalie said, her pulse thrumming in her wrist.

We're not leaving. I'll sound the horn, and he'll move aside.

"Shit, do you see all those people at the other end of the street? There's gotta be over a hundred protesters gathered. I can see a couple fires from here."

Gaither gave the engine a quick rev. The man in front of the car kicked the bumper and nearly knocked himself onto his ass, having misplaced his weight. Perhaps embarrassed, he did move aside, but Gaither and Natalie spotted the broken beer bottle he held in one hand. He jabbed the jagged, threatening end of the bottle at them as they glided past him.

As they crept along at a snail's pace, the crowd's numbers seemed to multiply, to swell. Some of the younger men zigzagged about like football players executing a play in the middle of the street. Without context, it might have resembled some grand game of catch. The crowd of protestors did not appear to notice the vehicle, a skulking machine in the foreground. Gaither put the Optima in reverse and slowly rolled back, angling the car along the curb as he went. He made sure to stop just beyond the yellow ring of a streetlamp above their heads. It would've lit them up like a target.

"Kill the engine," Natalie said.

Gaither turned the car off. They sat there, four eyes watching warily out of two tired, worn ones. The rain had finally thinned just enough to show them everything.

The Zigzaggers appeared to have splintered off from a larger group of people standing out in front a series of cement steps. A sign out front hung from a wrought iron pole and read **BILTMORE POLICE DEPARTMENT.** Natalie could've guessed the location without need of the signage. It was a scene she'd only just been remembering when Gaither pressed her about the town and what had happened there. Not to mention, cable news networks had been covering the unrest in Biltmore for the last four nights. The last she heard, the governor of Pennsylvania was weighing the option of bringing in the National Guard to put the protests to rest once and for all. There was no military presence yet, and Natalie was both thankful and fretful at the same time. A row of fifteen police officers in black riot gear formed a stoic line in front of the precinct's front doors. They held shatter-resistant shields, forming what looked like something of an impenetrable barrier. Still, the crowd appeared to be inching closer to the row of officers. They held up their votive candles and their homemade signs. Gaither and Natalie could make out a few of them in the murk. JUSTICE FOR LAURENCE CAIN! NO JUSTICE, NO PEACE! There was even a vaguely familiar Bible verse scrawled across a square of cardboard above their heads: "… they will know I am the LORD, when I take vengeance on them." Ezekiel 25:17. The shouting was loud as it was visceral in its effect upon Natalie and Gaither. Natalie shuddered. The Zigzaggers rushed all about, climbing up telephone poles and tossing glass bottles at the second story windows of the store fronts. Some of them wore dark bandanas over the lower half of their faces. Smoke bombs exploded, suddenly shrouding everything in a billowing grey curtain.

"No news vans tonight," Natalie said, surprised.

You don't see them? I do. Down the other end of the street. Further away than we are. You think they'd miss showing this? This skewed representation of furious anger?

"I *do* see them. Fuck if they aren't Johnny On the Spot. Back to frame their bullshit narrative."

Benefitting whom? Tell me that much.

Natalie thought about the question. "I guess it depends on who's telling *the story*, right? Conservative networks prop up the police. Liberal news lauds the victim. The truth lies somewhere in between, I think."

And what is that?

"Look, it's not simple, Gary. I know that. Racism. Bias. Mistrust. Misunderstanding. Abuse of power. And voila! You've got yourself a powder keg. And for what?"

I'm still waiting for you to tell me, Natalie. I've been more than patient.

"All right," she said. "Last Saturday night, a teenage boy named Laurence Cain was picking up some diapers for his mother and a packet of M&M's for himself at a Quik Mart. Apparently, when he walked up to the counter, he realized he'd forgotten his wallet back home. I guess he started panicking, and the clerk behind the counter must've misread this for Laurence going for a weapon in his hoodie. The clerk had already gotten off on the wrong foot with Laurence when the kid walked in. Told him to lower his hood. Something about a store dress code. Laurence, teenager that he was, didn't lower it. I mean, hell, I pulled the same shit when I was his age. Fuck authority, right?" A pause, gathering her thoughts. "The clerk, a twentysomething kid himself, told Laurence to get out or he was going to call the police. This was the last straw for Laurence. He was embarrassed he'd forgotten his money, and the clerk was giving him shit from the minute he walked in. So, he grabbed a handful of Bubble Yums from the counter and flung them at the clerk. Tells him, 'Go fuck yourself!' This is what the clerk told detectives.

"What Laurence Cain didn't know until it was too late was a man named Ronald Miller was in the store also. When he heard the commotion, he ducked down behind the candy aisle wall, waiting for his moment. I guess. Laurence stopped arguing with the clerk when he felt Miller's eyes on him. You know how you can just feel that, on your back? The side of your face? So, he grabbed another handful of Bubble Yums and spun around. Ronald Miller fired three rounds into Laurence's chest with his Glock. The kid never knew what hit him."

Gaither's voice was gravelly in the middle of her mind.

Neither did I.

"This Ronald Miller was part of Biltmore County's Town Watch Committee. It was later revealed he belonged to at least four different White Nationalist groups. His Facebook posts were a cesspool of Hitler quotes and racist cartoons and burning crosses. He wasn't even subtle about his hatred, yet the Town Watch had him anyway. They claimed he'd only been on the *job* for a couple nights and it wasn't a practice of theirs to screen an applicant by looking at their social media sites. Of course, hindsight is twenty-fucking-twenty, and now they say it will be a part of their screening process moving forward. But you can't get the toothpaste back into the tube, can you?"

The crowd of protesters, many of whom had locked arms with one another in solidarity, started up a chant that swelled to such a fever pitch, it penetrated the Optima's cab. It gave both Gaither and Natalie pause enough to stop their exchange so they could listen. At the same time, a series of hands shot up and seemed almost to sprout from the heads of the protestors. They worked together at unfurling a black banner with white writing running across it. The bodiless hands stretched the banner some ten feet across the tops of the crowd's heads, proclaiming its message to the line of police at the top of the stairs, to the Heavens. To God.

Between her ears, Gaither made a noise that hinted at curiosity. A question on the horizon. Then he asked it:

The Open Eyes Are Watching?

Natalie hesitated, weighing her words carefully. "The Open Eyes. They're a civil rights group. They organized in the wake of several shootings of black men by police officers. They exist to remind the people in the country who've either forgotten or never known all lives are precious regardless of skin color and will be guarded. Watched over."

And are their intentions true? Are they genuine?

"I would hope so," Natalie answered. "You'd have to ask them. I don't know their hearts."

You don't have an opinion, then?

"It's really not my place to say anything other than that a civilized society doesn't behave the way we've been behaving. What happened to Laurence Cain was first-degree murder. The facts that have been leaked to the press and made public point to that conclusion, and it's a heartbreaking one. People say the kid was just in the wrong place at the wrong time, but I reject that. There shouldn't be any *wrong place* anywhere in the world where a young man gets shot and killed for fumbling in his pockets and losing his temper."

It sounds like you have specific views, but you're afraid to voice them at the risk of enraging one side or the other. So you tiptoe? Is that it?

"I'd say any *tiptoeing* I've been doing around the topic of race relations is over and done with. I put that to rest the moment I agreed to help with your revenge errand. I could have said no."

I think that's only partly true. You had good reason to say you would. You want to see Danica again.

"Yeah, and how's that working out? I haven't heard a damned thing from her."

I explained that to you. She is on her way. She's on a higher plane, traveling backward. It takes time. That's all I can say. But she heard your summons, and Danica will be with you when you least expect it. And she'll make her presence evident when you need her most.

"I need her now. Christ, I needed her *yesterday*—"

The scraping sound cut Natalie off. At first, it sounded like it was coming from inside the car, a trapped bird or rodent clawing at the interior where it had gotten itself trapped. The hooded man who'd been standing in front of the car moments ago was walking along the driver's side of the Optima. He was running the jagged edge of his broken beer bottle along the side of the car, probably leaving a jagged silver scar from gas tank to door handle, where he stopped dead and started tapping the jagged spike of the bottle against her window.

Drawing his hood back, the white teenager with pockmarks and a shaved head sprouting blond fuzz leaned in. "You need to move the fuck on, white bitch! You think you can just hang around and rubberneck like some privileged ho? Move your flat ass on back to the suburbs. We be coming for you in your mansion sooner or later! *Get the fuck along!*" His eyes darkened, the sockets deepening. "Unless you wanna come on out? Maybe you want some of this!" He stepped back from the car, yanked his hoodie up to reveal a scrawny and sunken chest with cheap-looking, indecipherable tattoos scratched into his belly. "You want some of this shit, white bitch?"

Don't say anything.

"Start the car, Greg."

This young man's confused. I'm going to clear things up for him.

Before Natalie knew what was happening, she saw her left hand unlock the door and crank it open just as the boy moved to throw himself against it. The door opened hard and heavy into him, stealing his breath, and bending him over.

"Gregory, you're going to get me killed! Don't do this! You're using *my body!*"

I won't get so much as a scratch on you, Natalie. I promise you.

"No, I—"

73

But she felt herself climbing out of the car, and suddenly her heart was hammering in her head. The taut muscles up and down her arms pulled tighter, drenched in adrenaline. *I can't remember the last time I got in a fight! Too many years ago!*

"Gregory, stop! STOP!"

Gregory didn't stop. Instead, he seized the boy by the throat and lifted up off his feet, into the air.

Let me speak through you. Just for a moment.

"He's choking! You're killing him! Stop! Stop!"

Let me speak through you. Please. I'm not going to kill him.

"How?"

You know how. Let me open that door. You know how.

She did know how, and she let him.

Gaither spoke in her voice. Natalie felt completely and utterly hijacked. It terrified her; her own voice filled with such wrath.

The boy's face was turning blue. He offered a feeble kick at Natalie (*Gaither*) but it never connected with her (*him*).

"You're not helping things, you little shithead! I want you to go home, and I don't want you to come back here because I'll be waiting for you, and I will finish what I started. All it will take is a tightening of my grip. Say right around your windpipe. You feel my fingers around it right now?"

No response. Gurgling sounds, like soapy water running down a clogged drain. Another half-hearted kick.

"You're about to die. So I'm going to drop you. And you're going to run. Run home to your mother. This is not your fight. You're a fraudulent little fucker, and you're insulting Laurence Cain's memory. Run. Run away." With that, Gaither dropped the boy to the sodden asphalt. "Run. Now."

Natalie saw the crowd coming towards them in her periphery. They were running, the one's holding their votives either towing the line or walking behind them lest their candle flames flicker out. Inside, she sounded a warning. *They're coming. We shouldn't be here. They're going to think we're rubbernecking, just like this asshole said!*

"I see them. We'll leave this shit-heel for them to deal with."

Gaither surrendered his control over her voice. It felt for Natalie much like when he'd given her back control of her limbs. A warming sensation passed through her tongue, soothing and almost sexual. He turned to open the car door when the boy sounded something like a war cry behind him. Gaither stiffened too late, just as the boy's hands grabbed him by Natalie's shoulders and spun her around.

"Fucking *bitch!*" the boy screamed, his hands grabbing for her pants button. "I got something *for you!*"

"Greg, stop him!"

No need. Watch this.

Terror took hold of Natalie as her brain strained to steel itself against the oncoming sexual assault.

The crowd encircled them, a clamor of loud and angry voices swirling all about like their numbers stretched for miles rather than a city block. Three men from the crowd fell upon the boy and dragged him roughly backward. Natalie and Gaither felt the boy's hands try to grab at the top hem of her jeans before flailing loose as the crowd consumed him like a living, breathing leviathan of retribution. Their shouts were frenzied and unchained.

"-*buggin motherfucker!*"

"-*ain't gonna touch on no lady like that!*"

"-*done told you to get the fuck outta here!*"

"-*hold that pussy-motherfucker—hold him* here*!*"

One of the protestors-turned-saviors, a young black man with a powerful build and fire in his eyes, stepped to Natalie. There was no love in his gaze. Nothing of sympathy. "You shouldn't be here. There be knucklehead motherfuckers out and about. We got him. Get yourself gone."

Natalie/Gaither nodded and climbed back inside the Optima. She sighed, exhaling seemingly from the balls of her feet. It was not the closest she'd ever come to being raped, unfortunately. But it managed to awaken the sleeping dread lingering in the reptilian portion of her brain that stored away memories of when she'd come much closer years ago. Gaither backed the car up, cleared the crowd, and pulled a K-turn. Before pulling away, Gaither snuck a quick glance back towards the crowd that had come to their rescue. They were already moving back towards the police station, hauling the boy towards his own personal justice.

"Am I seeing this?" Natalie asked, breathlessly.

You are.

"So, they're going to hand him over to the cops?"

They are.

"I don't understand. I honestly don't understand."

Yes you do, Nat.

XI. TEARS NOT TO FORGET

The row of Harley Davidsons ran the entire length of the Motel 6's parking lot and framed the first-floor walkway like steel bushes and chrome hedges. Their owners appeared to have checked out the entire first floor as well. They had the doors to their rooms propped open to let the damp and humid air in. Their numbers were comprised predominantly of grizzled, road-hardened, white males, although Gaither spotted a handful of women in their midst and imagined there were perhaps a few more of them *behind the scenes*. The bikers sat in green beach chairs arranged outside their rooms, some stolen from the pool area. Clutching beer bottles in one hand and a cigarette or a blunt in the other, they dominated the front of the motel and put out a cautionary vibe. Leather and denim sentries with foul mouths, fouler breath, steely gazes, and most notably, heads shaved smooth. Gaither spotted swatches of red-and-black-checked shirt sleeves and cherry red Doc Marten boots laced all the way up to their knees.

And Gaither wondered to himself whether he would have dared pull into that particular Motel 6 parking lot if he weren't hidden inside the body of a petite white woman. He liked to think he would have, but there was no real way to test the hypothesis. Nevertheless, he did not hesitate to pull into a spot, even though Natalie told him she wanted to stay somewhere else.

"Greg, seriously, I *do not* want to stay here. I don't even want to breathe the same fucking air as those skinhead shitholes!"

Gaither turned off the engine as if he hadn't heard her.

This is where we're supposed to be. We're at the right place at the right time. You don't see it yet, but you will. I don't like it any more than you do but trust me on this.

"C'mon, man," Natalie groaned, "you're not the one who has to walk past them to the office. They're camped out all over the place. They're going to say something crude or insulting, and then I'm going to have to insist you yield the use of my fists back to me. Because I'm going to *have* to do something about that. I can't let any of their shit go unanswered."

76

I'm not asking you to, Nat. Just not tonight. Tonight, I want you to walk right by them no matter what. Steel yourself. All right?

"Again, I feel like there's something pretty damned important I should know that you're not telling me. I don't like this pattern between us."

Do you trust me?

"No, but ... fuck it anyway. Let's rock."

Natalie and Gaither climbed out of the car and started across the parking lot to the Office.

The neo-Nazis' first words cut her to the bone:

"BEST TURN YOUR DYKE ASS AROUND AND MOVE DOWN THE ROAD!"

"YOUR MOMMA SHOULDA' KILLED YOU IN THE FUCKIN' WOMB!"

Nat? Breathe. We're. Walking.

The group swelled with enough laughter Natalie swore she felt it in every bump of her spine, a wretched vibrational assault. Even as Gaither walked with *her* legs and swung *her* arms for balance, closing the distance between them and the office, Natalie made use of her peripheral vision to peek at the lot of them camped out front. She tracked them. Thought she saw a couple of them come up out of their green plastic chairs and start towards her and Gaither. But it was a trick of the frazzled mind. They rose to grab another beer out of a cooler, leaned in towards one another to share some private joke. Still, all eyes were fastened to her, and when she passed them, on her backside.

They whistled through their fingers. *"NOW THAT ASS IS TOO FINE TO WASTE ON A LEZZIE BODY! BRING THAT ON BACK HERE! LEMME TAKE A BITE OUT OF THAT!"*

The worst of it was Natalie could not even so much as bite her tongue in silent protest. Middle fingers shot up in her mind's eye, too many to count. Thousands. Stretching all the way to the horizon and beyond. Her cheeks burned, stung. They were all her middle fingers. Each one bore the small tattoo on the ring finger top knuckle. A small ankh symbol. And the thousand ankhs stabbing the sky filled her with some small resolve. It was enough to accompany her the rest of the way to the office door with its window glowing softly behind vertical blinds.

The clerk behind the counter started with her apologies before Natalie and Gaither made it over to her.

"I can hear them all the way in here," the woman said, cringing. "I'm so sorry. I wanted to turn them away, but I need this job. My boss would rent a room out to Joseph-freakin'-Mengele if he had the money to pay." Another send-up from the skinheads filtered into the lobby, clipping the clerk off neat as you please. She snuck a glance towards the office door, wrinkling her nose. "I'm going to set you up right next to the office. On the *other* side. You can go out that door right over there next to the magazine rack."

"You get a lot of this type around here?" Natalie asked

"No, thank God," the clerk gasped, her shoulder sagging. "But word around town is Jefferson Morgan is here in Biltmore. No one knows where he's staying, and if you were to even try and ask any of those fuckers out there where he is, they'd probably stab you in the heart, so …"

"You're shitting me," Natalie said, her intestines tightening and twisting. "Jefferson Morgan? With what's going on in Biltmore, that can't be a coincidence. Are they doing anything to find him?"

"The guy's slippery when he wants to be," the clerk said. "But something tells me he'll pop his head up. Hopefully, the FBI or somebody will be there to lop it off when he does. It's what you'd do to a snake, isn't that right?"

Jefferson Morgan?

"I just hope he shows himself *before* something bad happens. Not after, so he can gloat. That's usually more his style."

Who's Jefferson Morgan, Nat?

The clerk shook her head and ducked down to rummage underneath the countertop.

Under her breath, Natalie said, "Just wait, Greg …"

In seconds, the clerk produced the keycard, took Natalie's payment, then leaned across the countertop. "Those *things* out there? I know they're Morgan's people. Part of the New Reich."

Mm-hmm. Did you hear that, Nat?

Natalie couldn't exactly answer him, but she imagined he sensed her confusion.

That's the sound of the final tumblers falling into place.

"You know, we have one of the greatest Oktoberfest celebrations every year. I'm talking blowouts for the ages. You'd think Eyewitness News or CNN would've come out to cover *that* at least once in the last thirty years. That would've put Biltmore on the map for something *good*. But no!" The clerk handed Natalie the keycard for Room 113, flinched away. She threw up her hands, dejectedly. "When that poor boy was shot dead, it was like the news vans beat EMS to the scene. Even the kid's parents asked for the news outlets to keep their distance during their time of mourning. You would've thought they rolled out the red carpet for those anchor scumbags instead!" The clerk paused, chewed her bottom lip. "I don't know who's worse. The bloodsucking media or Morgan and people like him."

Gaither closed Natalie's hand over the room key.

The clerk reached out, closed her hand over top Natalie's.

"You dial zero-zero-one for the front desk if you need anything or you feel threatened in any way."

"All right. I will."

"I know where my boss keeps his gun. I'm serious. I don't give a *shit*!"

Around 2 a.m., Natalie came awake with the stark, disarming realization she might die tomorrow. It was more than mere possibility. If she believed everything Gaither had related to her about The Remainder Twins (and she did), there was serious danger afoot. This was no *errand*, as she'd called it earlier. It was revenge, and she'd read enough books and seen enough movies to understand such a thing was rarely, if ever, executed without some collateral damage. The *beings* they meant to kill, to cut down, were over a hundred years old. Obviously, they were skilled at survival. Otherwise, they would not have lasted so long. Not to mention, Gaither could neither confirm nor deny there were other Remainders walking the earth.

Yes, *this could be my last night on earth.*

Within, Gaither had gone silent. He did not wake with her. After she'd shown him on her cell phone exactly *who* Jefferson Morgan was, Gregory Gaither seemed to seethe at first, then to deflate inside her. Natalie had made sure to choose the most reliable source to show him. Now, a part of her wished she hadn't even referenced his name.

That's a bell I'd give anything to un-ring.

Morgan was a neo-Nazi and outspoken white supremacist, credited in part with pioneering the alt-right movement that gained momentum, and with that, serious scrutiny as well, in 2016 and 2017. His brash open calls for the resurgence of "imperialism" and "subjugation of other races" put him on the FBI's radar, although their surveillance had been soft at best. Natalie imagined the Bureau was of the *Bigger Fish to Fry* mindset when it came to fighting terrorism, and the homegrown threat was downgraded in terms of urgency. Consequently, Jefferson Morgan and his reviled "Nativity Movement"—which called for a purification and purging of diversity in the United States— continued to operate virtually unchecked by any law enforcement. Morgan was linked to everyone from Senators to lobbyists, CEOs to Union bosses, and never traveled anywhere without some portion of his loyal neo-Nazi followers flanking and protecting him from all sides. Even then, Morgan frequently wore disguises to ensure his movements here and there remained *free and uninhibited*.

She wondered if Gaither knew how all of this would end up. He made no secret about the fact he was privy to a great many things regarding their future together, or at least during the next twenty-four hours. Did he know her fate? If he anticipated her inevitable death at the hands of the undead Remainder Twins, he wouldn't have dragged her across the state to meet her end. Or would he?

So long as she (and Gaither) took the Twins down with her.

She could still hear the neo-Nazis at their alcohol-fueled carousing. They carried on like the impervious clan they'd built themselves up to be, untouchable and unaccountable to any rule of law or moral cues of civilization. Whether or not they were linked in some way to Jefferson Morgan didn't matter, although Morgan pretty much laid claim to and attracted most neo-Nazi factions to his cause. While Morgan maintained his hands were clean, they threatened and they beat and they abused anyone they damn well pleased and in many more instances than Natalie could count that came across the news wire of late.

The sick and disenfranchised will always flock together. And it's in their numbers that they can do some real damage. They fucking know that.

Gaither had explained to her the Remainder Twins were psychic vampires, two of many that had become "scattered to the four winds" (as he'd put it). They derived life-sustaining energy from the hatred and vile interactions among human beings who walked above ground, all the while dreaming and remembering endlessly while they shivered and squirmed like human-sized maggots (also Gaither's words)! Pale. Washed-out. Starved. Dead. And hanging by a thread of resilience as the decades unfurled themselves and further advancements in civil rights and discourse and equality made its glorious strides. Progress vibrated the Earth's tectonic plates in a much different fashion than when terrible events transpired like the attacks on 9/11 or Tiananmen Square or the Holocaust. They conducted a different tune. In a major key as opposed to the minor keys created by the tragedy of humankind. Cruelty.

Gaither had told her the Twins were weakened by such progress.

They could be gotten to. Now or never.

Yet, Natalie could not simply accept that all it would take was a stake to their hearts. A beheading. Their mouths stuffed full of garlic cloves.

No, it will take more than a physical destruction or some form of immolation. Their life's blood is derived from a flow of negative energy. Such a source will need to become compromised. Dealt a serious blow. But how?

Natalie almost didn't hear it when it started, she was so focused on this train of thought.

The small, brittle sound of weeping, like brambles snapping underfoot. Easily mistakable for something else. Perhaps nothing more than a phantom noise formed within a tired mind. Natalie was certainly exhausted.

It's Gregory.

No sooner did she realize it was Gaither, the sound diminished to such a low register she could barely hear it.

Don't be embarrassed. Gregory? What can I do?

No answer. Gregory Gaither sobbed inside her mind. His levee had finally broken. Natalie was surprised it had taken the poor soul so long to crack.

I'll leave you be. I'm sorry, Gregory. I'm so sorry ...

The weeping dried up, leaving Natalie alone once again with her dread and fear of future events.

That's when she decided to do something she swore she'd never do again. Natalie reached for the phone, casually noting the time on the bedside alarm clock as reading a little after two in the morning. It didn't faze her. She wouldn't call on her cell. She preferred the motel phone and its anonymity. Natalie punched in a number, settled back against the headboard, and waited through seven rings before a woman's sleep-worn voice filled the earpiece. Natalie sensed a visceral fear in the tone of her greeting.

"Yes?"

"Mom," Natalie said, "it's me."

A gasp.

Silence.

The woman on the other end burst into tears.

The last time Natalie saw her mother, Kathy Nolan had slapped her not once, but twice across the face. Natalie had just *come out* to her parents. The first slap stunned Natalie so thoroughly she did not know to get out of the way before her mother's hand swung around to strike her once more. Never before had her mother so much as raised a hand to Natalie. Not for anything. Not ever. Her father either.

Now, on the other end of the phone, her mother pushed words through the web of her own sobs. "Natalie, dear God! What took you *so long*? All these years."

"I'm sorry it's so late—"

"Oh Natalie, you don't know what it means to finally hear your voice again. It's …"

"Mom, I'm calling because I wanted to—"

"It's—*I don't know*—bittersweet."

"Bitter*sweet*?" Natalie gripped the headset so hard it clicked between her fingers. "I don't understand what that means."

"We were looking for you for so long," Kathy Nolan said, her voice tremulous. "Your father, he never got over it."

Natalie stopped herself from saying the words that sprang to mind on instinct. She did not want to damage what could be a peace between her and her parents. Being right was suddenly more overrated and wasteful than it had ever proven before.

"How long has it been, Mom?"

"It's been five years."

"Five years, huh?" she said. "And you've been looking for me?"

"Your father and I, we were sure you'd gone up north to New England for some reason. You always talked about how you wanted to live in Maine when you got older. Dad always insisted you're probably selling incense or designing homemade jewelry. Or maybe, you would be doing something with your sculpting. You always hated Philadelphia. Is that where you are now?"

"I only came back to Philly a year ago," Natalie said. She paused, then decided to pull no punches. "I was running a popular, successful occult shop in New York City with my wife. When she died a year ago, I moved back and opened another store. Lower rent, obviously. Less notoriety. But … it's going well." The lie tasted like a bitter herb, although she felt her mother deserved it. She didn't want to cede her mother any satisfaction in knowing Natalie had fallen into the red financially.

Silence on the other end.

"Your wife?" Kathy Nolan breathed. "I-I'm sorry for your loss." It sounded as cursory as a comforting word from a stranger on a bus. Then, it was as if the woman had suddenly come fully awake and been half asleep up until that point in the conversation. "Why did you hide from us? We hired a private investigator! Your father had to take a second job on top of his electrical work to pay the fees, and in the end, the bastard ran off with your father's supplementary income and never did a damned thing to find you. He was a fraud! B-but we didn't stop until we had to because there was no more choice in the matter—"

"This isn't why I called, Mom! So you'd have a chance to lay the second half of your guilt trip on me!"

"All right! Okay! Please!" Her mother sounded older, like it had not been five years but forty. "Please, don't hang up. All right?"

"Okay, I won't hang up," Natalie said.

A voice cut into the conversation; one Natalie knew instantly despite the fact it sounded like they were trying to speak to her through a tin can.

"Your mom wants to tell you she's sorry for slapping you." The voice popped and fizzed. Natalie felt her eyes burn, and pressure built behind her eyelids. "She doesn't go out much anymore. She just people-watches from the bathroom window where no one can really see her behind the curtain. Mom's afraid to go outside. She thinks her heart will stop or someone will kill her on the way to her car. The Wagoneer just sits. She doesn't drive it. It just sits."

"Mom?" Natalie asked. "Is that true?"

"Is what true, Natalie? I didn't say anything."

"No, *you* didn't. I'm talking about what Dad's saying. You don't go outside anymore?"

Nothing.

"Mom? Why would you think anyone's going to hurt you? No one's going to do anything to you. Do you understand?"

"*-it just sits-she doesn't drive it-it just sits—*"

"Dad! Hold it! I'm trying to talk to Mom! Mother-"

She cut in, her voice quavering. "What are you trying to do, Natalie?"

"About what? I'm just trying to find out why you won't leave the house. It can't be because of me. Dad?"

"*Natalie Evelyn Nolan!*" Kathy Nolan cried. *"What are you trying to do to me? Are you trying to get back at me?"*

"No, Dad just said—"

Through the buzzing and popping of a bad connection: "*-doesn't drive it-just sits—*"

"Dad?"

Kathy wailed. "WHY ARE YOU DOING THIS? PLEASE STOP! I DESERVE IT, BUT YOU SHOULDN'T MAKE FUN OF YOUR FATHER LIKE THAT! IT DIMINISHES HIS MEMORY!"

Then Natalie knew.

"Oh Mom, no. Dad's gone?" The tears spilled down her cheeks. Dappled her lap.

Natalie felt her mind tighten and a migraine bloom behind her eyes. "Mother, I-I-I didn't know. I swear I didn't know Dad was … oh, Mother, I'm so *sorry*."

In an instant, she saw the highlight reel of her memories with her father, from her earliest memory of him dipping her three-year-old bare feet down into rolling ocean waves, to the last time she saw him crossing the living room towards her as she backed out of the room after having been twice slapped by the woman who gave birth to her. Bill Nolan had not wanted her to leave the house, and he'd run after her beater Oldsmobile that evening as she drove down the street, away from him, and out of his life.

Forever now.

How? Why? She said he went back to working two jobs just to bankroll some crooked piece-of-shit detective to look for me. Oh no, God! Please, God, don't let it have killed him; aged him; drained him, not my Dad.

"So, you still think you can hear them?" her mother asked, in a small voice. "After all this time, you still think you can hear them? See them?"

"Yes, I do, Mother."

"N-never mind that. It's irrelevant. Jesus and Mary must have made up their minds it was finally time for you to pick up the phone."

"Oh, I don't believe in that fiction anymore," Natalie said. "I haven't since I left."

"Don't say that. It hurts my heart when you act so bold."

"I remember what you called it. My abilities? You called them my *sad grab at attention*."

"That's not correct. You're misremembering to hurt me—"

"All right. I'm going to hang up now, and then I'm going to yank the phone cord out of the wall!"

"No-please-Natalie-I'm sorry-wait-WAIT-I'M SORRY—"

Natalie held the phone away from her ear. She stared down at the headset, a sad and thoughtful expression tugging at the corners of her mouth and eyes as she listened to the frantic voice of her mother hissing out of the earpiece. It wasn't until the sound of her mother's begging softened, she switched the phone back up to her ear.

"Mom?"

"I'm here, Natalie. Don't hang up. I'm sorry."

"What exactly are you punishing yourself for? I don't want you to be afraid to live."

"Ah, your father. Maybe you do hear him. He used to tell me the same thing. He used to tell me I should at least go out and start the car once a day so the battery doesn't die. He couldn't stand the way I just let it sit in the driveway. I used to tell him he didn't care about me, just about the car. I was so hard on him towards the end, even though I knew he meant well."

"He always did." *I didn't leave because of him.*

"Natalie?"

"Yeah?"

A long pause, as if she had lost her train of thought. "I didn't mean what I said. I'm sorry I didn't believe you about the voices."

"They're more than just voices in my head."

Natalie's mother and father had taken her to get a CAT scan and an MRI, but neither had revealed any irregularities in her brain chemistry. Then, they had made the rounds with a handful of reputable psychiatrists once all physical possibilities had been ruled out. Every one of the psychiatrists had told Natalie and her parents the same thing. So long as the voices in question were not telling her to harm herself, then it did not enter their field, per se. They dealt in psychotic breaks or *episodes*. These breaks were normally signaled by sudden overwhelming internal commands from an unrecognizable voice instructing them to kill themselves or someone else. Natalie had never come across a spirit wanting her to do such a thing.

"Natalie?"

"Yeah, Mom?"

Kathy Nolan hesitated, producing a quick bleep of a sound before speaking again. "What, what was your wife's name?"

"Her name was Danica. Danica Kincaid. I loved her, and I'm certain she loved me back. And I was a real shit to her more often than I want to remember! But she always forgave me, and she always came back around." Natalie paused. "And earlier, you called me by my maiden name. Nolan. I'm Natalie Kincaid now."

"Oh, Natalie, I don't know about that. I just don't know."

"There's nothing to know, Mom. It is what it *is!*"

"*You can't expect me to call you—*"

"This was a mistake," Natalie said. "I'm going to hang up—"

"ALL RIGHT. YOU'RE NATALIE KINCAID. THAT'S WHAT YOU WANT TO BE CALLED, *ALL RIGHT*. All right, don't hang up."

"You hear me breathing, Mom?"

"Yes."

"Then I haven't hung up."

"Oh." Weighted silence. "Your father and I were worried about your epilepsy. That no one would know how to look after you."

Natalie wrote a word in the thin layering of dust on the nearby nightstand. "Funny thing. It's gone."

"It's—how   does   that   happen?"
"I still don't know."

Natalie had written her maiden name, *Nolan,* in the dust. Then, she wiped it off, sending dust motes into the air.

"Did a doctor confirm it?"

"I don't need a doctor. It's gone. I'm fine."

Lying, lying, lying for no other reason than I feel like it.

"I don't know that that can happen, Natalie—"

"Mom, I need to tell you a couple things," Natalie said, straightening up. She felt her back crack. She'd been leaning against the wood headboard too long. "And I don't want you to interrupt me until I'm all the way through it. Okay?"

"Oh … all right."

"I forgive you. I—I want to *absolve* you because I want you to enjoy your life. Because Dad won't be able to move on until *he* knows *you* are going to be all right without him. Do it for you and do it for Dad. Forgive yourself. It took me a long time, but I've finally forgiven myself for some of the things I've done. I don't know when or if we'll talk again—"

"Natalie—"

"I hope we do. I really do want that. But life is unpredictable, and it's important to plan for everything, even the bad stuff. The permanent stuff. So this is me, well, releasing you, I guess. That's the best way I can say it. Live your life, Mom. For yourself. For Dad. And if you can find it within yourself to do so, for me too."

"Are you in trouble?" her mother pressed. "I'll come get you!"

Natalie's jaw tightened as she bit back the urge to scream. She sighed, instead. "I love you, Daddy."

"*-love-you-too-Nat-Bear-*"

The sound of her father's voice, calling her by his nickname for her when she was small, choked Natalie, lodged a sob in her throat.

"Mom, I love you too."

"I never stopped loving you. Your father and I, we—never stopped. You're our daughter. You're our gem."

Blinking back tears, Natalie bit her lower lip. "Mm-hmm. Gotta go."

"Natalie-wait—!"

"Be well."

She hung up the phone. So it was just as Gaither stopped weeping that Natalie was overwhelmed with her own tears and grief. Finding out about her father's death in that way was somehow more traumatic than if she'd had the chance to kiss his forehead at the wake and hold his hand before they closed the lid of his coffin for all time. The shock of it, his quavering, staticky voice filling her brainpan was just as painful as when she'd seen Danica into the crematoria furnace, her body dressed in a lovely crimson evening gown Natalie always loved and dreaded thinking about how it had probably peeled and flaked off her in the furnace flames. *Too much death. All around! I can't breathe anymore. It's always with me!*

"Greg!" she cried out to the empty room, her mind buzzing with the skittering sounds of the Soul Static in the back of her consciousness. Natalie felt Greg near them, could see him hunkering down in the dark cavern of her mind. But he was no longer sobbing. His shoulders no longer hitched and jerked. He appeared calm, full of resolve.

And deathly serious.

Stern.

Like a man paralyzed by regret.

That was good, Natalie. What you did just now.

"Greg, I don't know that I can follow through with this. I feel weakened somehow. I should have *never* called her. Nobody saps my energy and confidence like my mother. No one."

It was a good call. You made peace with her. And your father.

"Yeah, you might have told me about my Dad so I wouldn't have to find out that way!"

I've told you this … I don't know everything. I only know more than the living. But I'm sorry for your loss.

The sound of a motorcycle engine revving outside, eliciting a grandiose burst of male cackling and whistles, hatched an angry heat in the center of Natalie's being. She sniffed, pulling back the reins on her tears, and stood up with her pillow in her arms. "I could *kill* them," she hissed at the closed door. "I could *just kill them* …" The hate for them was so strong, so cathartic, she believed it could have blown the door right off its hinges. That she could step out onto the balcony, follow it around to the other side of the office, and look out over where the lot of them were camped out in the weighted July humidity. That she could explode their gas tanks, one by one, on down the line, until the Motel 6 conflagration could be seen from fucking space. Explode them with her mind.

Sadly, Natalie had never exhibited any gift for telepathy.

Right then, she would have sold her soul for it.

Frustrated, she cried out and threw the pillow at the wall. This did nothing for her.

Natalie had no idea she'd fallen asleep until she came awake to the stickiness under her head, a sudden jolt, and the quick, fierce arrival of a migraine behind her eyes the likes of which she had never experienced before. Not even following one of her seizures. This was the worst.

It felt like dying.

"Greg! *Gregory!*"

"Natalie. I'm here."

The last residue of fatigue boiling off her, Natalie shot up on the bed and turned to her left.

Danica lay stretched out beside her, one elbow propping up her head.

"Dani?"

"Yes," Danica answered, solemnly, "it's me. I'm here for you. And there are some things you need to know."

"Oh my God, you're really here!" Natalie cried, reaching for her wife.

Danica took her hand in hers and squeezed. "I'm happy to see you too. But we have to talk, and it can't wait."

"There's so much to talk about, I-I don't even know where to begin!"

"I do. Keep your eyes on me and please just try and listen."

It wasn't a difficult task to do as Danica asked her. Natalie drank in the lovely vision of her wife, her eyes greedily consuming every inch of her. Danica's black hair hung to her chin in perfectly straight strands, and her heart-shaped face emanated the former flawless radiance of the young woman's olive complexion. Danica's mother had been Mandarin, her father white, which accounted for the oversized green eyes and proletarian trim of her nose. Upper lip larger than the bottom. Long arms and legs sculpted and extended early in life when Danica had been a dancer over at Maddie's Little Superstars Ballet Studio in their hometown of Philly. The profile of her body as she gazed up at Natalie rose and fell in dramatic peaks and valleys. Natalie felt her mouth water at the sight of such familiar curves, and the urge to kiss her wife consumed her in that moment. It managed to soften the pulsing pain in her skull, the sheer sight of the beautiful, departed Danica Kincaid. And Natalie did not take offense Danica had shed the dress she'd been buried in for a more knockaround ensemble consisting of black Converse, blue jeans, and her favorite hoodie that showed a unicorn farting a rainbow across the low slope of her breasts.

"Nat, eyes on me."

"Why?"

"Natty-cake, just listen and *all will be revealed*. God, you're the same."

"My head hurts so fucking bad."

"Something happened in the night. While you were out cold."

"Th-there's a lot of fucking blood, Dani!" Natalie's pillow glistened with a heavy coating of crimson. "Is-Is that all *my* blood?"

"Yes," Danica said, her gaze dipping down before resurging to meet Natalie's eyes once more. "Gregory is listening to us right now. I can hear him too. Just like you. He's still inside you, but he asked that I tell you what you need to know from here on out. He feels responsible. He's breaking right now."

"Responsible for what? Is he the one that made me bleed like that?"

Danica nodded stiffly. "Earlier, Gregory saw I had finally made it back to you. And he had a change of heart. About all of this. He wanted to leave your body. To free you. See, he loathed what he was doing to you, what he'd gotten you into. It bothered him more and more the deeper into it the two of you got. By the time you got to this motel, he was having serious doubts that taking down the men who killed him would accomplish anything or bring him any peace. Yes, he'd finally gain entry onto the next plane of his existence, but at what cost?"

"Okay. And he explained all of this to you?"

"He did," Danica said. "But only after the *accident*."

"Accident?"

"You remember earlier when Gaither explained to you why your head wound was gone? He said that when he slipped inside your mind and body, his presence was powerful enough he was able to heal your wound and fill in the hole."

"Yeah, like caulk. That's what he said. Filling in the imperfections."

"That's right. Only he hadn't considered the possibility there was the chance of a full reversal of your healing if he left you. When he attempted to separate from you earlier, the bore hole in your forehead opened again. There was so much blood all at once! The sight of it, running out of you like it did, just … sent Gaither into panic mode. You didn't wake up because the blood loss was so profound you were falling into a full-blown coma. Right before you dropped into that black hole of unconsciousness, Gregory repossessed you. And your wound disappeared again, but not without having spilled all that blood across your pillow first."

"Wait …" Natalie explored the area just below her widow's peak with cautious fingertips. The skin was unbroken but sticky with the tacky texture of her dried blood. She imagined if she were to check herself in the bathroom mirror right then, Natalie would find a bloody mask of her face staring back at her, eyes widened with terror and mouth screaming in a muted hiss. "So, so I'm all right?"

"Now you are," Danica said. "But this changes everything, Nat."

Of course, Natalie understood all too well. "If he leaves, I'll die. I'll bleed to death."

"Yes. And there's a reason this happened. There's a reason why Gregory can't separate from you without killing you."

"What are you talking about? It makes perfect sense. What more could there be to this?"

"Baby—"

"What are you *telling* me?" Natalie begged suddenly, bottom lip quivering. "What's *wrong* with me?"

"No-no-no-*honey*!" Danica sat up and reached for Natalie. Her hands passed through her, as if Natalie were a cobweb. To an observer, the awkward motion would have resembled a graceless air hug. "God-*dammit*! I can't even hold you. I want to! So badly! Now more than ever. Listen to me, baby! I-I don't want you to be afraid. You hear me? I'll be here, and I'm not going anywhere until this is all over. Do you understand me?"

Rocking back and forth, Natalie burrowed her face into the hard surface of her knees, drawn up into herself. "Tell me …"

"You have a brain tumor. Oh, honey, it's a brain tumor."

Natalie went still as a statue, and her big, scared eyes seemed to glow in the dark, radiating disbelief. "A tumor?"

Instead of confirming this further, Danica kept silent and allowed Natalie to process what she'd just been told.

When Natalie spoke next, her voice sounded like it was coming from some far-removed locale that muted her urgency and mocked her fear with tremulous echoes. "The headaches. The seizures. But … I thought Gaither was throwing me into those seizures. He played with the lights in the bathroom. The V-hold on the old TV in our bedroom."

Gaither spoke up, his voice slow and low like a mourner. *That was only partly my doing. I was exacerbating a preexisting condition, as it turns out. I was surprised how easy it was to put you into a seizure. It was too easy. I had no idea this would account for that. I'm so sorry, Natalie! I'm so damn sorry!*

"It-it's not your fault. It, it isn't."

Since the car accident, Natalie had attributed nearly every headache, migraine, stiff neck, arthritic joint, sore throat, and loose stool to the wreck and its fallout. None of these seemingly unrelated symptoms would have ever led her to consider the possibility of anything so serious. As a matter of fact, Natalie had gradually trained herself to abide the aches and pains. While they were downright debilitating at times, especially during the dead of winter and the wee hours of night, Natalie had reconciled herself as best she could to what she believed to be lingering after-effects of what could have been a fatal car accident for her as well. When she was younger, her grandmother on her mother's side had come to live with them after the old woman suffered a stroke in her rowhome. If not for the Life Alert button she had worn around her neck, Grandma Eve would have laid there on the floor of her kitchen with a nasty gash on the back of her head until death kissed her long and deep. She shared a bathroom with Natalie, and a night did not go by the old woman didn't rise in the dead of night to "make water." The groans and gripes she spoke into the darkness on her way to the bathroom every night told the story of a body whose aches tortured her with every movement. Remembering Grandmother Eve, with her stiff joints and clicking bones and moans of pain, had helped Natalie to train herself into keeping her own bodily ailments in perspective, because she'd lived for ten more years after the stroke and endured the pain as best she could, probably having counted herself lucky just in living on to the age of ninety-five. *If Grandma Eve could handle it and keep on smiling every day, then who the hell am I to complain?*

But Grandma Eve died in her bed of old age. The stroke had been minor. It had not killed her.

I'm going to die before I even see thirty.

This diagnosis baffled her as much as her epilepsy. There was no history of cancer or epilepsy on so much as a twig of her family tree. Yet, one had worked in concert with the other to murder her. *That's what this is … a murder. Epilepsy equals inoperable brain tumor.* A loathsome equation. A cruel determination.

Perhaps the worst part of that moment and its devastating revelation was she longed for human contact and there was none to be had in the motel room. She'd lived much of her life in the company of ghosts. Bloodless. Fleshless. Sometimes bodiless entirely. And Natalie did not realize it until right then just how much she'd taken human contact for granted. It wasn't that way so much when Danica had been alive. Once she was gone, Natalie had come to prefer seclusion to so much as a hand grazing her shoulder in passing.

I'm alone. I'm going to die alone.

"Don't you think that, baby!" Danica said, her voice swelling with concern. "I'm right here."

"No, I am alone."

Gaither's richly timbred voice filled her ears. *You're not. I'm not going anywhere until it's time for me to go. When you say it's all right. Not one second before.*

"But you can't leave me," Natalie reasoned, her rocking slowing to a stop. The motion no longer comforted her like when she was younger in the throes of an anxiety attack. Nothing comforted her. "Or ... you could, couldn't you? There's just no-no use in sticking around. Healing my wound. I've got a f-f-fucking ticking time bomb in my brain. Right? I mean, Danica? Are you sure I have it? How do you know?"

"It's hard to explain the *how* other than to say my travelling to a higher plane of existence has granted me certain intuitive abilities other spirits and seers can't ascertain."

Gaither said, *I'm a lesser spirit. Not fully enlightened. I'm earthbound.*

"I wouldn't lie to you," Danica added. "Not ever. Certainly not about something like this."

"All my life under this black *fucking cloud!*"

"No, honey!" Danica cried. "There's more to this!"

"Oh-yeah-sure-like-they're-going-to-have-to-bury-me-in-Potter's-fucking-Field-because-I'm-beyond-broke-"

Nat, Gaither said, *do you remember earlier when I called you out—rudely, I admit—about how you have no right to judge the intentions of that Open Eyes civil rights group? My words were sharp and unkind, and I'm sorry about that. I really am. But it's relevant. It's important for you to understand what I meant when I said those things to you. Do you?*

"I-I don't know!" Natalie blurted out, her cheeks burning. "I can barely think straight!"

I know, Nat. But it's all going to come clear.

Natalie fell silent. Outside, someone revved the engine on their motorcycle so exuberantly it threatened to shred her sanity. The noise gave way to a cacophony of raucous male laughter. That grated on her nerves, but not as aggressively as the mechanical grinding that inspired their mirth. She wanted to burrow down into herself. Neither one of them had any right to stop her, as she saw it. This was her cross to bear, and silence served her far better than lashing out or crying or raging against the dying of the light. She shut her eyes. Tears squeezed out from beneath the webbing of her eyelids as if wrung from her eyeballs like ripened fruit.

Gaither said, *We'll grieve until the sun comes up. Then you'll have a decision to make. It could be the most important decision you'll ever make. But it's yours to decide. Either way, we will stand by you. I'll stay with you until you're sleeping. Danica ... she'll be with you from now on. Whether you pass on in the next twenty-four hours or in the next few weeks or the next couple of months.*

But, Natalie? You have the choice to die on your own terms. Do you understand that?

Forewarned is forearmed, and you've felt like a blunt instrument for most of your life. Too blunt to make your mark on the world or leave an etching on the face of the earth that will survive you. Now that you know what you know, you have the choice to turn yourself into a weapon. A sharp fucking instrument that cuts and slashes at the bad guys. Leaves a mark no one will ever forget. And you have the power to get revenge on my behalf. You'd be serving my last wishes, and you ... you would finally have skin in the game. You remember? This is your chance.

Natalie opened her eyes and turned her head sluggishly towards the door where the mayhem of the bikers had swelled to another fever pitch of noise pollution. *Those pieces of shit ... I could kill them.*

Danica stirred beside her. "The Remainder Twins? They're about to become a bigger problem than the two of you anticipated. But Gaither is right."

Natalie tried to hold her tongue, but the words came tearing out of her. "What the *fuck* is he *right about*? If the two of you were any more cryptic, you'd be the engravings on the inside walls of the pyramids, for Christ sakes! You want to make me into a weapon? Yeah?"

Now, it was Danica and Gaither's turn to fall silent. They intended to let Natalie have her say at that point.

So, Natalie did not hold back. "All right, then you show me the way, and I'll be the weapon. I'll—how did you put it—leave my mark! But the first thing I want to do is I want to walk downstairs, and I want to shut those fucking bastards up! They're driving me crazy!"

Here's the deal, Gaither began.

XII. ALL STAGES BUT ONE

Natalie drew a bath and soaked her skin for hours. When the water went cold, she held still and did not rise right away. She relished the chill. The shock of the sensation drew her attention away from the plague of her own thoughts, now awash with the infection of pending mortality. But by the time she moved out of the bathroom, absently toweling herself dry, and moved to the cheap single-serve coffee maker arranged on the writing desk, Natalie felt as if she would collapse under the weight of her new *knowing*. It was an anvil balanced atop her head, pressing her down ever further into the rug. The ground. The dirt of death.

Danica lay across the bed, watching Natalie with the somber intent of a patient bystander. Gaither lingered somewhere within the wormy folds of Natalie's brain, but he had retreated into his own prolonged silence. Natalie felt a quick stab of anger thinking about how both vowed to be *there* for her, to bear witness to what she was meant to do, but they were not *in it* with her.

I'm the one with skin in the game, Greg. How's my cred now? I'm scared to fucking death!

Nothing from Gregory Gaither.

The feeling of resentment was blind as it was misplaced. She knew this. Natalie retracted her mental claws and poured herself a cup of black coffee. Greg was grateful, and she knew it. There was no gray area there. He'd made his gratitude known earlier. Hell, he'd wept like a child over what he would ask Natalie to do with her life while facing down her own death. He'd cried because he felt responsible for Natalie having developed an inoperable brain tumor. That the handful of seizures he'd induced had somehow grown the wretched lemon-sized cancer in her head. Birthed it. But Danica had talked him off his proverbial ledge, and Gaither hadn't uttered a word since.

Time was short as it was. Natalie hoped he'd come around *sooner* than *later*.

The coffee was half-grounds, half-liquid, and when she tossed her first mouthful back, it tasted like damp sawdust. It surged back up her throat, and she spit it out into the nearby trashcan. *Doesn't matter, anyhow! It's not like I need caffeine to wake me up! I don't know that I'll ever sleep again!*

In her mind, she felt herself cycling rapidly through the five steps of grief. Denial tempted her into meager disbelief for what Danica and Gaither had told her. Only until the swift kick of a Doc Marten burst through the thin glass of such a false notion to make room enough for Anger to boil over. To simmer and burn and then to burn off the surface of her brain like fog hovering above a Kansas wheat field at mid-morning.

Her Bargaining reminded her of the gospels that tell of Jesus's agony in the Garden of Gethsemane before he freely and willingly gave himself over to the Roman guards and then to the Cross. This is not to say Natalie experienced any sort of God-complex when it came to her mission and what she meant to do with what was left of her life. It was just she *Bargained* very much as Jesus is said to have done with God. *Let me off the hook for this, if you can? Why not someone else? WHY ME?*

As for Depression, it only deepened within her. It had been with her for so long as it was.

Lost in such thoughts, Natalie had no recollection of having dumped the rest of her coffee down the bathroom drain, or of having opened the blinds wide. It was only when she came to, blinking at the white haze filtering through the sheers, that Natalie knew she'd been functioning from muscle memory and nothing more for the last couple of minutes.

"Dani?" Natalie said, turning away from the shine of the windows. "I won't make it to the Fifth Step."

"Acceptance?" Dani asked. "I know it. I'm sorry."

"And that's all right? That sounds healthy?"

"No," Danica answered, softly. "No, none of this is fair to you."

"Too *fucking* bad for me? Is that what you're saying?"

"Of course not. I'm saying too bad for them." Danica nodded her head towards the door.

The sounds coming from the parking lot. Noises that had held all night.

XIII. THE SPANGLER WOODS HORROR

Raymond Charles had buried his father a week ago. The old man had been one of those obstinate diabetics who believed Type II meant *eat what you want,* and Type I meant insulin and certain death. The old man's steady diet of Big Macs and Beefaroni, a menu he cultivated and stuck to right after Raymond's mother died, was what sent him to the ER seven days ago complaining of a tightness in his chest. Within twenty minutes of his arrival, Raymond's father was knocking on heaven's door. This meant several things to Raymond and his family. It elicited a range of emotions. That July morning, though, Raymond felt the loss worse than ever.

The forty-something steelworker named Raymond Charles trudged through the forest with his hunting rifle slung over his right shoulder and Dad's hunting rifle slung over his left, all the while trying in vain to keep his eyes clear of the tears that kept coming. He held the simple urn containing the ashes of his father close to his barrel chest and prayed there weren't any rabbit or snake holes in the terrain, hidden well beneath the crunchy, thick carpeting of leaves and underbrush. He had chosen to wear his father's rifle for this ritual of tribute. In life, his father had always said the firearm felt like an extension of his arm and granted him a temporary sense of control over the world around him, if for only the few hours he and his son spent every year on their hunting trips. Raymond counted himself lucky he and Dad had been able to spend one final trip together last Thanksgiving weekend.

Now, the tug of the rifle's strap against his shoulder felt as comforting as his father's hand had when the old man pulled him to a stop so they could set up a blind. Raymond could only hope this final step in meeting his father's last wishes would work as something of a salve for his grief, but the gaping hole inside of him could not be filled with any sort of symbolic gesture.

Ever since he was eight years old, Raymond and his dad had gone out just before dawn on Black Friday to bag themselves a pair of Pennsylvania bucks in this same stretch of woodland. Spangler Woods. They had admired the same fox den for the last ten years every time they passed by it a mile and a half into the forest's northeastern perimeter. This was where his father had specified his ashes be scattered. Ten paces from the entrance to the den itself to limit the chances of one of the animals pissing on his dusty remains.

Now, Raymond approached the fox den and thought of shooting into it before the ritual at hand. Just emptying all of his ammo into the hutch, then scattering the mortal remains of his father to the four winds and heading back home to drown himself in rum and Cokes until he snored the rest of the day away.

Of course, that's not what his father would have wanted—for his son to turn psychopath because he lost his old man earlier than expected.

Just the sight of the fox den hurt him down deep. He imagined his father crawling out of it on his hands and knees in some strange supplication before telling his son it had all been a trick. A lie. That he was very much alive, his humor just as off-color as ever. But Raymond had to abandon the reverie when his father drew close enough and raised his face to the dappled sunlight above, revealing a worm-eaten visage and a hole in his cheek.

Dad is gone. And I don't know what the fuck I'm even doing out here. Honest to Christ!

They were never supposed to hunt those woods. The **No Hunting** signs were posted every quarter mile along the forest's border. But Raymond's father chose to pay no mind to them. He said he'd pay the fine because it would be worth it. The way Raymond's father explained it, he'd hunted Spangler Woods with Raymond's grandfather since long before the signs went up. "Ever since the liberals got the governorship of the state, they been imposing their hippie tyranny on everyone else," Raymond's father told him. "I vote a Conservative straight ticket every two years. Not my governor. Not my problem."

Still, it had nudged at Raymond's conscience every year they stepped inside the perimeter, ignoring the posted signs and, by proxy, the law. So many times, Raymond had wanted to remind his father the forest was most likely off limits to hunters because of its immediate proximity with the historic Gettysburg Field, as well as the role the old woods themselves had played in the conflict itself. Not to mention, the secret Democrat inside of Raymond protested. Then, he remembered he was more loyal to his father than the political party he'd never told his father about.

Shit, he knows now, doesn't he? He knows I bleed Blue. Oh well, Pop.

"Probably knows more now than I ever wanted him to."

Twenty paces north of his position, the crunching of dead leaves.

The crisp snap of a tree branch rang out, sounding like ten of them breaking underfoot.

Fuck hunting season, Raymond thought, his face hot and fresh tears blurring his vision. *This one's for you, Pop!*

Raymond took a knee and swung his backpack down onto the ground. He unzipped it slowly, to mute the sound of the zipper, and stowed his father's urn inside along with a wrapped tuna sandwich, a Slim Jim, and a Fanta. He set the bag aside. Then, Raymond silently lowered himself down to the forest floor, into a prone position. He removed his father's rifle and laid it down next to him in the leaves. Then he slid his hunting rifle off his shoulder and sighted through the scope, searching the vicinity for the familiar flash of brindle buck fur.

"All right, Dad," he said to the rifle lying beside him, "here we go. Guide my sights. Guide my hands."

The deer seemed to appear out of thin air, slipping an elm tree trunk and sliding into view as if on a treadmill.

"Oh *Christ*," Raymond breathed. "What in the hell's wrong with that thing?"

The deer was slender, its limbs precarious, so finely built, Raymond would not have been surprised if it simply toppled over, its limbs folding under like the legs of a card table. They wobbled like the limbs of a newborn fawn, but this was a full-grown deer. Its body was rife with big, black, and bulging tumors. It was not a buck. But it was the only animal Raymond had seen that morning for miles, and he wanted to finish the hunt. The tradition would die after that day, and Raymond decided right then he would never revive it. Raymond and his wife were childless.

Something deep inside of him, a second voice, not his father, told him not to shoot this particular animal. No, Raymond should leave the woods and fast. And not merely because the animal looked frightening in its appearance.

When the animal turned its small head towards him, Raymond clamped a hand over his mouth to stifle the scream.

The deer's eyes were black tumors, grown completely over its eyes. It looked like some unholy god had stabbed onyx stones into the animal's ocular cavities, and taken Its time doing so.

"Jesus, I gotta do it. Gotta put the poor thing out of its misery. That thing's cancer on four legs."

It's also most likely blind, but it looks like the fuckin' thing is staring straight at me.

Raymond waited until his shooting finger went still, then he slid it out from behind the safety guard. He curled it around the trigger. The first time Raymond ever went hunting with his father, he had been inclined to shoot the buck in its massive, pronged head. Raymond's father had explained how important it was to aim with precision, not for himself, but for the sake of the prey. A lung shot too far back wouldn't kill the animal. It would send them bucking into the brush, trailing blood across the forest floor detritus and the musk of fear through the air. Raymond remembered his training and his father's words. He sighted on an invisible line directly up from the back of the front leg, between one-third and one-half the way up the body.

He squeezed the trigger.

The deer's hip exploded into a red flap of meat. It leapt what looked like five feet in the air before landing slipshod on three of its four legs. The fourth leg buckled, and the animal awkwardly fell face-first into the brambles and dead leaves before gracelessly finding its way back onto all fours and bounding out of sight. Raymond tried to track it for a kill shot. It lost him, breaking left, and disappearing behind a large stand of skeletal branches bound in ivy and brambles. He didn't shoot up off the ground like he used to in his younger days. Raymond found his knees and strapped the backpack on. He stood, his body jumping with adrenaline. He nearly started the chase after the animal without his father's hunting rifle. Thankfully, his eyes happened upon its muzzle sticking out of the debris when he was giving himself a quick dust-off.

"Fucker."

Stringing his father's weapon over his shoulder once more, Raymond bounded through the underbrush, kicking up leaves and twigs in his wake. The forest had never seemed so deep. He had only recently started going to the gym, walking the treadmill for twenty minutes at a brisk five miles an hour. This was what kept him from getting winded immediately. He gave chase for what seemed like an eternity to his lungs and heart. Raymond was certain he and his father had never made it this deep into the woods, having bagged their prizes well beforehand. He was miles in.

He'd never seen the need to panic out there with his father.

Dad always knew where we were and how to get back!

"Fuck-fuck *fuck!*" he cried. "This was a *mistake.* God-*dammit!*"

He saw bright red splashes of blood spanning what looked like another forty kilometers before him. The Tumor Deer was gushing like a stuck pig. *I didn't miss the mark that far off! My aim ain't as true as Dad's was, but Jesus-H-Christ!*

Raymond continued tracking the crimson trail.

The animal had banked a hard, deliberate left, as if it held some sort of specific destination in mind. Raymond followed it, nearly turning his heel in his Timberlands. His left boot squished down into a muddy mold in the ground, and when he pulled it back out again, it created a sound like two people kissing with luscious lips.

In an instant, Raymond looked down to his ruined boots as they kept pace beneath him.

When he looked up again, there was a ramshackle-looking house blocking his path. The blood ran right up to the building's only entryway, a threshold without a door. He'd never seen the structure before. It looked like an old schoolhouse, dating back perhaps to the nineteenth century. He'd seen pictures of such buildings. One-story. A-frame roof. Simple edifices. Nothing grand. How had this place escaped notice? How had the historic society not cleared the area around such a historic landmark and renovated the place to something of its former glory? The schoolhouse had been painted red, but moss bearded a good bit of it from the ground up and concealed nearly three-quarters of its former shade. Pale slivers of exposed wooden planks smiled out from behind the flaking paint job. Whoever had built the schoolhouse had done it for keeps!

Dad would have been impressed! And he wouldn't have just stood outside the place with his mouth hanging open! He'd go in, and he'd search out the prey.

Raymond approached the threshold. Holes were punched into the roof like it'd been struck by lightning over and over during its lengthy time standing, as if tendrils of hot, white electricity straight from the palm of God had miraculously struck down between the patchwork of treetops to stab and bludgeon the rooftop of the little, squat building.

To burn the place down?

That's Old Testament wrath, right there!

But sure enough, Raymond saw the scorch marks ringing every hole in the roof above.

If Raymond hadn't watched his step, he might have dropped ass over teakettle into the recessed dirt floor inside. The drop-off was steep in its descent. Its deepest point easily measured six to seven feet below the surface. It would have meant a broken neck for Raymond Charles out in the middle of nowhere. No Christian burial. Just food for the worms he saw quite clearly in the loose muddy earth below, dipping in and out of the drudge.

The interior looked like it had once housed corpses in a mass grave.

And there was no sign of the Tumor Deer.

Baffled, Raymond turned himself around, searching for some sign of the blood trail having resumed somewhere perhaps further off. But it was as if that same great hand of God that had showered the rooftop of the schoolhouse in numerous stitches of white lightning strikes had also reached down in the matter of a moment to scoop up the dying, deformed animal and carried it back up into His loving arms.

Since Raymond had lost his father, a lot of things he had believed or taken for granted in his life were given closer, more scrutinous, and, in some instances, painful examinations. Among such tenets was Raymond's belief in God. Odd as it was, while he'd read on the internet most people doubted the existence of God after losing a loved one, he had turned all the way back around to face and embrace his faith. For years and years, he'd kept his Catholicism in the corner of his eye. Of late, he chose to face it full on.

But here?

Here was nothing of God or goodness or grace present nor accounted for in the schoolhouse.

The old structure only renewed Raymond's sense of loss, and on a much deeper and crippling level.

He lowered his rifle. Shut his eyes. A tear squeezed itself out from under the flap of his left eyelid and skated down his cheek to drop into the mud at his feet.

Raymond's whole body felt like it was wavering. He felt drunk. Overwhelmed.

He had not yet cried for the loss of his father, but his wife told him it would come. How could he not have known this expedition would be just the thing to break him down emotionally so he could mourn properly?

"Open your goddamn eyes, pussy!" The voice of his father was strained. Compressed.

Raymond's eyes flashed open.

He screamed.

His father, Earl Charles, was buried up to his neck in the dirt floor of the farmhouse. The surface of the muddy ground at the bottom of the

(grave)

trench rumbled like bubbling lava. Then the old man's hands burst through, and he scrabbled at the loose, wet earth for some kind of purchase. He wriggled around, struggling to unsheathe his upper body from the mud.

"Dad?" Raymond stood there, mouth agape. His hand loosened from around the butt of the rifle. It tumbled down into the

(grave)

trench.

Earl Charles grabbed for it. The rifle had become wedged in the side of the hole. The old man curled his chubby, porcelain-white fingers around the rifle's stock. He pulled himself up and out to just above the soiled loincloth he wore. Other than that, Earl Charles was naked.

"Dad, what … where's your suit? Dad …"

They had indeed cremated the old man in his favorite charcoal grey suit, the only suit the man owned, as it had been designed by a Big and Tall manufacturer. The old man's viewing casket was what is known in the undertaker business as *double-wide*, like they were burying him in a house trailer. Somewhere between then and now, Earl Charles had shed his suit. And as the old, overweight man slid the tips of his bare feet out of the hole, Raymond could see his father had also shed a good bit of his skin from his belly, left thigh, forehead, and shoulder blades. Green-grey, slippery flesh gleamed where its covering had been sloughed off.

Raymond lurched and gagged. He folded over onto his knees.

Vomited down into the hole.

Snot bubbled in his nose as he sobbed with wet, red eyes.

"*Oh God, help me. Dad—*"

"You always *were* a fuckin' terrible shot, son!" the old man grumbled. "Now, they'll be coming! All of 'em! You picked the wrong *fuggin'* animal to shoot at! Din't you hear me in your ear telling you to *let this one go*? That this one's *different? Off-fuggin'-limits?!*"

"I didn't know it was you, Pop! I swear!"

Raymond doubled over, burrowing his head into the small of his turkey neck. He hadn't inherited his father's huskiness. He squeezed his eyes shut.

Earl Charles scoffed at his son. "You wanna see what you got in store when *you* go, son?"

Raymond recoiled when the cold, clammy, and dirty fingertip grazed his knee.

"You wanna see, Ray?"

"*NOIDON'TWANNASEE—*"

"GOOD-CUZ'-THERE-AIN'T-NOTHIN'-*TO*-SEE! BUT THERE'S

PLENTY O' DIRT TO TASTE! TO EAT! THERE'S PLENTY TO FILL YOU UP!"

The ground at the bottom of the
(grave)
trench bubbled up and over.

The hole birthed an abomination of a man before Raymond's eyes. His eyes widened, and his mouth opened in a scream that never sounded. A dry hiss escaped his throat as he blankly surveyed the horrid living corpse before him. The man was built like a broken kite stuffed inside a white sheet, and his body was caked in mud and grime. Grubs and earthworms and other vile insects dripped off him as he moved in a series of stiff tics and swipes of his arms. A dark moustache covered the man's upper lip. His eyes were the color of curdled milk. The meager dark strands of hair atop his head were slicked down to a misshapen skull. The white scalp shone through the profoundly thin follicles. The man leveled its blank gaze at Raymond. While Raymond could not see where the irises were aimed, he was dead certain they'd landed on him.

I'm running a fever! This isn't real! Feel your head, Raymond! You're coming down with something. Don't be afraid.

He hadn't noticed how light both his shoulders felt until Raymond saw that he'd dropped both his and his father's rifles down into the
(grave)
trench.

The rifle! Get the goddam rifle! NOW!

Just as shock had begun to fog his brain to uselessness, Raymond dropped down onto his stomach and crawled down halfway into the hole. He reached for the rifle, only a foot shy of his searching fingers.

Raymond gritted his teeth and inched his way precariously further past the lip of the grave. His tongue swept across his chapped upper lip as he touched the tip of his index finger to the stock of the rifle.

The pale, naked corpse opened his mouth and let loose a shredded scream. "*Yank-eeeeeeeeeee!*"

Raymond's hand curled around the stock. He yanked the weapon up the side of the incline as the corpse made its own sad grab for the rifle at the same time. His heart thumping like a jackhammer between his ears and heating his cheeks, Raymond fumbled the rifle up off the muddy incline. The muzzle came up, and he worked his finger around the trigger as the corpse moved to within a foot of him.

The blast was deafening. The cordite like a death musk.

The pale corpse flinched. It felt itself, searching for any entry-point or wound the bullet could have inflicted. Its mouth stretched into a great, gaping maw as something resembling a knowing in its milky eyes widened them in their cavernous sockets. After inspecting itself with groping, sinewy fingers and finding nothing resembling a wound, the corpse angled himself around at the bottom of the hole and with a viciously abrupt motion, drove its hands down into the hole from which it had only just emerged.

With a brittle grunt, the corpse pulled at something submerged in the dirt. The corpse straightened, ever so slightly, drawing it beyond the filthy surface like some bony crane working to unearth a treasure.

Another pair of hands were tightly curled around the corpse's wrists.

They gave way to a second pair of pale, starved arms.

Raymond watched this unfold before him like a man swept up in some fever dream born in the wake of a horror movie marathon the night before.

"Oh Christ!" he cried.

Raymond scrambled up and away from the lip of the drop-off, holding fast to his father's rifle. His own rifle lay stowed away behind him, safe and sound. He raised himself up onto his feet once more and moved blindly backward, out the way he'd come in. But not before witnessing the hands in the hole giving way to the upper half of a *second* corpse who'd been hidden away moments ago beneath the dirt and mud.

I hit 'em! Hit the bastard, whatever it is!

The second corpse's neck had been cleaved through by the rifle's bullet when it fired down into the ground, and its head listed severely to the right. Half of its neck had been blown away, exposing a yawning red wound that appeared to scream silently. A desperate look of shock tugged at its features, stretching them back toward its ears like an ill-fitting mask. Oddly, the blood did not gush out of the gaping wound right away. When it issued from his opened neck it did not pour forth. It sprayed and fanned outward as if it were being funneled through a pair of cupped hands. The second corpse's mouth hung open, slack-jawed and soundless. Two massive fangs, gored in gleaming red, protruded from its upper gums. Then, the left one dropped out of his opened mouth, disappearing into the turned earth.

The right fang followed suit, dissolving into the dirt.

That was enough for Raymond. More than enough. Had he stood his ground any longer, Raymond was dead certain he would have lost the will and means to run from the horror unfolding at the bottom of the

(grave)

trench.

Shoving off his left heel, Raymond ran from the schoolhouse and did not look back. Not even when he swore he heard the incessant snapping of twigs underfoot behind him. Then right at his heels.

He did not see the Tumor Deer lingering just outside the red schoolhouse, lingering and tracking the hunter until he disappeared behind a copse of trees. Then, without warning, it bounded after Raymond Charles with all the frenzy of a starved, stalking creature.

XIV. COME TOGETHER

John Tarvill could not close his brother Henry's mouth. It was widened into a soundless scream. After pulling Henry all the way up out of the ground, he tried to squeeze his brother's jaws shut again, but they were as rigidly unyielding as the mouth of an opened vise. Henry's body had swiftly turned against him, staging a rapid revolt sparked off by the wretched, yawning opening in the side of his neck. John laid his brother out in the dirt, but he could do nothing other than grab at the flesh of his face, pull at it like he would have pulled at hair if it were still on his head. The skin was loose and offered a good amount of play as John pulled the flesh and the thinner, web-like skin away from the bone in utter lament.

The Remainders had never before known such vulnerability, and now it had been visited upon them in such a debilitating shock and awe manner, the strength of their evil resolve seemed to have fled them in favor of self-preservation.

Now, death smiled upon both from a distance not so far removed as before.

Death stared down at them from the lip of the

(grave)

trench, biding *its* time. Because it really was only a matter of moments before they would have no other choice other than to give themselves over to the finality of things. They could not cheat any longer. There would come an end for them. A conclusion.

Then, they would pay for their crimes and their *cheating*.

What John had not counted on was how directly tied to his twin brother his own survival truly was. The suffering of Henry passed into John, burrowing into his suddenly porous cells, flesh, blood, and brittle bones.

Henry …

Henry's eyes roved ravenously about, unable to fix themselves upon John.

Henry …

But Henry's eyes fluttered, shut, even as the rest of his body continued to

102

twitch and jiggle like a fish pinned to the end of a hook. The sight of Henry's coveted fangs dropping out of his gums sent John Tarvill into a panic. Through the decades, they'd encountered a number of wounds while securing their prey or moving amidst the *living*, but they had all proven superficial in nature. Blood acted as a great solvent in every instance, and they tore the offending prey limb from limb, not merely to get theirs but also as an act of quick, frenzied retribution. Never had either of them suffered the sort of wound or disfigurement Henry sustained from the bullet of the vile interloper's hunting rifle. John laid his hands on his brother. Henry lay prone on the ground.

I will bring the Yankee back, Henry.

Too weakened to transfer a coherent thought to his brother, Henry merely stared with his mouth stuck open.

John climbed precariously up the side of the trench. He pulled himself up and out, found his bare feet. Naked, pale, and skeletal in build, John Tarvill burst from the schoolhouse.

He did not have to search far, no further than a few yards from the threshold.

The Yankee's body writhed and twisted half-heartedly, impaled on a low hanging elm branch. The sharpened end of the branch protruded from the center of the Yankee's billowing coat. Gleaming crimson fanned outward from the mortal wound, even bearding the man's jowls in thick, globulous red. His arms were bloody stumps, ending in craggy icicles of bone sticking from his shoulder blades. His legs were gone. Shriveled and dead penis and testicles dangled uselessly between the Yankee's thighs. John looked on in sheer wonderment as this new adversary shuddered, sucked in a worthless lungful of the cold air and died.

Incredulous, John Tarvill turned around and around, searching for so much as the snap of a branch or the twitch of a bramble pile.

Nothing.

Then, a craggy voice, relaxed in the same Southern drawl John and Henry had used in life, sounded between his ears.

We're all here.

It was not Henry. His brother had been struck dumb.

You know me.

The recollection was faint. Too faint to register.

I'm your maker.

Now, it was John Tarvill's turn to be struck dumb with bewilderment.

Meet us on the battlefield. It's begun.

XV. IN THE FIELDS, THE FORESTS

In all the years Robert Harvey had played *colonel* for the mock-Union Army (seven years that summer), he never felt more self-conscious about how bloated his stomach had become than that July. That morning when he'd stood in front of the full-length mirror in his bedroom, with his trusty Labrador named Millie watching him from his queen-sized bed rather than a groggy wife, Robert had found he could not suck in far enough.

Not without cutting off the air to his lungs.

There had never been a need to maintain any sort of healthy build until that morning. Robert worked as a history professor at University of Penn. Before that, he'd chaired the English department at an inner-city parochial high school. Many of his male colleagues developed bellies, and their asses had done the old *secretary spread* because most of them gave up walking around the class while they lectured. They sat on stools in the front of the classroom. Some even took to delivering their entire lessons from their desks. His friend from that high school, Herbert Winthrop, himself a bachelor by default, had told Robert, "Teaching is show-business for ugly leading men." And Robert had taken comfort in that. It fit his lifestyle, his ever-widening waistline, and his carelessness when it came to how he looked every day when the school bell rang at seven-thirty every morning.

So, no impetus to change. To exercise. To shave off some poundage.

As far as his role as a reenactment actor was concerned, Robert had seen enough of those old vintage photographs, grainy like the photographer had let a spider spin a web over the lens, to know many of the soldiers on both sides of the Civil War conflict had been fat asses. Sure, most of them were boys with grimy faces and fear, intermingled with a dislocated sense of urgency stamped into their features. But the older men, the ranking officers? Not a Brad Pitt or a Schwarzenegger or a Rambo among the lot of them. Their guts, in many instances, rivalled Robert's own. And he'd hoped he did not have to get in any kind of shape to cut a convincing Union Army colonel for their annual July third reenactment of the Battle of Gettysburg.

Then he had gotten a call the night before from Fox 4 News, the local station out of Gettysburg. They wanted to send one of their beat reporters out to Gettysburg Field to interview him for what they called a "color segment," the kind that typically wraps up a broadcast around eleven at night, all neat as you please before beddy-bye. He agreed, of course. The turnout of paying spectators to his event had taken a considerable dip in the last two years. A feature might just drum up interest among residents, and Robert knew Fox 4 broadcasted to the five counties surrounding Gettysburg as well. It could be just what he and his fellow Civil War enthusiasts needed to generate the type of revenue they needed to make sure the show would continue. This prospect was as important to Robert as giving a good lecture or inspiring his students. History was sacred to him, the Civil War an obsession of his ever since he could walk, and his father had taken him to an exhibit at the Franklin Institute of the period's preserved artillery.

But Robert made a mistake, one he wished he could have gotten back. He'd asked the caller from Fox 4 which reporter they were sending out. He knew all their names and who they were. When the caller told Robert he would interview with Tonya Lafferty, two things happened that nearly caused him to drop the phone. The strength went out of his legs for a millisecond. And Robert Harvey realized he had let himself turn into a behemoth pushing two-fifty at only forty-three years old. The insecurity had always been there, but he'd become something of an expert at tamping it down.

This time was different.

He didn't sleep soundly, his dreams broken and scattered across the cosmos of his unconscious mind with free-floating images of Robert stuffing his face as a kid even after his father tried to cut him off while his mother indulged him with thirds and sometimes fourths. He thought about his own mortality, something that had never nagged at him before. He thought of how many pallbearers he would need if he kept along the path he was on. Dying young. Alone, save his trusty Lab, Millie, who just might outlive him if he didn't wise up and opt to have his goddamn jaw wired shut.

Robert was up that morning before the sun faintly glazed his windowpanes. He had also dreamt of the reporter, Tonya Lafferty.

They just had to send their hottest reporter, didn't they! She must have really screwed the pooch over at the station to have gotten stuck with this assignment!

Before he had left for Gettysburg Field, Robert had tried to do some crunches, his costume boots tucked under the sofa in his living room. After five, he had drummed up just enough endorphins for himself to ride the high for some of his commute. He drove to the field in a funk, thinking of what his first words would be when Tonya Lafferty approached him with her microphone and cameraman in tow.

It should probably be along the lines of: It's a great pleasure to meet you! *How about that? You don't want to creep her out, right? Shake her hand, not too hard. Look her in the eyes, but not too long. Just enough to create a rapport before the interview.*

"Mr. Harvey?"

Robert spun around, the rise of his bootheel cutting into the damp grass of the low bluff.

There she stood.

Tonya Lafferty.

"Um, y-yes," Robert said, his eyes unblinking and alert. "It's a great pleasure to meet you." *Yes, exactly like you rehearsed in the car. Good show, Bobby!* "I—"

Behind him, the reenactors tested the cannon, and Robert jumped like someone just goosed him.

Tonya Lafferty was even more strikingly gorgeous (and taller) than she looked on Robert's forty-eight-inch plasma screen TV at home. He knew some of her backstory. Former Miss Pennsylvania in 2014. A brief stint starring in commercials for Lowenbrau and Wheat Thins that somehow led her to hayseed country with tractor pulls and car shows on alternating weekends year-round. She wore her thick and wavy black hair long, draped across the red blouse she wore paired with a black skirt. The ground was sodden, and she'd planned for such a condition, but Robert couldn't help but to smile just the same when he noticed Tonya's beat-up sneakers. Perfect for walking through damp grass on a hot morning. Her eyes were big and brown with amber flecks encircling her pupils like planets around an eclipsed sun. Perfect olive skin showcased a smattering of lightened freckles across the bridge of her nose.

In other words, she was the woman of Robert Harvey's dreams.

Tonya already had her hand out, finely manicured nails done up in a seafoam blue polish. Her smile may very well have looked plastered on, almost like it hurt her from overuse, but Robert chose to read it as a genuine display of emotion.

He reached out to shake. He looked down at their hands clasping one another, and in that split second, Robert saw the way his belly shoved his navy-blue Union button down shirt up and over his belt like a suspended avalanche of flab.

Leave it, you idiot! Just, be yourself.

"Mister Harvey, is it? I'm Tonya Lafferty. With Fox 4?"

"Yes, of course. I know who *you* are."

A cameraman trailed behind her who looked like he could quite possibly harbor the same insecurities about his weight as Robert. He balanced his camera across the wide ridge of his left shoulder. It sagged there in his arms while he waited for Tonya to signal him to switch on. He wore a ratty grey hoodie, black chinos, and blue Converse that looked like a dog's chew toys. A rumpled Pirates baseball cap was screwed down onto his bullet head. Robert saw the guy blow a bubble with his gum, and after it popped, he spoke up in a heavy Boston accent.

"Hey, Tanya?" he said in a thick Southie accent while balancing his camera across the wide ridge of his left shoulder. "We maybe wanna get dahn' on the field for a betta' shaht? I'll take a panoramic shaht from heah, then we'll go dahn?"

"Oh," Tonya said, switching her attention between the cameraman and Robert, "are we allowed to get that close, Mr. Harvey?"

"Robert, please. And yes, I'll bring you to the tent where I will be standing. As the colonel, I'm forced to do a lot of standing around. Apparently, *they* did a lot of that during battle, unless their forces were shrinking rapidly. Then they dove into the fray head-first."

"All right, Trey," Tonya told the cameraman, "get the wide shot and then we'll go down." She turned her lovely brown eyes back to Robert, and he felt blood rush to his inner thighs. "Hope I don't slip on my way down. I don't think these sneakers have much sole left."

"Got the shot!" Trey piped up behind them, perfectly comfortable with living in the background. "You wanna' go dahn' there now?"

Robert and Tonya were ready. He led them along the low bluff to where it dipped just low enough, they would not have to step down the steeper slope. Robert's big, black boots, Tonya's tennis shoes, and Trey's Converse all squished along in what became a cacophonous series of sound devoid of rhythm. Robert snuck a sideways glance at Tonya trudging along beside him and thought he saw a hint of annoyance tugging at the corners of her mouth and turning down her eyebrows. He was surprised by the stab of offense he felt in his gut at her expression. Not everyone is a history buff, but a moment ago, she'd looked jazzed to be covering the event. Right then, in that glimpse of an instant, Robert thought he might have seen the reporter with her mask off, so to speak.

"Man, this is *so* damn cool!" Trey exclaimed, surveying the mock *theater of war* spread out for a quarter mile across the opened, uneven terrain of Gettysburg's famous field. "Up close, you feel like you're in it, man! Just like you're dahn' in it!"

Robert nodded. "Thank you. We work hard to honor all the soldiers who fought in this bloody war by maintaining painstaking accuracy. We studied the journals of many of the men who fought in this battle, and records of all maneuvers which took place. We perform it in near-perfect consequential order. Every stitch of clothing is woven of the exact material the Union and the Confederacy wore. Canteens. Weaponry. Facial hair styles of the day. The placement of cannons and commander tents? All where they were staked and arranged during the battle.

Trey grunted, a type of approval. "You guys use fake blood and all?"

"No, that's strictly forbidden by the National Historical Society. It would be disrespectful to spill so much as an ounce on the same hallowed ground where real, living, breathing men bled their last for their cause. I tend to agree."

'Yeah," Trey pressed as they neared the tent and he continued goggling at the *theater of war* to his left in all its tragedy and glory. "But you guys can't help but tear up the ground heah' and there. Moving stuff arahnd. Setting up the tents. Running arahnd, fighting and stuff. Kicking up wet grahnd."

"Trey!" Tonya interjected. "Don't push!"

Trey shook his head. "Just a curious mind. That's all."

"Fair question," Robert said, comfortable with leaving it there.

"So, Robert," Tonya said, the lilt in her voice having returned, "what are we seeing here? When does it start?"

"Well, when it comes to *the start*, we have to adhere to how it *started* historically. General Lee did not initially give the go-ahead for the battle to ensue, and he was not present when the First Corps, Army of the Potomac arrived on this very field and provided reinforcements to Brigadier General John Buford's weakened cavalry. The men were exhausted from their trek, and the relief was welcome. That is who you see on the field right now. Union men. Standing over there at the tent's entrance is *our* John Buford. The silver-haired fox with the bushy gray moustache." Robert cut a sharp salute to the fake *Buford*, who returned it steadfast. "The fact that the Cavalry were not the first ones here is the reason many believe God smiled on the Union and abhors slavery in any and all forms, because this early arrival allowed for the Union soldiers to gain the high ground in advance of the Confederate arrival. That's what we're standing on right now, the very peak where our Union boys set up shop, waited, and ultimately picked off enough of the Confederacy that they turned tail and ran after three days. Of course, this left fifty thousand men dead on both sides."

Tonya nodded. "And when did the Union soldiers arrive?"

"Lee discovered that the Union army was on its way to the as-yet unknown town of Gettysburg, and he planned to arrange his army at the crossroads in town. But he and his forces arrived on the second of July. The Union forces were already in place by the time Lee arrived with his men. There were confrontations before they met on this battlefield in particular, and Lee did manage to drive some Union forces back through town to what's called Cemetery Hill. But that's a half-mile south of here, and it's not like we could carry out the reenact in the middle of what's now a busy area. Just think of it this way, Ms. Lafferty. The Battle of Gettysburg lasted three days. We had to figure out a way to somehow condense the events of three days into six hours, and we included *only* the portion of the battle that took place right here. That's why I said earlier we strived for a *near-perfect* unfolding of chronological events."

The three of them walked towards the slope upon which the Union soldiers were gathered and forming regimented lines. There was a distinct electricity in the air around them, like the moments preceding a thunderstorm. A purple-bruised blanket of clouds rose over Spangler Woods, unfurling beyond the treetops. It unrolled, blackest where it touched the canopy of waving elms, a premature night peeking at the valley of actors, darkening every inch of ground as it approached. Paced and steady. On its way.

Robert shrugged off his annoyance at such a daunting development. It had been Tonya's own Fox 4 news that had predicted clear, sunny, and hot all day.

No mention of a storm. Tornado. What have you. The question was on the tip of his tongue to Tonya when she acknowledged the error herself.

"Drizzle in the early morning," she said, lamenting the sky herself. "That's what Dan Defelice said last night on the eleven o'clock? Nothing about the apocalypse! Good God, look at that skyline!" She paused, snatched at her hair to pull out some volume, and went on. "Let's try and beat the rain. So, where are the Confederate soldiers right now?"

Robert smiled to himself. "They are waiting. In the parking lot. You know, for their cue." He noticed Trey's quick little smirk, swallowed his irritation, and then turned to Tonya Lafferty with an ingratiating smile. "Ms. Lafferty—"

"Tonya."

"Tonya, why don't we step back from the breach here and you can ask your questions?"

"All right," she agreed, and seemed to produce a microphone from thin air when, in fact, she'd been holding it at her side the entire time. "Trey, if you could arrange us by the tent, we'll use that as a backdrop along with the men walking around. Make sure you catch someone on horseback as well. The kids will love that, Trey?"

Trey was staring off to his right, along the densely packed tree line along the field's northern perimeter. His mouth hung open, unhinged, and adding another chin to the two already there.

Tonya's lips pulled into a white line while her eyes seemed still to smile. "*Trey?* What's wrong? What are you—"

"Shit, man. I heard this place was haunted, but ..."

Robert turned to him. "It does stand to reason why you'd think that."

"No, dude. You don't get it. I see faces. White pale faces. I just saw a shit load of them. Standing just inside the forest perimeter. You ever seen anything like that?"

Robert scoffed. "No. Sorry to disappoint."

"Yo, Tahn, I'm gonna film the woods for a quick second. See what I catch."

"Trey, Robert needs to get started soon, and the sky looks like it's about to open up—"

"Jesus," Trey gasped, his right eye already behind the viewfinder as he panned across the field and swept the tree line. "Jesus Christ. There must be, like, a hundred or so of those motherfuckers!"

XVI. ACCEPTANCE

Natalie was up, ready, and in position before the bikers even stirred. She'd snuck down to her car around nine-thirty in the morning and climbed inside, unseen by the lot of them. She attributed their delayed reflexes and relaxed attention to the effects of the beer they'd been swilling all night and the different drugs they'd shot or smoked.

For a group of separatist assholes on a *mission,* they certainly seemed to be far more interested in playing grab ass with the women, firing up the bong for a few more hits of smoky courage, and killing time like it owed them a debt rather than tending to the devil's business. Their numbers had swelled overnight. When Natalie had first walked across the Motel 6 parking lot and endured their pathetic, obscene catcalls, she vaguely remembered there having been roughly about ten to fifteen of them. Sometime during the night (one the *assholes* had not let pass quietly by any stretch), another ten joined them. The parking lot was tagged in zigzagging burnout tire marks. Chrome, polished to a high sheen, formed something of a barrier in front of the entire first floor row of units.

Some of them had gone inside to the rooms and crashed—probably hodge-podge on top of one another. A handful of others, mostly men (save a couple who'd snuggled up under a blanket atop a chaise lounge), had lingered outside in the wet heat. They sat up in uncomfortable lawn chairs that looked like they had been toted along for their trip. They slept with their heads nodded forward and baseball caps pulled down low over their brows. By slow degrees, the lot of them stirred while Natalie watched them from a spot farther removed from them than the one Gaither had parked in the night before. She observed them like a scientist squints one eye into a microscope's eye-tube at some toxic strain of the flu or *the plague.* They sped up in their motion, many of them probably gaining more momentum after having pissed the last of the alcohol out. Many of them appeared whimsical, boasting gloating smiles or clapping one another on the back for no real reason.

And Natalie wondered how the hell such a group of hateful pieces of shit dared to smile in the pale sunlight of a perfect summer morning like they deserved the simple joy of existence. It was in times like these she was certain if she were still a practicing Catholic, that would have been the moment she experienced some crisis of faith. A real schism of her inner spirituality. She remembered a poem she'd read back in high school by a guy named William Blake. He was a cool cat for his time and far ahead of it, according to Mr. Devlin. The poem was called "The Tyger." A stanza that had stayed with her since high school rang out clear and daunting as a funeral knell in the center of her mind while she watched the White Supremacists lock motel doors behind them, pack their shit into duffels, strap that packed shit to the backs of their bikes, and wait.

When the stars threw down their spears
And water'd heaven with their tears:
Did He smile His work to see?
Did He who made the Lamb make thee?

William Blake was wondering how the same God who created the meek and mild lamb could have created the fearsome *Tyger* with the same Hands.

This same God who had created men and women like the crew of evildoers saddling up across the parking lot from Natalie with murder on their minds and hate forged upon the hot anvils of their brains, hardened to a deadly, unforgiving tool of destruction. This same God had created Danica and Gary, two good people cut down in the prime of their lives, simply *because?*

Natalie grabbed her cell phone off the passenger seat then navigated to the mobile contact number for Dan McCausland. He had been blowing up her phone ever since yesterday afternoon. Grand total of seventy unanswered calls from Dan-O. Yes, Natalie felt bad for ignoring her last and only close friend in the whole wide world, but she suspected he would forgive her in time. Future circumstance would pave the way for a swift reprieve, she imagined. Finality has a way of settling all debts. She pressed the green call button. She did not have to wait long. The other end of the line barely made it through one ring before Dan's panicked voice filled her ear.

"Natalie! Jesus-Christ! What'd you turn your fucking phone off?"

"No," she answered, calmly. "I heard every ring. I never turned it off. Out of respect for you."

"If you *really* wanted to show me some respect, you would have—I dunno—*answered the goddamn phone!* Not run off with *my* car!"

"I couldn't."

"Why not? You're calling me now. What changed? You grow a conscience in the last couple of hours?"

"You're not that far off, Dan."

"You. Fucking. Played. Me."

"I know. I'm sorry. That was never my intention, and I'm sorry things happened that way."

"You used me. And don't hand me that shit that it wasn't your intention. I don't think you understand how out of my mind I've been!"

"I know—"

"No, you *don't know*, Nat-my-dear! I think I bombed my exam this morning because I was out of my gourd with this bullshit."

Danica leaned in towards her, coming off the backseat. *Tell him where he can find his car and then tell him goodbye. You've got to treat this like a Band-Aid. One motion. Right off! Otherwise, you're not doing him any favors, and you know how many he's done for you through the years.*

"Nat? Hello?" Dan's voice sounded stricken with panic now.

"I'm still here."

"Just-just *tell* me where you are, and I'll come to you. I-I'm not mad. I'm just … I dunno. But just clue me in, will you?"

"Dan, do you remember how you stuck your neck out for Danica and me back in high school? At The Tarps? Those rich-bitch girls were giving us a hard time and they were crashing our get-together. And you basically told them both to get lost and fuck off? Knowing full well they were popular, and they could ruin you and your reputation for coming to the aid of two teenage lesbians? You remember that?"

"Yes. But I don't know what that has to do with what we're talking about, Nat."

"Oh, it's got more to do with what I'm talking about than you could possibly imagine."

"How so?"

"Because I'm going to pull a *Dan McCausland*." She looked out the windshield and saw one of the bikers emerge from the last room to be locked up and vacated. He strode over to a close-knit group of his racist peers, who appeared to have been waiting on him. When the biker swung the backpack off his shoulder and started unzipping it for the other men to look inside, men who then formed a circle around him while he did this, Natalie felt her pulse quicken and the flurry of second thoughts she'd anticipated flashing across her brain in rapid succession. "In about, oh, a half hour, depending on how much longer I have to wait."

"Okay, pulling a what?"

"I love you, Dan. You're the brother I never had and always needed, and I'm sorry to have to leave it like this—"

"*Nat!*"

"—but you'll be able to pick up your car in Biltmore. The place that's been all over the news for the last couple of days. It'll be parked down the street from the police station in town. The worst thing you'll face is a ticket for the meter. I'm sorry, but I don't have any change on me."

"Biltmore? Pennsylvania? You're not far. Not *that* far so just wait—"

"Save a lot of lives, Dan-O. I love you."

Natalie hung up. The coils of her intestines seemed to flip over. Nausea tickled her stomach lining, an invisible finger drumming up unrest. She rolled down the window and tossed her cell phone out. Rolled it back up again.

Gaither's voice washed over her, and she welcomed its calm and resolve, traits it had been lacking for some time. Until right then when she needed it.

Keep your eye on the guy with the backpack. Don't lose sight of him. It looks like they're getting ready to roll out.

One of them, a tall, elder-looking man wrapped in denim from head to toe and sporting a grimy Confederate Flag bandanna over what was most likely a bald, liver-spotted skull, burst from the motel office. He was thumbing through a money roll. He stuffed the bills into his back pocket and joined the cluster of men and Mr. Backpack. A couple of them nodded their heads, satisfied with whatever Mr. Backpack showed to them. Confederate Flag Bandanna fished a crumpled pack of cigarettes out from inside his denim jacket. Mr. Backpack clapped a heavy hand upon Bandanna's shoulder, shaking his head *No!* insistently.

Fucking idiots to the end, huh?

Everyone sitting inside Dan McCausland's stolen Optima agreed.

One by one, the crew of miscreants climbed onto their bikes. They kicked their engines on, and the sound was like the sky imploding. Natalie jumped at the sound, even though she expected it to be louder than hell. In the signature line of a motorcycle caravan hitting the blacktop, they fell in behind one another and opened the throats of their engines with long, smoky coughs. Deep bronchial expulsions. And when the last of them, Mr. Backpack as it turned out, carried up the back end, Natalie put the Optima in Drive and started after them.

XVII. CIVIL WAR II

Robert Harvey chuckled, his cheeks reddening with mirth, like some kind of Cavalry Santa Claus as he regarded the spooked cameraman.

"It's only your eyes playing tricks on you and your mind corroborating," he said, slipping back into the somewhat patronizing tone of the college lecturer. "You've heard all the stories about this site. I've heard three times as many as you, and I can assure you they are nothing more than that. Shivery campfire tales to help us all cope with the unexplained."

Tonya was staring at the tree line. Her heartbeat had sped up a bit, but not enough for her to confess to it. Still, she saw nothing either. "Trey-Trey-Trey," she said, shaking her head. "What *are* we going to do with you?"

Trey scoffed. He kept filming. "Digital doesn't lie, Tahn. Just wait 'til I play this back for you later for edits. You'll see. They're standing right there. All the way dahn the line. So many of 'em. Just wait!"

Robert smiled dotingly. "And yet you don't sound the least bit spooked at the sight of them."

"That's because they're one of about fifty apparitions I've seen and committed to film in the last five years. I'm a ghost hunter when I'm naht shooting the news."

"Really, now?" Robert's eyes twinkled.

Tonya picked at the bottom hem of her skirt. It was starting to ride up. She yanked it back down, then picked up both her sneakered feet to draw them out of the sinking, sodden ground of the hill they were standing on. Airily, she confirmed Trey's story. "I've seen some of his footage. Made me a believer. But in this case, Trey? I think we just might be seeing what we want to see."

The compulsion to sneak a second glance at the tree line was more powerful than the first for Robert Harvey, but he refused to give in to the instinctual curiosity. It was important to him to cut more of an academic figure than some sophomoric, overgrown child who still played dress-up and *played at war*. There was also the fact that the statements he meant to convey to the pretty reporter before him required he project just such an air of seriousness. *This cameraman is easily half my age, and I'm not about to play along with his bullshit for the sake of being amicable.* He wasn't sorrowful, not even if it cast him in a stuffed-shirt negative light with Tonya Lafferty, his ideal woman. "I'm ready to answer any questions you may have," he said, gently prompting the reporter to steer things back towards the purpose of the meeting.

"Of course, of course," Tonya said, sounding like someone shaken out of a dream state. She slipped into professional mode as seamlessly as if they had *not* just been talking about phantoms hiding in the forest a moment ago. Clearing a stray lock of black hair from her eyes, Tonya Lafferty cued Trey.

The cameraman was delayed in guiding the lens away from the adjacent forest, centering its focus on Tonya and Robert, whom she moved into the shot with a soft hand at the small of his back. Trey muttered something under his breath.

Tonya smirked. "Something wrong, Trey?"

"I said *they're gone.*"

But Tonya thought she'd asked a rhetorical question of the cameraman and was already rolling her finger, counting down from three.

Two—

"I'm here with Robert Harvey, chairman of The Gettysburg Historical Society and moderator of the reenactment organization. Every year on July third, Robert and some two hundred actors, teachers, people from all walks of life who share a common love of history, come together to commemorate the pivotal Battle of Gettysburg on the yearly anniversary of its final day in what was initially a three-day confrontation. Robert, how long does it take every year to put all of this together?"

Robert's grin started out normal enough, but by the time Tonya held the microphone out to him, that grin tilted sideways. "We start rehearsing maneuvers the first week of February every year. Our cast was growing like wildfire for about ten years straight, and it got to the point we just had no choice but to turn people away. Otherwise, the battlefield would have looked more like the audience at a rock concert than a field of orchestrated battle."

"I'll bet. This looks like a lot of fun! And not just for the actors and history buffs, but there looks to be a little something for everyone. You have women dressed in period garb stitching up uniforms and serving refreshments. Children who come out with their families get to pet and even groom horses. You offer pony rides. All of this on top of enjoying a wonderful display on this sacred landmark where people of all ages and from all over can experience the awe-inspiring spectacle that—honestly—makes you feel like you just stepped out of a time machine. At least, that's how I feel standing here with you, looking around at all of this."

"Yes, it can be a bit disorienting at times, especially for the actors. They speak in the authentic dialects of the time. They only use words and phrases that were a part of the English lexicon in the eighteen-sixties. We do try hard to achieve an authentic, ah, *experience,* that even the most studied and seasoned Civil War buff would be hard-pressed to find an inaccuracy."

"Mm, sounds like a challenge to you *history buffs* out there who've never been."

Robert laughed. "I guess that's exactly what it is."

You can't back down *from what you wanted to say* now? *You promised your colleagues you'd speak your mind on the topic. Not just because it's something close to their hearts, but because it's obvious the spectator turnout has been dwindling every year, and this year is by far the lowest of all. You* know *why that is, and you need to educate people whenever you can about the importance of erasing the errors of history.*

"—and how long have you been doing this? I spoke to some locals, and they claim it's become something of a sacred tradition around these parts."

"Yes, and it has. But it didn't start with me, or really any of us you see here today. My grandfather was taking part in these reenactment activities when he was younger than me. This has been an annual event since the mid-fifties, although on a much smaller scale. It wasn't nearly as painstakingly accurate as it is now because they simply did not have access to the documentation we have now with the internet. But they did their best, and their hearts were in the right places, so ..."

"And it's your hope that *your* grandchildren will continue with the tradition?"

Robert pursed his lips. "Right."

"I'll bet."

"And I would like to address the elephant in the room about this tradition. I understand there was a planned protest that was set to be staged here condemning the event. They wished to shut us down, but they were denied a permit and given a stern warning they would be jailed if they showed up and tried in any way to interfere with what is, and always has been, a powerful vehicle for honoring the memory of those brave soldiers, on *both sides of the conflict,* alive and in our hearts. Does progress show us the Confederacy was on the wrong side of history? Yes, of course it does."

Even as Robert spoke, he could sense the reporter gradually moving the microphone away from him by almost undetectable degrees. Tonya Lafferty also appeared to be wilting somewhat beside him as he spoke, and Robert suspected his statement would most certainly never make it to broadcast. Still, he felt he had to try to clarify things and to stick up for the event he had given his heart and soul over to for much of his adult life. He'd fielded a handful of death threats from anonymous callers who rang his phone in the dead of night, stopping his heart and breathing in some instances, only to threaten his life should he proceed with the reenactment. A few of the calls worried him to the point he had seen fit to wear his Glock in a shoulder holster underneath his costume, only the second time since he'd gotten his gun permit he'd actually worn a weapon on his person. They called him *racist. Confederate sympathizer. White supremacist.* Ten students dropped his American History IV class over two weeks, and he'd never lost one before. And he took it all in stride. That's who he was, who his single-mother raised in a one-room house in southern Indiana. She never backed down. Neither would he.

Robert pressed on.

Not realizing Tonya had given Trey the Cameraman a hidden hand-signal out of Robert's view signaling him to cut the feed. To mime that he was, in fact, still rolling. Not the first time.

"Let me be clear," Robert said, his face flushed and eyes serious as a heart-attack. "When that-that *demon* named Jack Swain walked into that Baptist Church down in Mississippi and shot four innocent African-American churchgoers for no other reason than to kill someone different from himself, he acted apart from those who do not and would *never* subscribe to the sick and profoundly flawed principles of white nationalism. And we are *legion*! That's the reality. He is part of a small, twisted sect of people who are living in the darkest portion of our nation's history. But-but to erase any trace of that dark history is a mistake that will cost us dearly. We not only are obligated to preserve the triumphs of our past so we know how to repeat them, but we are also obligated to preserve the elements of our darker history and the warning signs that led to these things so we *do not see these terrible institutions put back into place.*

"So, Tonya, I thank you for yielding me this time and letting me put it across that we won't ever let this die. When it comes right down to it, we're all history buffs before anything else. And as human beings, we should all make a point of being students of history, the good and the bad. All of it—"

"Uhm, Robert?" Trey interrupted. He'd stopped pretending to film Robert and had shifted the aim of his lens off to the right once more. "Do you *know* those guys? Coming out of the woods?"

Then, Tonya and Trey had both turned their attention away from Robert.

"Coming out of the woods?" He blanched at Trey and did an about-face.

The pale faces burst from the tree line, now full-bodied monsters. The Confederacy actors had only just begun to file into the expansive clearing leading up to the base of the plateau where the Union soldiers were rushing about, making last minute adjustments to formation and artillery placement. The pale faces from the forest vaguely recognized the rules of engagement as the opposing *sides* moved into proper formation.

There was a time the pale faces would have obeyed and fallen in line as well. That was when they'd lived and breathed, all brethren of the human race. Now the rules no longer applied to the pale faces, and they cast them aside as a corpse tosses off a muslin while limping among the gravestones.

No, there were no rules. And the absence of such allowed for mayhem, unhinged and terrifying, to ensue at a dizzying and breakneck pace. They flooded the hilltop and the clearing below in equal measures of speed and violence.

The small group of spectators assembled near the parking lot sent up a collective scream that seemed to pierce a hole in the bloated and black cumulus clouds hovering above the field like an old zeppelin partially obscured by a dreadful mist. Hard, stinging rain fell upon Gettysburg Field. Children, and wives, and uncles, and brothers, and sisters and grandparents scrambled beneath the morning sky awash in night. They sprinted to their cars, where they could garner some semblance of safety closed inside a steel machine with interlocking doors. But they could not leave. Would not. Their loved ones were outside. The spectators and family members, everyone, could only wait and pray as the biblical rainfall thumped against the roofs of the cars.

Tonya Lafferty did not immediately respond to what her eyes were showing her. To *whom* or *what* was swarming them with the speed of sound and intensity of lightning. It was as if the forest had vomited this army of pal, or satchels, or weapons, or shoes, for that matter) like it meant to expel an agitating meal from the pit of its belly. When it all finally registered, Tonya screamed, flung her microphone down, and turned to run. Her treadless sneakers did not support such a quick, graceless movement, and she fell face down in the dampening, overgrown grass.

Trey the Cameraman did not stop rolling until it was evident he should turn and run, maybe even abandon the camera in favor of saving his skin.

A voice blared inside Trey's skull, like the great reverb-heavy announcement of a master of ceremonies at a rock concert.

No one's gonna hurt you. I won't allow it. So long as you keep filming. All of it.

Guided by pure muscle memory, Trey returned his left eye to the viewfinder and panned the camera across the field. He could not reconcile his mind to what he was seeing.

The inside of Trey's skull lit up with another blast from the disembodied voice.

Grab the woman! Get her up! I will meet you there!

"Oh Christ," Trey breathed. He couldn't help but sneak a glance all about for the source of the voice and its admonitions. "Hey, Tahn-ya?"

Robert was helping her to her feet. Tonya was slathered in mud along her right side.

"Get behind me, and stay behind me," Robert told her, and she did just that.

The swarm reached the actors at the bottom of the hill first. Confederate *actors* intermingled with their undead, ultimately authentic counterparts. The clash was as sickening to behold as it was to hear. The pale faces pounced upon the actors as if spring-boarded from the spongy, sodden ground. And some of the actors, not paralyzed by the threat running towards them, had already put their authentic weapons to good use. Those who had them, unsheathed their swords from the scabbards and swung on their attackers, lucky to land a blow before their throats were ripped out. Many more, equipped with the standard knife-edged bayonet, saw better results, impaling a pale one only to struggle with freeing it from their body before they were overtaken by the swarm and torn to pieces.

The threat of violent protests had prompted many of the actors to wear a gun in a holster underneath their costumes, along with Robert. Many of them had also gotten calls in the middle of the night or notes left on their cars issuing unnervingly specific threats to the actors should they take part that year

The irony was not lost on Robert when he shouted to the other Union actors scrambling about on the top of the hill. They had their concealed weapons out. The pale faces slowed for but a moment as the bullets caught them in their thighs, shoulders, arms, and legs. Several them dropped when a marksman or two in the Union actor crowd aimed true and blew the backs of their heads out.

"Stop filming and help us, you dimwitted shit!" Robert screamed at Trey.

Trey's lips tremulous and tongue barely functional, he shook his head in the negative. "I-I gotta keep filming to keep them off! I can't stop, dude."

"What in God's name are you talking about?"

"Oh Christ, man, it's a massacre. I gotta shut my eyes, I'm gonna ..."

Trey turned to the side, his camera dipping down, and stooped to vomit something yellow into the grass.

The intellectual-oriented portion of Robert's mind tried to override and undermine Trey's words, but the reptilian self-serving section of his frontal lobe won out. His limbs were drenched in adrenaline. He felt like some divine power had plugged him into a live wire, blue sparks skittering around under his skin. *What if Trey's right? What if? What then?*

Trey nearly dropped his camera as his stomach muscles clenched again, wringing him dry as a washrag. Robert rescued the camera just before it went crashing into the wet grass. He fitted his left eye behind the viewfinder. He wondered how filming the horrid events unfolding around him might figure in to saving him from the murderous pale faces.

But Robert did not continue filming for this reason alone.

He needed to see what was happening to the actors down in the clearing. He felt responsible. He needed to gain a lay of the land. A quick at-a-glance. Then, he could assess what his next move would be.

What he saw closed a fist around his heart.

The viewfinder had fallen upon one of the actors, a young man and son of one of the Union soldier actors who was battling bronchitis back at home that day. The boy's face was a bloody, glistening mask with ever-widening eyes of shock. His mouth stretched into an endless scream as one pale face bit into the side of his skull with what looked like the elongated tusks of a sabre toothed tiger. The thing's pale face had folded up and backward somewhat to allow for the emergence of the menacing fangs out of its mouth, and the top of the thing's skull resembled an accordion bag drained of air. The boy's eyes rolled back white. One pale face devoured the boy's head while another worked on his leg, whipping its head back and forth with all the frenzy of a great white tearing meat away from bone.

I can't remember the boy's name, oh, Christ! Please, what is his name?

Stretching for what seemed like miles in some nightmarish mirage, similar scenarios played out to their violent and fathomless ends. A field saturated anew with blood, screams, strife, helplessness, and terror.

"Dude, hand me the camera! They're coming!" Trey already had his hands around the big, weighty camera.

Pull your gun, you idiot!

Robert let go. Then he set about undoing the top half of his uniform, unbuttoning the buttons as quickly as he could, to reveal the holstered weapon gleaming gunmetal blue by his considerable breast. He drew it out, lined up the sights, readying himself somehow.

Tonya stood beside him, her once pristinely primped dark hair now fallen across her face like black, frothing snakes. She looked haggard, frightened, impossibly beautiful, and ready to put up a fight beside them. Some last stand.

The pale faces closed the distance to the Union camp perched at the top of the hill.

A line of actors fired and fired on them while others stabbed at them with their bayonets or sliced at the thick, gelatinous air with their swords.

Still, they came. Closing the gap.

Twenty yards.

Fifteen.

Ten.

Just as the pale faces and the Union actors became entangled with each other, torrential screams pealing out of mouths opened to the sky and catching rain, one of the undead continued on towards the spot where Robert, Trey, and Tonya stood their ground. Two brawny, bearded actors launched themselves at the thing. He swept them back as effortlessly as if he were wiping dust from the shoulders of his Confederate uniform. Big as his two attackers had been, they matched neither the thing's height nor his width. The Undead Man was a moving mountain, lumbering towards the three in wide arcing strides. His eyes strobed red with every footfall as if one motion prompted the other. Long, dirty black hair, hardened and matted into dreadlocks, hung in his face like fat sausage links. His jowls were massive, teeth even more so. They extended down halfway over his expansive chin. He wore the standard robe-like uniform swathed around his massive frame. The fabric had been torn away, leaving a gray flap that hung open to reveal a chest beneath, hatched with blue and green veins against a chalky hue. His belt had somehow remained cinched around his wide waist, but it heaved, not from any respiration but because the Undead Man's belly was swollen to bursting. He exuded an unmistakable air of authority, and Trey was certain when he heard the Undead Man speak, the voice would match the one that had commanded him moments ago in some psychic exchange.

The Undead Man stopped before the three, an unsettlingly small divide of five feet or so.

Red flashed and swirled around his eyeball like a crimson electrical current.

Then, Robert, Tonya, and Trey's skulls throbbed with the thumping of the Undead Man's voice between their ears. His mouth did not move in speech, and the terrible presence of his elongated fangs revealed why this would be.

Speech was an impossibility.

I'm Corporal Roger Creel, Confederacy. I made these men. All of 'em.

Robert trained his handgun on Creel's heart, then moved the sight to the man's skull. "Then you can make them stop. Say the word. Y-you're the one in charge."

Can't do that. Wouldn't do that, even if. Creel's red-strobing eyes touched upon Tonya over Robert's shoulder, *even if the purty lady made the request.* Creel straightened, the buttons down the front of his tunic looking pressed to their limits. *You been making a mockery of the South for too long. This battle was supposed to be* our *turning point. Not yours. And y'all celebrate this like this is what God wanted. I'm here to tell ya, folks, there ain't no God and there never was. If there was, you think He would abide the likes o' myself and my men? No, we keep on living. And this is by* my *design. Call it a contingency plan, in case something like Gettysburg happened and the world loses its way. We're here, and this is the shot heard round the goddam world, jack! S'why I insisted you keep on filming and showing what we doin' over here to everyone. This is a rally to arms, and we know—we seen—we ain't alone in our beliefs. We got sympathizers all over the goddam spinning earth!*

"You're a—a sickness," Robert said, trying to steady the tremor that suddenly built up in his hands. "Whoever—*whatever* you are? There's no place for you or anyone like you here. Here or *anywhere.*"

Y'all made a big fuck-all of everything, and it's quite lit'rally killing me and my men. And we been around longer than you and your daddy and your daddy's *daddy. Et cetera. We thought you'd all wise up to your erroneous ways. Letting the brown people flood through the southern border so they come and they take the jobs of the southern man? You been* muddyin' the water *for too god-dam long and now it's just too fuckin' dirty to be ignored. Not for one. More. Day. We hoped you'd come to yer' senses. But you been killing us, and you been murdering all that nature intended! Thought you'd honor the natural order o' things and the class system handed down from one generation to the next over the course o' hundreds o' thousands o' years. But y'all wanna go against nature itself. So now? You're gonna deal with the most* un-na-tu-ral *reckoning anyone ever seen.*

Tonya snared Robert's shoulder in her hands. "Shoot him! What are you waiting for?"

"I-I can't get a shot! He's-he's *doing something* and I can't—"

You fat shit, The Undead Man scoffed. *You couldn't hit a woodchuck at five paces on a sunshiny day, even if I* wasn't *fuckin' with ya' like this!*

The Undead Man had ceased to be a solid mass. He'd divided into an array of shifting, shuddering partial profiles and cross-sections of his massive frame. Robert felt both drunk and nauseous just looking upon him and trying to line up what had ultimately become an impossible shot. The sight of him hurt his eyes, but that was not all. A great, choking sadness took hold of him the likes of which he had not experienced since the day he buried his mother five years ago. Before he realized what was happening, Robert Harvey was blinking tears out of his eyes. The gun slipped from his hands.

The Undead Man jabbed a thumb at Trey the Cameraman. His eyes burned like the surface of the sun. *You jus' keep that rolling. Come up close. I don't want you to miss this.*

Today the Old South rises! Tomorrow, the old world falls! Then he fell upon Robert Harvey and Tonya Lafferty with a ferocity Trey had not seen outside the animal kingdom, framed within the pages of a National Geographic. With powerful, ambidextrous hands, The Undead Man tore their throats out and lifted them both to his mouth, lapping at their spouting blood.

All around, the *Union* fell to the *New Undead Confederacy.*

And Trey the Cameraman, who had always wanted to document something of consequence, something award-winning, never stopped recording.

XVIII. THE BACKPACK

Natalie had not thought much of the overcast morning sky when she'd first set out following behind Mr. Backpack and his gang of hatred. It looked like and felt like rain, but that was all. In fact, Natalie had found it suitable the weather should match the dark things afoot in the town of Biltmore. She had no idea what to think when the sky did not drop an ounce of rain, and yet the clouds had not only darkened to an ink black, they had also vanquished the sun altogether. At ten-thirty in the morning, the sky was pitch as night. There was no moon or sun to lend some semblance of normalcy to the otherwise frightening change in a cycle taken very much for granted over time. And while Natalie knew there were some places on earth where it was dark for six months straight out of the year, alternating to daylight for the other half, this drastic change in the atmosphere filled her with a deeper depression than that which she was already victim to.

She asked the question and felt stupid immediately after. "Are they doing this?"

There's a strong vampire among them,) Gaither answered inside Natalie's mind. (*An elder. A Maker, even. They would have the power to control the weather in this way. Perhaps even the proper rotation of the earth.*) Gaither paused, then added, (*It makes sense. In darkness, they can move about freely without fear of natural sunlight. From what I've learned of The Remainders, this is a new ability, an evolutionary adaptation that the older generations of Undead were incapable of.*

"What … like flippered feet? The primordial ooze? Along those lines?"

Along those lines.

"I imagine Darwin never could have dreamed he'd need to take into account *survival of the fittest* amongst the Vampire Legion."

A legion that feeds on hatred,) Gaither said. (*That's new, too. Psychic vampirism. Talking less than two hundred years old.*

"Well … I hope to God this will strike at the heart of them. That it'll make a difference."

123

We have to try, Gaither said, then lapsed into a brief silence, as if he could offer no real assurance. Then, he went on. *They're trying to spark a race war. It was never about trying to reboot the Battle of Gettysburg. They're bastards, yes, but time has made them wise enough to know they can't possibly remake history.*

From the back seat, Danica added in a saccharine tone, "Cable news has made that into an art form. And one of these days, we're going to find out where George Orwell kept his time machine. How else could he have known so much?"

The words *race war* caused Natalie's hands to quickly squeeze the wheel, bringing the white ridges of her knuckles up against the thin webbing of skin like four pearls in a row.

Gaither had decided not to retake control of her arms and legs as before. The ghost understood how dramatically the original plan had changed. And Gaither knew the part Natalie would play in this new plan would not involve the Twin Remainders as he had wanted, but they would suffer by proxy, and that simply would have to serve his purpose. How he had wanted to punish the Twins—wielding an axe with Natalie's hands and driving it down into their tendon-knotted pale throats while they slept in the dirt; setting their still-screaming heads on fire and watching the muscle and then bone turn to black porridge before his very eyes.

There was always the question as to what such actions might have done to Natalie's mind. To watch *her hands* swing the blade; *her arms* douse the decapitated heads in gasoline; *her fingers* strike the match alight and touch the flame to the thin, gas-soaked hairs of the Twins' heads. All the while, a spectator to such things. No power, nor will to stop any of it.

Yet, Natalie Kincaid had agreed to it all.

All of it. And not only because she longed more than anything to reunite with Danica. Natalie's motives had evolved in the last twenty-four hours. Now, as they drove in fits and starts of speaking, both Gaither and Danica understood the woman driving the Optima along a back country road in the haze and drizzle of a July morning was not the same woman who'd set out from South Philadelphia. Natalie was as focused and devoted to the new cause as if it were her plan and her plan alone. She no longer moved through life with love fueling her every step.

It was hate.

Hate with a side of resolve.

Peace of mind?

She was not there yet.

Out the windshield and a quarter mile down the stretch of one-lane blacktop, the brake light of Mr. Backpack's motorcycle flashed as he rounded an especially sharp turn and disappeared behind a copse of elm trees. Natalie had been following that red brake light like the North Star for the last half hour. Not because she depended upon Mr. Backpack so she would know where she was going, Natalie knew where they were going. She'd known since the night before. What mattered, the reason for the *tail*, was so Natalie could see where Mr. Backpack and his band of racist misfits meant to set up their *home base*, as it was. The bikers were not all heading to the same place. They'd be sending Mr. Backpack further along, and they'd lie in wait like the *cockroaches* they were. Then—

A sudden stab of doubt cut into her heart and stole Natalie's breath.

Danica came up off the backseat. "Babe, you all right?"

"*Mm ... yeah-fine ...*"

"Because you were just gasping for breath."

Gaither said, *She's all right. It's not a seizure, Dani. I know that's what you're afraid of.*

"Close, but no cigar, Gary," Danica said. "I'm worried her nerves are going to come unraveled and she's going to get herself caught or *worse*, b—"

"Guys, you're both talking about me like my parents used to do at the dinner table with me sitting right there. I hated it then when *they* used to do it, and all you're doing right now is upsetting me. I can't lose my nerve. And nerve is all I've got. I need to hold onto it for dear life. So would you both *please* talk *to* me, instead of *around me*?" Biting her lip in irritation, Natalie rounded the sharp turn and felt her heart quicken when her eyes found Mr. Backpack's red taillight in the dark like a light house on the banks of a deadly rock shore. "Now, I need you both to promise me what I'm about to do *will* stop the other ones. That it will cancel this—and I still can't believe this is where *we* are—this *race war* The Remainders mean to spark?"

A pregnant silence ensued. Then, Gaither spoke up. *There are no guarantees, Nat. I'm not going to lie to you. But we know The Remainders feed off hate and they thrive in the throes of tragedy and injustice at its worst. This would function as the equivalent of taking the nipple away from the baby if that baby's mother's name happened to be Rosemary, if you catch my drift.*

"Knowing what we know and ... to do nothing? ..." Danica stalled then picked up the rhythm once more. "Even if The Remainders shrug this off and they achieve their goal, well ... at least we will have done the right thing. The human thing."

The Static Souls crouched in the back of Natalie's consciousness like patient fans of a rock band held back by fences and police presence raised their collective voice. The collaborative cacophony of men, women, and children's raised voices and screams of insistence clamored for Natalie's attention. They had not left her. She'd merely managed to mute their collective wailings and incomprehensible ramblings and imploring words and last-ditch efforts at communication. Now, as her thoughts raced through her mind at a dizzying rate and disoriented her, the Static Souls took advantage of this frazzled state. They sensed it was now or never. They sensed the futility of their circumstances. Some fled her mind altogether, returning to the ether of the atmosphere.

Others lingered.

Begged. Pleaded.

The initial pressure of a migraine formed along the crown of Natalie's shorn skull.

Natalie almost lost sight of Mr. Backpack's taillight, the pain in her head and the terrible clamoring of the Static Souls forcing her to shut her eyes for a second.

"Fuck off! *All of you!* I'm retired! As of right *fucking* now! I! Can't! Help! You!"

Danica whispered in Natalie's ear. "I'll deal with them. I'll do my best. We're close." Natalie swore she felt her wife's breath, real and tangible, on the sensitive cartilage.

The woods halted on either side of the one-lane road, making way for single-story ramshackle abodes to ride the now two-lane roadway close enough Natalie could see inside many of their bay windows. Toys lay scattered across patchy lawns, their bright colors muted by the gray weather and intensifying rainfall. A skin-and-bones rottweiler cowered just under the slanted eaves of a porch, its attention slow and attitude forlorn. The news stations and cable networks described Biltmore as a largely working-class town "with the same problems as most city boroughs." Problems like crime, poverty, unrest, and impatience. A tenuous thread of hope slowly unraveling. Well, the thread had not merely snapped in Biltmore when a Town Watch member shot and killed an innocent black man, the very patchwork of the town's community had come undone, leaving a naked body of contempt and violence in its wake.

Natalie watched Mr. Backpack's red taillight glide past the left turn that led onto Main Street. He kept straight on, just as Natalie and Gaither and Danica already knew he would, leading up the back for his crone Brothers and Sisters. So she drove past the turn, Milton's News and Smoke rearing up beside her on the left in all its mopish white-siding anti-glory like some dormant ghost.

There was an uneasiness in allowing herself to be *led* by Mr. Backpack. But it was no less uncomfortable than when she'd given up control of her arms and legs to Gaither so he could drive. She envisioned the motorcycle crew of villains leading her off a cliff obscured by the fog and darkness of an unnatural nighttime. *They'd kill themselves in order to rid the world of one more lesbian? I don't think so. They're cowards. Otherwise, they'd do this completely different from how they plan to do it.*

Mr. Backpack's taillight beckoned Natalie onward like an illuminated demon. She felt the pull of it start to take hold of her with its building hypnotic quality. She followed it through two right turns at intersections sparsely populated by other motorists.

But Natalie slowed to a stop when she realized their destination lay at the end of a wide, long slant of driveway on her right-hand side. Seeking something to block the view of her vehicle, Natalie threw the car into reverse and angled the car alongside a nearby bus stop enclosure that provided just the right amount of cover for the Optima. A little old woman wearing a powder blue rag on her head and clutching a gigantic handbag to her sunken chest sat silently inside the enclosure. She squinted out at the suspicious car and scowled at them before turning her eyes aside.

Good. Mind your own, lady.

Natalie snatched up her cell from the center console. Her view of the gas station down the road was unobstructed, but distant. There was a remedy. The wonder of the iPhone! She thumbed her camera app open, trained it on the gas station a little under one kilometer out, and then zoomed in until the full desolate character of the place slipped into perfect view.

The snaking driveway fed into what looked like the snug, abandoned parking lot of a mom and pop gas station called Mooney's Body Shop and Petrol. A single gas pump island stood in the center of the lot, an orange cone blocking it off from public use. Out of order. So much for the *gas station* promise made by the glowing black and white sign waving ever so slightly as it hung above the entrance to a small office with various cigarette brand stickers in its windows. The bikers performed their signature choreographed backing-in along the side of the small body shop adjoining the office and pathetic mini-mart.

Both garage doors of the body shop were down when the bikers pulled in. Natalie watched one of them raise up and a grossly obese man emerge with a Slim Jim poking out of one fat fist. He wore dark horn rim glasses, a stretched-out white tank top, and camouflage cargo pants tucked into maroon-red boots like the ones many of the bikers were sporting. A sodden Pirates baseball cap sat loosely atop his oversized head, and long, greasy red hair hung to his meaty, sloping shoulders.

"Mr. Mooney, I presume?" Natalie seethed, maxing out the zoom feature. "You pork-fed piece of shit."

Another man exited the garage after Mooney. This one stuck out like a sore thumb amongst the slovenly man and the bikers flanking him. The second man wore charcoal slacks, and a crisp, white dress shirt buttoned all the way up. No tie, which Natalie always considered an odd fashion statement and rather Amish-esque. He carried himself like the spoiled rich kid he'd been before the darkness took hold of him and the extreme, unwavering hatred laid siege on his brain. A tall, handsome man, he sported a perfectly coiffed pelt of dark hair swept high across his head like any politician with any hair left to style. As a matter of fact, the sonofabitch would have fit it in seamlessly on a debate stage with other candidates vying for the Presidency.

The founder of The Nativity Movement.

The Devil personified.

"Holy shit," Natalie said, "it's him. Jefferson Morgan. These are his people." Then, she stopped, foolishness touching her and reddening her cheeks. "But … you both knew that. You knew he was here, that this was *all* him."

Gaither waited to answer.

Now do you understand how important this is? How effective it will be?

"You might have told me," she said, somewhat stung. "Because then it would have been a *no-brainer* for me."

The older man who wore the Confederate Flag Bandanna was the first over to Morgan and Fat Man Mooney, who looked profoundly concerned with the odd nighttime heavens more than anything else. Morgan and Flag Bandanna Man shook hands. Two quick, stiff pumps, as if one man were challenging the grip and the strength of the other and vice versa. The other men flooded up behind Bandanna Man, and hands pumped hands at such a psychopathic rate with smiles beamed from seemingly all of them, that Natalie had to turn away to keep from retching. She knew what they meant to do. They knew what they meant to do on that sad and dreary morning, and yet they all grinned like they had just arrived to an especially festive birthday party.

Gaither scoffed loudly within.

Hold on to that hate, Nat. You're going to need it later when you think you might turn back.

"I don't know how I feel about that," Natalie said.

"What's that, babe?" Danica asked.

"Oh … never mind. Wait, *where's Mr. Backpack!?*"

In the shifting cluster of denim-clad bodies, Mr. Backpack, a nondescript member of the crew as it was, seemed to have dropped out of their ranks without Natalie noticing.

"How is that possible? I had my eye on him the whole time, the sonofabitch—"

He's there, Nat! Gaither erupted.

"*There.*" Danica pointed out the windshield at the moving blurb of grey and black crossing the field spread out like a bumpy, fuzzy wet blanket. "Right *there!*"

Natalie spotted the signature bulging backpack strapped to the rider's shoulders as he took his especially rocky shortcut back to Main Street.

Fat Man Mooney had raised both garage doors, and Jefferson Morgan, along with a good bit of the gathering, had already crammed inside. Others hung outside, finishing off a roach or lighting a fresh menthol. Shooting the proverbial shit. The rain had pulled back in intensity, and now a weak spray misted the Optima's windshield.

Natalie drew a deep, belabored breath. Her head throbbed worse than before, but that was to be expected at this point. She kept picturing Fat Man Mooney staring up at the black sky and the falling rain with an intermingling of dread and concern.

It was an image that ran in an endless loop across her brainpan, even as she pulled a quick, squealing U-turn and pulled back out behind Mr. Backpack.

Natalie parked the Optima in roughly the same area as the night before on Main Street and set out down the sidewalk towards the crowd of protesters, whose numbers had swelled to three times the number it had boasted the "natural" night before. She had Gaither, a firm but comforting voice in her head, and he talked her down the road. It was right and proper this should come down to Natalie and Gaither in the end.

Danica temporarily parted with them right after Natalie parked the Optima, setting about the task of fulfilling her part in the operation. Her spirit moved in the opposite direction of the protesters. In a matter of moments, her thin and ethereal form disappeared into an alleyway between True Value Hardware and Bette's Flower Shoppe. Both stores were shuttered to the darkness and the threat of confrontation.

The protesters were halfway up the cement steps leading up to the Biltmore Police Department. Their numbers spilled out a quarter mile on either side. The signs were out in force, each painted message cutting to the meat of the matter and the promise there would be no peace without justice—an adage and play on words as powerful now as it had been in the sixties. Natalie saw old men and women leaning on their younger children or leaning on a cane with wet eyes and mouths drawn into bloodless lines of contempt. There were strollers parked here and there, mothers rocking their children while they raised their signs high enough not only to be read but noted by the row of stoic police officers in full SWAT gear guarding the entrance.

Natalie remembered it was only twelve or so hours prior the protesters and police had come together in a brief, albeit tenuous, moment for the sake of apprehending a man who'd tried to assault and quite possibly rape her right outside her car. *When it matters, they will unite in a common cause.*

From there, who knows?

The protesters noticed her approach one person at a time. A nudge here, a head nod in Natalie's direction there, as she mixed into the crowd with a gentle, knowing smile on her face and in her heart. There were questions as to who she was. Who did she *think* she was? The people seemed to favor that among other things she overheard, and before Natalie had even moved in among them deeply enough, the Optima had disappeared from view, the mystery of her presence both confounded and enchanted (and, in some cases, angered) the multitude. But the protesters also seemed to part around her, as if anticipating her next step and direction before she made it. She kept her head down, and Gaither told her to lift her chin.

They're going to stop giving you the benefit of the doubt real fast if they see you looking shady. Look up and look everyone in the eye. You hear?

Natalie knew she would have to conduct an inner dialogue with Gaither while among the protesters. Otherwise, they would have wasted little time in expelling her from their numbers in a matter of moments.

I haven't heard anything from Danica. Do you think she's okay?

No doubt she's fine. Probably waiting for Mr. Backpack to make a call or take a call from his boys back at the auto body. That will give her a better idea of the time frame. If they're waiting for something specific before they do their thing. Some sign or someone giving a speech. Could be anything. But once Danica gains intel, she'll hit you up via that direct line in your mind. In the meantime, we keep moving and mingling until we make it to the newspaper vending machine. Then—

Danica's voice cleaved off Gaither's words. Her trademark calm and unassuming tone had turned to a panicked, pressing delivery: *The DA is going to speak out on the steps of the precinct. He'll be announcing whether they'll be indicting Ronald Miller for first-degree murder. Mr. Backpack just took a call from Morgan back at Mooney's Garage, and that's what he told him. Apparently, they were just going to do it on a whim until they heard on the news there would be a high-value target on Main Street also. I don't know if this is good for us, or if it's worse!*

High-value target.

All the major news networks, local and cable, had already set up their shots on the knoll in front of the precinct. Natalie could see them haggling in nondescript ways and angling for what they deemed the best shot. And although Natalie did not count *clairvoyance* among her psychic talents, she felt she could pretty accurately predict the future, at least when it came to those news networks and how they would each bend and twist and manipulate whatever the DA said in his speech or the protesters' reactions into something parallel with their *side's* narrative. She felt as confident about her prediction as she was saddened by the fact that they would all lie, perhaps even spinning *her* actions into something convenient for themselves.

It was almost enough for Natalie to call it quits right there. To call the whole damned off.

You know they're going to, Nat. But the people standing here? The people who are here? They'll know the truth, and I know that every single one of these people will make sure the truth is told about you.

The crowd was getting antsy, and it was no wonder. Many of them had probably been there for the last four nights. They'd been rained on and shouted down, and now there was the distinct possibility the DA would come out, speak briefly and just long enough to confirm their worst fears: there would be no justice for Lawrence Cain.

Gaither, I'm flying blind right now. We have no idea when the DA will be out to speak. It could be any minute for all we know.

Check the news feed on your cell phone.

She wondered why it hadn't occurred to her before this. Natalie fished it out of her pants pocket and quickly navigated the web to one of the cable news network's live feeds. Sure enough, a blow-dried and pouty-serious newsman filled the small screen while up in the right corner, a smaller screen framed a blonde newswoman wearing a clear rain slicker and standing near the cement steps leading up to the Biltmore precinct a few feet away. "Gotta love the twenty-four-hour news cycle, Gregory," Natalie said, not caring who heard her.

The news ticker running along the bottom of the cell phone screen announced in bold red and yellow lettering **HIGH ALERT**. Natalie could remember when such a provocative tagline embedded in the ticker of a news program used to actually mean something, and people ought to pay attention and stop whatever it was they were doing. Underneath these words, the *actual* ticker read: BILTMORE DA EXPECTED TO RENDER DECISION ABOUT INDICTMENT IN MOMENTS.

Oh my God, that doesn't tell me a damn thing! What now?

What now, Nat? Time to head on over to that newspaper bin, make the grab, hurry back to the Optima without drawing too much attention. Then we—

Don't tell me to hope for the best, Gaither!

I was going to say pray. And I don't care who to, you just pray!

Danica was not waiting for Natalie and Gaither in the parked Optima when they made it back, and they were relieved not to find her there. There was no concern because Danica Kincaid was pulling double-duty and had moved back down Main Street shortly after communicating her intel to Natalie and Gaither about the DA's pending speech and what it would trigger.

She'd left Mr. Backpack huddling behind a big green dumpster in that alley between the florist and the hardware store. The poor bastard looked more scared than excited. Danica left him in that alley as she'd found him, tremulous from head to toe like it was December instead of July and praying to the same God as Natalie—just for polar-opposite ends. *This piece of garbage is* actually *praying to God to watch over* him*!* Him?

Danica wished she could have shown herself to him in that alleyway. To frighten the living shit out of him.

Maybe even stop his heart with terror.

But she was needed down the road.

Walls were of little consequence to her, and Danica Kincaid slipped inside the precinct as cleanly as a whisper of wind through a small opening between window and jamb. Inside, the main foyer of the Biltmore Police Station was vibrantly alive and overflowing with activity. Men and women, in and out of uniform, raced to and fro, shouting questions or answering someone else's inquiry; sucking at Styrofoam cups half-filled with cold coffee or carting an armful of manila file folders somewhere. Occasionally, one or four of the detectives or uniformed officers cast a glance towards the back of the foyer where a thick oak door polished to a high shine, stood closed and sealed off to them. *Ah, they're waiting for that door to open and for Mister DA to emerge with some news. Let's go pop our head in, or our whole body even, and see what we can't do to delay him just a tad.*

The precinct's staff passed right through her, and Danica couldn't help but smile to herself as each of them shuddered like they'd walked through a draft or under an air-conditioner vent. They thought nothing of it, and she was counting on their obliviousness. Danica banked to her left, where a maze of desks and officers in various states of occupation were seated or pacing or taking part in the impromptu dart game taking place just outside the unisex bathroom. *Nothing like a game of darts to divert their attention from what could very well be a riot on their hands right outside those double doors over there. The DA probably has a car waiting for him out back so he can make a quick getaway after he gives the crowd the bad news. Pussy.*

With unseen hands in graceful motion, Danica moved alongside a vacated desk that just so happened to be rife with all kinds of office supplies. A red stapler. Blotter calendar. A three-bin stack loaded with stacks of papers and fat, colorful folders. One of those small block calendars on a plastic stand that provides its owner with a new "Shakespearean insult" for every single day of the year. It was an orderly desk, worthy of someone in the grips of some serious obsessive-compulsive disorder. Regardless, Danica had to concentrate. Focus all her energy and funnel it down into the thumb and index finger of her right hand. She held out her hand and wiggled her fingers. And after a few worrisome moments, she experienced that familiar warmth as it suddenly bloomed inside the ethereal confines of her hands. Her fingers. It was fleeting and tenuous as it was draining for Danica, and she would not have been able to transport, let alone lift, anything heavier than a paperclip.

Luckily, that was precisely what she managed to snatch out of the little plastic bin on the desk.

A simple paperclip.

If anyone noticed the floating paperclip, none of them let on for fear they'd be called out or referred to the staff psychiatrist at once. By the time Danica had transported the clip over to the closed oak door with the DA and his staff behind it, she was fatigued beyond anything she'd ever experienced as a *lighter being* or *spirit*. The limitation surprised her, but Danica didn't dwell on it. She'd seen what lies beyond, and such a setback was of little consequence in the grand scheme of existence.

The blinds were drawn over the full-length glass panels on either side of the door. Danica shrugged and passed through the door. Inside, she found what appeared to be more of a boardroom than a wing of a police precinct. A long buffet table ran down the center length of the room and various black swivel chairs were either pulled in or shoved backward from the large wooden slab of furniture. One of the chairs looked as if someone had just leapt out of it, for it was still spinning out. Four men and two women were huddled together on the other side of the room while a tall, lanky man with obvious blond hair plugs and swimming in a charcoal gray suit paced along the rear wall. He was hissing into a cell phone, and his cheeks were flushed. Jowls loose. Beady blue eyes ringed and tired looking.

Oh Mr. DA, better tell whoever you're on the phone with you'll be running late.

Danica slipped out of the boardroom and stood once again before its locked door. By the time she had bent the paperclip out of shape and turned one end into a jagged hook, her fingers felt like what she imagined her grandmother must have experienced during her final living years in the grips of horrid arthritis.

This'll buy you some time, Nat.

Danica shoved the hooked end of the paperclip into the door's lock. Wiggled it around until it broke off inside.

She popped back into the boardroom and tried to thumb the lock open.

Jammed.

Hurry up, babe.

XIX. SKIN IN THE GAME

The engine was knocking under the Optima's hood, and it sounded more human than mechanical in its sound. Of course, when Natalie saw the *Low Oil* red light come on inside the recessed dash beneath the steering wheel, the noise became some cause for alarm. They were two blocks out from Mooney's Auto Body, and while Natalie and Gaither had not heard any further update from Danica back at the precinct, no news was not necessarily good news in this case. They both craved the sound of Danica's voice, the update, and just how close they were to the endgame.

"What kind of idiot lets his oil levels get low enough to seize? My God, the guy's going to be operating on people's fucking brains before long! Are you kidding me right now?"

Just keep going! It won't matter if we leave the thing dead down the driveway from Mooney's Auto.

"Oh, I think it might matter to Dan more than a little bit," Natalie said, seething as the knocking grew louder and its rhythm increased speed. "Then again, shame on him for not hitting a Jiffy Lube in the last freakin' year!"

That's when Danica's lovely, low, and smoky voice broke through inside Natalie's mind like a radio station tuning itself in. *I have the DA penned into the back office of the precinct. You should hear him and his staff hammering on the door like a bunch of banshees! Honestly, you'd think the room was on fire the way they're carrying on. They have maintenance taking the doorknob off!*

Natalie followed that same roundabout road that led into the long driveway up to Mooney's Autobody. The squat building looked like it had somehow sunken even lower into the boggy ground than before when they'd been there. Natalie wondered if the place was built on swampland and the earth had finally decided to swallow up the sacks of shit who populated its grounds for the last however many decades. Swallow them up once and for all.

"We just pulled up," Natalie said, then remembered there was no real need to say it out loud. "I'm going to roll halfway up the drive and walk the rest of the way on foot. How much time do we—"

Oh shit-oh shit, he's out! He got out! They're getting ready to walk out now, Nat!

"Okay-okay-okay!"

Nat, I love you! I love you so much! I'll be right there!

That was the rub of it, though. Natalie was aware Danica could be there in two shakes of a lamb's tail. That wasn't an issue. It was that Natalie began her walk up the driveway to Mooney's Auto Body and came to realize with every step that this was a walk she would have to make alone. It didn't matter who walked beside her or had taken up temporarily lodging in the frontal lobe of her mind. And every time she felt herself growing even a little bit comfortable with her decision or gathered some small sense of resolve, it was trampled by the quick, roughshod bounding hooves of a horse spooked by something it had seen in the back of her brain. Something unfathomable and without logic. Ruled by the many and wondrous musings of human beings and their guesswork about what their lives have meant or will come to mean as they continue to draw breaths. As much as Natalie wanted to slow her step, as she'd begun to trot along with the weight of her package now bouncing against the buttons of her spine, she knew she could not slow up. If anything, she should jog. No.

Run.

Then Gaither's voice sounded, soft and ponderous.

(It's time for me to leave you.)

"I—I know," Natalie replied, and her eyes filled instantly. She armed the tears out of them as quickly as they came over her. "Gotta do what you gotta do."

Hesitation, then he went on.

You were asleep when I left your body back at the Motel 6. You probably don't remember much about what happened, and I don't want you to be frightened or alarmed when your wound opens back up. The moment you feel me leave you, it will reappear, and if what happened before is any indication of what to expect, you're going to bleed out very quickly. In fact, there's a very good chance you will be dead before—

"Gregory," Natalie broke in, picking up her feet and coming up along the broken blacktop of the barely-there parking lot out front of the auto body shop. "Can I ask you something?"

Anything, girl.

"Was there *any* chance—any at all—I could have lived? You know, beat the cancer?"

Silence. The weighted kind.

The burr hole in your forehead hasn't been treated or healed or covered. If it had been, maybe it could have developed a natural plug. But the brain cancer is too far along. You'd have weeks, Natalie.

She tried to think of what she could have done, relationships she could have tended to or nurtured before the last bell tolled for her. Perhaps Natalie would have been able to leave her mother with something more than she had, offered the woman a more meaningful sense of closure. Visited her father's grave, or

135

held the urn containing his ashes in her arms if that was what he'd chosen. Spent some time with Dan if he'd see her after the stunt she pulled. Something told her Dan McCausland's capacity for both forgiveness and sympathy was as endless as the sea.

Then, the pull of Danica's presence and the promise of rejoining her cast a deeper and lovelier shadow over all other possibilities, and Natalie understood love. The kind she shared with her late wife usurped all other obligations or terms for making amends.

That's gotta be okay, then.

At closer inspection than before, Natalie discovered the structure did not merely house a small, spare convenience store, but also wrapped around into a one-story housing unit that looked out over a wide, uneven field cut with intersecting tributaries like veins feeding into the wet, sloshing heart of a lake thirty kilometers north. It was far too pretty and inviting a view for the likes of the scum that inhabited the crappy abode rising before her like some demon monolith. Jefferson Morgan and his bikers were all crammed inside, not a one of them sneaking a quick smoke or a moment of what was probably much-needed breathing room. Unless the garage also doubled as an off-shoot of the main house and no longer functioned as a business that serviced and reshaped damaged vehicles, Natalie imagined they were all inside standing shoulder-to-shoulder. Crowded around a TV set with rabbit ears, waiting for a certain DA to make his much-anticipated announcement.

There's a basement. They're all down there. Wish we could just run a hose down there through a ground-level window and just drown 'em like rats.

"Yeah," Natalie said. "But this is better."

I don't know how to say goodbye. I don't know how to even begin to thank you, Natalie.

"I'm glad I could do something for you. To help you … move on." Natalie breathed, approached the closed garage doors. She swore she could taste her beating heart between her teeth. "So, let's just do this like we'd do with a Band-Aid. One time, right off?"

Goodbye, Natalie. Godspeed, my girl.

It started in the balls of her feet, a building tremor not unlike the beginning inner rumblings before one of her grand mal seizures. Then the sensation as it rose up her legs and converged briefly in her stomach, that of feeling full-up, reminiscent of the period of time immediately following a Thanksgiving meal with all the trimmings. Then, it hit her heart, and she felt it quicken before returning to its usual standard flubbing rhythm. By the time it reached her head, Natalie felt like she needed to either chew a stick of gum or hold her nose closed while breathing out through it; the pressing need to pop her own ears, like she was on a plane that had just lifted off the tarmac.

And Gaither left her body and mind, the sensation like an unsheathing.

Natalie stood there before the closed garage door, shuddering and drenched in rain. She felt like a husk, peeled away and emptied of its contents. Like a stiff wind might blow her across the field, over the nearby lake with her feet skimming the water's surface.

Then, she heard the audible sound of her wound *uncorking* along her shaven hairline.

Blood, thick and sticky and coppery, spilled down the front of her face. It ran into her mouth, and she gagged on it, the sheer volume of it, as it tried to reenter her body.

Her legs turned to rubber. The ground seemed suddenly to grab at her, as if seeking to pull her down into it.

The carefree cackle of laughter behind the garage door triggered her next move.

Natalie rapped three times on the door, rattling it in its tracks.

All merriment within stopped dead.

She swore she heard someone inside say, "Don't fuckin' answer. That's what the Closed sign's for, you dimwit …"

There was no way of telling who was coming to roll up the garage door in response to her knocking. The narrow windows set into the garage doors at eye level were blacked out.

"*WHO'S IT?*"

When Natalie tried to conjure words in response, it was like her inner well of even the most basic English had run dry. The joint in her right knee gave without her permission, then the other, and she pitched forward, just barely bracing herself against the garage door, which rattled angrily back at her in answer. Natalie felt it on her skin, its tackiness, and was certain she would make for quite a picture when they found her outside their doors.

Wearing a mask of blood, like a merchant of death.

That is what I am, aren't I?

Their dead reckoning.

Sliding down the garage door, her hands raking down its surface and finding no purchase, Natalie made certain to roll down onto her stomach, even amid her own collapse.

The garage door rolled up, producing a sound like the thunder of the gods.

Natalie angled her crimson-caked face upward towards the person standing above her.

Fat Man Mooney, flanked by the bikers. Beyond and within, she could hear the sound of a television blaring on. The polished, clipped speech of a news anchor.

"… and now, we go to our live feed in Biltmore for DA Breakwater's remarks …"

In a velvety haze, Natalie watched as Fat Man Mooney dropped the Snickers he was holding and wheeled around, shouting something her ears could not make sense of. Then, they all disappeared from her rapidly narrowing periphery. Retreating.

With the last swirl of breath in her lungs, Natalie said:

"Surprise, motherfuckers."

Then the black Jansport backpack strapped to Natalie Kincaid's shoulders exploded.

EPILOGUE-ACTORS

...and John Tarvill barely made it off the Gettysburg field in one piece. Still, he was not long for the world, and somewhere beyond his reach and comprehension, he swore he heard the black, boiling clouds above laughing as the first pinprick ray of sunlight pierced the night sky above, branding his skin at once. It flaked away from the gamey flesh beneath like parchment on fire. Then it fell away from his bones like it had been slow roasting for centuries. By the time John Tarvill, one-half of the once immortal Twin Remainders, had scrambled through a quarter mile of the underbrush and back to the old red school house, he was little more than bones clicking together and slowing down with each and every tic of motion. He was a clock winding down. The sounds of gunfire and inhuman wailing were still ringing off the hills, the valleys, the mountains by the time John Tarvill laid eyes on the schoolhouse. He died loosely holding the pile of bones that had been his brother, Henry, in his own skeletal hands. When authorities came to scour the woods in the hours and days that followed what came to be known as The Second Civil War, they came across the Twin Remainders.

One skeleton embracing a pile of bones.

The other Remainders?

The Maker of The New South did not stand by his infantry, but this was not his fault. One instant, the big, imposing corporal was forcibly moving a man with a video camera on his shoulder around like he was some evil puppeteer. Shoving him forward. Moving him left. Panning him right, like the poor little man were merely a dolly for the camera itself. The next minute, a Union actor walked right up behind The Maker and with one sure, sweeping slash of his sword, he beheaded Roger Creel. The Maker did not so much fold over in eternal death as he crumbled, then rolled like an avalanche of quivering, dead flesh spreading out across the ground. Then, Roger "The Maker" Creel began to flake away as John Tarvill's skin had done. Then, the flesh. Then, lastly, the brain burned out like an old spark plug, and the eyes fell out, as if some higher power had designed it to happen in just that way.

So, The Remainders had no option other than to watch themselves wither away to brittle and breakable bones before their eyeballs dropped out of their heads like grapes from their vines.

The other Remainders similarly experienced the terrible mutiny of their own brains and bodies against them in an instant. They dropped their arms to their sides. They fell to their knees, and they laced their hands behind their bent heads. Union and Confederacy soldier actors kicked and clawed and beat them with heavy, hammering fists. The armed actors fired into their previous aggressors until their weapons dry-fired. Then, some of them reloaded, the actors who'd actually seen reason to bring more than what they'd loaded into their handguns the night before. And The Pale Faces went down like great sacks of meat, sprung-leaks spouting and fountaining gouts of black, viscous blood that did not sink into the Gettysburg ground as much as it coated and smothered the grass like tar.

It was not a war. Not a fight. It was a slaughter. A purging of hate and intolerance given human form and made to walk and savage and infect the world, all the while drawing terrible sustenance from the very abominable behaviors of humankind that had reached something of a critical mass in the last century and a half. In the end, when the people in the parking lot had seen fit to leave the safety of their vehicles and they'd crept back to the roped-off sidelines of the battlefield, what they found would be written and chronicled and argued over for decades to come. But no amount of belaboring the point and the end-scene of this second, stranger Civil War would diminish the irony in the conclusion those spectators witnessed that day. Men and women dressed in the uniforms of both the Union and Confederacy working together in a common cause. That of survival. Then, when they raised their hands in celebration and they hugged and kissed one another, how curious and yet satisfying it appeared to the spectators and everyone in attendance. These actors symbolically bridging the gap of two regions at home under the same flag and freedoms.

Symbolically.

Yes, but symbols exist within the same realm as dreams.

And all good things begin with a dream of them.

August 5, 2019 to December 4, 2019
Fairless Hills, Pennsylvania

DALLAS TELLER'S KILL LIST

"He thought, in fine, that the dreams of poets
were the realities of life." "I thought in my
heart how seldom, even in this world, justice
fails to overtake the murderer, and to enforce
the righteous judgment of God, 'that whoso
sheddeth man's blood, by man shall his blood
be shed'."
-*The Vampyre*
John Polidori

"The dead can't be repaired or come back to
life or be normal again. It's irreversible." The
wounded "are like collateral damage, I guess.
I regret that they had to be wounded rather than
the bullets just missing them or something."
-James Holmes
Colorado Mass Shooter

I. EDUCATOR OF THE YEAR

You know they only chose you for the award because of what happened to you. It's a pity award, man!

At thirty years old, Conor Crenshaw had made history the night before by winning the prestigious **EDUCATOR OF THE YEAR** award. Never in Bucks County had someone so young and with such a short period of service received the award. No one had been more surprised than Conor that morning months ago when the principal called him down to his office during Conor's prep period to tell him he'd been selected by a panel of his peers, administrators, and the superintendent of schools.

While Conor had harbored no illusions of grandeur, that didn't mean he would have said no to the honor. Nor would he have stood up there as he did last night to a rousing standing ovation *before* he even delivered his acceptance speech, only to proclaim in his humblest tone he would like to share the award with *this* Bio teacher or *that* Psych teacher. That was never going to happen. Why?

"Because I worked hard for the acknowledgement," he told himself. "And if it's got anything at all to do with what happened to me, *it's not a pity award!*"

Muscle memory drove him to school that Thursday morning, January 29, 2019. There was so much he felt he needed to hash out about the night before and the deep-seated sense of insecurity that plagued him about the award.

Good thing the traffic was sparse that morning. His trusty ole muscle memory drove him through a *very* red light at the intersection of Veterans and Daly Road. The assailing of horns wrenched him out of the all-consuming back-and-forth he was having with himself, but the outward consciousness was short-lived, and once he made it cleanly to the other side of said intersection, Conor Crenshaw dove back inside of himself. What few people knew was that it was actually where he was most comfortable.

For as long as Conor could remember, talking to himself felt as normal as drawing breath. Any Freudian psychologist could suggest the habit was born of the fact Conor's father had left on a business trip to Italy when he was still small and never came back, abandoning Conor and his mother. Conor trusted in this mental processing, no matter how screwy it came across to other people in his presence. And the smart-asses who had caught him in the act, when he thought he was alone in the faculty lounge or in a Men's Room stall at Baldwin High School, always said the same thing: "It's all right to talk to yourself, Conor, so long as you never start answering back."

I'm not always talking to myself. Sometimes I hear a voice or two I don't recognize in my head. The neurologist says it's a byproduct of what happened *to me.*

The incident.

That's how Conor referred to it, both inwardly and outwardly.

"I've been offered administrative positions three different times, and *every single time,* I turned them down. You want to know why? Because I belong in the classroom. I care about the kids, cliché as that sounds. And I want to perfect my craft as a teacher. That's the measure of an educator, baby. That's my reality! And—you know—look! I'm not looking for a pat on the back, but I've mentored some twenty-five students into Ivy League colleges. I give of myself whenever possible. I co-moderated the Student Council until mom got too sick. I helped the Creative Writing Club produce their first lit mag in ten years! I give blood every damned year … I mean … Jesus … this is starting to sound ridiculous. What am I doing?"

Trying to validate yourself. Like a parking pass.

Ever since *the incident,* Conor found himself grasping sadly for words while speaking and thinking. His neurologist called the condition *Word-Searching.* He attributed it to the damage done to the portion of Conor's brain that controlled speech. This nearly spelled the end of his teaching career before he even hit his ten-year mark. An educator who is frequently at a loss for words in front of a classroom full of students seemed to Conor as the equivalent of a guitarist trying to play before Madison Square Garden with the low and high E strings missing. Luckily, Conor managed this impediment much better in front of an audience than when he was by himself.

During that morning drive, Conor was finding it more difficult than usual to find the right word.

Not to mention, he felt his anxiety spiking.

Conor could only attribute it to the post-traumatic stress disorder he'd developed shortly after the incident.

The attack—

"*Shit!*" Conor cried, stomping down on the brake.

The steering wheel rose like a living thing to strike him. It hit him square in the forehead, and exquisite pain immediately pulsed behind the rugged bone. Thunder clapped inside his skull, and he felt his stomach turn over as the world went black and cold for what seemed like an eternity. Stinging bile climbed his throat, and he nearly vomited down the front of himself as he came away from the thing that had battered him. Conor shut his mouth, the bile pooling behind his teeth and sizzling against an opened sore along the interior of his left cheek. His chest muscles ached, spasmed, and unclenched.

The cold, black void washed away, and Ferry Road bled across his vision as he stared blankly out his windshield.

The blue Dodge Neon was stopped dead in front of him.

The car appeared to be backing up.

Know me.

Conor felt the warm wetness gather along the rim of his upper lip.

His hand flew to his mouth and came away red. His nose was gushing.

"Oh … dammit," he moaned, and pinched his nose shut. Awkwardly, he jostled around in the driver's seat and craned around to search the back with frantic eyes. His gym bag was stowed there. Conor grabbed for it, gracelessly worked at unzipping it with one hand, and after succeeding, he yanked a pair of black sweat shorts out of it. Conor swung back around, his ribcage pulsating with stabs of soreness. He cried out and clapped the shorts over his face, mindful to replace his fingers to hold his nostrils closed. He shut his eyes.

You. Know. Me.

The blood slowly dripped back down his throat, nearly engaging his gag reflex. The fist of a migraine had formed behind his eyes, but dizziness came and went just as quickly.

He felt eyes on him while he nursed his bloody nose.

Conor took three deep breaths, tossed the stained shorts into the passenger seat, and set about clearing the blood off his face like a cat. Wet fingers. Dab. Scrub. Repeat. He straightened his tie, sighed from deep within, and climbed out of the car.

The sun was a torch driven into his eye sockets.

He braced himself along the edge of the driver's side door and found his equilibrium once more.

"Never traffic here!" Conor muttered to himself. "What-what's happening?"

Road work? The impromptu kind?

"… already running late."

The driver of the Dodge Neon he'd almost rear-ended climbed out of the car. Conor thought he recognized the middle-aged woman. She wore a fleece Eagles Football pullover and pajama bottoms with lipstick-kiss prints up and down the legs. Her blonde hair was pulled into a haphazard ponytail that looked off-center when she turned her head for a moment to scan something up ahead. Mrs. Glassman. Tommy Glassman's mother. They'd met in his classroom only a week ago for Parent-Teacher conferences. Tommy was failing and needed a swift kick in the rear to avoid summer school. Of course, Mrs. Glassman had looked much more put-together. This woman standing beside her car looked like she had only just rolled out of bed. Maybe even out of the woods after having been missing for days.

Damn you. Know me. Hear me.

A phantom voice. The neurosurgeon had warned him about these auditory hallucinations. But he could have done without one of them right then.

Conor approached her with his hands up in supplication. "I'm so sorry. I wasn't paying attention."

"Oh Mr. Crenshaw? I'm-I'm so sorry! Are you all right?"

With a stiff neck that felt stuffed with ball bearings, Conor nodded. "Fine."

"I ... what's happening at Baldwin?"

"I dunno," Conor said, blinking the spots out of his eyes. "What's happening at Baldwin?" He stopped beside Mrs. Glassman's car and cast a wider glance up ahead, where he saw a lineup of stopped cars stretching some four blocks down. Then, his eyes found the flashing police dome lights obstructing the traffic.

Mrs. Glassman made a strange *tsk* sound with her front teeth and tongue, then fished her yellow iPhone out of the front pouch of her oversized hoodie. Chewing at her upper lip, she moved her index finger rapidly across the cell's screen. "I-I just dropped Tommy off at school, and then I get *this* from him right when I'm pulling back in my driveway. I drove back."

She handed her phone off to Conor. He scrolled down to Tommy Glassman's first text, sent to his mother at 7:22 a.m.:

Tommy: Mom, come back! I'm gonna sneak out through the gym. Will meet u in the back of school. I don't care what the principal tells us to do. SOMEONE IS HERE WITH GUNS IN THE PARKING LOT! SCHOOL SHOOTER!!!

Conor's face felt tight as he handed the cell back to Mrs. Glassman, who now wore an expectant expression on her face. *Christ, she thinks I'll know what to do? She's waiting for me to advise her, and I don't know shit! We're both in the same darkness. And I think my nose is un-clotting.*

"All right," he said, "I'll call in to the school. Maybe I'll get someone." A wave of dizziness hit him. He steadied himself against the side of her car. "I'm sorry, do you have an aspirin, by chance?"

"Oh, I think I do." Mrs. Glassman ducked back inside her car and came back out with a bottle of Ibuprofen. She handed it to Conor, who shook four of the brown, football-shaped tablets into his palm and dry-swallowed them. "Are you sure you're okay?"

One of the tablets stuck in his throat. He winced, forced a winsome smile. "I'm fine."

He brought out his cell, accessed Baldwin High's Main Office line, and punched it in. He motioned towards the line of cars before them with people in them and engines running so they could keep warm on such an unseasonably chilly morning. "They're waiting for the *All Clear* signal. That's protocol. You should text your son to stay put wherever he is."

The office line went to voicemail on the seventh ring.

Mrs. Glassman cast a nervous glance in the direction of the school, which right then seemed like an impossible destination for them both. "He said he's in the cafeteria. That's where they're keeping most of them. The cafeteria and the gym."

"That's good," Conor said. "Just text him to sit and stay."

A terrible image flashed across Conor's mind, that of Baldwin's two receptionists, both grandmothers and tough cookies to boot, lying dead on the floor behind their desks. Shot up and leaking gleaming crimson. Their eyes wide and filmy as they stared vacantly up at the ceiling tiles, and perhaps beyond into the void.

His cell phone beeped in his ear, cutting through the ringing tone that stretched on and on without engaging voicemail.

Conor looked at his screen:

**INCOMING CALL
MIKE D.**

I dunno whether to laugh or worry!

This was usually the range of emotions Conor anticipated when Mike Distefano called him on his cell. Before Mike took the job at Baldwin as its Director of Student Life and Main Disciplinarian, he taught American History I and II in the classroom next door to Conor's room. They were fast friends from Conor's first day there. Now, the poor guy spent most of his day dealing with problems and doling out punishment, all of which seemed greatly at odds with Mike's former jokester demeanor.

Conor took the call. "Yeah, Mike, what—"

"Where are you?" Mike's clipped voice filled the earpiece. He sounded the way he did when he needed to put a student in place, to cut through the proverbial bullshit of the moment. "Where are you *right now?*"

"Where am I?"

"I know you're not *here*, Conor. You on your way?"

"I was," Conor said, switching his gaze from the row of cars in front of his to the onslaught of new vehicles backed up behind him. "Ferry Road's a parking lot right now. What's going on, Mike?"

"The parents," Mike sighed. "Dammit, I told all the kids *not* to text their parents. It would cause a lot of chaos and we needed to keep the road out front clear for any EMS if we needed them—"

"Whoa, EMS? What's. Going. On?"

"Any parents near you right now?"

They're swarming. "Yeah."

"Walk away from them."

Mrs. Glassman was not the only one who'd sidled up alongside him, trying to glean some new information. A mother and father, both dressed in what looked like their gym clothes, and an older, somewhat stooped "Auntie" had converged upon him. Their eyes searching. Seeking. Their ears wide open. Looking at him with supplicating expressions.

Smiling thinly, Conor slipped past them and moved into the loose gravel of the narrow breakdown lane. "Folks, I'll be right with you," he said to the parents, who had begun to graze along the road like sheep. "Give me a minute." He turned completely away from them. "Mike? I just read a text sent from Tommy Glassman to his mother about a school shooter in the parking lot?"

"Tommy-fucking-Glassman? Jesus!"

"Mike?"

"We're lucky. You remember how I said at our faculty meeting a couple months back how close we are in relation to the Comstock Police Department? That quarter-mile radius meant the difference between our shooter climbing inside the windows of the Main Office after he sprayed them with a goddamn AR-15, and the police arriving on the heels of that and taking him down while he was trying to load another magazine."

Conor rubbed the bridge of his nose. Flashes of red and black danced before his eyes. "Oh my God. Did he hit Delia or Mary?"

"No," Mike said. "Mary was under the desk loading more computer paper into her printer. Delia was getting coffee in the lounge. When I tell you this was a *Hail Mary* kind of situation, I mean it. So much went right that could have gone so very wrong."

A cluster of parents had gathered a few feet behind Conor. He snuck a glance at them, his face unreadable on purpose. "All right. So … the shooter's in custody?"

"Yeah. They already got him in the back of one of their cars. But I want you to wait a little bit before coming in. Let us release the kids to their parents and get the rest onto buses and out of the driveway. Then, I'll give you a call and you come in."

No problem there. Conor's Honda was officially boxed in. He saw them from the corner of his eye, and a sudden sense of paranoia stirred within him that he could not place. They all seemed to be sizing him up, their eyes searching him. It seemed to stretch beyond that of mere concern for what was happening in the school with their children. No, the parents sitting in their cars and staring out the windshield at him, the parents standing in a loose huddle behind him, even the ones making their way towards him, their eyes hooded and mouths set; they all seemed to look to him as if he were somehow the root cause.

That Conor Crenshaw, beloved and award-winning English teacher, was guilty.

He shook it off, but some of its sticky and irritating residue clung to the inside of his mind like a paste. "I can't go anywhere if I wanted to, Mike."

"Don't tell them anything other than everything is under control and we will be releasing their children to them very shortly. Can you do that?"

"Got it. And once I can make it the rest of the way, I'll—"

"Conor, just listen," Mike said, an edge crowding out all remnants of the funny guy who used to have a classroom next to Conor's room. "We'll call you to come in when they're ready."

They?

"Well, who's *they*?" He knew Mike wouldn't refer to the other administrators as *they*. It had always been *we*, at least ever since Tony Stadt took the job as principal.

Mike sighed. "The police. They want to talk to you. After they cart the shooter away and make it back."

"Me?" Conor could feel the eyes of the parents all around him. For an instant, he imagined them coming at him like an angry mob of villagers like in the old monster movies he used to watch with his mother every Friday night. Prodding at him with spears and waving torches at him. Immolating him, right there in the middle of the backed-up residential road. Conor's cheeks stung. He blinked his eyes twice and refocused his attention on the call. "Why would the police want to talk to me?"

"I know I'm going to catch shit for this, but you should know going into the interview. To some degree."

"Okay ..."

"The shooter. You know Dallas Teller? He's a Junior?"

A strange thing happened to Conor right before he answered Mike Distefano. The *word well* from which Conor Crenshaw extracted and arranged his vocabulary in such a way as to communicate turned up dry as a bone. Had he tried to raise the metaphorical bucket up out of that well and look inside it, Conor would have found nothing inside but an empty interior. Not an article. Verb. Noun. Adjective. Proper noun. In that instant, he had no idea what those terms even meant, and Conor had made a living and a name for himself teaching young people how to arrange words into the most effective and meaningful ways. The doctor who had worked on Conor, operated on his brain and somehow staved off what could have been irreparable brain damage from the beating (the *incident*), had warned him there was the chance of forgetting words here and there. But there was also a further impediment, one that could prove more severe. He could not recall the name of it, but he knew it was a condition whereby he'd forget how to speak.

"Conor?"

Mike's voice sounded like he was calling down to Conor from a great height.

Then a buzzing erupted in the back of his skull. It felt like his head was a honeycomb that had just been whacked with a baseball bat and the bees had become frenzied in response. And yet, it was frightening and deeply *pleasurable* all at once. The sensation stimulated the pleasure center of his brain. A rush of disorientation, coupled with the dopamine headiness that follows a powerful orgasm, seized Conor Crenshaw by the brain stem, and he was at its mercy.

"Conor, you there?"

I'm here ... but I can't come to the phone ...

When he opened his mouth, the voice that came out of his mouth and its message were not of Conor Crenshaw or from him. But he spoke the words just the same, operating as more of a conduit than a thinking human being. *"Come. Home. Conor. Mama. Needs. You."*

"What're you talking about, man? You *with* me?"

Then, all at once, Conor's *well of words* overflowed its walls and spilled over into his brain pan. "Sorry, Mike. A parent tried to grab my phone to talk to you."

"So you don't know Dallas Teller?"

"Nope. I've heard the name, but other than that, I couldn't tell you what he looks like."

"Well, he seems to know you. Or, at least, he seems to have a very serious problem with you."

"Oh yeah?"

"Yeah," Mike said. "Teller had a *Kill List* tucked into his back pocket when they took him into custody.

Conor. Come. Home. Mama. Is. Dying—

"A *kill list?*"

"Nine students. One name crossed out. And one faculty member."

Conor felt his stomach drop twelve floors, well below the soles of his shoes. "My name?"

"Yeah, Conor. Your name."

II. DALLAS TELLER

One hundred and twenty-seven parents picked up their kids outside Baldwin High School forty-five minutes later. The cheese buses took care of the rest. In between, bus drivers argued with parents and relatives almost exclusively through the use of their horns until the logjam in the parking lot finally filtered through, clearing the way for an oddly serene and clear March morning to take center stage. The teachers fled shortly after, many of them meeting up at The Wharf Bar three miles west to discuss. To vent. To hold one another. The last time they'd come together at The Wharf, Christmas Break was fast approaching, the New Year after that, and the possibility for improvement and greater days.

Not quite a promise, but if it were, that day in Baldwin High School history would have broken it.

Conor Crenshaw had expected the call from Mike Distefano once the road cleared and the students were gone. Once his car was freed up from its position further down Ferry Road, he drove to the Denny's five miles north of Baldwin. Initially, he'd planned on going in, wrapping his hands around a sub-standard cup of black diner coffee, and concentrating solely upon trying to steady his palsied hands. They had been all over the wheel the entire drive over to Denny's. Frightening in its involuntary nature.

Ultimately, Conor could not bring himself to get out of the car. His thoughts were terrible and taunting.

He'd told Mike Distefano he didn't know Dallas Teller. Now, sitting there in his car with only his thoughts and a slow-building sense of focus, Conor remembered he'd sent a referral to the Guidance Counselor about Teller. Something had happened.

Something happened before *the incident.*

Before I was attacked.

"What did I do to this kid?"

Conor laid his forehead against the lightly vibrating steering wheel. He'd left the engine running. The sensation against the thick, rugged bone of his brow seemed to stimulate the subtle, vague hatchlings of recall. He shut his eyes and tried to mentally seize the formless, murky memory. To drag it out into the light of remembrance. But the memory was slippery. Greased. And it retreated further into the darker, unconscious recesses of his impaired mind. Hiding from him. This was how many of the memories he'd formed *before the attack* teased him.

The operating neurosurgeon had given him no guarantee he'd recover all his memories, but it wasn't an impossibility. They could come creeping back, little by little, parsing themselves out. Often, recovering a memory felt like fishing inside his brain. Casting out a line, feeling the tug on said line, then quickly working to reel the memory in before it dropped off the hook and disappeared back into the fathomless depths of the untapped portions of his mind. Sometimes, he caught the fish.

More often, the fish slipped him entirely.

This fish? The fish named *Dallas Teller?*

"You're my great white whale, Dallas Teller. But I'll hook you. Call me Ishmael, you little fucker."

His cell phone rang on the passenger seat, skittering about in the bucket as it vibrated at the same time.

Conor snatched it up. The number on the screen was Baldwin's main line. Not Mike Distefano.

He took the call. "Hello?"

"Conor, it's Tony." The principal sounded like his voice could give out any second. "Where are you?"

"Uh, I camped out at Denny's down a-ways. Waiting for the call."

"Can you come back?"

"Of course," Conor said. "I'm on my way."

Tony Stadt did not say goodbye.

In the brief pocket of silence before the line went dead, he heard another voice.

Not his own.

Bad blood, Conny! She's poisoning me ...

His mother.

"Conor?"

Principal Tony Stadt sat at the head of the long cherry wood table inside the Conference Room. The school's guidance counselor, Mary Marguerite, and the Studies Director, Victoria Rosner—the oldest staff member in the entire building, as well as the most wizened—flanked him on either side. Mike Distefano was not in attendance. The principal was a young guy for his position, only a few years older than Conor and twice his size. Stadt was a bear of a fellow, with a big personality one did not mind having imposed on them. He was the kind of man's man who clapped you on the back so hard your teeth rattled, and your breath caught in your throat. But that was okay too. Stadt was *good people*, by all accounts. High-and-tight haircut, a residual effect of his time spent in Iraq.

Mary Marguerite, the guidance counselor, stared warily at Conor as he entered, her fingers arched and fingertips standing on end along the tabletop like a white spider. Mary Marguerite bristled noticeably when they locked eyes for a moment.

Victoria Rosner held her silence at the table. She had been twenty pounds heavier before facing down and beating breast cancer only five years before. In that time, she'd compacted into a small woman made larger by shoulder pads and billowing pant suits.

"Take a load off, Con," Stadt said, waving him over to the chair beside the guidance counselor.

"Kids are all gone?" Conor asked, lowering himself into the seat and folding his hands in his lap.

"Yeah," Stadt said. "We waited to call you back in until every last one got picked up." For a moment, he adopted the same cautiously aware expression as Mary. "How you holding up?"

"Well, you know, I'm at a loss," Conor said, spreading his hands and letting them drop back into his lap. "Mike told me it was Dallas Teller. And I gotta tell you, I've had minimal interaction with the kid at best."

Marguerite stiffened beside him. She angled her whole upper body towards him. Conor hadn't noticed the folder on the table before her until she opened it and slipped a paper out. She slid it towards him. "Conor? I understand you … *we* recognize the physical trauma you had experienced has affected some of your memory about certain, ah, events which had taken place prior to that. But-"

"Mary," Conor said, cracking an easy smile, "you don't have to choose your words so carefully. No need to pull punches. I'm working through it." He glanced down at the paper. "What's this?"

"You filed this in my office a few months back. Could you verify it's accuracy for us?"

The words **STUDENT REFERRAL NOTICE** ran across the top of the page. Beneath that, the professional header of the school's Guidance Office inched its way down the page in centered, short bursts of words. "Do you remember filing this in my office, Conor? It would have been two months ago. Mid-February."

Conor skimmed the document. It was a Referral Notice for Dallas Teller to meet with Mary Marguerite as soon as possible. He signed in his wide, flamboyant Hancockian cursive at the bottom. In the Comments section, he'd written:

*In the Men's Room, Dallas grabbed my arm
and said, "I'm awake now, Mr. Crenshaw.
Wide awake." Dallas appeared to be under
the influence of some kind of controlled
substance. His eyes were glassy. His pupils
were dilated. This young man is in crisis and
should meet with you as soon as possible. If
you have any further questions, please don't
hesitate to reach out to me directly.*

Mary cleared her throat, her eyes boring into the side of Conor's head like a laser.

"I was going to say you submitted this to Guidance a month after your attack. Is it accurate to assume you were of—and please don't take offense at this—of *sound mind* when you made this report?"

"You mean, did this really happen or—I dunno—was I *off* when I wrote this?"

"I wasn't going to say *off*, Conor. I assure you."

"A hallucination, then? My mind playing tricks on me, so to speak?"

She shook her head, folded her arms. "Of course not. Nothing like that. But you *did* tell Mike Distefano you ... er ... couldn't even tell him what Dallas Teller looks like. And you told the three of us just now that you've had *minimal* contact with the boy. Now, I understand you're probably shaken by the events of this morning. We all are. I'm not trying to marginalize how you'd be feeling right now, knowing this young man came here to hurt you specifically. But ..." Marguerite stalled, lowering her eyes to the high shine of the table. She breathed out and shifted in her seat. "Your story seems to be ... evolving? No contact, then *minimal* contact. And it's important we have all our ducks in a row before the detectives arrive."

Stadt leaned in, steepling his hands on the tabletop. "I think what Mary's trying to say is we believe you, and there's no question your concern about the kid was genuine and your heart was in the right place when you made the referral. We just need you to go on record that you had a strange—some would say random—exchange with Teller. With us. And the brass when they get here. Can you do that?"

"What? Like an affidavit?"

"No," Stadt scoffed. "No-no-no. We want to share Mary's notes and that referral with the detectives, and its important you verify its authenticity. I mean, we understand your nerves are frazzled. That's probably an understatement. So you forgot about filing the referral. The incident in the Men's Room. All understandable."

Conor straightened in his seat. "Mmm, I think I remember now. Dammit, I don't know how the hell I could have forgotten. Something did happen between Teller and I."

That's when the beehive in the back of his skull buzzed as it had before. Like someone had just whacked it with a bat, driving an army of frenzied bees out of their haven. The sound was deafening. It trampled the words of the guidance counselor as she spoke to Conor, her eyes pinched and brow knitted as she pointed at the Referral Form. Then, through the building, maniacal buzzing of hundreds of *mental bees* inside his skull, another voice (one he vaguely recognized) bloomed in his head like a blooming black flower.

Your mother is dying, Conor. It was bad blood. Your wife.

"Conor? You with us?" Stadt stared at him from the head of the table, concern building behind his unblinking green eyes.

Mike Distefano had just come in, followed by two men Conor did not know but could only assume to be the detectives in question. Everyone was looking at Conor now, even the newcomers dressed in their slightly rumpled suits and carrying Styrofoam cups brimming with black coffee from the urn in the faculty lounge. Collectively, they made Conor feel as if he were in the presence of some Lovecraftian beast with a thousand unblinking eyes, sizing him up and greedily salivating. His anxiety was a pressure on his ribcage he could not shake.

Both detectives took seats across from Conor. Mike Distefano hovered by the windows along the back wall.

The detective who sat higher in his chair spoke first, holding out his credentials in a plastic sleeve for Conor to have a look at. "Mr. Crenshaw," he began, plaintively, "my name is Detective Winthrop. This is my partner," he waved his hand at the slight looking man sitting next to him, "Detective Grimes. We're from the Comstock Borough Police Department. We wanted to talk to you about Dallas Teller." Winthrop turned to Tony Stadt. "What does he know so far?"

I'm sitting right here, Conor thought. *You could ask me, Detective.*

Principal Stadt briefed the two detectives about what they had already revealed to Conor.

A stick of irritation wedged itself inside Conor's chest. *Either they're all worried about laying a glove on me because they think I'll wilt like a flower, or they think I'm hiding something and they're working an angle.* Whatever it was, he did not want to sit by while they discussed him like two parents at the dinner table musing over what exactly they should do about this problem child in their midst.

"Driver's Ed," Conor blurted out, tossing up his hands.

"Mr. Crenshaw?" Detective Winthrop raised a bushy salt-and-pepper eyebrow. The guy's left ear wiggled at the same time, which would have amused Conor in any other setting.

"I teach Driver's Ed here at Baldwin. Dallas Teller was in my class last semester. He didn't do as well as he would have liked, in the classroom or on the road. I took him out for a mock road test to prep him for the real test. He was nervous. Shaking. And, I think he might have been on something, but I couldn't prove it. It was the same sort of look in his eyes I encountered in the Men's Room. Just a thousand-yard stare. The kind of thing you see in the gazes of veterans. I've never seen it in a student's eyes before Dallas Teller. Long story short, he nearly got us T-boned over on Street Road when he crossed through a red light and a cement truck was barreling towards us in the opposite direction. I failed him for the road test. And he did *not* take it as one to grow on. He was angry. I tried to reason with him, but he wouldn't have any of it. The next time Dallas Teller said anything to me, it was in the Men's Room back in February. Just as the Referral Form states."

"Here's the Referral Form," Marguerite said, sliding it towards Detective Winthrop, who clapped one big paw down on it before moving it between he and his partner so they could both have a look.

It was the as-yet-unspoken Detective Grimes who spoke next, lifting his basset-hound brown eyes to match Conor's expectant gaze.

"Any idea what Teller meant when he said, 'I'm awake'?"

"No idea," Conor said. "The kid sounded troubled, and the way he said it, you know, it sounded almost like he was broken from reality."

Grimes did not blink. "So, you … recommended him to Guidance?"

"I did."

"And it never occurred to you this student may very well have been sending you some coded message? Maybe even to some other people he felt had wronged him in some way?"

"This boy needed kid gloves, you know? Not another hit to his ego. And, I also thought he needed an intervention about what I deemed to be an addiction to some controlled substance. I mean, Teller was not all there when he said this to me. I assure you."

Winthrop turned to Mary. "So, he met with you, we can assume. What was your assessment, Ms. Marguerite?"

She cleared her throat. "Well, I wish I'd had the presence of mind to bring my notes to this interview. I gathered a rather sizable write-up on Dallas Teller. I could go get it if—"

"That won't be necessary. What was your overall feeling about the boy? Your diagnosis?"

"In my professional opinion, Dallas Teller is a textbook depressive. I believe he's been self-medicating but failing a road test was not the triggering event. No, he had clearly grown accustomed to the relief alcohol and cold medicine was offering him. It's all in my notes. He confessed to drinking regularly before school and downing Nyquil every night so he could sleep. He complained of night terrors. I asked him how long he'd been experiencing them, and he said something very strange in response."

Winthrop leaned in, resting his arms on the lip of the table. "What'd he say?"

"He said he couldn't remember ever *not* having the night terrors. That there was no *before* that he could remember when he slept soundly."

"Did you reach out to a parent?"

Mary nodded firmly. "Yes, and I did not let him leave the office until I reached someone. He gave me his mother's cell phone number. I called that number, and her voice mailbox was full. It wouldn't let me leave a message. Dallas told me she works full time in a lawyer's office. Ms. Teller is a paralegal, apparently. I got her at the office, and I explained to her I had her son in my office and what had transpired between Dallas and Mr. Crenshaw in the Men's Room. That he'd confessed to abusing alcohol and other substances. The woman sounded like you could have knocked her over with a feather. She left work and met with me and Principal Stadt."

Mike Distefano cut in. "Why wasn't I included in this meeting?"

Principal Stadt, arms folded across his barrel-chest, offered a curt nod Mike's way. "You were in Disneyworld that week with your family. Remember?"

"February?" Mike asked, his brow crinkling. "Right. But, still, someone might have made me aware of what happened. I would have wanted to go another route entirely."

Winthrop leveled his gaze at Mike. "What would have been your course of action?"

"All due respect, Mary," Mike said to the guidance counselor, his eyes hooded, "I would have suspended him and placed certain mandatory demands on him *and* his mother. A complete psych-eval. Weekly, documented therapy sessions. If necessary, the kid would go in-house someplace."

"I'm sorry, Mike," Mary said, a sardonic edge to her tone. "*I* performed a complete psychological evaluation right here. In this building," she said, stabbing an index finger into the surface of the table. "*In*. Guidance."

"Then my question to you would be——"

Winthrop held up his hands. "Everybody, cool your jets!"

"——how in the *hell* did we end up here when all the warning signs were there?"

Principal Stadt slapped the table with the flat of his palm. "Dammit, Mike! Just because the kid's depressed doesn't automatically make him a future school shooter. I mean, my eight-year-old is on Prozac for her depression, and I gotta tell you, I can't possibly imagine her throwing on all black, getting her hands on a gun, and shooting up her elementary school. If you ask me, the stigma mental illness carries with it—in twenty nineteen, mind you—is the reason so many kids suffer in silence. They don't want to be labeled. They feel desperate, but that doesn't equal a call to violence or-or mass murder." His face was a blooming rose, and he backed off some for a second before continuing in a much more contained voice. "Now, Mary shared her notes with me, and we talked with the mother. We talked with Dallas. And it was a *joint* determination, mine and Mary's, that he did not pose a threat to the school. The kid's sad. Father killed himself when he was three. Mom put herself through college and lifted herself up by the bootstraps. Granted, she admitted she is not around for Dallas as much as she would like. But she's doing her best. So, when I tell you there was *no way* anyone could have seen this coming, that's the truth."

Detective Grimes asked, "You don't think this boy was in desperate need of rehab? For his addiction?"

"Of course," Principal Stadt concurred, albeit somewhat begrudgingly. He was neither comfortable nor willing to sit in a hot seat. Not even for a couple of detectives. "But his mother pleaded with us to allow him to finish out the year. She told us she would administer at-home breathalyzers to Dallas. And she'd lock up the medicine cabinet that day. This woman was deadly serious. We believed her. What's more, Dallas agreed to all of it. He broke down, and he begged us to let him finish Junior year. We believed him."

"Well," Winthrop said, "it sounds like the mother's doing all she can do."

"I agree," Principal Stadt stated flatly.

Conor found he could not hold his tongue for another second. "No, she's good. Truthful. But Dallas Teller? He probably should have won an Oscar for the performance he put on for all of you."

"You think so?" Mary snapped at him, her eyes flashing.

The black flower voice whispered in his ear.

Steer them into the rocks. We are nearly finished.

"I feel responsible," Conor said. "I do. I should have brought this to Mike when he came back from Florida. I'm sorry, Mary. I mean no disrespect. This was my error. I fell for the kid's lost little boy act. Not just in the Men's Room. I was going to pass him for the road test at first, even though he almost got us both killed. I felt sorry for him. It's my weakness. I identify too much with the students. All of them. I always thought if I approached them on their level, I'd find a way in so I could teach them in a meaningful way. But Dallas Teller? I read him wrong. I got it wrong—"

"You don't want to travel down this road, Mr. Crenshaw," Winthrop said. "I've seen it enough times. Sounds like you gave the boy more credit than he deserved, but that doesn't make you the orchestrator of this mess we've got here. And that brings us to the next thing." The detective brought out a small notepad with a pen woven through its wire spirals. He thumbed it open and flipped through a few pages before stopping. He folded the rest of them over and slid the pad across the table to Conor. "These are the names that appear on Dallas Teller's list. He had it in his back pocket all crumpled up when we took him into custody. The paper itself is being logged into evidence, of course. Do you recognize any of those names?"

Conor picked up the pad, his eyesight still strained from the bump he'd taken on the head and the subsequent migraine pulsing behind his ocular cavities. It read:

The Dead

Mr. Crenshaw (Room 113)
Harry Hasting (Room 113)
Joe Brickman (Room 117)

Delaney Lindberg (Room 218)
Michael Malone (Room 218)
Pete Mason (Room 218)
Tara Neeley (Room 220)
Valerie Parent (Room 238)
Steve Teague (Room 315)
Stacy Kennedy (Room 131)
/////////////////////////
In infernis arderet!

The Dead.
My name at the top.
The Dead.
His mouth went dry.
"Conor?" Winthrop prompted. "Do you?"
The pulse behind his eyes sped up. Black spots blinked like broken traffic lights.
"Uh, yes," he answered. "I taught all of them."
Winthrop shifted in his seat. "Were you close with them?"
Conor set the pad down before him. "*Close* to them?"
"I mean, it's my understanding you're one of the more … popular teachers? Students gravitated to you for advice. Popped into your room more frequently than other teachers? That sort of thing. I know my children each have a favorite of their own where they go to school. Nothing untoward, I would assume. Is that the case with these students as well?"
"Well, yes, it was that way. But I have a good relationship with a lot of students. I try not to play favorites."
"Were any of them … your favorites? At least in their own mind?"
He rubbed at his eyes. They flared in response, and he tried not to wince. "I, you know, I have no idea what's in their minds. I only know I always try to make myself available for those who need something or just want to say hi. I mean, some of them, I can tell you, some of them are more self-sufficient than others. Some of them need more of a guiding hand."
"All right—"
"That's not to say I don't follow protocol. With the girls."
"By protocol, you mean?"
Stadt interjected. "We require that all of our teachers leave their doors open at all times. We also strongly encourage our faculty to meet with students in public areas whenever possible. This goes for our female instructors as well, you understand."
Winthrop grunted gruffly. "Can you think of anything else that would connect them to one another? Besides a fondness for you?"
Conor shrugged. "I can't think of anything." *Can't I?*

The beehive inside his skull rose from its previous low drone to a feverish buzz, as if from a thousand furious yellow jackets.

He had no idea Mike Distefano was reading the list over his shoulder. "Two questions?"

Winthrop nodded. "Sure."

"First, what are those squiggly lines at the end of the list?"

The two detectives exchanged a winsome glance. The nondescript one, Grimes, folded his thin arms across a rail of a chest. "The actual list had something crossed out. That's what they stand for."

"It's aligned with the rest of the names, though."

"Yes," Grimes said, "it was."

"Well, was there another name on the list?"

After a beat, Grimes nodded. "It would fit."

Stadt gasped. "You can find out who it was, can't you?"

"Apparently, Dallas Teller went to great lengths to make sure the name was indecipherable. He used what looked like a pen along with a black permanent marker to cross it out. Lotta layering."

The principal flopped back against his seat, his eyes shut and mouth set. "Christ," he breathed.

Mike reached for the pad, scanned it. "Second question. *In … infernis … arderet?* The tagline at the end."

"Latin," Grimes answered. "It translates: 'Burn In Hell!'"

Conor noticed Mary staring openly at him with eyes that had shed their concern altogether and now favored an open suspicion. A dread. He clutched his skull like a ball in play. The bees were stinging the slipper folds of his brain. "I feel responsible. I should have done more. To help them. To help *him*."

"No," Mary said in a deadened tone, "it doesn't make you responsible. It makes you … *Educator of the Year*. Isn't that right, Conor?"

"All right, Mary," Mike Distefano said, peeling away from the windows. "That's enough."

Conor's spine straightened. "You want to tell me what you're driving at?"

Winthrop waved his hands in the air like a ref rejecting a field goal. "We're getting off track, people!"

Mary turned to face Conor.

"I'll tell you why, Conor," she began. "Because in my opinion, you carry yourself around many of our students in a far too *familiar* way. It's always put me off, but I dismissed it because you're the most popular teacher at Baldwin and no student has ever come to me with concerns about you. However, the number of students visiting my office has spiked in the last couple of months. Students with depressive symptoms. Anxiety issues. Granted, some of these kids have always kind of flown under the radar. They're not social. They don't belong to any clubs. Many have discipline records. But there are also a number of students who have *also* come to my office in tears. Shaking. A member of the student council. The captain of the Cheerleading squad. May I have that pad, Mike?"

Begrudgingly, Mike handed it off to her.

Mary studied the names.

"Student Council? Delaney Lindberg. She's here. Another who'd just been inducted into the National Honors Society. Oh my God, there she is. Stacy Kennedy. And … one of our cheerleaders?" Her face suddenly pinched, Mary flung the pad back onto the table. "She's there too. Valerie Parent!"

Winthrop retrieved the notepad, quietly.

Mary turned her wide eyes to the ceiling, then let them land on Principal Stadt at the head of the table. "I understand the list is a mixed bag, on its surface." She jabbed a thumb at Conor. "Besides the depressive symptoms and the social anxiety, all of which have cropped up in their lives within a two-week span, they all complained of sleep issues."

The air in the conference room thickened. The only sound was that of Detective Winthrop, whose breathing sounded wet and sloshy like his lungs were a washing machine in its second cycle.

Conor shook his head. "Correct me if I'm wrong, Mary, but isn't insomnia a common symptom of depression?"

"It is," she responded, curtly. "But *night terrors* are not. And these students not only described having terrible, haunting night terrors every night, they described their experiences in the *exact same way*."

Principal Stadt said, "Mary, I know we're all on edge right now, but—"

"They all told me they could *not* remember having ever gotten a sound night sleep. Never, Conor."

Winthrop was looking at Conor now.

Mike Distefano.

Detective Grimes, with his big, mopey brown eyes.

Vice Principal Rosner, no longer hunkering into her chair like the fireplug Buddha she'd been the entire time, had come up off her back rest.

And Conor Crenshaw saw all of them once more as the Lovecraftian creature with a thousand eyes, all boring into him with an expectant, unblinking focus.

For a minute, Conor wished for the sound of the psychopathic bees buzzing in the back of his brain. He sure could have used some counsel from his own conscience, the right response.

"So," he blurted out, flashing his trademark smile and perfect, whitened teeth, "in your mind, you think there's a direct connection between myself and all of these students with their insomnia. Because Dallas Teller gripped my arm in the Men's Room back in February before later complaining of the same sleep problem?"

Mike Distefano moved into Conor's purview. "Mary, this is beyond the pale for you. I don't know where your mind is right now, but Conor was nearly the victim of a school shooting. And you're *what*? Beating *him* up and employing some seriously false and—I gotta just say this— *fucked up* logic to cast blame on him?"

Mary and Conor glared at one another like they were the only two people in the conference room.

Principal Stadt knocked on the tabletop. "Mary? Conor? That's enough. Understood?"

Detective Winthrop slid the Referral Form back to Mary, who slowly swiveled back around to face everyone else. Her lips were bloodless. Her cheeks were flushed.

"Listen, Conor," Principal Stadt said, his voice gravelly from overuse, "I think it would be best if you just went home. Take the rest of the day off. Maybe even take a couple days. No one will fault you for that." His eyes flashed at Mary before flicking back to Conor. "We're all with you. Make no mistake about it. You're one of *us,* and we will get to the bottom of this. So you won't feel you have to look over your shoulder for the rest of your career. You're a young guy. A good teacher. Dedicated. We all watched you collect that award at the ceremony last night, and it felt like you were taking home that thing for all of us. For Baldwin. We're sorry this happened." The Principal heaved a sigh. Glanced over at the two detectives. "I'm sure if Detectives, er, Winthrop and Grimes need to speak with you further, you'll make yourself available. Because we know the *what.* What *almost* happened here this morning. But we still need to ascertain the *why.* All right, Conor?"

Beside Conor, Mary stiffened. If one were watching her closely enough in that moment, they would have caught jaw clenching and pockets forming in her cheeks before smoothing again once more.

Conor glanced at her, a fire in his belly lapping at the top of his throat. Then, he nodded, moved to get up. He shook hands with everyone around the table. Mary did not offer him her hand. She kept it under the table in her lap. He shrugged it off because that is simply how *Educator of the Year* Conor Crenshaw treated negativity and negative people, at least in his outward displays. He dismissed them. One of the many things his colleagues like about him, as well as his students. No need to shatter expectations for what they'd get and had always gotten from a stand-up guy like Conor Crenshaw.

On his way out of the conference room, he remembered something that hadn't meant much before the meeting. Before the morning of *the Kill List* of Dallas Teller's, his near assassin.

Mary Marguerite was the only faculty member who had not come to the awards ceremony the night before.

The beehive in the back of Conor's brain buzzed the whole ride home.

But his conscience was completely mum.

III. OTHER VOICES

Conor crept up to bed like a man who wished never to wake up. His shoulders slumped. His feet slid along the tile of the foyer, to and fro, from the cupboard to the refrigerator to pour himself a glass of Merlot, then up the steps and into the master bedroom. The sun blazed through the sheers over the windows. Conor remedied this immediately, yanking the heavy mauve drapes closed. He stood there in the interminable darkness, clutching his glass of wine, and strained to shut out the voice in his head that had hounded him incessantly the whole drive home. The voice was a rich baritone. It did not belong to him. Yet, during the meeting, Conor had convinced himself it was indeed his conscience guiding him through what had proven to be a trying series of exchanges that may very well have won him a forced sabbatical.

The thing of it was, all the while he tried in vain to close off the voice, Conor also strained to identify it.

He wondered if he had a concussion from banging his head against the steering wheel. *Aren't hallucinatory voices a sign of that?*

As Conor stood there sipping at the red wine, his eyes blurring and unfocused, his thoughts spiraled downward until they grazed the bottom of his essence where his deepest fears resided.

Am I losing my mind? I heard my mother's voice. An unknown voice on top of that. Hounding me, for God's sake! Is this what the surgeon was talking about when he mentioned aftereffects? Echoes? If the voice was some kind of echo, it possessed some source of sound. Conor begged to know the source of the sound. To hell with the *echo*, if that's what this was. Who had drilled this mantra into his head if they were echoes of a past conversation?

He tossed back half the glass. The top of his head tingled, not an unpleasant sensation, but it did not halt the voice, now more his aggressor than before when it had been his advisor.

His mother's voice again.

Bad blood, Conny! Come home! Dying. Your wife ...

"I am home!" he cried. "Goddammit! This is my home! You're not making any sense!"

Then, as if that were all it took, Conor found himself drawn into a conversation.

With himself?

And it felt as familiar as slipping into an old pair of worn jeans.

Come home. To mother's house.

"Mother's ... house?" He turned away from the dark draperies as if he would find the speaker standing there behind him. The queen-sized bed was made up to its usual perfection. Maddie, his wife, would have it no other way. The ornamental pillows were piled waist high against the wrought-iron headboard. Conor always hated having to take them all off and arrange them beside his nightstand every night before they went to bed. He strode across the bedroom and set his wine down on his wife's nightstand. With a wide sweep of his arms, Conor drove all the little annoying pillows off the bed. He wrenched the blankets back and slipped inside, not caring how lying around in his pressed slacks and Brooks Brothers shirt, red tie knotted loosely around his throat, would muss the whole ensemble and require a trip to the dry cleaner. He knew he only wanted sleep, and if not sleep, then only to shut his eyes. "Mother's house?!"

Come home. To mother's house. You been gone so long.

"Hey, fuck off! *Fuck off!* I've always, *always* been attentive to my mother! And how dare anyone accuse Maddie of being anything other than a fucking saint. The way she took over care for Mom after my attack. My wife is a saint!" His head hit the pillow hard. It was stiff and felt like a rock. Conor ripped the pillow out from under and threw it across the room. Something crashed. Shattered. "You're not real! This is ridiculous! Fuck! *Off!*"

If sleep did not escape him, Conor resolved to call Dr. Burdon, the surgeon, when he woke up. The kind, doting Indian doctor had given his business card to both Conor and his wife, told them they could call him for any reason.

Ungrateful son ... I got ... bad blood.

The voice thumped off the back of his skull like a ping pong ball, but Conor barely flinched. The wine had already begun to work on his empty stomach and poor brain. The wonderful, wondrous sensation that precedes sleep, that of one's body melting into the mattress, overtook him. His every cell oozed with soft, lovely repose, and it felt so good in comparison to the morning Conor had lived through, he felt tears pinch at the corners of his eyes. Tears of great relief.

He only half-heard the voice in his head before deep sleep claimed him. It did not register.

Your mother is finished. The Queen is dead. There is need for another.

He dreamt of a naked man; his body painted from head to toe in what looked like turpentine that gleamed against his skin. Sinewy build. Skulking. The man's face rose out of depthless darkness, ebbing and flowing as if he were riding an ocean current. The sounds of clicking in the voice. Chattery teeth, perhaps. Elongated fingernails drumming an iron surface. Something. He felt himself spinning out, whirling amid some invisible whirlwind he could neither see nor find his way out of. Buoying him upward, higher and higher until the rolling gray heavens seemed to dip down. To nuzzle him with its cold and its damp. Grating at the skin of his cheeks. Peeling his face away.

"Ah-*nah*!"

The blankets were wound round Conor's whole body threefold, and when he rocketed off the pillow, it felt like someone had strapped him into a straitjacket. He yanked and tore at the sheets. They were stuck to him with his own adhesive sweat. His arms flailing, Conor knocked the phone off the nightstand just as it started to ring.

Conor scrambled off the bed, barely finding his feet. The voice on the other end of the line was shouting, fretful and frightened.

He snatched up the receiver, juggling it gracelessly in the air before finally bringing it up to his ear.

"Hello? Who is it?"

"It's your *wife*, for God's sake! Where have you been? Why aren't you answering your cell phone?"

"Oh … I … I must have left it in the car. I-I'm sorry, honey. I … oh *Jesus*—"

"Why didn't you call me at work?" Maddie Crenshaw pressed, somewhat breathless. "I have to find out about it from one of my coworkers?"

"I'm all right," Conor lied. "It-it's okay. The police got there before the kid made it into the school. They took him away and let all the kids go home."

"Who is he? Did they tell you?"

(*I'm awake, Mr. Crenshaw*)

"Just some troubled Junior boy."

"Did you know him? Was he in your class?"

"I—babe—I knew *of* him, but, you know, b-beyond that …"

A pause on her end. When she broke the silence, Maddie's voice was wracked with trepidation. "I'm going to come home. You don't sound good, Con."

"No—"

"Con!"

"Baby, no!" Conor insisted, glancing all about in the darkened bedroom. He thought he'd heard someone standing beside him. A creaking of the floorboards beneath the rug. The electrical sensation of someone standing within his personal space. He swiped his hand out at the air beside him. Nothing. But still. *I'm not alone. I'm not.*

"What does that mean, Con?"

"What?"

"You just said *you're not alone.* I don't understand."

"Oh … I'm still half-asleep. Coming out of it."

"I don't know what to make of this. I mean … I *dunno* what I mean … so you're okay?"

"Hey, er, Maddie?"

Maddie sighed. "Yes."

"I have, well, kind of a strange question to ask you."

"O-kay. What is it?"

Conor licked his lips, shut his eyes. "Have I always … talked to myself?"

"You mean before you were attacked as well?"

"Yes, exactly."

"Why do you ask?"

"Please! *Honey* … could you just answer my question? I've had … I've had a *day*, Maddie."

Another sigh. "You've always talked to yourself. If you remember, when we moved in together, it took me a while to get used to that quirk of yours. You tricked me so many times into thinking you were talking to me when you weren't. I'd hear you in another room prattling on, and it was strange at first. But I learned how to differentiate between when you *were* talking to *me* and when you were, you know, just trying to sort things out. It's not a big deal. Everyone's got a voice in their head. It's your conscience. It's also your mind problem-solving. Some people just need to, I dunno, broadcast what they're hearing, while others can hold it inside."

She's going to think I'm cracking a joke, but I have to ask. I fucking have to!

"Did you ever hear me answer myself?"

"You mean, have I ever heard what sounded like you were having a conversation with yourself?"

"Right."

"Well," Maddie said, "the weird thing about that is you *did* slip into a dialogue pretty often *before* the attack. I was worried about you for a little while there. You remember I asked you if you needed to talk to somebody. I mean, you were just under so much pressure. I always thought you were taking way too much on at school. Trying to be Superman to everyone. And after the … after what happened, I was certain you needed to offload some of your responsibilities. But I never said anything because I thought you'd be able to tell me when you were feeling overextended and we'd figure it out from there."

"After the attack?"

"Oh, Con, you've had a traumatic day. Are you sure you want to get into this right now?"

"Maddie? After the attack? How was I?"

"Talking to yourself?" Maddie sounded flustered, like her attention had somehow divided against her will. "You stopped."

"All together?" Conor could feel the start of a lightness from within begin to hatch. It was a sense of a relief, a warming sensation emanating from his solar plexus. *The voices aren't real. It's just my body trying to tell me I'm doing too much. It's stress—*

"No, not all together. You still talk to yourself. But not nearly as much as you had before."

It's all right—you're all right, Conor—hold it together.

Maddie breathed into the phone. "And no more dialogue. You stopped answering yourself after your attack at McCauley's Bar."

The sudden spray of what sounded like a bottomless handful of nails flung against the siding of the house made Conor jump. It was not hail season, but that's exactly what he imagined he'd find had he rushed to the window and parted the heavy blinds. Then, his mind submitted to his imagination, a dark animal at play within Conor Crenshaw, and he saw himself looking out the window and finding not hail stones interspersed with fat rain drops but hooded figures floating in the air just outside. Clicking their yellow, elongated fingernails against the pane at a psychopathic rate. Rolling their fingers across the window's surface. Creating hairline fractures in the glass. Weakening it.

Conor turned away from the curtained window and strode across the bedroom, trailing the long phone cord behind him.

"Conor?"

"Yeah? Yeah, I'm here."

"I'm talking to you," Maddie said, frustration flaring her words. "I asked you a question."

"I'm sorry. I must have zoned out."

"Do you want me to come home? I feel like I should be there with you."

"What time is it?"

"What?"

"What time is it?"

"It's a little after one."

"Stay at work," he said. "Stay where you are. I'll talk to you when you get home. I'll tell you everything."

Not quite. Not exactly, Conor. You're still piecing it all together yourself. You don't know everything. *But you will remember.*

"My God, is that rain?"

"Yeah … it just started over here too."

"All right, honey," Maddie relented. "I'll call you in a little bit to see how you're doing. Just promise me you're okay."

Behind him.

Clicketyclackclicketyclackclickety

Conor shuddered from head to toe, but he did not turn around. Would not let himself.

"Con?"

"Yeah?"

"I'll bring home Chinese, and we'll watch the new *Ray Donovan* OnDemand. All right?"

"Good. Sounds good, honey."

"I love you."

The dull throb of the call-waiting tone filled Conor's ear.

Behind him, out the window, the

(nails)

hail dissipated, giving way to a steady tinkling rain.

"That's the other line," Conor said. "Could be school."

"All right."

Conor took a deep breath and clicked over to the other line. "Hello?"

"Yes, this is Officer Kramer. Bensalem Police Department. Is this Conor Crenshaw?"

His breath caught in his throat, clicked against his epiglottis. Ever since Conor could remember, he'd had just this sort of involuntary reaction to the stern and stark gruffness of a police officer. It had been two police officers, with a rumpled-suit detective in tow who was not unlike the two Conor had spoken to earlier at Baldwin, who'd delivered the news to a four-year-old Conor and his mother that David Crenshaw, husband and father, was missing. With their black-brimmed hats over their hearts, they'd talked about how they were in communication with Missing Persons in Genoa, Italy, but the clues they'd managed to gather pointed to an accident while scaling the Apennine Mountains. Conor's mother told him David Crenshaw had always been something of a *thrill seeker*. That she wasn't surprised he'd tried to climb one of the most dangerous mountain ranges in the world without a guide or partner. His father had been in Italy on business. He worked as an independent consultant, advising and guiding various large-scale merchants through what were oftentimes painful growing pains associated with the branching-out process.

While he could rely on the old photographs of his mother and father to see what his father looked like, Conor could not remember the sound of the man's voice. His mother possessed no audio recordings of David Crenshaw, sadly. And he remembered with acute bitterness how everyone in Comstock had turned a cold shoulder to the both shortly after the patriarch's disappearance. Conor wouldn't come to discover the reason for the drastic change in their neighbors and the kids at school until one of his classmates told him his mother was a *bag lady* and had taken to begging for handouts from anyone and everyone who would listen. Conor knew they were poor, but the fact they had a roof over their head and food in the refrigerator dispelled the myth they were destitute enough for his mother to panhandle behind his back. His mother developed a blood disease shortly after the disappearance of his father, and she was unable to work any longer at the Diamond Diner as a waitress. The government dole had kept them afloat, carrying with it a stigma all its own for those who knew how the Crenshaw's subsisted.

Yes, Comstock had proven a cold and uncaring place for the mother and son, and Conor never forgot it. Neither did his mother, who grew more and more embittered towards its inhabitants as the years went by.

"Mr. Crenshaw? Is this you?"

"Yes, Officer. I'm Conor Crenshaw. Is something wrong?"

In the background, a CB gurgled and muddled Officer Kramer's first few words in response.

"I'm sorry, Officer. I didn't catch that."

"—asked is your mother Matilda Crenshaw?"

You've failed us, son. You're weak. You must be reminded.

It hurt when Conor blinked his eyes, like a gnat had attached itself to his cornea. He clutched the phone with both hands, squeezing it until it clicked.

"I am. Is everything all right?"

"Mr. Crenshaw, we're over at your mother's house. We received a call from a neighbor who was concerned they hadn't seen her in almost a week. They also mentioned you usually come every day to see her. That you hadn't been by in months. Your mother lives alone?"

"Yes. But my wife has been taking care of her! I've been sick, you see."

Bad blood. Your bitch-whore wife.

Officer Kramer cleared his throat. "I'm sorry to have to tell you this, but we entered your mother's home and found her at the bottom of the cellar stairs. She's dead."

"But my wife ..." Conor clutched his head. The bees were awake, bouncing off the inside of his skull. Glancing off the tough bone. Awake. Alive. "She's been taking care of Mom and her transfusions."

"Transfusions?"

"M-my mother ... she had—*has* a blood disorder. Porphyria."

The words pushed their way out of him without his having to think about it.

And they felt like a lie. There came the quickening of his pulse which usually accompanies the telling of an untruth. The stirring in the gut. The guilt. And with that lie, which had come so easy to him, the floodgates of Conor Crenshaw's memory banged open and his brainpan was awash in everything his poor brain had failed to remember in the months following the attack at McCauley's Bar.

"What is that?" Officer Kramer repeated, his patience wearing thin on the other end.

"She's *not* dead! She *can't be dead!*"

"Can you come, sir? We'll be here—"

Conor spun around and hurled the phone at the curtained window. It shattered the pane behind the heavy mauve curtains, and the torrential winds outside sucked at the fabric, pulling it through the break in the pane and then inflating it like a balloon. The curtains looked like they were breathing. The sound of the fingernails against the glass started again, only now every tap knocked pieces of broken glass away to be taken away by the Gulf Stream gusts that had traveled all the way north to hammer Conor's house in southeastern Pennsylvania. To drive him insane with the sudden onslaught of seemingly lost or repressed memories.

Of who he'd been.

The monster he was. The puppet.

The *Educator of the Year* who wore a human face to conceal the predator beneath.

Conor strode towards the window. The curtains had parted just enough the rain rushed in, falling sideways, and dappling his face. He drew the curtains all the way with a violent sweep of his hands.

Clicketyclackclicketyclackclicketyclack

They were waiting for him, just as he'd expected they would be.

Hovering.

Dancing on air.

His brothers and sisters.

The family he never had and always wanted.

"I'm ... awake."

He picked a shard of glass up off the windowsill and got to cutting.

IV. RECONSTRUCTING THE EGO

(*Six Weeks Later*)

Maddie Crenshaw had only ever spoken to Baldwin High School's Guidance Counselor in passing at a faculty holiday party or Commencement Ceremony. Even then, Maddie always got the impression Mary Marguerite was cross with her for some reason. So when Maddie got the call from Mary Marguerite six weeks after her husband opened his wrists and nearly died, the mystery of the guidance counselor's veiled animosity only seemed to deepen for her.

"Mrs. Crenshaw, can we meet?" Mary Marguerite had asked, calling Maddie at her job, of all places. "I wanted to talk to you about Conor."

This had rubbed Maddie the wrong way at first. "About ... my husband?"

"Yes, whenever you're free."

"He's doing better, by the way. Thanks for asking." Maddie had almost hung up the phone on the snooping little bitch, but Mary said something that convinced Maddie it was more than worthwhile for the two of them to meet.

"I'm sorry," Mary said. "I'm glad he's doing all right. But we've got a situation that has been evolving over at the school. With some of our students. All of them were rather close to Conor."

Now seated towards the back of the narrow coffee shop ten miles north of Baldwin High School, Maddie tried not to let her imagination get the better of her.

What if Conor did something to his students? What if he—oh God, I can't even think about it.

The coffee shop was littered with hipsters and businessmen, slumped in their chairs and blinking fatigue out of their eyes as they stared into over-bright laptop screens. An old couple stared vacantly across a booth table at one another, nursing their Earl Grey teas and looking resigned to the fate of the rest of their days. The sight of them hurt Maddie's heart. *I don't know that Conor and I will ever have that. Not now.* Sipping her pumpkin-spice latte as she peered over the top of the rim, Maddie stuffed the regret down when she saw Mary Marguerite slip inside the shop.

The woman looked like she'd just evaded a stalker. Mary snuck a glance behind her, out the glass panel of the entrance door. Then, satisfied, she nodded to herself and swiped a bottled water quickly off a nearby cooler shelf. There was no line in queue, so she dropped three dollars on the counter for the barista, then without a word between them, Mary surged towards the back of the shop like she'd just felt the nip of an aggressor at the heels of her flats.

I don't remember her looking so— harassed? Terrified? Like a paranoiac.

When Mary reached the table, her smile was visibly strained, as if it were painted on.

"Thank you for coming, Mrs. Crenshaw," she muttered, slipping down into the seat across the small, oval table from Maddie. Mary did not look at Maddie straight on, which seemed even more perplexing, as most counselors are big on eye-to-eye contact. Body language. The guidance counselor's body language told a story to Maddie of paranoia, at least the beginning stages of something full-blown. Mary sat with her body angled sideways, nearly out of her seat altogether.

"Please," Maddie said, "call me Maddie. May I call you Mary?"

"Yes, of course," Mary agreed, and popped the cap off her water. She took a swig and her cheeks flushed. "I'm sorry. I'm, I'm pretty spooked."

"Why? What happened?" Maddie cast a curious glance towards the front door, almost expecting to find some shady looking character peering in through the glass. There was no one.

"I just … I've never been frightened or unnerved by … children. I…"

Mary stalled, opened her eyes wide, smoothed down the rumples in her skirt, and when she looked up at Maddie again, it seemed like there was a completely different woman sitting there. "How are you holding up, Maddie?"

The question itself touched a nerve inside her that nearly called tears to her eyes. Maddie managed to hold them at bay. "It's lonely. Crippling, at times. You know, I have no family. No siblings. It's just me. My co-workers have no idea what happened. I won't tell them. They'd look at me a certain way from then on, and I like where I work. So, to hear someone ask me how I'm doing?" Maddie paused, chewed her lip some. "Thank you. For asking."

"Well, I've got nowhere to be," Mary said, winsomely. "I don't have my daughter. So you take your time. And I'll take my time. Would that be all right?"

"A daughter?" Maddie asked, brightening some. "What's her name?"

"Her name's Jenny. She's five. And she's well, she's on the spectrum, so it's been challenging, especially with my husband and I living at separate residences. But somehow we've made it work." Mary's eyes turned vacant for a moment, then she snapped back. "But … back to you, Maddie."

Maddie nodded, started slowly. "I would need this to stay between the two of us."

"Of course," Mary obliged. "I'd ask the same from you."

Maddie nodded.

"I … I gave the school a *very* abridged version of what happened with Conor. To protect him. And to make sure when he gets better, he'll have a job to go back to. Right now, though, it's really in God's hands whether he ever gets back into a classroom. It's going to be a long road."

"Your husband, he's greatly admired among the students. Some of it is a healthy admiration, like the kind a young adult reserves for a parent or a sports hero. But, Maddie, there is also the *unhealthy* side of admiration, which morphs into idolatry. Hero worship. Blind allegiance."

"You make it sound like my husband's moonlighting as David Koresh or something. Why are you doing that?"

"I'm only working from the knowledge and the experiences I've gathered thus far regarding Conor and, namely, his favorite students. And you should know, your husband admitted to having a close relationship with all the students on the potential school-shooter's kill list."

Maddie's eyes flashed. "Is that why you asked me here? To blacken my husband's name? To cast aspersions about a man you barely know yourself? His background? Any of it? Or are you merely making assumptions because you have no other way of explaining why this happened! What are you, some kind of sadist? Do you know what I've been through already?"

Mary nodded. "I'm sorry. I want to understand. I don't mean to sound presumptuous … and I'm probably wrong about a great deal of what concerns me. It's just …there are these nine students. The very same students on Dallas Teller's kill list. They've formed a formidable cluster. Seemingly out of nowhere. It's more dramatic than I originally explained to you."

"My God, *you're* the Guidance Counselor here!"

"Maddie, please—"

"It makes perfect sense to me, and I don't even have a PhD after my name."

"I know what you're going to say—"

"Those nine kids are clearly bonding because they're badly shaken by the fact they were nearly shot and killed by some psycho."

"Maddie, if you'll let me finish?"

Some of the hot blood that had engorged Maddie's cheeks flushed away, and she gathered herself. Quietened.

Mary took a breath. "None of them know they were on the list."

"What? Nobody told them?"

"We decided it would be better that they not know." Mary paused. "That's not to say the parents haven't banded together to demand the identities of the marked students be released. But we're holding strong against that. And the superintendent agrees with our stance."

"Well, I guess that makes sense."

"And Conor——"

"Again, *what does that have to do with my husband?*"

"Maddie," Mary said, evenly, "the situation has evolved in the last month and a half. Well beyond what I've just told you."

Maddie avoided Mary's eyes, her head shaking continuously as if on a swivel.

"There are nine of them," Mrs. Marguerite said in a low voice, like she feared being listened in upon. "The students on the list. Five girls and four boys. A few of them are discipline problems, but there are also a few scholars, the captain of the Cheerleading team, even the Junior Class President mixed in with them. This rarely happens. Cliques don't normally mix with one another so dramatically." Mary hesitated. "They have started to see themselves as an extension of your husband in his absence. Spray paint tags have been showing up in stairwells. Bathroom stalls. The gym locker room was graffitied so horrendously the whole place has to be repainted."

Maddie looked at Mary, an eyebrow raised. "And what's the tag?"

"*Crenshaw's Children,*" Mrs. Marguerite said. "I know this is the *nine.*"

"The *nine?*"

"I'm sorry," Mary said. "I know how it sounds. But it's how I've been referring to them. And *Crenshaw Children?* They walk through the halls *nine across.* No one behind and no one in front. And the halls are not wide enough to accommodate that sort of thing. Not to mention, there are lockers on both sides. Students standing there trying to gather their books or take a sip of water or check their look in the mirror, even. So, what do you think has been happening repeatedly in the hallways when The Nine walk nine across while students are at their lockers?"

What Mary Marguerite was describing reminded Maddie of some great robotic hand sweeping down the hallway of Baldwin, unyielding and destructive.

"Well," Mary said, "it's just what you'd imagine. They keep moving, oblivious and blind to the other students in their path. A Sophomore girl turned her ankle when one of The Nine tread on her and turned it under his shoe. The girl's parents complained, and we hauled all nine of the kids in. They were very apologetic and insisted it was nothing more than a *goof.* But, sure enough, a few days later, The Nine were walking side-by-side wide across the halls once more. Banging into the freshmen. Oblivious. Trance-like, even. I caught them doing it once." Mary stalled, drummed her fingers along the edge of the small oval table. "Their expressions. Their … eyes."

"What about them?"

"They looked strained. Not in control. Helpless."

"Helpless?"

"Mouths pulled back into these rictus grins. Skin tighter than normal, like they'd all taken their faces off and then just stapled them back on." A breezy sigh. "I *know* how this all sounds. I really do."

For a minute or so, neither woman spoke or looked at one another. They nursed their beverages, Maddie sipping while Mary pulled long and deep from her Fiji water bottle.

The old couple nearby stood up, and the old man laid his hand across his wife's back as she navigated their way towards the door. That small, simple gesture filled Maddie to bursting with the need to stick up for her husband. To *have his back* just like that old man had his wife's back, quite literally.

"My husband tried to take his life that night, Mary."

Mary blanched at her. "I-I ... the way it was explained to all of us was—"

"I know what was said because it's what I told Tony Stadt. The fact a boy had come to the school to kill him had shaken him to the core. And I said *we*, as a couple, decided it would be best for him to take a leave of absence. But ... yes, that night, Conor tried to kill himself. And I had to fight for weeks to keep the hospital from three-oh-twoing him. When someone tries to kill themselves or shows they could be a threat to someone else, the hospital works in accordance with the police to determine whether that person should be *committed*. That's what three-oh-two means. And I almost lost that battle because Conor refused treatment. He refused to take their meds or participate in their groups."

"Why wouldn't he want to get better? I don't understand the resistance."

"Because, Mary, my husband believed he didn't deserve to live, let alone feel better."

Mary made a motion as if to say something, but her mouth clapped audibly shut and she settled back against her chair. "Okay," she said, "I was wondering about two things. I was hoping you could shed some light."

"Regarding Conor?"

"Yes," she said, then added, "and not to pry. These teens seem to have developed some form of obsession with your husband beyond the norm. I'm only trying to make sense of all of this because it sounds very much like I have nine students at Baldwin who are suffering from mental illness or anxiety, in the very least. And this? This is an anomaly, to put it lightly. After what happened six weeks ago, I've got to make sure every move we make with these kids is a well-informed one. You understand? Will you help me?"

It took a moment. Maddie sat there staring at Mary with vacant eyes. Inside, she was deliberating. Finally, she nodded stiffly, after having come to the disheartening realization Conor would probably never teach at Baldwin ever again. This would not tarnish his reputation, and if the guidance counselor dared to break the sanctity of the conversation, it would not hurt Conor as much as it would hurt the woman's reputation for being a decent human being. "All right," Maddie said. "Go ahead."

"As cliché as this is going to sound, what do you know about Conor's childhood? His background?"

Maddie paused, contemplating her words. "Conor did not have a healthy upbringing, to be honest. He may have thought he did, but I disagree. I tried not to lock horns with him about his mother, even though we never got along. His father disappeared while on a business trip overseas. They never heard from him again. Conor was too young to really remember much of anything about him, but his mother explained some things. Apparently, the man was something of a … a thrill-seeker? He was a consultant for business, domestic and abroad. As Conor explained it, his father had business in Italy. While there, being the man he was, Conor's father had worked hiking into his travels. He vanished in the Apennine Mountains. They never heard from or saw him again."

"And how do you think that affected Conor?"

"Wow, I really am starting to feel like you're going to charge me a fee at the end of this conversation, but … okay, well do I think Conor growing up without a father affected him adversely in some way? I don't even have to think about my answer, sadly."

"Really?"

"I think when his father disappeared, his mother cracked and decided her son would fill the void of her husband. And I mean, if the woman had her way, Conor would have … I dunno."

"Are you saying Conor's mother craved a physical relationship with Conor?"

"All I'm going to say is Tilly Crenshaw has always wanted her son all to herself. According to Conor, no girl he ever brought home made it through the front door without Tilly insulting them, then feigning ignorance. She knew what she was doing. She punished Conor a lot, grounding him not for weekends. Not for weeks. The woman grounded him for months if he didn't roll up the toothpaste from the bottom. Conor missed out on his entire Freshman year, all the socials and the dances and the mixers. Tilly grounded him for a year. Wanna know why?"

Mary nodded.

"She'd sniffed out his personal journal and read about Conor's— his first time."

"So, young Conor would have been fourteen the first time he had sex?"

"No," Maddie said, shaking her head derisively. "He says it was, but I don't believe him."

"Why?"

Maddie paused, a tear forming in the corner of her left eye. It held its precarious position until she blinked. That sent it skating down her cheek. "Because Conor has this tic. He … he's always—for as long as I have known him—talked to himself. It's … I'm sorry, it's just."

"Don't be sorry," Mary said, snatching her purse off the table and fishing inside for a thing of tissues. She slipped one out, and Maddie accepted it without a word.

"It's just, the last conversation, I mean *real* conversation I had with him was that night. And he was asking me about his habit of talking to himself. He couldn't remember how often he did it before he was attacked. He also couldn't remember there were many times I had heard him carrying on entire conversations with himself when he thought I wasn't around. It practically stopped altogether after the attack. I can only assume the beating he took, in the head especially, must have somehow affected the part of his brain that longed for such a thing. I dunno."

"It doesn't make sense that Conor craved affection from the very woman who made his life a living hell during his formative years."

"Not to mention, he was the doting son as an adult," Maddie said, almost lamenting this. "He told me his mother suffered from a blood disorder called EPP. I can't remember what that stands for, but it's rare. The woman initially refused to allow any nurse to come in and care for her, but Conor can't give her the blood transfusions she needs, so Tilly had no choice. Every other day, Conor would meet the nurse at Tilly's house and he'd oversee things so, you know, the woman didn't try anything or become abusive to the caregiver. But that wasn't enough for his mother, and she placed such high demands on his time. He went over there two, sometimes three days a week just to care for her on his own. I went out and got her a Life Alert bracelet so Conor wouldn't have to worry, and he wouldn't have to go over so often. The woman wouldn't take it, let alone wear it, and she sent him back home with it. Conor bought her a wheelchair because the blood disorder weakened her. He said she refused to use that either, but that stayed. He said he insisted on that, at least."

"What is this disorder? What do you know?"

"I know it's an iron deficiency in the blood. Conor told me the iron is called *heme*? Her body doesn't produce enough of it on its own. This causes extreme photosensitivity, and, according to Conor, if Tilly dared to go outside during the day, her skin would blister." Shaking her head morosely, Maddie paused and went on. "Conor said she developed it at an advanced age, which is an anomaly in and of itself. Usually, EPP is a children's blood disorder."

"Sounds like a lot of pressure for Conor."

"I mean, I know you shouldn't speak ill of the dead."

"Oh, I'm so sorry!" Mary gasped. "When?"

Maddie looked right at her, deadpan. "Conor got the call she was gone right before he ... before he tried to kill himself." She wet her dry lips. "*That* was the hold this woman had on her son."

"But why would he do that?"

"Because he felt responsible for her death, I imagine."

"If he was doing everything you say he was doing to care for her, then I don't really see how he could blame himself for her death. How old was she?"

"Sixty-two." Maddie fell quiet. The handful of patrons buzzed and sipped at their drinks while a Leonard Cohen song droned on in the background from the speakers in the ceiling. "If there's anyone who should feel at least a touch of guilt, it's me."

"Why is that?"

"After Conor was attacked, his memory was impaired, as you all know at Baldwin. That was common knowledge. But even the level of *that* severity was not fully communicated. My husband's wishes. And I honored them. He didn't want to leave teaching, and he didn't want to be asked to leave. As far as I know, he continued to do well in the classroom. He got that award. *Educator of the Year.* I know a part of him thought it was just a pity award for the guy who nearly died on a South Philly street a few months back. He never said this outright to me, but I think he would have if the award ceremony hadn't taken place the night before his breakdown. Our conversations since the breakdown have been ... spare. Strange."

Mary sipped at her water, replaced the cap. Nodded, sympathetically.

"I had to take over the duties of caring for Tilly. Conor just couldn't remember to get over there like he used to. There was some kind of block there that had formed. He had stopped talking to himself, at least whenever I was around him. It was almost as if a better part of him, a calmer and more rational part of him had emerged. Something good born of something horrific, if a violent attack can be viewed as a blessing in a way? It set something right inside him. He had found inner peace like never before. I didn't want to disturb that, so I saw to Tilly. I called the caregiver service Conor told me he'd hired to administer Tilly's transfusions." Maddie stopped cold, lost in thought.

"What?"

"He was giving her the transfusions himself," Maddie said, her throat dry and voice scratchy. "There was never any nurse. I got that much out of him. But Conor became upset. Distressed by my questioning him, so I let it go. Honestly, I don't know how the woman didn't die with Conor giving her the transfusions. Where did he get the blood? How did he make this all happen without the help of a nurse? I wanted to ask him so damn bad, but he was so fragile. So I let that go too. I made the arrangements to have a nurse meet me at Tilly's. I was going to set this right. See, I knew this was because Tilly probably guilted him into doing it himself. She probably flat-out refused to have anyone else come in.

"A part of me looked forward to telling her who's boss for the first time in her life. She had no sway over me. She never liked me. I could've cared less for her if she wasn't my husband's mother. I met the nurse at Tilly's house. Tilly lives over in Endsley, in one of those post World War II A-frame homes. People call the place 'A-Town' on account of the fact every house bears the same exact cookie-cutter architecture. The nurse—her name was Milly Stone—was this nice black woman with a handshake like a bear. Strong hands. Kind eyes. I liked her right away.

"Tilly didn't want either of us in the house, and she even went so far as to grab the phone to call the police. She wanted to report us as intruders. But I knew she was bluffing. Tilly was beyond melodramatic, and I knew she wouldn't want the cops there either. So, I waited until she relented, tossed up her stick-like arms, and seemed to surrender. Milly the Nurse readied the equipment at the kitchen table and Tilly sat there. But she started muttering something to herself. Over and over. Like a prayer. I was close enough to hear some of what she was saying." Maddie paused, continued. "The woman was praying to ... her husband. His name was Robert. I heard it. She must have been worse off mentally than I realized.

"I should have known better," Maddie said, grimly. "When Milly tried to stick the needle into Tilly's arm, the old woman took her hand and bit into it so deep, blood started gushing immediately. It happened so quickly. I couldn't believe the old woman had the strength in her jaw or teeth sharp enough to do such damage. But the wound, after I helped Milly bandage and disinfect it … the teeth marks were so deep and jagged it looked like she'd been mauled by a dog."

"Maybe dementia?"

"Oh no," Maddie protested. "That woman knew exactly what she was doing. And if Milly the Nurse hadn't been in the field and experienced things ten times worse than what Tilly did to her, we probably would have been sued. Milly went out to her car and came back with these padded gloves that went all the way up her arms. She told me to hold Tilly's head still. The woman tried to bite me, but I got a good hold on her, and Milly was able to deliver the transfusion. It made the old woman vomit a half an hour later. By that time, Milly was gone, and it was just me and her. Tilly was weak. Couldn't put up a fight. I told her right then and there how things were going to be from then on. I pulled no punches."

"Did she have anything to say?"

"She called out to her husband a couple times, head lolling all over the place. Her voice weak, barely there. 'I can't wait any longer,' she said, probably to him too. 'You have to come now. It can't wait any longer. I've been poisoned!' I can only assume she was trying to guilt me into feeling bad by saying she wanted to be with her dead husband. Or that I had somehow poisoned the old witch. For the man to come and, I dunno, *take her away from their evil daughter-in-law*. I dunno. But the nurse kept coming. Every other day. The transfusions ran like clockwork. And I had assumed the role of caretaker. Conor … it was almost like he'd forgotten he even had a mother. And, I know how this is going to sound, but I think that was why he seemed more at peace. I let him forget about her."

"It sounds like it was for the best."

Maddie withdrew her hands from the table and dropped them defeatedly in her lap. She dropped her gaze, sniffed at the air. "You don't understand. Conor refuses to believe she's dead. He insists that Tilly can't die. Conor insists I … I buried his mother alive. He even tried to attack me when I told him that I'd seen to her burial and the headstone was coming soon. I consulted with his psychiatrist at the clinic where he's staying, and she told me while the anti-psychotic pills he's on have caused hallucinations and paranoia in some patients, the number is so low it's negligible. Conor is still on the same cocktail of meds. And he is singing a different tune. It's a tune I've never heard him sing before. If I'd heard it from him before I said *I do*, I can assure you I would have run for the hills. I want to believe it's the meds and his doctor will eventually see that and switch him to something else. But I don't know how much longer I can hang on. It's all just wearing me down to a little nub." Maddie hesitated, added, "It won't be long before I feel like I'll need to check in at the clinic for an extended stay."

"Maddie, have you ever heard of *gaslighting*?"

Maddie shook her head. "No."

"It's a psychological term for when someone who is mentally ill manipulates a loved one by insisting so fervently their delusions are real that the loved one begins to doubt what reality is. They want to believe the sick person isn't as delusional as it seems, so they try to reconcile their rational mind with that of the false beliefs. That's called *gaslighting*. And it's what your husband is doing to you. And you can't let him, Maddie. Do you hear me?"

"I-I don't believe anything that he's told me. I mean, how could I?"

"Give me your hand, lady," Mary said, offering her own across the table. After a moment, Maddie's hand slipped out from under the table and she took it. Mary could feel the tremor coursing through Maddie's fingers. "Keep after that psychiatrist of his. If this is not *your husband*, then the psychiatrist needs to adapt to that fact and change Conor's med regimen."

Speechless, Maddie Crenshaw could only turn her head away to stare off into space. She sucked the inside of her cheek thoughtfully. But no words.

Mary gave Maddie's hand another nurturing squeeze. "Why don't we go?"

"No," Maddie said, looking at Mary with sodden, swollen eyes. "No-no-no. You said you need to know everything so you could help these children. Maybe even my husband. And … I trust you now. I don't think you're the enemy."

"I never was. I only want to help. But if you want to talk later—"

"I want to get it all out," Maddie insisted. "Because I don't want to sift through all this—this *shit*—ever again!"

"All right."

"Conor's attack."

"Are you sure?"

"He's not a bad guy. I know how all of this makes him look; like he's too whipped by his own mother to put me first. But he tried to keep everyone happy. His mother. His students. Me. And if I blame anyone for the mess we're currently in, I can trace it all back to his mother. And not just because he was *at* that bar the night he got beat up *because of her*!"

"How?" Mary asked, while inside she couldn't shake off the question, *How do you not see you never really knew your husband at all? How can you still take up for him like this?*

"McCauley's Bar was where his mother and father met thirty-five years ago. And so when Tilly read in the newspaper a little while back that the space had been recently purchased by a Wawa and they were going to gut the bar within the next couple of days, she asked Conor to pay a visit there before they closed their doors forever. There were live bands. Bagpipes. Green beer, even though it wasn't St. Patty's Day. An Irish bar, you know! Tilly was in no condition to go to the event, so she sent Conor there. She wanted him to ask the owner, Casey McCauley, if he could have one of the photographs on the wall. Casey had a section of wall designated for all the photographs of couples who met at the bar or got engaged there. He called it the 'Wall of Venus.' I guess he was kind of a romantic himself.

"So Conor did as his mother asked. He decided to stick around and watch the festivities, even though he didn't know anybody there. The way he describes it, the exact moment he sat down there were five guys hanging out at the end of the bar who just started right in on him. Shouting things like 'Can't believe you'd come *back* after that bullshit you just pulled!' and 'You *must* have a death-wish, mother-effer!' Conor had *no* idea what they were talking about, and he thought it would pass if he just kept his head down and drank his beer. The bartender came up to him and gave him this weird once-over like he was making sure Conor was old enough to drink there or something. Then, the bartender walked down to the end of the bar and got into an argument with the five guys who were giving Conor such a hard time. Conor heard the bartender telling them 'It ain't the guy! Now, you're upsetting the good people here who just want to have a good time! Do I gotta throw you out?' They kept on arguing, but finally relented, and it looked like they had settled some. They were still eyeballing Conor the whole time, only then they kept it on the downlow. So, Conor had his word with Casey McCauley about the photograph of his mother and father, got it along with a fond clap on the back from the owner, and then Conor settled up. He walked out.

"The five guys followed him out onto the sidewalk. They kept on, something about Conor owing them the money he stole from them earlier in the day. Again, Conor had no idea, and he tried to convince them they had the wrong guy. 'You're wearing the same fucking ratty-ass Phillies cap you had on earlier. Now I *know* there ain't two pieces of shit like that on two asshole heads!' I saw the police video. There was a camera mounted on the light pole just outside. No sound, but I could only imagine what they were saying. Negating everything Conor was saying. Inching closer to him. Circling him like a bunch of fucking sharks. Three minutes must have passed.

"Then, my God, it was so chilling to watch—especially without any sound—the five of them just stopped cold. They all straightened up. They pulled their hoodies up over their heads, and then they just started beating Conor. Mercilessly. For five minutes. No one was around. I imagine anyone who had been around wasn't about to jump in the middle of it. I had to have the detective who showed it to me turn it off when they started kicking him in the head. They had on boots."

It hadn't occurred to Mary just how tight her grip had become on Maddie's hand until she saw her own knuckles had become white pearls pushed up against thin skin. "Oh, I'm sorry." She lessened her hold but did not let go. Mary imagined Maddie would not have wanted her to if she had. "It was mistaken identity, you said. What prompted them to do this?"

Maddie laughed desperately. "A beat-up Phillies cap. Wrinkled and sunken in all the right places so Conor looked enough like the guy who, earlier that day, had stolen tip money those five guys had left on the bar for their waitress. They called the guy on it, but he had played dumb and walked out. And the five guys weren't nearly drunk enough nor angry enough to go after him. Not to mention, the bartender talked them out of it, and they were much more reasonable only a few beers in. By the time Conor came walking in, the men were trashed, and they couldn't see straight. All they saw was that my husband had on a hat similar to the thief's hat, enough black scruff on his cheeks to resemble the thief's facial hair, and Conor probably stood to the same height. That was all they needed. So they beat him, and he almost died. They lost him twice on the way to the hospital."

"Oh God," Mary sighed. "I ... I feel like a broken record. You must forgive me for sounding like one, but I *really* had no idea ..."

Sniffling, Maddie nodded. "Again," she muttered, "I was trying to protect Conor. And now ... I feel like I've lost him all over again. Maybe for good this time."

"Oh, Maddie."

"He's not Conor anymore. My husband is *gone*. He's ... it's like he's finally gone crazy. Unless the things he's been spouting out in the last six weeks are the truth and this is who Conor *really* is. The other *Conor*, the 'Educator of the Year,' the loving husband; that was the delusional side of him."

"Let's not jump to—"

The bell on the door to the coffee shop chimed, drawing the eyes of everyone inside. Maddie looked toward the entrance. Mary craned around in her seat, and when she saw them filing in from the street, the air went audibly out of her like she was deflating.

"Mary?"

"Ssh." Mary swiveled back around to face Maddie Crenshaw. Her face looked pinched, tightening by the minute. She mouthed something to Maddie, but she didn't understand at first. Mary leaned in, grasped Maddie's hand once more. "The *Nine*."

They did not make an entrance like any typical grouping of teenagers, all giggles and sarcasm. The Nine (as Mary had dubbed them) entered The Coffee Bean like they were filing into a viewing, waiting to say goodbye to a loved one for all time. They snaked sullenly through the aisles of the coffee shop and silently filled two booths roughly five feet from where Mary and Maddie were seated.

When Maddie had first started dating Conor and he was a newbie teacher, it was annoying how many of his students they would run into no matter the setting. Aside from the bar where Maddie and Conor wet their whistles together, she and Conor could not go anywhere without someone calling out to "*Mr. Crenshaw!*" from across a crowded supermarket or a bustling restaurant. They joked about how Conor had become a "small-town celebrity." They'd also made light of the whole phenomenon by saying his students were like his *children*. "Children with a thousand eyes," Conor had said, laughing while

Maddie tried not to let it get to her that they never had any privacy when out in public.

They're like my children. I swear he said that.

They were looking at Maddie and Mary. The Nine.

Maddie's initial instinct was not to dread them, but rather to laugh at them. Just like she'd laughed over and over at the varied, diversely experienced troublemakers serving a Saturday morning detention in *The Breakfast Club*. It did not take much effort at all to identify which of The Nine filled the roles of *the jock, the princess, the brainy nerd, the freak, and the criminal*. They were all there, seated a skip and a jump away, with their wrinkle-ringed, bloodshot eyes boring into her and Mary like their minds had all been wiped. There was more than one *criminal and freak* rounding out The Nine. This was also no surprise to Maddie. It made sense.

Crenshaw's Children.

No, The Nine! Maddie's brain screamed.

"Hey!" one of the boys called to them. He was wearing a jean jacket a size too small for him and sporting longish black hair that looked like it hadn't been shampooed since infancy. Fat flakes of dandruff stood in the severe part down the center of his head. "Hey, Mrs. Marguerite! Why didn't you say *hi* back! We saw you outside and we waved, but you didn't say *hi* back!"

Craning her neck in their direction, Mary nodded stiffly. "Hello, Harry. I didn't see you."

"Yeah," Harry Hastings said, "but there's no way you didn't hear us! Why didn't you say *hi* back … Mary?"

Mary turned around all the way, her cheeks blooming red. "You will address me as Mrs. Marguerite, Harry. Do you understand?"

The other kids shook their heads dismissively. The *cheerleader* did not drop her eyes or move her head. She looked like a piece of waxwork.

Harry Hastings blinked vapidly. "But … you didn't say *hi* back?"

"Yes, well, you're just going to have to get over it, Harry. Aren't you?"

Maddie moved to grab her handbag off the floor of the coffeeshop, a sign she hoped Mary would interpret to mean it was time to go.

But Mary did not get up to leave. She stood, her back rigid and mouth a bloodless line as she moved closer to The Nine in their booth. "I know you followed me here from school. I saw you. Waiting on the front sidewalk until I pulled out of the parking lot. Then, you followed behind me."

The *cheerleader* blanched at this. "How did we manage to do *that*, Mary?"

"You will call me *Mrs. Marguerite, Valerie Parent!*"

"You were in a car, and we were on foot. How could we have kept up with you?"

"Are you calling me a liar, Valerie?"

Valerie glared up at Mary, slack-jawed like she'd just been slapped. Then, the cheerleader echoed Harry Hastings. "You … it's just … you didn't say *hi* back."

Mary folded her arms, bit her lower lip. Her eyes flashed with scorn, sweeping the faces of the nine students spread across two booths. "What is wrong with all of you?"

The hairs on the back of Maddie's neck stood to full attention. *These kids are on something. Damned if I know what.*

Mary kicked the side of the booth nearest her with the tip of her flats.

"Out with it! I'll see you all in detention before you'll disrespect me like this. You are representatives of Baldwin High School no matter where you are. That means you are to conduct yourselves as young ladies and gentlemen at *all times*!"

A girl in a big black sweater with holes cut out of the wrist for her to poke her thumbs out of cleared her throat and looked up at Mary. The pockets under her eyes were so pronounced, Maddie found herself wondering just how long a person could go without sleep before insanity set in or death took them.

"Something happened, Mrs. Marguerite," the girl said in a flat tone, her face as void of emotion as the others. "I-I don't understand, Tara. *What* are you talking about?"

"She's gone."

"Who's gone? You're not making any sense."

"We need you to get a message to Mr. Crenshaw. From all of us."

At this, Maddie stepped up, yanking her handbag back up her shoulder. "I'm Mr. Crenshaw's wife. And before you ask to have a message relayed to him, I'm asking you to cool it with this *Crenshaw's Children* business. No more graffiti around the school. That's it. You were all his favorites, I'm guessing? What do you think Mr. Crenshaw would have to say if he knew you were defacing the school using his name?"

It was as if Maddie were not even there, had not said a word. The Nine did not let go of Mary Marguerite with their eighteen eyes.

-my students have a thousand eyes-

Harry Hastings slapped the tabletop with the flat of his right palm. "*Just …* say *hi!*"

"I'll be calling your mother tonight, Harry," Mary culled. "The moment I get home. Do you hear me?"

The boy tilted his head, savant-like. "*And the phone, it rang and it rang.*"

"*and rang,*" Valerie Parent, the cheerleader picked up the thread.

"*and rang,*" Tara Neeley, the girl with the black sweater full of holes kept it going.

Then, it became a chant that drowned out Mary, although she did not give up. She raised her voice in return to be heard.

"*What* are you *playing at*? All of you?"

Maddie edged in closer to Mary, touched her arm. "Let's go. We're getting nowhere. They're just kids testing our limits. That's all."

The barista had come out from behind the counter, and she was cutting a path right towards them. As she drew closer, her hand shot out, index finger stabbing at the air in their direction. "Either order something and lower your voices or leave! I mean it!"

"and *rang* and *rang*."

Maddie tugged on Mary's arm, trying to lead her away. The barista stood a few feet away, hands on her aproned hips.

That's when Valerie Parent's finger fell upon Mary's free hand, encircling her wrist with the strength of an iron manacle. Mary remembered the girl's eyes as having once been a deep, clear blue. Now, they shuddered within the sockets so quick glimpses of black bordering the eyeballs showed in so brief an instant, it might have been imagined. In a small, childish voice, she begged. "So soon?"

It cut Mary and Maddie to the bone.

The barista ripped off her apron and surged forward just as Maddie pulled Mary out of her path and roughly guided her towards the door.

They burst through the door just as the red sun in the west melted into the pitching treetops of a copse of elms across the street from the coffee house. Neither of them questioned why it was they were running the moment their soles hit the cement walk. It was an unspoken understanding, they needed to escape. There was no other way to explain it. Sheer primal *flight* winning out over *fight*. Because they had no idea who they would have fought. Children? Petulant children?

They crossed the street and dodged the two-way traffic. Somehow, the two women had joined hands, another inadvertent reaction to what they'd just witnessed at the coffee shop. Valerie Parent's eyes floating in seemingly oversized black cavities. Maddie's hands were shaking in Mary's palm. They did not break stride until they reached Mary's black Volvo a block down. Out of breath, they braced themselves against the side of the car and hung their heads, gasping for breath.

Mary was the first to catch her breath. She straightened up, spun slowly around with her eyes upturned to the darkening twilight sky. She looked almost to be searching the shifting clouds for some answer to a question not yet asked. Then, she stopped dead and cast a wary glance back in the direction from which they'd just come.

"Mary?"

Mary turned to Maddie.

"Why are you crying?" Maddie asked, in a spellbound voice.

She had no idea what Maddie was talking about until a breeze tickled the cold tears laying on her cheeks. "I'm ... I ... I don't know."

"Are you all right?" Maddie took the woman's hand once more.

"Did that just happen? I-I don't even know."

"It happened."

"Then why, why do I feel like I'm dreaming right now?"

Maddie moved in front of her. "You too?"

"You?"

"Yeah," Maddie said. She paused, as if second-guessing herself, then said, "You know how when you know you're dreaming you sometimes get an idea to, I dunno, act a certain way or do something you would never do when you're awake?"

Mary nodded, fishing in her bag for her crumpled pack of Parliaments. She drew one out, offered one to Maddie who begged off, and lit her smoke. Thoughtfully pulling on it and blowing out slowly, Mary Marguerite leaned against the car and listened to Maddie.

"I thought of … I can't believe I'm saying this, let alone to a guidance counselor at my husband's school, I thought of strangling that cheerleader. Right there in the middle of the coffeehouse. Just wrapping my hands around her throat and squeezing. Until her face turned black."

Mary stood there, quietly smoking.

"I had to actually concentrate on *not* doing that. I thought I was going to lose control and just, I dunno. I have no idea."

"My mind just went black. Soft. And blank."

"They're just smart-ass kids."

"Maybe. But every one of them—and I do mean all nine of them—come from a broken home. No fathers. He either died or he ran off."

"Are you sure?"

"*Crenshaw's Children*, Maddie. This explains some of it. Their loyalty to your husband. In the absence of a father. This is textbook *imprinting*."

"So you think what we just saw was *his* doing? His influence?"

"I don't know," Mary said, once more casting her eyes to the darkening sky above. "I honestly don't know."

V. CLINICAL

The Bickby Clinic in Haversham, Pennsylvania sat a full acre off Bluebird Road. The clinic was not fenced in, and the sprawling lush green grass surrounding the single-story complex was deceitful in its beauty. Within, the screams and cries and prayers for merciful death rang off the mint-green walls as incessantly as a healthy heart beating its rhythm. Even when the clinically depressed and suicidal cries ceased as the sun set over the back perimeter of elms, clustered into a tight-knit web of wood and bramble and putrid life, the *sundowners* with their caterwauling and incomprehensible ramblings spiked and terrified the staff and the other patients until the evening dosage of Haldol was administered into the meat of their backsides. Somehow, the staff of RNs and techs and visiting psychiatrists had learned to abide by such rumbling chaos in their midst as one grew accustomed to the ticking of a clock on the wall after a short time. The staff manned the central desks of each unit and moved through the halls soundlessly with their faces blank and eyes empty, calming the patients in low and doting tones, replacing shitty sheets, offering noise-cancelling headphones to those patients acutely sensitive to any conglomeration of sounds, and, in general, carving out as much a semblance of normalcy as was possible in an edifice that housed the schizophrenic and the homicidal under the same roof as the clinically depressed, the borderline, and the hopelessly melancholy.

Conor Crenshaw was busy underneath his bed in the Stat Unit. Its frame was bolted to the floor, so he couldn't merely slide it aside. Consequently, he had no choice but to slide underneath on his belly. The staff conducted regular rounds of every room in the unit, populated with suicidal patients, paranoids, and catatonics. Humphrey, the big black psych tech who had a smile for Conor for the first couple weeks into his stay but now regarded him guardedly like one will hold a pit bull in the corner of their eye for any hint of a switch being thrown, would be ducking his head into Conor's room in three minutes. Conor had to work fast. Humphrey visited like clockwork, and he would no doubt seize Conor by his legs and drag him out from under his bed. And Conor would lose his shit, because he just couldn't help himself. Conor's newfound hatred for authority had only just occurred to him when he entered Bickby. He could not allow for anyone there to make a fool of him or to impose their will.

There was only room for one man to impose his will on Conor Crenshaw. For anyone else to impose anything upon him struck Conor as sacrilege of the highest order. Thus, he fought bitterly against every pill they shoved at him. He slapped and punched and kicked. Of course, the staff won the day, and they'd been winning ever since, administering every dose directly into his bloodstream by way of a syringe. But Conor vowed revenge. It chilled his heart and kept him company at night in the darkest hours of his soul. Revenge.

Goddammit, he'll be here any minute, and I'm not done yet!

With graceful fingers despite the hurriedness of his motion, Conor picked the pieces of gauze bandages apart until they barely held their shape by wispy, cotton strands. He rubbed them against the roughness of his palms, coarsening them into something of a threadbare webbing. He'd snatched a handful off an unattended cart just beyond the Nurse's Station and hoarded them, something he'd been doing every other day for the last couple weeks. It was with these gauzes, once they'd been reduced to a run of roughhewn webbing, that Conor set his trap under the bed.

Conor removed the previous gauze-web from the wood paneling along the floor and glowered over it briefly before continuing. The seconds ticked away in his mind to when he'd feel Humphrey's meaty hands around his ankles. He felt along the white-washed paneling bordering the tile floor for the slightest imperfection in the sculpted wood. Any snags. There were several. Conor quickly hooked the web of shredded gauze onto the snags in the paneling until he'd drawn it a foot across. It hung down to the floor.

There! There it is! Even a daddy long-legs would be fooled!

That was the point. Sort of. Bickby Clinic had an insect problem. One could even call it an infestation of sorts. He'd heard the staff complaining about it. A silverfish floating in their coffee. Wolf spiders scuttering across the top of the copier. Roaches crunching under the nurses' expensive nursing shoes while they're walking the hallways. They may have called in an exterminator, but Conor had not seen anyone fitting that description since he'd come there. He assumed (hoped, at least) they would continue to put it off until Conor re-established *the connection.*

So far, Conor's *catch* was never disappointing. There were some days he would retrieve the artificial web under his bed where he'd find twenty to thirty of the little buggers caught up in the trap. Some were even still wriggling and writhing against the silken bondage it had become ensnared in. Never less than ten of them. All manner of insect, seemingly drawn to the trap like it beckoned to them with the ruse of rotten food or decomposing scraps to be feasted upon. In fact, they served Conor in a similar way.

It was all very ritualistic. He did not snatch them up and stuff them into his mouth willy-nilly like a gluttonous child at a buffet. No, Conor had learned from a young age he must first *honor* them for their service to him. Their nourishment. The *benefits* they granted him when he took them into his mouth and down into his rumbling belly. Into his bloodstream. Then, to all points of his anatomy where their accumulation strengthened Conor's strength. To his brain where their microscopic proteins bolstered the connection between Conor and the voice.

Ah, The Voice! How I miss your Voice! And all the smaller voices. I am lost at sea.

By the time big Humphrey ducked into Conor's room with his clipboard and wide, searching eyes, Conor lay stretched out across his single bed. A tattered, unabridged copy of *Les Misérables* lay opened at his feet. One of Conor's favorite classics. There was also the fact the big book perfectly concealed the gauze-web trap he'd removed from under the bed moments ago.

Conor's belly grumbled. He smiled a lopsided grin at Humphrey.

Waved.

"Almost time for Visiting Hours, eh?" he asked the tech.

Humphrey ticked something off on his clipboard with his tongue tucked firmly into the corner of his mouth. He snuck a glance at his wristwatch. "Ya' got about five minutes. Wife coming today?"

"You know it, Humphrey. The woman's a saint. She's my life."

"Pretty lady," Humphrey grumbled, his eyes leaping from the page to land on Conor. "How'd you land that one?"

"You know, I ask myself that same question every damn day of my life, Humphrey-ole-boy. And I keep coming up with the same sorry answer every time."

"What's that?"

"Because sometimes, the gods just smile. I mean, The Big Man can't hold a frown all the time, can He? The day I met my wife, I think that was one of the days the gods actually *smiled*."

"Interesting theory," Humphrey droned, turning to go.

"Have the gods ever smiled on you, ole boy?"

Humphrey stopped in the doorway, back still to Conor. He rolled his big shoulders. After a moment, he said, "Have a good visit." Then he was gone.

Conor waited a beat. Then he sprang into motion, snatching the book and tossing it onto his pillow. He took the gauze-web in his hands, holding it before him like a holy book opened to a sacred prayer.

"Father, thank you for these small gifts of insight and sustenance," he whispered. "May they increase our bond ever further."

Eyes wide and tongue lolling out of his mouth like a hungry mongrel, he picked the trapped insects out of the gauze and swallowed them down one by one in rapid succession. Twelve in all. He saved the centipede for last because it still lived, straining to free itself and only working its way deeper into the weave work. It tickled his throat all the way down, and he could have sworn he felt it trying to climb the sides of his stomach for a couple seconds before the acid within burned it down. When he finished, Conor crumpled the web up to its tightest, smallest ball and stuffed it under his pillow. He'd throw it in the garbage after he finished with the ritual, for it was not finished.

It was time for *the communication.*

The sweat sprang across his brow, smelling pungent with desperation. Indeed, he was despairing and had been ever since they'd forced medication into his body. The Lexapro. The Haldol. If there was one thing Conor was certain of, it was the antipsychotic that had driven The Little Voices and The Voice from his mind like children chased off a playground at dusk. It had been his mother who'd shown him the trick with the insects. She'd shown him how to make use of them to re-establish his telepathic connection to The Voice. The Voice he had thought to be merely the advisory voice of his own conscience since the attack in Philly, but now had proven itself once again to be that of Conor's long dead father.

The Little Voices…

The children. But not mine.

Crenshaw's Children.

The Father's Children. And my brothers and sisters.

There was a time Conor and Maddie had talked seriously about starting a family. He couldn't remember what decision they'd come to, if any, and could only guess the whole idea simply shriveled in both their minds as a result of neglect. That was all right with him. If Maddie never arrived at a decision to bear him children, it was no longer of any consequence to him. In service to The Voice, that of his father, and to his mother, Conor had grown his family. A happy, blessed byproduct! New brothers and sisters. And his mother had seen to all of them. All Conor had to do was bring them, one by one, to his mother's house and she would "work on them." That was her way of describing the *transformation,* one that amounted to each teenager entering her house with the firm belief their mother was the woman who'd birthed them and their father was either the "sperm-donor" piece of garbage that ran out on them, or the "stranger who'd died before they knew him." Either way, they had all entered Conor's mother's home fatherless children with struggling mothers, and they left a half-hour later in the car Conor had taken them out in to "practice on the road" for the Driver's Education course, their belief systems shattered and reconstructed in the same instance.

Conor was their brother.

They were *Crenshaw's Children.*

Conor's father's children.

One big happy family.

And being out of contact with my brothers and sisters is enough to drive me mad. Clear out of my skull!

He had been out of contact with them all for weeks. It was vital that he communicate with them. And he'd consumed close to one hundred and fifty of the wretched Bickby Clinic insects. Here and there, he'd thought he heard them, but they were faint and indecipherable in their words. That meant more nourishment. More traps set under his bed. And faith. Above all else, faith!

Conor drew his legs up into a crisscross-applesauce position and straightened his back. He lifted his chin slightly, sniffed at the air, which smelled of disinfectant and the muted stench of shit. He shut his eyes, his own inner monologue surging forth in one frantic burst of words and fearful sounds. After some resistance, Conor swept it aside to provide a silent, empty stage for The Voice to swell within his mind. He focused on the timbre of The Voice, as if this would strengthen his summoning. But the absence of sound in his skull quickly gave way to the renewed effort of his insistent conscience and its begging. Pleading.

You've got to release the little ones. You're killing them. Slowly. It will take years, but you are killing them. Make no mistake. You must fight this, no matter how long you've been at mother's mercy! Mother and The Voice.

Soundlessly, he moved his lips in supplication. "Boys and girls … I need you. If you can't speak to me, then … come to me. I'm here. I am *here*."

It was one of the young girls who answered him, her voice as thin and precarious as a precious string of sounds carried not just across miles and miles, but beyond ages of time.

"We … hear … you."

His stomach somersaulted at the sound of her voice. The steady insect diet had worked its wonders. Mother had not lied to him—he had begun to suspect what she'd told him might prove to be nothing more than a way of comforting him. Then, Conor felt the shame in his gut that accompanied any doubt he harbored about Mother's counsel. The woman was in peril. Great danger, in fact. And Maddie, his wife, was responsible for the entire debacle. Conor's mind's eye, which had grown especially unruly during his stay at Bickby, showed him a dreadful image. One that had been haunting him ever since his wife told him during one of her visits how she had "seen to Tilly's burial, and a headstone should be ready shortly."

How Conor had raged at her! The staff had needed to sedate him with nearly three times the dosage necessary to calm him. He had bitten at any exposed skin. He had round-housed the air and nearly clipped Humphrey in the side of his massive head.

Still, Maddie came to visit every other day.

It used to be every day, Conor. At first, it was every day, except Friday, of course. No visiting hours on Friday. Now, it's every other day. She's pulling away.

The young girl's voice trembled between his ears and shook his skull.

"WE … HEAR … YOU."

"All of you have *failed*," he hissed in a low, rapid, and serpentine whisper. "Let it be known to all of you. You *failed* to protect The Mother, which was your charge. She is buried. The Mother is buried, and she is *not dead*. Her blood was forcibly polluted by outside forces. She is badly weakened. She has been in the ground for a month and a half, deprived of The Blood that could heal her. I couldn't reach you when they locked me in this godforsaken place. But you knew—you *understood*—it was your responsibility—your *duty*—protect The Mother as you would Your Father! So it is *your fault* if The Mother didn't survive the interment."

The clock on Conor's wall read 7:29 p.m. Visiting hours would start in one minute. Perhaps less.

Maddie would be waiting. Humphrey would come for him any minute. It was imperative The Nine not merely understand but agree to act.

But the young girl was silent. In place of her sonorous voice, Conor could hear the low-register hum between his ears. Barely detectable, and yet audible enough to threaten insanity should it persist for too long.

"Acknowledge me, you little—"

"*What— Are—Our—Orders?*"

Conor told them in a frenzied string of words.

The young girl (Conor was certain this was The Cheerleader) accepted his order, and suddenly Conor's mind was empty. No low hum. Nothing.

Then, there was Humphrey filling his doorway once more, and his voice was an avalanche falling all around him.

"—wife's here, Crenshaw! Didjoo' hear what I said? She's waiting on you!"

"Coming." Conor Crenshaw flashed his trademark smile, the very same that had charmed students over the last eight years into behavior just shy of hero worship, and strode out of his room to see his wife.

Madison Crenshaw, who had recently begun to toy with the possibility of going back to her maiden name *Bradley,* pulled up a seat at the table across from her husband and set one Dixie cup of decaf coffee before him and the other at her place. Patients milled around with loved ones, some wearing bathrobes or threadbare pajamas, and for every one Madison smiled at, another returned it while the rest set her with a longing look like they were on the verge of begging her to break them out. Across from her, Conor drummed his fingers on the table, staring at the plume of steam rising out of his coffee cup. His eyes, big basset hound brown ones, were more alert than usual. He looked like he could barely contain whatever disjointed thoughts were racing around his brain.

She opened her mouth to say something when he cut her off in a plaintive voice.

"I really don't know what it is the world wants from me, Maddie."

Shifting in her seat, she smoothed the palm of her hand across her brow and took a breath. "I don't understand what that means."

"Oh, come on. You know *exactly* what it means."

"No. No, I really don't."

"Well, if you kept in touch with my psychiatrist regularly, you'd know he thinks I have a—what did he call it—a *persecution* complex. So let me ask you this. I've had my freedom taken away, and I'm locked away with all these ..."
Conor waved his hand at the other patients crammed into the small leisure

room. "… these walking shells. I mean, these people, they've got *real* problems, Maddie. Me? My eyes are open. Everything I worked so damn hard to maintain, to cultivate, is crumbling, and I tell Dr. Reddy this. I bare my soul. Tell him 'Hey, Doc, I *really-really-really* need to get out of here because there are people outside these walls who are counting on me to protect them. To-to *herd* them so they don't all run off a cliff.'"

"Con, we've been over this. And I *have* been in touch with Dr. Reddy. We speak three times a week. I'll admit I haven't spoken with him today, but I'll reach out to him first thing tomorrow, and I'll find out what's going on." Maddie paused, her gaze glancing off the dull tabletop surface, then lighting on her husband again. "I wonder if …"

"You wonder what?" Conor steepled his hands, nearly upsetting his cup of coffee.

"I wonder if you hear me when I say things to you. I mean really *hear me*."

"Mmm, well, you haven't exactly said anything of real consequence just yet. But, yes, you're my wife, and I always listen to you."

"All right," Maddie said, evenly. "Do you understand me? Believe me when I tell you your mother is gone? That she died six weeks ago—"

"Here's what I understand … honey. And stop me if I start in about *anything* that's untrue. I find out my name was on a *Kill List* penned by some pissant. The kid was going to shoot me dead, along with a bunch of other kids. So, I weather that as best I can. Then on my drive my home, it hits me. Someone wanted me dead. *Me.* And I've given my life—my *fucking* life—to those Baldwin brats! I get home, and I crawl into bed, but there's no rest because I have these nightmares that'd make your hair stand up, babe. Real dark stuff! I wake up in a pool of sweat to the phone ringing. The police officer on the other end tells me my mother's dead. And *here's* the rub." Conor stabbed his index finger down into the table so violently the digit bent to a near ninety-degree angle. His lips peeled away from his teeth to reveal a mouthful of black flecks in between each tooth. "There is no way … no way in *hell* that Mom's dead. I know it. I wanted to tell the officer to hold off on tagging and bagging her until I made it there. I could've cleared it up for them in a matter of moments. Then I saw something. I saw something outside our bedroom window."

Maddie's eyes narrowed. "Where? In the backyard?"

"No-no-*no*! Hovering. Hovering-hovering-hovering-in-the-air. I remember the rain. It was pouring rain. There was hail. And I thought it was the hail hitting the siding I was hearing. It wasn't. It was a scratching. A scraping. Then-then-then something just took hold of me. It wrung me out. I felt the strength just, you know, *ooze* out of my muscles. And this-this command just exploded in my brain. A bright blast. Fireworks and words. Saying I should pick up the broken glass on the floor and kill myself because I … well, I failed *him*. He would come for me because I let Mother die. My own mother. His … his wife."

"Oh, Conor, your *father*? No—"

"Yes. It was what I'd been working for all these years. To bring my father home. I did everything he asked of me. I made ready the way, just like he said. Otherwise, he couldn't come back. You see a man *needs* his father." Tears formed in Conor's eyes. His teeth, mottled with unidentifiable bits of black and brown, snapped shut so viciously it was audible. "The world is a cruel, unforgiving place for a child who's never known their father. Then, to find out Father would return after all these years, but he meant to punish me for Mother's death. To wait. The anticipation of what Father's brand of punishment would be. I couldn't live in such suspense, Maddie."

"Con, what have you got between your teeth?" She made to stand. "Why don't I see if they'll let you use a mirror at the nurse's station so you can clean your mouth."

"I'm trying to come clean, goddammit!"

"Con, please—"

"Now or never, Maddie. Or you'll never know, and I'll never tell! Never!"

One patient across the room, a rotund, middle-aged woman in a wrinkled house dress dotted with pink flowers, shot out of her seat, screaming and smacking herself across the face. Her husband, a rail-thin man with a shiny bald head and tweed jacket, rose, rushed to her, and laid his hands on her meaty shoulder blades. Mr. Tweed Jacket shot a death stare at Conor and Maddie, all the while whispering into the woman's ear. A sizable black tech rushed into the room, his head whipping to the right and left in search of the source of the woman's triggering. Mrs. House Dress quietened, her whole body shuddering and heaving sigh after sigh. Mr. Tweed Jacket pointed at Conor when the tech looked at him, and in seconds, he stood towering over Conor, who seemed not to notice as he glared up at Maddie. She lowered herself back down into the seat. The ghost of an embarrassed smile passed over her lips.

"It's all right," she told the tech. "I'm so sorry. It won't happen again."

The tech folded his arms, cocked his head. "This is a place of healing, ma'am. I can't have this kind of thing. Once more and you'll have to leave. We'll have to sedate your husband."

"Understood," Maddie muttered, mortified.

"Conor, you got me?"

Conor shrugged. "We understand each other, Humphrey. Always have."

Humphrey stalked off, shaking his head.

Once the big tech was out of earshot, Conor started back in. "After what happened at the bar, the beating, I had a hard time remembering things. My responsibilities. Readying the way."

"I know that. That's why I took over caring for your mother."

"See, you know. You *know*! I was Forgetful Jones there for a while. I could teach. That-that was like riding a bike, honestly. But other things, important things, they just got away from me. I was responsible for the welfare of others. My kids. My students. I promised them I'd be there to guide them. To mentor them through their ... their *growing pains*. Their transitioning. They must have felt abandoned. First, their fathers! Then, Mr. Crenshaw!"

Crenshaw's Children. Dear God, what did he do to those kids? Who is this person?

Conor chuckled, a dirty and almost wicked sound. "Worst of all? My father was trying to communicate with me, and I … I thought it was just a voice in my head. Like, my conscience or something. I forgot who it was. Who *he* was! So I treated the voice like an annoyance more than anything. But I swear to God, I didn't know! I did not know it was *him!*"

"Wait a minute," Maddie said, gasping. She shut her eyes, kneaded the bridge of her nose. "Just. Wait." She paused, short of breath. "How long have you been talking to your *father?*"

"For all of my adult life."

"So, all those times I thought you were just talking to yourself—"

Conor glowered at her. "Now, don't you *say* it, Maddie. Don't."

But Maddie couldn't hold it back. "You've been sick all that time, and I … I never picked up on it. I-I could have gotten you help long before it came to this. I … God … I could have."

"You could have run," Conor said, his voice hollow. "You can't now. We're married. You, my dear, are part of the *family*, and soon we'll all be joined again. Don't worry. I'll help you to transition, just as I've helped the children. Only, I *need*—must get the *fuck* out of here—"

"The *children?*" Maddie visored her eyes, lowered her head as the tears pushed themselves out of her eyes. "Oh dear God, Conor. What have you done? They're just kids. I thought you cared about them."

"I do," he said, laying his hand palm-up before her. "Take my hand."

In a blur of motion, Madison Crenshaw batted his hand aside. She moaned low in her throat. "You've been living this double life. You're nothing but an-an actor. Just a lying, deceitful actor. Two-faced sonofabitch. *Educator of the Year?* You piece of shit." Seething, Maddie held her voice down, barely reining it in when it threatened to climb in volume and intensity. "You're a predator. A sociopath. I don't see an ounce, not a *fucking* ounce, of remorse in you. I only see … pride. Fucking pride. You should see what you've done to your … *children.*"

"You've seen them?" Conor straightened in his seat, like a bolt of lightning struck his spinal column.

Her cheeks sunken. Eyes sodden. Hands curling into fists under the table. Uncurling. Over and over. "They are little horrors. Just little *horrors.*"

"They're lost without me, that's all it is. They must feel unmoored. Have some compassion, Maddie."

"They followed Mary Marguerite from school," Maddie said. "They're stalking her."

"Mmm. That Mary Marguerite. If she's not careful, she will be sucked in."

Speechless, Maddie could only stare vacantly across the table at the man who had once been her husband.

Conor dove into the silence and went on. "You've been speaking to her? Mary-fucking-*Marguerite?*"

"She's told me more about my own husband than *my own husband*."

"I forbid you to see her again."

"You ... *forbid* me?"

"I can't protect you if you keep in contact with her. I'm offering you fair warning. This is too important. There is too much at stake where I'd be able to call him off if you were to find yourself ensnared in that bitch's obstruction."

"Protect me from *him*?"

"She will get you killed."

Her cheeks stinging and red, Madison Crenshaw stood like a shot. She armed the remaining tears from her eyes. "I won't be back. This is the end, Conor. I lost you. You're not here anymore."

"Maddie—"

"*No!*" she cried. "You hear me. You listen to me, Conor. Your mother is dead. Your father is dead. He disappeared when you were five years old and was declared legally dead. This was a long time ago. And your wife? Jesus Christ, your *wife* will find out what you've been doing all this time! This sick little delusion that drives you to do *God-knows-what!* You want to threaten me? Huh? Your *wife*? I'm going to find out all there is to know, and then I'm going to make sure that three-oh-two stands and you never *ever* have the chance to hurt another child. I'll fight to my last breath to make certain you never get out of here, you sick bastard."

Conor was on his feet so fast Maddie flinched.

"I have a far reach, Madison!" he fired back, his eyes dancing in flames. "Beyond these walls! You have no idea what they can do! What *he* can do! I'll stand aside and let them do what they do! You hear me?!"

"You'll rot in here!"

"And you and Mary-*fucking*-Marguerite will die screaming!"

That's when all hell broke loose in the Leisure Room.

VI. "WALKING DREAM"

Term Paper turned into Mr. Ronald Leone by Ms. Valerie Parent, Second Semester, 2019, Baldwin High School

Valerie Parent
English Language Arts III
Mr. Leone
Period 8

"The Walking Dream":
Narrative Essay

It's looking like this diary my mom bought for me last Christmas is shaping up to be more of a dream journal that anything else. Oh well, I don't think Mom would complain if she knew this. After all, she couldn't have spent more than $5 on it at Five Below. It was probably a last-minute gift, a stocking stuffer or something. Either way, I'm getting more mileage out of this cheap-o gift than my new Timberlands or my Apple Watch. So cheap-o versus trendy and expensive wins the day. If you're reading this right now, Mom—A) don't you have laundry to do—and— B) why would you suddenly start giving a shit what I've been up to?

But seriously, if Mom asked me questions like "How's life, Val?" or "Is there anything bothering you?" or "Are you getting enough sleep?" I think I'd have to answer her just like this. "Well, Mother, where do I begin? I don't feel alive. Not in the literal sense. Not in the proverbial sense. I haven't felt alive for months. My eyes are open, and I see the world around me, but none of it makes sense anymore. I feel like a newborn learning how to speak and understand for the first time. All over again, in my case. My grades are dropping because I'm having a hard time with what used to be the most basic tasks for me—long division, vocabulary, essay-writing. Sure, I can spill my guts out all over this five-dollar diary like nothing but give me a writing prompt and I will fail. I'll freeze. My mind goes el blanko. I think this must be what it's like to die. To have your brain shut down for a long enough period of time that when it finally comes time to reboot up again, a lot of data (memory) has been lost. Maybe it'll come back (recovered). Maybe, it's lost to the ages forever.

"Oh, and, Mother, as to your third question? The one about getting enough sleep? Less and less, sorry to say. But that's to be expected, according to Tilly. The change-over from sleeping at night to sleeping during the day will happen gradually, and it will turn my world upside down at first. Tilly promised the time will come, if I don't fight the change, when I'll come to hate the light of day and come to love and cherish the dead of night, 'almost in a sexual way—a sexual kind of love for the dark.' Tilly's words, not mine!

"Answer your questions, Mom? I think it's good to be pre-emptive.

"The problem? Even after all this time, I'm still not entirely sure if Tilly's even real or not. I mean, she could be real. But every time I think of her, I can't see her face in my mind. Her features run like watercolors. And that's how my dreams unfold a lot of the time, which makes me think maybe Tilly is of my dreams, not of this world. I'll tell you this, if I dreamt her up, she's part of the most lucid dream state I've ever experienced."

Real or imagined, Tilly's like the mother I wish I had.

Which is what makes what I'm about to write about so hard to do.

Man, I'm crying all over the pages. See that dot? That one right there? And this one?

I'm sorry ... sorry-sorry-sorry.

I'm crying over a nightmare, like a four-year-old. Crying about an old woman who may or may not even be real. It feels a lot like crying over a character in a book who dies unexpectedly. You wouldn't do that, right? I wouldn't. Well, that's not entirely true. I cried when Professor Snape died, but we won't get into that.

There was me, Joe Brickman, Tara Neeley, Stacy Kennedy, Pete Mason, Harry Hasting, Delaney Lindberg, Michael Malone, and Steve Teague. A mixed bag if ever there was one. In the dream, it was late. Had to be the middle of the night. Cold. The moon was big and fat and red, and there's a name for that, but I'll ask Alexa later what that is. I don't want to lose my train of thought. We were walking through St. Luke's Cemetery. I don't know why we weren't in a car with the lights off. That probably would have made more sense than walking there the whole way. St. Luke's is ten miles away from my house. Joe Brickman and I were leading everybody else along, like we knew where we're going. The paved blacktop driveway that snakes its way through the cemetery is hard to navigate in broad daylight, but somehow, me and Joe knew exactly where to go.

Gravestones twinkled for as far as the eye could see. The miniature portraits of the dead and buried fastened to the markers cast flashes of reflected headlights all about as late-night drivers (the bar crowd) drove past or made a turn onto Glastonbury Drive along the east perimeter of the cemetery. A nest of rabbits emptied out in a burst of motion and blur of grays and browns off to our left. We didn't startle. Immune to the ole "jump scare," I guess. That's not to say some of us weren't afraid. I was cold, shivering in my parka and yoga pants. I shook and shuddered not just from the frigidity of the evening, but because I've never liked cemeteries. I don't do well at funerals. My mother forced me to attend my father's funeral when I was five. I should have never been there. My father died in a car wreck, and they did a poor job of putting him back together again. I remember being able to pick out the oddness of his appearance in the casket, even at five. The angle of his head as it lay against the satin pillow, not quite flush with his throat or sitting right. It was the head of a man who'd been decapitated by his own windshield, as I would later come to find out.

It's strange, a short time ago, I wouldn't have been able to write about that without crying or having a panic attack. I feel nothing. It's like I'm writing about someone else's dead father. I'm ... I feel my sympathies for this world slipping away. The people I loved don't mean as much to me as they did before. Before what? I don't know. The string that connects me to my life and to this existence is ... stretching ... straining ... groaning ... I feel like an astronaut tethered to his space shuttle and floating out in space but the tether is weakening and the astronaut doesn't care; he wants the stars and the blackness of the void to take him away from all he ever knew.

Joe said, "She's buried along the back fence. It's this way."

We left the blacktop and trudged off into the tall, neglected wheatgrass sprouting up around our sneakers, where we did not tramp them down, leaving a trail of footsteps. The graves were fewer and fewer the further back we walked. The stones were simpler, their messages reduced to the dead's name and their year-span. No quotes. No "Loving Mother" or "Proud Father" or "Gone Too Soon" for the teenagers like us who killed themselves or crashed like my father. I noticed a few of the stones were no bigger than the size of a red brick, and there was nothing chiseled on them. They were literally markers and nothing more. Someone's buried here, but damned if I know!

"Stop," Joe said, halting before a three-feet by eight-feet patch of dirt that lay untarnished by so much as a blade of grass. "Here."

The nine of us gathered around, encircling the grave like watchers. It was Delaney Lindberg, the scholar among us, who noticed the deep fractures in the dirt of the grave, a spiderweb of deep grooves sinking down into the earth. The ground was not packed, and it ought to be considering Tilly Crenshaw went down into the ground six weeks ago.

Delaney made a musing sound. "The ground shifted. That's all. Pockets down below collapsed, and that's why it looks like this. The dirt moved. It cracked."

Something told me she was wrong. Call it a second opinion from somewhere deep inside.

It was Pete Mason, whose nickname was Goalpost, referring to his bad teeth and the large gaps between them (a nickname that won anyone who dared use it in front of him a broken nose or raccoon eyes), who brandished a shovel seemingly from nowhere. I couldn't remember seeing him with it beforehand, but in dreams, things tend to fuzz-out here and there. Time expands and contracts. Stacy Kennedy, the lead actress in the last three Baldwin musicals, brought out the second shovel and wasted no time stabbing the diamond-shaped edge of it into one of the larger fissures in the dirt. Pete Mason followed suit, switching to the opposite side of the grave and stabbing at the ground like it had wronged him in some way.

The rest of us stood loosely gathered around what became a black, gaping maw in the ground in what seemed like minutes. I had stood by and watched Pete and Stacy laboring with their shovels, scooping up the crumbly dark dirt and pitching it over their shoulders without any care for replacing it later on. We all stood by while they worked. I would have felt strange about not pitching in if the cemetery and its strange, alien sounds didn't start to work on my nerves. They both thrilled and unnerved me, and I couldn't decide whether the sounds of the cemetery felt like home or the place where my nightmares originated from.

And time is a funny thing, as I've said.

I blinked, and when my eyes flashed open again, not only was the grave dug out, but everyone was lowering themselves down into the hole. Quickly, I moved in and dropped down into the grave with the steadying grasp of Joe interlocking with my right hand. The smell of old dust and shit and mud hit me. Something wriggled along the nape of my neck. I swatted at it, and my hand came away with the squashed, oozing bits of an earthworm and a couple white grubs. Pete and Stacy had done a commendable job of hollowing out the area around the silver casket so all of nine of us could stand around it without turning an ankle or lodging our feet between the casket's base and the grave wall.

"The lock is broken," I said, stooping to examine it more closely. The hasp was not just broken, though. It had been obliterated, the steel bent out of shape and barely hanging on to the frame of the casket itself. I touched it, and the entire mechanism dropped off into the caked dirt at my feet.

Joe nodded to all of us, and we knew what he meant without words. He was standing beside me in the hole. He worked his fingers in between the lid and the base, pulled upward with an extended grunt that inspired Pete and Harry to immediately spring into motion. The lid would not budge. The three of them pried at the lid. It offered a quick clicking sound, two surfaces separating slightly. The boys straightened back up and exchanged confused glances with one another.

Pete shrugged, his brow a map of worry lines. "It's not locked, for Christsakes! What's holding it shut?"

Stacy said, "Rust, maybe?"

We grumbled our half-hearted agreement to this. That did not solve the problem, of course. None of us had noticed Steve Teague had lapsed into silence. He stood there at the head of the casket, frowning down at its tarnished surface. Then, it was as if someone suddenly roused him from a trance. His eyes lit up, quite literally. His pupils turned white as he raised them to look at each of us. His gaze felt like a penlight sweeping across each of our faces. His smile was wide, lips the red of a woman's lipstick, and top teeth longer than they had been before. They had extended so far down over top of the bottom row; you could barely see them at all. Steve's teeth had also turned in on one another as they'd grown downward. He said, "We have to ask her. She'll open her casket for us if she consents."

"What if she doesn't consent?" I asked. "Mr. Crenshaw was very clear in his instruction."

Steve moved down onto his haunches and leaned in towards the casket, his lips nearly grazing its dirty surface as he spoke to the grave's inhabitant. None of us could hear his precise words, but they sounded imploring in their delivery and tone. That was good enough. He straightened, the pudge of his belly hiking up his Fortnite t-shirt. He raked it back down over his paunch and nodded, satisfied.

Inside the casket, something shifted.

A mournful cry, helpless and infantile in its delivery, worked its way out of its interior.

I felt that same sensation of great fatigue pushing on me, pressing my shoulders down to the earth. It felt like some strange kind of gravitational pull, like the equator lay right beneath my black Converse. I have no idea if the others were experiencing anything similar, but I'd wager a guess they had. I bent under the invisible weight, bracing myself against the casket. That's when I felt the vibrating hum emanating from within, like someone had locked an idling chainsaw inside instead of the body of Tilly Crenshaw. I saw the others had doubled over also, splayed their hands along the top of the casket like I had. Tara and Pete started gagging. Joe skipped that step entirely, vomiting blood and bile in a projectile stream.

Before Joe's bodily fluid had a chance to splash against the top of the casket, the lid flew open and the spray spattered Tilly's face and upturned chin. Her mouth was opened wide. To catch Joe's spew.

The force that had been compressing me changed course all at once. I suddenly felt myself being pulled towards the great, gory, and gaping maw of Tilly Crenshaw. I couldn't fight it, and barely tried because it felt … right? I don't know. Her mouth widened to an impossible diameter. Her jaw had unhinged. The top of her head folded up and back, buckling like an accordion bag. Then, Pete rammed into me so violently I puked down the front of my black acrylic sweater. The nausea wasn't there a second before. Then it was. Pete's bloody vomit flew past my face, missing my cheek by barely an inch. We were all vomiting thick, syrupy blood. It was being drawn out of us.

Called forth.

Towards Tilly's ever-widening mouth and snapping picket-fence rows of teeth bursting out of her gumline.

Delaney clapped a hand over mouth, holding her purge back. She looked at me, her pupils gone to white now like Pete's had a second ago.

I heard her voice in my mind, wild and terrified. "She's siphoning us. For blood. She's empty. Her blood was polluted. Something about *transfusions?* She needs our pure blood. Crenshaw warned us this might happen."

It was Joe Brickman who turned rogue first.

"Knives out!" he cried, his chin gored a deep and gleaming crimson. "Knives out!"

At first, I thought I hadn't heard right. My ears were ringing, and I couldn't process anything because I was too busy trying to rein in my spasming stomach muscles. Clutching my stomach with one hand, I lunged for Joe, who'd brought out a straight razor he'd stolen out of the bathroom vanity. It still had flecks of his mother's leg hair along its edge. "What are you doing? We're here to save her! To bring her back home."

The Voice of Our Father nearly split my brain in half when it erupted between my ears.

SHE CAN'T BE SAVED! PUT HER OUT OF HER MISERY! SHE MUST BE DESTROYED! KNIVES OUT!

Joe raised his blade up, his hands and the blade trembling above Tilly's throat, roped in corded veins and stained a sickly blue and green shade. "You heard?" he asked us.

Stiffly, I managed to nod my head.

Then, we all drew the knives we'd brought with us. The knives we thought we'd be using to open our veins so our Mother, Tilly Crenshaw, could drink her fill from each of us. After all, she was our Maker. And the Blood is the life!

To rise up and to kill her in her casket?

It was erotic. Exciting.

It was dreadful. Monstrous.

One by one, we climbed atop Tilly, her body writhing and contorting beneath us. It was near impossible to straddle the woman. She bucked like a bronco and almost threw Pete clear. All two hundred twenty-five pounds of him. Joe stabbed his straight razor down into her throat, releasing a gurgle like water from a dying fountain. Before this, Tilly's blood would have burst out of her like a geyser. But she had been trapped underground and had not hunted nor fed for the better part of a month and a half. She'd been infused with *incompatible blood,* "over and over by Mrs. Crenshaw." Until the build-up of the blood poisoned Tilly and weakened her to a death-like state. It must have seemed like an eternity for her, arms pinned to her sides by the narrow confines of her coffin. Barely enough room to turn onto her side. She'd managed to break the casket's lock. She'd managed to move the earth piled atop her casket enough to bring those fractures into the packed ground the way we'd come to find it at first arrival. But that must have sapped her of more strength than she could afford to lose. Right before I stabbed the steak knife from my mother's cutlery drawer into her sunken stomach, the stab of remorse stayed my hand for a moment. I started crying. Then, I burst into laughter, the two emotions battling for dominance over each other and failing equally.

This is what a descent into madness must feel like. I was sure of it.

Tilly found me with her eyes, full black orbs that had crowded out any lingering semblance of humanity, and I struggled to tear my gaze away. To turn my head from her as I freed the knife from the wound. It had snagged under the coarsened skin, which had hardened to a hide over time. I couldn't bring myself to look to my right or to my left because I could barely endure the peripheral view of the others as their arms raised and lowered at a psychopathic rate, puncturing the old woman's chest. The blue dress she'd been buried in gleamed purple.

Perhaps the worst of it was that Tilly Crenshaw could not even derive the strength to ward us off with her hands or to kick out at us with her feet once we put enough holes in her. Tara and Joe and Stacy were panting and grunting. With my eyes closed, it would have sounded like a threesome rather than an execution.

Execution.

When Tilly's head dropped back down against the satin pillow, we slowed to a stop. Joe Brickman dipped down to Tilly's ravaged throat.

(DO NOT DRINK! HER BLOOD IS TAINTED! DO NOT!)

Joe drew back, as if slapped.

I felt a sickening, all-consuming urge to do the same as Joe had nearly done. To drink my fill. Before I could give in to the overwhelming temptation, Michael Malone seized me by the shoulders and held me back.

I couldn't bring myself to look at Tilly's ruined body. Warily, I looked from one to the next then the next. All their cheeks were wet with tears. What would this leave us with? How would we be after having done this? To The Mother. Under the direction of Our Father? Tilly's face turned aside. Her body went slack. Defeated. But the muscles of her face clung to a terrible expression I am certain was the shock of betrayal.

The night seemed to hold its breath, afraid to exhale.

We were a machine run out of fuel, and thankful for it.

I thought I heard someone let out a dreadful gasp just outside the grave. A whistle sounded from what had to have been a dry pair of lips. I felt ice in my veins. Then, Joe leaned in closer to the body of Tilly Crenshaw. "Listen," he said.

The sounds I'd just heard were coming from the wounds we'd inflicted on her.

A gasp.

A weak whistle.

It stopped just as soon as it started.

I'd had enough. "Can we go?"

Pete bristled beside me. "Shouldn't we at least fill the hole back in? Shut the casket?"

Henry asked, "You offering?"

Joe socked Henry in the shoulder. "Enough," he said, "we stay until the job is done. We all help. This was The Mother. Or did you forget that Henry? Dipshit!"

There was rarely ever arguing with Joe Brickman when an order came down. We gave one another a leg up and out. Pete Mason was the second to last out, and he reached down with his overlong, orangutan arms to haul Joe out of Tilly's yawning, black grave. Henry, perhaps to slip back into Joe's good graces again, took up a shovel, and I grabbed the other. My arms ached from the frenzied downward arcing of my hands as I'd helped to kill Tilly in her casket under a fattened blood moon. Gradually, muscle memory kicked in, and before I knew it, I was hauling the last of the dirt to what was now a waist-high pile over the hole. I tamped it down, then Henry did the same.

When I turned away from Tilly's filled-in grave, I found myself standing there alone. I thought they'd left me there alone in a cemetery with the souls of the unsettled whipping all around me and riding the wind that suddenly kicked up.

I spun around. They were all gathered around something in their midst, offset by a lone maple to their left. I could hear Joe's hushed whispers.

"Guys?" I called to them.

Joe waved me over without a word, listening intently to something or someone I couldn't see.

I strode over to their huddle and broke in.

At first, I moved to rub the tiredness from my eyes. I gouged at my eyes with a closed fist, struggling to clear them of what I was sure had to be a hallucination. But when I drew my hand away from my face, the wretched animal still stood a few feet away, between a pair of leaning tombstones. It peered at me; its bulbous, nightmarish eyes boring into me in much the same way Tilly's had done while I stabbed her. It was a deer, at least that was its underlying shape and mass. This was a sickly animal, however. Initially, I mistook the black bulges all over its body to be dark stones embedded in its taut flesh. It wasn't until my gaze flitted back to its staring eyes, I realized I was looking into two giant tumors that had grown out and over the animal's eyes. The deer was riddled with tumors, what looked like eggplants in the pale moonlight.

I waited for it to say something, to hear its voice in my head. After all, it had just communicated with the others. Still, a part of me was thankful it chose to trot off rather than to penetrate my mind. I dreaded what the thing's voice would have sounded like to me.

I turned to Joe. "Was ... that?"

"Our Father? No. But The Tumor Deer is of Our Father. That's what It said." Joe paused. He cast a long, sideways glance in the direction of the departed Tumor Deer, then he went on. "Do exactly as I say."

VII. "TRUST, BUT VERIFY"

Mary Marguerite finished reading the three printed pages of Valerie Parent's essay and laid it face down on her desk. Matt Leone, the long-term substitute for Mr. Crenshaw, had brought it to her earlier, expressing his concerns about its "disturbing content." The students in his 8th period class had been tasked with writing a narrative about something that changed their lives in a positive or negative way. According to Mr. Leone, most of the students had chosen to write about relatively benign topics like getting their license or the first day of their first job. He'd also gone on to say a few students had written about the death of a parent, one student even having penned a paper that told the brief, harrowing, true story of riding dirt bikes with his best friend on a residential road and then having to watch helplessly when said friend got hit by a car and was killed instantly. Mary would be speaking with that student, if for no other reason than to check in with him. To decide if further counseling might be required.

But Valerie Parent? The head of Baldwin's varsity cheerleading squad, whose heart-shaped face, long blonde hair, and vibrant blue eyes graced the front of Baldwin's High School brochures, the *face* of the school ever since she'd entered its front doors as a chatty, friendly little Freshman girl? How does such a student entertain such horrid nightmares? It was possible. Mary was not so close-minded or prejudiced in her understanding of the teenage mind that she could close herself off entirely from the possibility that even a young girl like Valerie harbored a dark subconscious. Molestation, some form of abuse, be it physical or sexual or verbal, prompted such a preoccupation with such desperate underpinnings. Mary knew more about Valerie Parent than most of the student body, only because she had always stood out among her peers by her own design. She did come from a single-parent household, but her mother was a mainstay at bake sales and had briefly been President of the Parent-Teacher Association before bowing out of the position due to the fact she'd been promoted at her job to "lead buyer" for a major department store chain.

207

Valerie and her mother lived just beyond the invisible blue-collar border town of Comstock, which fed Baldwin with the largest percentage of its students. She came from money. Her father had left a lot of it to her and her mother when he died in a car accident years ago.

Her name had also appeared on Dallas Teller's now infamous Kill List. She was one of what Mary had come to call The Nine.

Matt Leone told them they had to write about something that happened *to them.* It was quite possible Valerie had had such a dream, as terrible as it was. Usually, when a student turns in a paper like this, it's a cry for help. Had she found out she could have been killed that day had Teller carried out his carnage unchecked? That would be enough to give anyone nightmares, even the strongest of individuals. Hell, look what it had done to Conor Crenshaw.

There's more to Crenshaw than meets the eye, and you know it! That's not the same! And it's quite plausible, if anything, he had a hand in Valerie's inner turmoil.

"The kids loved him, Mare," she told herself, shoving the stapled papers away. "It's not uncommon for students to form a fan club around that type of teacher. It's not the first time you've seen something like that happen. Some teachers just have a way, a charisma about them that draws people to them. Conor Crenshaw had that. The rare gift."

She paused, glancing over at the window of her office.

She craved a cigarette.

The need for nicotine often hit her hardest when she decided to forgo her medicine regimen. That day, she'd opted to skip her antipsychotic meds. She felt they tended to dull her thoughts, and Mary was a woman determined to gain as much insight into the mystery of The Nine as she could. It required a sharpened mind above all else. Mary had decided that day, as she'd done occasionally here and there when she saw fit, to depend solely upon her Xanax supply as needed. That and cigarettes.

Her mouth was dry. Her thoughts were frazzled.

"But we know now there was another side to him. His wife didn't even know about that other side of him. The guy somehow managed to hide some form of psychosis from his students. From his colleagues. For years and years. Then … then he gets his head caved in. He loses a substantial amount of memory. The darker side prevails in the face of the Kill List situation. He cracks. And, from what Maddie told me, there might not be any way back for him."

All right, what about the tags all over the school? What about Crenshaw's Children?

In all reality, she had no proof it was The Nine who'd vandalized the school. When Conor had been there, the kids (and there were a lot of them from all walks of life) held him in their hearts like people worship celebrities. The list of suspects swelled far beyond that of nine students.

"Those nine teenagers could not be more different from one another. The odds of those kids in particular gravitating towards one another in a high school culture has to be a-thousand-to-one. Yet, they've become inseparable in the last six months or so. It just doesn't happen."

Why? Because you've never seen it in your fifteen years as a Guidance Counselor? That renders it an impossibility. You've never seen the Northern Lights, yet they remain a phenomenon also! Why don't you get the girl in your office and ask her yourself? Is the essay a dream, or something … something more?

Mary reached for her phone and punched in the number sequence to access the school's intercom. "Would Valerie Parent please report to the Guidance Office? Valerie Parent, report to the Guidance Office! Thank you!"

She hung up the phone, decided after she wrapped up the meeting with Valerie, she'd sneak a cigarette in her office. Walking out to the courtyard and having a cig was no longer an option. Mary had made the mistake of confiding in a couple of her coworkers she was trying the nicotine patch and trying to quit. If any of them were to suddenly catch her smoking, she would have felt not only weak but a sense of shame that did not entirely make sense to her. She was only human, yet that fear of being viewed in such a way by others stuck in her craw.

Then again, it made perfect sense the more she parsed it out. The licensed therapist in her knew damn well there was no way to run and hide from her own academic mind. *Doug called you weak all the time. He told you it was a big reason why he now has custody of Jenny. A weak mother will only raise a weaker, more vulnerable child. And with Jenny's autism, she could not afford to be made weak on top of that.*

The phone buzzed. Mary snatched it up, pushing all thoughts of her estranged husband and the loss of Jenny from her home out of her mind, for the time being. "Yes?"

One of the secretaries in Mike Distefano's Student Life Office. The cranky one, of course. "Did you get my Absentee List from this morning?"

"Oh, I … I haven't finished going through my emails yet."

"Valerie Parent is absent today."

Mary sighed. "Oh. All right."

"FYI, it's an *unexcused* absence."

"No one called her out of school this morning?"

"No one called. And we've got a number of students with unexcused absences today."

A number of them?

Mary wanted to ask how many, but she knew what Marcy would tell her. *Check it yourself!*

"Thank you, Marcy," Mary said, laying her hand flat atop the downturned essay and pulling it back towards her on the desk blotter. "I appreciate it."

Marcy rang off. The secretary had something against proper phone etiquette, such as saying *Goodbye* at the close of a call. Mary had learned a long time ago to not take it personally.

Suspicion gnawed at her mind like a rat biting at a scrap of cheese. The number of questions she'd had before this bit of information was relayed multiplied to a staggering amount, and Mary sat there for a beat to rein in her thoughts. She could feel her chest tightening and did not notice her hand had balled into a fist atop the essay until she looked down and found it sitting there, the knuckles bloodless and white.

Mary nodded to herself, some of the tension within softening, and she woke up her computer lock screen with a jiggle of the mouse. She navigated to her emails, scrolled down to the one labeled Absentee Report-3/23/2019, and opened it. She scribbled the names of all the Juniors onto an index card and shut the email. Then, Mary pulled open the drawer beside her left hip and thumbed through the files inside. She brought out a blue folder and opened it up before her. It was a copy of Dallas Teller's Kill List, the very one the police had found on his person the morning of his attempted infiltration of the school:

The Dead

Mr. Crenshaw (Room 113)
Harry Hasting (Room 113)
Joe Brickman (Room 117)
Delaney Lindberg (Room 218)
Michael Malone (Room 218)
Pete Mason (Room 218)
Tara Neeley (Room 220)
Valerie Parent (Room 238)
Steve Teague (Room 315)
Stacy Kennedy (Room 131)
/////////////////////////
In infernis arderet!

Just reading it again, Mary forgot to breathe, and it wasn't until she finished scanning The Kill List she realized she was growing lightheaded. Baldwin was one of the few schools in the county that still offered Latin as an elective. She'd checked Dallas Teller's roster out of morbid curiosity after that fateful day and had been surprised to find he was indeed enrolled in the class. That would explain the sign off, which translated to *Burn In Hell!* Those three words. Her eyes went back to them over and over again before Mary finally tore her gaze away to check the Kill List names against the names of the Junior absentees on her index card.

The unexcused absences.

All nine students on Teller's infamous list matched the names of the students who had not come to school that day. Had not called out either.

"What are their parents thinking?" she asked her empty office. Protocol involved calling the parents in the event of an unexcused absence. But Marcy hadn't mentioned they were in the process of reaching out to the parents or guardians. Why would she? The woman barely knew how to field a phone call without coming across as a snarky bitch. Marcy Cartwright played a lot of the dealings in Student Life close to the vest, and Mary had had many an argument with the woman about her tight-lipped way of handling student affairs. *The question is … do I call Mike Distefano himself to find out where they are with this? Sidestep good ole Marcy? She'll hit the roof!*

That made it almost seem worth it.

Mary fumbled in her purse beside her desk, drew out a crumpled pack of Parliaments.

First things first. A cigarette would calm her nerves. She located her bottle of Xanax and partook of one more as well, which did not soften nor slow her frantic thoughts like the sweet and sour taste of a nicotine hit as much as it turned her into jelly from head to toe. And even that took a few minutes.

Your mind keeps running to the worst-case scenario. There is an explanation for all of this. How much of this is legit, and how much is withdrawal from your meds? Hell, you didn't even report the students at the coffee shop to Tony Stadt because you're not entirely sure they were as bad as you remember. You can't trust your own thoughts off meds, and you need to get back on them before you do some real damage. Or don't you remember what you did with Jenny?

Her desk phone rang.

See? Probably Mike with an update about the kids!

She was all too eager to snatch up the phone, fumbling it at first before pinning it between her shoulder and cheek while she worked a cigarette out of the pack and prayed it hadn't broken in half.

"Guidance Office?" she said.

An automated female voice answered. "This is Hulmeville Prison. Will you accept a call from—*Dallas Teller?*" The name was a recording of Dallas himself, his voice manic sounding.

Slowly, Mary set the pack of Parliaments down on her desk and gripped the headset tightly.

Evenly, she said, "I will."

"Thank you," the automated voice said.

Then, all at once, Dallas Teller was in Mary's ear.

"Miss Marguerite? Man, thank Christ you picked up! Thanks for taking the call."

"That's fine, Dallas," Mary said, shutting her eyes. "How are you?"

"They're gone, aren't they?"

"Who's gone, Dallas?"

"The others."

"I-I don't know—"

"You've been calling them The Nine, I think? Them. They're gone, right?"

"What do you mean *gone*? Do you know something?"

What could he possibly know? He's in lock up, Mare.

"Please-please-*please*, Miss Marguerite! I already know. All right? I already

211

know what's going on. You're the one who has questions. And I want to tell you everything. Because you're the only one who'll fuckin' *actually* listen." A pause. "You were always a good listener. A real straight shooter."

"Well, I-I … Dallas, how did you know I call them The Nine?"

"Call it a blessing and a curse how I know," Dallas rambled, like a racing a clock. "I know more than I ever wanted to."

"Dallas—"

"Like, I know what I was going to do to *them* is *nothing* compared to what's happening to them right now. What he wanted to do to me. *And* what *they're* gonna do to all of you when they come back."

"Dallas, who is *he*? Are you talking about Mr. Crenshaw?"

The laugh on the other end came crawling out of Dallas, slow and low and creepy. "Nah. Things have changed for Mr. Crenshaw, that *fuck*! He's out of the game. He just don't know it yet. He's out. So's Tilly. There's been an adjustment. And I want to—I *need to tell you what's happening!* Please, will you come? Talk to me! I'll tell you everything you need to know!"

Mary's heart was throwing itself against her ribcage. Drawing in a deep breath, she envisioned her center, the core of her being, and concentrated all her efforts on bringing her body back to a homeostasis that would allow her to regain her poise and center herself.

"Miss Marguerite, *hello*!"

"Three o'clock," she said, shuddering in her seat.

"Thank Christ!" he bellowed. "You won't regret it."

"I hope not, Dallas. I truly do."

"Thank you."

"You're welcome."

She moved to hang up the phone when she heard Dallas still talking. She replaced it to her ear. "I'm sorry, I missed that last part."

"I just said I wanted to show you how grateful I am by giving you a bit of good news."

"O-kay."

"Your daughter said *Mommy* for the first time at school today."

"Excuse me?"

"Jenny?"

Mary's breath caught in her throat. *What. Is. Happening?*

"Okay, Miss Marguerite. Thanks. I hope that makes your day."

A dial tone.

When the door to the visiting area of Hulmeville Prison wheezed open twenty minutes after Mary had taken a seat by the window, as far from the other inmates and their visitors as possible, she was not prepared for the arrival of Dallas Teller. He'd always been unusually tall, angular, and gangly for a seventeen-year-old boy. The more literate students at Baldwin had taken to calling him "Ichabod Crane" early on. Mary had met with Dallas a handful of times in the last three years before Conor Crenshaw's fateful referral, and she'd inquired each time about his diet and verified he had access to at least three square meals a day. The boy confessed he ate like a bird and was self-conscious about eating in front of other people. He skipped lunch at school as a result. But the boy in prison orange with his hands and feet shackled who made his way towards her with his mouth set and slanted somewhat sideways looked like a husk of the Junior she'd come to know during her meetings with him.

Dallas Teller stood six foot four. It would have proven an imposing height if the boy did not look to have shed twenty pounds in the last six weeks. He walked with precarious, wobbly steps that made it seem like he was walking atop stilts and trying to remain upright. When Mary was younger, her parents took her to the Ringling Brothers and Barnum and Bailey Circus. The Stilt Man was a fixture under the big top, and when her eight-year-old self had encountered the performer gliding slowly by her, she had crowded herself into her mother's skirt and dropped her Sno-Cone. The Stilt Man had terrified her. Seated there as Dallas nodded to his handler, a short and squat black man in a khaki suit with the letters DOC stenciled across his chest, Mary felt that old familiar dread seep back into her muscles and startle her already nervous mind.

He nodded shallowly at Mary, sweeping his long, stick-like legs down around the seat across from her at the table and then disappearing them underneath. Dallas laid his hands down on the table. The handler seized the manacle's chain and connected it to a steel loop poking up out of a hole in the center of the table. Then, he retreated into the background, taking up a position by the window a few feet away.

Mary glanced out the window, uncertain how to proceed. The way she saw it, there was no suitable *ice breaker* for such an encounter. The air seemed sour and heavy, like humidity with weight behind it. The sky outside the window was crawling with pregnant grey clouds, slipping and colliding and mounting one another, building towards what AccuWeather predicted as a *thunder snow* event. Spring and Winter brawling it out behind a heavy, smeared pane of glass.

Spreading her hands in her lap, Mary turned to look at Dallas, who gazed at her expectantly.

She gasped, a closer look revealing the unthinkable.

"Oh my God, Dallas," she said, leaning in. "What did you do to yourself?"

He looked at her befuddled, eyes blinking slow. Then, his hands crept to his throat, where a deep purple and red bruise peeked out from under the collar of his orange jumpsuit. It ringed his neck. Mary could see the subtle indentation in the boy's taut flesh. Dallas's eyes widened, like he'd had no idea it was there.

That wasn't it, of course.

"This? This I did not do." He told her this like someone tired of being disbelieved. There was no fight or insistence in his tone. He sounded sunk.

"Dallas, dear God. Did someone in here do that to you?"

He shook his head. "It wasn't an inmate." He paused, licked his chapped lips. "Everyone in here thinks I strung myself up because that's how they found me when they came running in to my cell. But someone did this *to me*."

"Who was it?"

The boy looked at Mary for a long time, silent and still. Mary felt like they were the only two people in that room, even though a two-year-old was screaming bloody murder across the way and trying to work himself off his mother's lap so he could hug his felon father, who looked thoroughly disinterested in such a thing. Thunder clapped, flickering the lights of the visiting room. Wind hurled itself at the windowpane like a bird attempting suicide. Then, Dallas Teller went on, as if prompted by the knell of violent nature outside.

"Well, this seems like as good a lead-in as we're going to get, so." He straightened in his seat, his head coming up above Mary so he had to look down on her. "Miss Marguerite, I'm gonna need you to promise me you'll keep an open mind and that you'll take every word I say to you as Gospel, as my mother would say. Can you agree to that, so I don't open up my veins right here in front of you without good reason?"

"I-I, well, Dallas, I'm going to try to … I'll hear you out. I've got questions. They're mounting, it seems. By the hour. And I don't know what you're going to tell me but let me say this. I *want* to believe you. Because things have been happening ever since that morning."

"Tell me," he said, clasping his hands before him like an earnest priest.

Mary traced an invisible circle on the tabletop, a common fidget of hers. "I'll tell you I had a heck of a time tearing myself away from school this afternoon. I had to lie to them and say there was a death in my family and I'd just gotten the phone call. Even then, Principal Stadt looked like he didn't believe a word of it. But he waved me out. They're trying to get in touch with the parents. Of the students? No luck with any of them by the time I left. The kids … there's a fear they've all gone missing."

"I told you they were."

"No, you only said you knew they were absent."

"I *said* they were gone," Dallas insisted, gently. "And they are."

"Nine students are missing, Dallas. And all of their parents seem to have vanished as well."

Dallas dropped his head down. Then he lifted his chin up, his mop of brown hair sweeping back from his high brow. "Are you sure you want to know where they are?"

"Of course I do."

"They're dying," Dallas said. "The Nine." He paused, his eyes wide and hands shaking inside the handcuffs. "Their parents? They're all dead. Murdered."

Mary felt the bottom drop out of her stomach. The weight of Dallas's revelation took time to penetrate her understanding, but when it did, she felt tears prick at her eyes and her face crinkle. The shock she felt was palpable, like a living thing smothering her with big, flat palms. "What?" she managed, breathlessly.

"I know how it sounds, and I know how *I* sound telling you this. You think I'm glad or I don't care. I do. But I tried to do something about it. Now?" He lifted his shackled hands an inch off the table, rattled the chain for effect. "My hands are tied. Literally."

"What do you mean they're dying? The parents? Dead? What are you saying?"

"I'm saying The Nine are busy dying. And the end game was always to rise and slaughter the *false* guardians. The parents. The Nine are changing over. While you and I are sitting here talking. It's a process. The last five months have led up to this. The Nine have been exchanging their—" Dallas drew back, looked at Mary with narrowing eyes. "They were swapping blood with Tilly Crenshaw. Mr. Crenshaw's mother. Kind of the way lovers swap spit and it makes them feel closer to one another? Only, this was more of a mutual transfusion. A blood line running both ways. Joe Brickman was the first one. This year, anyway. Mr. Crenshaw brought him to his mother, to Tilly's house, dropped him off there, and when he came back for Joe, the blood line was established. Mr. Crenshaw did this with The Nine. Every one of them. And he did it with me." Dallas's eyes flashed with knowing, almost a gloating. "But it didn't run as smoothly with me as it did with the others. I wasn't supposed to come to during the *exchange*. I did. That's what I meant when I told that motherfuck Crenshaw 'I'm awake.' I was. He had no idea what I was talking about because of what happened to him. When he got his head knocked around and lost a lot of his memory. He didn't remember what he'd been doing to us, and it's possible he forgot all about Tilly and the whole goddam arrangement."

He's lying about the parents. He's being provocative. He's wrong. Has to be.

"Okay-*hold up*-hold up-*please!*" Mary held up her hands, eyes closed and nostrils flaring. "Just slow down. Please. My head is spinning."

"All right, sorry. I know we only have an hour, and I been waiting to spill all this for someone who'll listen. See, cuz I told all the fuckarows I could in here. Told my lawyer. Fired him when he tried to talk me into an insanity defense. Told the police. They all told me in so many words to *go fuck myself!* Hell, I even made the mistake of trying to tell my bunkmate. He knocked me around for 'wasting his fuckin' time' and then he transferred out. I haven't gotten a new mate since, but I don't give a shit, see? I—"

"I have questions you said you'd try to answer. All right?"

Dallas put up his hands in mock surrender. "Go ahead."

"You said *this year*. That Joe Brickman was the first *this year*. How long has whatever this is with Mr. Crenshaw been going on?"

He looked at the ceiling, sniffed. Then he looked at her with calculating eyes. "However long he's been a teacher. I remember I asked him one time how long he's been teaching, and he said, like, eight years."

Mary laid her trembling hands flat on the table, trying to steady them against its stiff surface. "Eight years? You say he's been doing something to his students for as long as he's been a teacher."

"That's what I'm saying."

"And what has he been doing to these students for eight years? Has there been sexual abuse?"

"You're not listening, Miss Marguerite," Dallas said, his hands curling into fists. He leaned towards her. "This isn't a molesting thing. Let's get that straight. If that's what it was, Joe or Valerie or me, we would've kicked his nuts in right off the bat. This is more of a *mindfuck*. And that's in the simplest terms."

"How do you know all of this?"

"Ah," Dallas sighed, leaning back and folding his bony arms across his rail of a chest, "this is where you're really going to have to stretch the limits of what you ever believed possible. I'm just going to put it out there because I know everything, I'm telling you is the truth and every bit of it can be verified. And I hope you do. Verify all of this. Not because I want to get out of here on a technicality. I want to prevent what's coming." He hesitated. "When Tilly tried to, you know, establish the blood line between her and I, I said I woke up while my mouth was clamped down on her wrist and her mouth was clamped down on mine—"

"Dallas—!"

"Wait-*just wait*! I told you I came to before she could finish. And I never went back there. I knew what was happening. I was awake. But during that brief period before I snapped to, I came away with an … ability, I'll say. While I'm not a part of their little coven, I'm plugged in to everything they've been doing. Everything with Tilly. Mr. Crenshaw. And with The Old Man. I'll call him The Old Man. For now. So, I'm priv—priv—"

"You're privy."

"Yeah, I'm privy to all of it. The only one I can't get any kind of a read on is The Granddad. That fucked-up looking deer."

"The what?"

"Nah, The Granddad's insulated. Top of the food chain. He's The Revelator. His mind. Can't get in. But that's no big deal because he's more of a watcher. An outside observer who only steps in when he's looking to get things back on course." Dallas paused. "You're looking at me a certain way."

Mary drew back, a nervous grin playing about her lips. She turned aside, measuring the darkening skyline absently. She took a deep, heady breath in, blew out through her nose, and clapped her hands along the edge of the table. "Okay," she said, her tone an intermingling of amusement and dread. "I want to believe you. I said that. I meant it. But, Dallas, it sounds to me like you may be suffering from a break from reality, which is common in people who've been abused for a prolonged period. It's an escape hatch for them."

"Oh, don't you do it, Miss Marguerite! Not you too!"

He tried to stand, only to have his manacled hands yank him back down into his seat. He gritted his teeth, the gums red and inflamed.

Mary waved him back down, just the same. "Don't go, Dallas. Please. I promised you I'd listen and try to believe what you tell me. I'm not in the business of breaking promises. Especially not to my kids. You'll always be a Baldwin student and my allegiance—my loyalty—goes to you just like any other student. So, I'm going to ignore my training. Years and years of experience with troubled young people. And I'm going to treat you with dignity by listening and *trying* to understand you and what drove you to do what you tried to do that morning. But you have to understand, it's like you said. I'll trust, but I'll also verify."

"Hey, listen, those were my words, ma'am. Check me when you leave here. Only don't wait too long or all of this will be for nothing and a lot of people are going to suffer. Comstock? The way you know it now? It's going to go away. It's all just gonna *go away*."

Mary nodded, took another breath, and braced herself. "So, Mr. Crenshaw would take you and the other nine, *along with however many other students through the years*—"

"Two to three per year. He was new at it. It took years for him and that bitch-whore mother of his to get it right. Lots of trial and error. And again … you don't believe me, there's got to be back files on students at Baldwin in your office going back eight years. Look for alumni that committed suicide. Disappeared. Anything that smacks of foul play. Check me. I'm serious."

"I will," Mary said, flatly. "How did Mr. Crenshaw manage to get you to his mother's house unsuspecting?"

"Driver's Ed, ma'am. Road time."

"Driver's Ed. So he drove you there? To his mother's house?"

"Nope, we drove ourselves. The fucked irony of it. He took us out on the road in his car, and he told us where to drive. He'd take us the highway route, so we'd feel like we're being tested, and, you know, getting a feel for the road. But the whole time he was directing us to Tilly's house. Get there and he tells us to stop for a minute, if we don't mind. That it's his mother's place and she just got some furniture delivered. She's older. Late-fifties, maybe? She needs some help moving it around inside to the right room. The same line of bullshit every time. So we park. He walks us up to the back door. Opens the screen door, then the storm door. He says, 'After you,' and he … he waves us in. And then … *fuck me*."

Dallas Teller's eyes were suddenly brimming with tears. He put his head down.

"Take your time," Mary told him, waiting patiently.

After a minute or two, his head came up off his forearm. His spine clicked at the sudden motion. His eyes were slitted and red, his nose a runny mess. He wiped it away with a bare arm and went on.

"The crazy thing is, Tilly is *not* a bad looking woman for her age," he said, shaking his head as if in disbelief at his own observation. "In fact, she's what you'd call, um, I can speak frankly?"

"Go ahead," Mary said, cautiously.

"A MILF? Or a GILF at least." Dallas looked at her, searching for recognition of the term in her eyes. "They stand for—"

"I know what they stand for, Dallas. She's an attractive older woman. You can go on."

Blushing just the same, Dallas nodded stiffly and continued. "Yeah. She looked almost like an older version of a hippie, you know? Long, straight blonde hair. Real skinny. Like—what do they call that look—*waifish*! That's it! I know the other guys in The Nine must have, you know, wanted to get it on with her the minute they saw her. I know I'm not alone in this. And that ... that attraction, at least for the guys ... that helped her to bring our defenses down faster than if she were a hag. I'm sorry, but I'm only being honest."

Mary nodded. *I know there was statutory rape in the mix here. I can't deny it. All signs point to this. Even if the boys took part and not the girls, I'm going to nail someone's ass to the wall for this. I'm just sorry this bitch isn't alive for me to bury her in lawsuits.*

"Tilly's eyes were another story, though," Dallas muttered, his gaze distant and unmoored. "I remember she was waiting for me in the kitchen, and the second I set foot inside, she stepped in my path. She took me by the shoulders, and her eyes immediately set to work coaxing my ... I wanna say my *soul* ... out of my body? Or my mind? Maybe both. I don't really know where the soul resides, but I can tell you everybody's got one. And when someone starts tugging at it, trying to pull it out of you like a mechanic sliding an engine block out of a car, it hurts so bad you either black out or your mind just sort of slips into autopilot. And when *that* happens, it's so completely vulnerable to the power of suggestion, any at all, I think I would have slit my own throat if she told me to. With those eyes. I would have. With a smile on my face.

"It's hard to describe what I saw when I looked in her eyes. At first, they were just regular blue eyes. Big with long, light eyelashes. Really pretty eyes." Dallas paused, examining the surface of the table as if it would stir his memory further. "But when she took me by the shoulders and her eyes started trying to dig my soul out of my body, they turned into, I dunno, a pair of movie projectors. I don't know how to describe it. You know how when you go to the movies and you look at the back wall, you can see that lighted line of dust in the air and you can see the projected film in that dust? That's what I saw when her eyes changed. The dust in her kitchen illuminated the images she was projecting into my eyes. The images filtered through my eyes, and they became a weird kind of movie playing against the back wall of my skull. I ... I'm probably not making any sense."

Dallas sounded defeated, like his own words were failing him in their limitations. Mary was surprised at his choice of certain words, the quality of them. She'd seen Dallas's standardized test scores for the last three years, and they weren't so hot. Yet, the seventeen-year-old was far more well-spoken than any such test would have predicted. Casually, Mary wondered if this sudden advancement in the boy's ability to communicate was not also a byproduct of whatever contact he'd had with this Tilly person.

"You're doing fine, Dallas. I can picture what you're describing. That's good. Go on."

A smile that seemed more rictus than joyful came and went from Dallas's face.

"The movie wasn't like any movie I ever saw before," he said, an expression of revulsion infecting his features little by little. "The pictures, the quick little blips of action … they were edited together so tightly it got to the point I could barely differentiate one thing from the next. Maybe that was the point because it worked on my mind on a subconscious level. You know, like the way advertisers use subliminal messaging in their commercials to make someone crave their product without knowing why or how? That's it."

"Do you remember any of what you saw?"

"Mmmm … it's embarrassing … but I *did* ask you to come here. So I'm just going to."

"Dallas?"

"It was just a mess, Miss Marguerite," he said, tears gleaming once more in his eyes. "Just glimpses. All of it. A baby being born to a corpse inside a casket while a bunch of mourners look on … oh God, that was fucking horrible." He leaned forward, clutching his head. "My bedroom. At least, it looked like my room. All my posters were gone, and there were bloody handprints all over the walls. The ceiling, too. My mom pacing so fast she was a blur of motion. I think she was crying, but she might have been laughing. It sounded interchangeable. Seamless? I dunno. The Tumor Deer—I told you about him, *ole Granddad*—he was standing up on the altar at my church. On his hind legs. His front legs were long, and they had human hands at the ends. He held up a wafer. You know, The Body of Christ? It's a Catholic thing. The parishioners were screaming like they were being disemboweled or something." His breathing sped up. He clutched the edge of the table with hands gone bone-white. "Oh Christ, I saw myself. Inside a casket. Alive. Clawing at the roof. Worms and maggots swarming me. I-I can't-I can't—"

"Okay, all right, Dallas," Mary said, reaching for him. "You don't have to go on. You must have been terrified."

The corrections officer who'd been standing by peeled himself off the wall and stepped up to the table. "Ma'am, no touching! First and final warning!" He turned to Dallas. "You cool, Dallas?"

The boy didn't answer. Didn't move. Then, he mustered a small and barely detectable nod. He raised his head to look up at the corrections officer, whose name was stitched into the breast of his khaki shirt. **OFR. PRINCE**.

"Damn, Dallas! You got a nosebleed."

A rich stream of red was running from his nostrils, into his mouth. His teeth were bloodied when he turned back to Mary.

Officer Prince pulled the radio attached to his lapel up to his mouth. "Yeah, I'm gonna need some tissues. Inmate has a nosebleed."

It might have made Mary laugh if it weren't so surreal. If her head was not spinning out.

Mary smiled warmly. "It's okay, Dallas. I get them all the time. If you want to stop, we can leave it there. I know how hard this has to be for you."

"No," Dallas exclaimed. "*No-no-no!* Just let me clean myself up. You can't leave yet. There's more."

The doors to the visiting room banged open, and another guard, a female this time, bounded over to their table. She handed Dallas a handful of tissues. Officer Prince lingered a bit longer, until Dallas had cleared his face (smearing some of it). He tilted his head back, held it that way for a beat, then lowered it back down. Clutching the bloody handful of tissues in one fist, he waited until Officer Prince stepped forward. The guard had already donned nitrile gloves in anticipation of taking the bloody tissues from Dallas. He did so, and after verifying Dallas was okay to continue with the visit, Officer Prince retreated once more to his post a few feet away.

"Yeah," Dallas said, as if he hadn't missed a beat. "It was pretty bad." He cast his eyes out the window, absently regarding the fat snowflakes swarming the windowpane like fat white flies. "Miss Marguerite?"

"Yes, Dallas?"

"Can I tell you something without you judging me?"

"Of course. We've come this far, after all."

"At the time, all the things she showed me. Those terrible glimpses? They didn't upset me. I think … I think they excited me."

"What do you mean they *excited* you?" Mary stiffened.

"Like, sexually."

She felt the stifling feeling of being boxed into an ever-shrinking room. A compactor. The visiting area had seemed bigger when she'd first come in. Now, she felt like if she were to spread her arms wide, they would hit the walls on either side of her.

"It's okay, Dallas. But you can look back on it, and your finding it upsetting proves that your sexual response to it previously was nothing more than a manifestation of your hormones. Nothing more. Sometimes, a teenager's hormones act more strangely than the teenagers themselves. That doesn't make you a bad person."

"You sure?" His eyes were glassy, desperate.

"I'm sure."

"Good," he said, somewhat satisfied with her diagnosis. "Anyway, I told you I wasn't supposed to come out of this-this *state*. It was supposed to subdue me until the *exchange* was finished and Tilly led me back upstairs and guided me out the door again. With no memory of what happened. I'm sure if you were to ask any of The Nine if they remember any of what I just told you I can remember, they'd have no idea what you're talking about. They all left Tilly's house with minds as clean as slate. As far as they knew, they'd been on the road with Mr. Crenshaw the whole time."

"What was happening when you came to?"

"I told you," he said, exasperated. "I was in the basement. She must have led me down there. Taken me by the hand or something. I remember how it felt, slipping her grasp. I was digging myself out of a grave. Moving the dirt aside, somehow. It was packed tight, and it was really hard to slither through, but that's what I did. I fought. I remember how hard I fought. It was my grave. I was trying to escape my own grave. And I did it. I got out. Pulled myself up and out. Then, the next thing I knew, I was on my knees, and Tilly was leaning forward in a rocking chair towards me. The cement floor was so cold. My legs were numb. And … it's like I said. Tilly was drinking from a wound she'd bitten into my wrist. I had her wrist in my mouth, and I was drinking from her. And, I can tell you I've tasted blood before. You know, when you cut your finger and you suck on it to try and stop it from gushing? Tastes like an old, dirty penny. Coppery. Tilly's blood didn't taste anything like that."

Mary didn't say anything. She suspected he would continue of his own accord.

Dallas bit his lower lip, teeth pulling at the fatty flesh. "It tasted like, like the best swallow of fruit juice you could possibly imagine. Like some kinda nectar of the gods. It was just *so* fucking good. I-I didn't want to stop drinking. But I did. I pulled away. And I booked it out there. I was dizzy. I don't know how much of my blood she'd taken out of me. I almost fell flat on my face going up the stairs, but I made it all the way out of the basement. Through the kitchen. I escaped out the back door. I didn't meet back up with Mr. Crenshaw. He was waiting in the car. I cut through a bunch of neighbors' yards until I found a bus stop. I tried to take a Septa bus. They wouldn't let me board. My mouth was ringed in blood. It was all down my shirt. I was covered in it. I must have looked like a fucking psychopath. So I walked the ten miles home, keeping to the shadows as best I could so no one saw this bloodied teenager roaming the streets.

"For the next couple of months, I felt like I was stuck inside this waking dream. Everything looked like it was covered in a thin layer of gauze. I thought of telling my mom I wanted to get my eyes checked. Maybe I needed glasses. But I just couldn't be bothered. I couldn't bring myself to ask for help.

"I went through the motions. School. Home. Maybe two hours of sleep a night, and it was broken. I kept seeing Tilly with her mouth clamped around my wrist. Only she was a lot older. She looked twice her age. Wrinkly. Her skin was yellow and shot with blue lines. Her veins, I guess they were. And The Nine. I had nightmares about them. Those poor bastards. I don't blame them. They were as oblivious as I was. In the nightmares, they would corner me at school. The lunch room. Bio class. A bathroom stall. They'd punch and kick and slap at me until they got me on the ground. Then … then the knives came out. I always woke up the second before they, well, they got down to business. Every. Goddam. Night. And I was losing my mind.

"My grades dropped. I'm sure Academics noticed, and I waited to be called to their office. That never happened. I did manage to convince them to let me drop the Driver's Ed course. I told them I was having panic attacks out on the road, and they let me lose that elective. Thank Christ they did! I couldn't bear to sit in Mr. Crenshaw's class, let alone catch a glimpse of him in the halls. Getting swarmed by students like some kind of Messiah! The man is the fucking Devil, Miss Marguerite. I know you had your suspicions about him. That something wasn't right. You were on the money. It's been wrong for a long time. And he needed to be stopped. I remember the day he came strolling into the Men's Room while I was in there. He came up to the urinal right next to mine, and I know he *knew* what he was doing. He was trying to intimidate me. To get me to break. I thought he might try to work some mindfuck on me again. And I wasn't gonna let him. I remember he tried to say something to me. That's when I grabbed his arm and I told him. I laid it out for him. I wanted him to know that I was onto him! I knew what he did to me. How he tricked me. I told him I was *awake.*

"By the look in his eyes, I could tell the guy had *no fucking idea* what the hell I was talking about. Then I remembered. It was all around school. He got beat up bad, and it messed up his memory. He looked at me the way a sensitive little kid looks at you when you rag on his mom for no reason. Hurt. Shocked. It made me mad that he couldn't remember what he'd done to me. To all of us. He may have gotten his head bashed in, but he got off easy, if you ask me. Way too easy!

"I had enough. Had my fill. That day, I went home and I made my list."

"The people you wanted to—" Mary broke off, sickened by the word that hung in her mind, unspoken and unimaginable.

"Yes. It would be stupid to deny it, wouldn't it?" His eyes widened with a strange delight. "I went to a lot of trouble for what I still think was a good cause. I got to work right away. I hit up a coin shop over by the Neshaminy Mall. I bought up a whole bunch of old silver coins. They're surprisingly cheap. Mom keeps her *Rainy-Day* money in her underwear, so I had to dig through her panties to get to the baggie full of ones. No fun, but what can you do? Next, I hit a craft store and bought myself a mini art furnace. It's about the size of a shoebox. And, with the help of a couple YouTube videos, I managed, through a lot of trial and error, to cast twelve silver bullets down in my mom's basement. She works odd shifts. She had no idea."

"Silver bullets?"

"You can't kill them with regular ammo. It's gotta be silver."

Mary felt a lightness of being for the first time since she'd sat down with Dallas. It was welcome, if not surreal, considering the context. "All right," she said, "I'll bite. Take me all the way down the rabbit hole if you must."

"If you haven't figured out what The Nine have become, what Tilly was, then I guess I haven't done a very good job explaining."

"You believe they're all vampires." It wasn't a question, even though Mary heard it as such in her mind.

Dallas looked at her, his mouth set and lips bloodless. His jaws were clenched, digging little divots into his cheeks. "They are. And silver bullets aren't just for hunting werewolves. I thought so too. It's true. And like I said. Like we agreed. Check me out on all of this. Verify. You'll find I'm telling the truth, and that I drafted that list with the sole intent of killing a coven of vampires. And Mr. Crenshaw, the sonofabitch Renfield-wannabe who tricked them all into it. All to please his mother and his father."

"And someone else you obviously changed your mind about. The person you scribbled out."

The teenager tore his gaze away and cast his glare over her left shoulder. "Right," he blurted, uncomfortably.

"I don't suppose you'd be open to telling me who it was you *changed your mind* about?"

"What does it matter?" he countered, mildly irritated. "I was going to spare that person. Now more than ever, I'm proud of that decision."

"That's fine." Mary cleared her throat. "So, is Conor Crenshaw a vampire also?"

"No," Dallas said flatly. "His father refused to turn him. His father didn't trust him. But he turned Tilly, his wife. She would prove useful to him, and he trusted her about as much as a husband trusts his wife. He had plans for her. He tasked her with populating his coven, because he wouldn't return to Comstock until he knew he had his loyalists. A coven's main purpose is always to protect and serve The Master. Or … as The Nine has come to know him, The Father."

"A father to a group of *fatherless children*. Is that the connection? Is that why he chose them?"

"Yes," Dallas said, seeming pleased Mary had finally begun to connect the impossible dots on her own now. "It's why he chose me too. My dad died when I was three. I never knew him. He was a war veteran. Served three tours in Iraq. He hung himself in an empty warehouse a block from where we live. I don't have enough of a memory to mourn or to miss him. But dad was also a bona fide *gun nut*. Mom kept his collection to remember him by. And she was responsible, so don't go thinking she left the gun safe open one day out of carelessness and that's how I got a hold of Dad's AR-15. No, she's not to blame. Her lack of imagination as to where to hide the key to the gun safe? She could've done better there. But even if she *had* hidden the key in a better hiding spot, I would have found a way. There's *always* another way when someone sets their mind to killing."

Mary shifted uncomfortably in her seat. Covertly, she checked her watch while rearranging herself. Fifteen minutes left. *I've got to get out of here. I can't believe I'm still listening to this. Dallas Teller is a victim of abuse with an elaborate imagination. Nothing more. He's using that imagination to justify his actions and to escape the reality of his life, post-abuse. Dammit, Mary, just get up and LEAVE!*

"You want to go," Dallas said. "I know. And I understand."

Somehow, his *knowing* sapped her of the motivation to get up and get out. Mary found she could not do so even though she wanted to. She felt a strange kind of containment. A submissiveness she could not shake. "I'll leave when you're finished."

"More questions? Questions giving birth to more questions. Sorry about that. If it's any consolation, Miss Marguerite, I'm not ... uh, *privy*, to all the things *I* want to know."

"Like what?"

"Well, for instance, I don't know how Conor's father came to become a vampire, let alone such a strong and domineering one." He touched his finger to the small divot in his chin thoughtfully. "My theory? He was taken. Turned. Left for dead. Died a *natural* death and was born into darkness. Someone—or probably some *thing*—took him by surprise and left him no choice in the matter. Then they left him, continuing the long line of *fathers abandoning or leaving their children.* His Maker abandoned him. And so on and so on. The world we live in, eh, Miss Marguerite? Soul-crushing."

"Mm, it sounds like you know enough. Do you know about what The Nine have taken to calling themselves?"

"Yeah," Dallas said, rolling his eyes. "And I think it's stupid as shit. *Crenshaw's Children?* I mean, come the fuck on!"

Mary shrugged. "Doesn't really make sense, does it? If these teenagers were in search of a father figure, and they found it in this, this Vampire Father-Master-what-have you, then why would they call themselves Mr. Crenshaw's children? You said he's not even a vampire."

"I know. I said it's fucking stupid. It's idiotic. But it fits. You just have to think it through a little more."

"How so, Dallas?"

"Crenshaw isn't just Conor Crenshaw's last name, now is it?"

Mary felt the lump in her throat slide into place, shrinking her air canal. "Crenshaw *Senior.* The Father. And ... Conor's father."

"Real dipshit, right?"

Silence.

Crenshaw's Children. The Father's Children.

Fatherless Children.

"They all have a father again."

"Yes. And they will do whatever he tells them to. They're missing, but they'll be back. But they won't be who they were when they come back. They're dying now, like I said. The next time you see them ... you better run. As fast as your feet will take you. Don't try to save them. Don't try to be their *guidance counselor* or try to be the hero. You can see what happens to the *hero* in the end." Once more, Dallas Teller drew her attention to his manacles, shaking them in the air as he'd done at the outset. "Not to mention you're marked."

"I'm *what?*"

"That's another reason I needed to see *you* in particular, Miss Marguerite."

224

She could not help her mind suddenly seizing upon the image of The Nine trailing her while she drove from school to the coffee shop to meet with Maddie Crenshaw. The impossible distance they'd covered and equally improbable time they had all made, keeping up with her car while on foot. All of them.

"Their feet don't touch the ground, Miss Marguerite," Dallas said, once more answering Mary's unasked question. "Not the way yours and mine do. Other than the slight arch, our feet plant themselves on the ground from heel to side ridge and all the way up to the little piggies gone to market. When *they* walk, it's an optical illusion that our minds are more than happy to fill in the blanks, so it makes sense to us. Their toes are the only parts of their feet that touch the ground when they move, and even then, it's barely a grazing contact between one and the other. When you and I look at them, we see what we want to see … or what *they* want us to see. Full foot contact with the ground. In actuality, they're practically hovering at all times. That's how they did it. How they followed you on foot."

"You're telling me they were, what, *flying?*"

"Yes," Dallas said, clearly more comfortable with both stating and discussing the impossible and the miraculous with her than he was initially. The teenager was emboldened. He sniffed loudly, hesitated, then Dallas Teller practically extended the entire upper half of his body across the table to make for a more covert exchange between them. "Okay," he said, his voice low and rasping. "All right. Full disclosure, Miss Marguerite. I-I can't keep this from you. It's gonna sound sick, and it's going to make you think I'm a pervert. You may even tell me to go take a flying *fuck*, for all I know. But at least I will have told you. I will have done my part in protecting you." He chuckled darkly. "Because I am pretty certain I'm not getting out of this place any other way than by gurney. Zipped into a body bag. Whatever The Father decides to leave of me when he's done with me—"

"Dallas, if you feel your life is being threatened in here, I can talk to someone—"

"Please," he cut her off, holding his palms up in supplication, "no need. All I want you to do is to listen and to remember my intentions were pure."

"Dallas—"

"I crossed out *your name* on the list," he said. "It was you. And I'm sorry but let me explain.

"Me? What-why?"

"Let me *explain*," Dallas pleaded with her now.

Mary's mouth hung open, her eyes wide and surprised as Mr. Crenshaw's eyes had been that day in the Men's Room when he'd had his run-in with a boy named Dallas Teller. She swung her legs out from under the table and abruptly stood up, buttoning up the front of her coat.

"This was a mistake," she said, not looking at him. Her gaze landed on all things around Dallas Teller, but flinched away from the teenager himself like the sight of him head-on could blind her. "I have to go."

"Oh no, Miss Marguerite!" Dallas struggled to stand, bracing himself along the lip of the table and barely gaining purchase as the grapples bit into his wrists. "No, please! Don't go! Wait!"

"Please don't contact me again, Dallas—"

"You don't understand!"

"The day I come to *understand* a word you've been saying, they'll have to come for me with a straitjacket!"

"I saw you! I *saw* you! In my visions! I-I didn't-I *couldn't* tell you!"

"You need help, Dallas! I hope you get it."

"I was embarrassed, Miss Marguerite! I'm sorry! But I saw you in the visions! At first, I couldn't be sure it was you. It was all quick clips and edits bleeding into one another and cutting away, and it made me sick, and I felt like I was coming apart inside! Then I was *certain, dead certain,* it was you!"

She turned and hurried back towards the double door entryway.

Officer Prince came up behind Dallas, planted his hands on the teen to lead him away. "C'mon, Dallas."

"The Father, oh Christ, *he was fucking you! The vision showed me!*"

Mary wheeled around, her blood pressure up and profanities pressing at her lips and twitching along her tongue.

What she saw put her back on her heels at once.

What had been a nosebleed before had become a thick, flow of mucous and blood pouring out of Dallas Teller's flaring nostrils.

And his eyes.

His mouth.

His ears.

With his tongue and teeth tacky with blood, Dallas cried out. "You're the mark, now! *Miss, Miss, Marguer—*"

Dallas Teller's legs gave out. The manacles that had locked him to the center of the table yanked against his hands and arms, and the rest of Dallas did not so much drop as slide somewhat underneath the table itself. He dangled there, hovering between a prone position and sitting. Blood now poured from every blessed orifice and opening. The back of his pants was stained crimson. The front, as well. It ran down the orange legs of his prison jumper, purpling the stiff fabric.

"*DALLAS!*" Mary lunged across the room, handbag sliding down her arm and past her hand. Its contents spilled out across the linoleum tiles. "*OhmyGod!*"

Officer Prince lunged forward as if spring-loaded. He unlocked the manacles from the steel ring in the table, then braced the back of the teenager to lower him onto his side without the boy striking the back of his skull against the unforgiving floor.

Mary crowded in, already having worked herself out of her coat and rolling up her sleeves.

"Ma'am!" Officer Prince screamed. "I need you to stand back!"

"I-I can help you! I know CPR!"

"I'm happy for you, ma'am, but this boy's bleeding out faster than a quadruple amputee! Just *keep BACK!*"

But even Officer Prince suddenly appeared at a loss, leaning over the now spasming body of the boy with his hands in the air and his mouth pulled into a tight knot of concentration. A dark red pool crept across the tiles from underneath Dallas Teller's body.

Blood splashed up Mary's pant legs, kicked up by the boy's involuntary motion.

He's-dying-right-there-on-the-dirty-floor.

Immobilized, Mary stood there and fought with all her might the overwhelming need to be of some help. She looked at Dallas.

The fact he'd somehow managed to turn his head to look her in the eye during his final death throes stole Mary Marguerite's breath at once.

He mouthed a word to her. Then his body gave a terrible shudder from crown to toes and Dallas Teller went still in Officer Prince's arms.

One word.

Mother.

VIII. WHAT WOULD THE NEIGHBORS SAY?

When Maddie Crenshaw pulled up in front of Tilly Crenshaw's house, she found the young twentysomething blonde pacing in the driveway with her hands double-fisting two cups of Wawa coffee and a look of consternation laid plain across her face. It looked like the realtor, a young woman named Terry Nolan, had just received terrible news, like a loved one died, or her condo had burnt to the ground.

Maddie had just hung up with the caretaker of St. Luke's Cemetery, who'd called to tell her about some "disturbance" to Tilly's grave. Maddie had asked him to elaborate on the word, and what the caretaker described sounded far less than what he'd implied. "It looked like someone—prob'ly a couple of people—dug her up and then, I dunno, buried her again," he'd said. And it wasn't that the news hadn't fazed her. It did indeed give Maddie pause, but not enough she felt the need to make the trip to the site of Tilly's grave to inspect and commiserate any further with the caretaker on the matter.

And it's not because I never liked her! Not because she didn't like me either!

She killed the engine, turning away from the realtor, who had stopped in place and was now eyeing Maddie's Subaru cautiously. "Oh, Tilly," she said to herself, face turned to the other side of the street, "you're more trouble dead than you ever were alive. Dammit.,"

It vented some of the frustration she was feeling, and by the time Maddie strode up the driveway of cracked, crumbly, black asphalt, she found she could muster some small smile of greeting. The realtor had called her there, asked to meet. More great news tied to the *old bitch* weeks in the ground.

"Hey, thanks for meeting me, Maddie."

"Of course," Maddie said. "We're going to freeze out here. Why don't we go in, and we'll talk?"

Terry Nolan shook her head, a shudder that either signaled cold or dread shaking her body beneath the black pea coat hanging just past her thighs. "Here," she said, handing the second sixteen-ounce of joe over to Maddie. "I brought this for you. I know it's cold, but there's no way we could go inside and have a chat, even if we both wanted to."

"Why? What's wrong?"

"Here," Terry nodded over towards the sidewalk and led the way, "let's walk and talk. And drink a little liquid gold, huh?"

Maddie fell in line. She sipped at the coffee and relished it. Briefly.

"So what is it?"

The realtor walked stoically along, her eyes measuring the cement terrain before them as if in meditation. "As I'm sure you're aware by now, the house is just not selling. I've done close to thirty walkthroughs. Young couples. Families. All walks of life and income. And each time, I've run into the same obstruction. I'm not talking a credit issue. Not the interior layout. Nothing to that effect. I only wish it were one of those things, but in every instance—and I do mean *every instance*—they cut the house tour short before we even made it out of the foyer. Now, I haven't been doing this for years and years, Maddie, but I can tell you with confidence this is *not* the norm. There's something else going on here. In there, actually." She paused, perhaps expecting Maddie to answer. When Maddie didn't, Terry pressed on. "So, you've got to decide which way you'd like to go from here."

From the first phone call, when Maddie had called to retain Terry Nolan's service at her Re/Max office in Warminster, and right up until this conversation, the realtor had always used the word *we* when it came to their working together to sell The Crenshaw House. Maddie had recognized it at once as the realtor pairing herself up with her client for the sake of building and cementing a rapport. *We. We'll sell this house in record time. We will set the initial asking price high at first. We. We. We.*

Now, walking beside the young realtor, Maddie was acutely aware of how that *We* had become *You. As in, this is our goodbye and you're on your own with this shit heap of a house from here on out.*

"Let me stop you, if you don't mind," Maddie interjected. "It's only been a little over two months. Now, I know these things take time. You must know it too. I mean, when my parents sold their townhouse, it took a little over a year and three price drops before anybody made a real offer. And their house was immaculate."

"So you understand what sort of, well, property we're working with then?" The realtor cast a sidelong glance at The Crenshaw House as they cleared its perimeter. There was something in the young woman's eyes Maddie could not place but did not like either. "Mrs. Crenshaw, you made it clear to me you and your mother-in-law weren't exactly close. Do you have *any,* and I do mean *any,* affection for the house?"

What a strange question. "None," Maddie said. "I'd sooner see it bulldozed and be done with it."

"Good," Terry Nolan breathed, as if she'd been let off the hook. "That makes it easier to speak frankly, knowing it won't offend you."

"What? Is that what you think I should do? Just take a loss and move on? There's no chance it might sell?"

"No," Terry said, curtly. "And it wouldn't even work as a rental."

Maddie didn't say anything. She listened absently to the hypnotic clicking of the realtor's black heels along the sidewalk. Sipped at her coffee and worked at letting go of any prospect of making money off the house where her husband had grown up. And where his mother had, no doubt, fostered serious abandonment/attachment issues within him from the cradle onward. It suddenly seemed right and proper the house be razed or immolated.

"Okay. Did any of them tell you what the problem was exactly? Anything at all?"

"I hand out Feedback Cards to every prospective buyer," Terry said. "Not everyone turns them in, which is to be expected. But there have been a handful who have provided a reason for not moving any further."

"Like what?"

"The house gave a number of them an *unsettling* feeling. A few even questioned *my* ethics, because they were certain something bad had to have taken place there at some point to leave such a bad … *residue* behind. Their word, by the way. And I'm obligated to disclose when a murder or a suicide has taken place on a property. So, I'll ask you. Did something happen here you're not telling me, Maddie?"

"Other than the woman of the house dying here after what had to have been days on the floor of the basement? Nothing but that. Is that relevant? I mean, houses are put up for sale every day when the owner dies. And you knew that. I told you the circumstances."

"You did tell me that. But there's nothing *beyond* that?"

"No," Maddie said, emphatically. "I would've told you. I'm not playing games here."

"Mmm." The realtor lapsed into a brief silence. It started to annoy Maddie, these pregnant pauses. "One of them wrote that they felt like they were being watched when they walked back out to their car. Not by me. They were specific about that. Someone was watching them. From one of the windows upstairs. Frankly, I was shocked they wrote that on a Feedback Card. Most people wouldn't put themselves out there like that. They'd simply move on in their search. End of story."

"Well," Maddie said, "did you ever feel anything along those lines? You've been through the whole house. You would have experienced something, right?"

"One gentleman even wrote that his wife's bipolar depression spiked on the ride home from visiting the house."

"Jesus."

"I'll show them to you, Maddie. This is real."

"Oh, this is *bunk!*"

"Whatever it is, the house is not going to sell. It will not turn a profit. And you've got a decision to make."

Maddie stopped dead, wheeled on the realtor. The fire of irritation in her eyes was not for the realtor, but rather the old woman who continued to complicate her life from beyond the grave. "Fine," she said, "I'll agree to another avenue after I see for myself what everyone else is talking about. I want to go inside, and I want to see if it makes me feel something similar to what they've described. If I do, then we'll talk about abandoning the sale. I'll wash my hands of the whole thing."

"Mrs. Crenshaw, as I've said—"

"Yes, you said we couldn't go in *even if we wanted to*. It's a strange thing to say, Terry. I think you know that. But I insist. Let's go in and see what all the fuss is about. Let's see if you can make me a believer."

Terry Nolan grabbed Maddie's shoulder, firmly. "You won't make it past the kitchen."

"Why is that? What the *hell* is going on?"

"What's going on? The house smells like death! Like something has been rotting inside for a very long time. Last week? There was nothing of the sort. The place smelled like the Yankee Candle I burn in the living room on Open House days. It smelled like fresh linens. You don't want to experience it. Believe me."

Only, Maddie did. She said so.

The overwhelming odor was not new for Terry the Realtor, as it was for Maddie Crenshaw. But the muddy footprints stamped across the cheap, bendy linoleum tiles of the kitchen were. The moment Terry unlocked the side entrance, which entered into the kitchen, the smell she'd described, that of death and a long-neglected tomb with a body left uncovered to the elements of decay, wafted an awful, hot breath in both their faces. It doubled Maddie over because she was not prepared for it. Terry managed to pinch her nose shut and breathe through her mouth as she filed inside.

The kitchen was as it had been when Matilda Crenshaw herself prattled around within, banging pots and pans around or fixing her only son, Conor, his favorite sandwich—toasted bologna and ketchup. Dark wood cabinets stared dully downward at them like blackened eyes.

Terry took a knee and touched the footprints. A closer inspection revealed the prints were numerous, mashed on top of one another to the point they blended nearly into a hodge-podge of brownish stamps that did not stop at the basement door across the kitchen, but appeared to continue on beneath the door itself. Downstairs. "These are dried," Terry said, confounded. "This was not here a half hour ago when I arrived and popped my head in. The smell was, well, it was a bit weaker earlier, if you can believe that. These—these just happened."

"How many are there?"

"Impossible to tell. All I know is they weren't here before, and now, not only can both of us see them plain as day but they're dry. Dusty, almost. Like they've been here for decades, drying out over time."

Maddie inched her way further into the kitchen. She pinched her nostrils closed while cupping her palm across her mouth just enough so she could breathe in and out comfortably. She followed the barefoot markings away from the basement door, not able to confront their implication just yet.

Terry sniffed at her fingers, which now bore some of the brown stuff that had flaked away. Her gag reflex seized her at once, and she tasted the vomit rise in her throat and pool in her mouth. No choice but to swallow it back down, wretched as it was. "Blood," she said, a feather tickling her epiglottis. She did not speak with her tongue, but rather *around* it so as not to set off another round of sickness. "Blood and feces."

"Look here." Maddie was craning her neck to look upward. Then her head swiveled. "The prints are all over the walls. The ceiling. They're everywhere, walking every which goddam way."

Maddie turned to Terry just as the realtor's sick burst out of her and splashed the tiles so viciously the sound was more solid than wet. "*Oh Ggoddd ... godda geddouttahere!*" Her mouth still stretched into a great maw that would no doubt precede another round of vomiting, Terry surged past Maddie and banged out the screen door.

The terrible sounds of the realtor heaving her guts up just outside engaged Maddie's own gag reflex as the sickly smell of rotten eggs and rancid meat hit her like a swift, stunning backhand. She barely staved off her own sickness. Her hand had fallen away absently when she looked up at the ceiling and found what looked to be the starting point for the dizzying array of footprints stamped across every surface of the small kitchen. A hole yawned down at her a foot from where the cheap chandelier was bolted to the drywall. Vertigo took hold of Maddie as she stared up and through the hole, which looked wide enough to permit the passage of a mid-sized body through. And beyond that, Maddie saw the second-floor room directly above had a hole punched through its ceiling as well.

Can't be.

Can't.

Beyond the hole in the second-floor room, a third hole in the roof of the attic gaped with jagged teeth of wood and plaster and shredded shingles. It looked like the great mouth of some monster with blackened teeth. Only inside the mouth of this particular monster, Maddie found she could see the darkening skies above. Black, fattening clouds tumbled over top of one another as if clamoring for the attention of something out of view. Maddie tried to lower her head, to turn her eyes aside from the open seam in The Crenshaw House's seemingly parallel universe.

Something pulled at her. Hands inside her skull, clasping her poor brain. Yanking it upward as if to free it from her head.

A migraine bloomed, pulsing and paralyzing, in Maddie's skull. She screamed. *I don't want to see anymore. I won't look. I'm leaving. Something wants me gone. I'm going. I'm going, I swear to God—*

"Maddie!"

Behind her, Terry the Realtor seized her by the shoulders and led her roughly out the way they had come in.

"The ceiling!" Maddie cried. "Did you see? Goes all the way to space! I saw a face all the way up … but it wasn't God, no it wasn't God—"

"Come on," Terry pressed, holding her about the shoulders and leading her down the driveway with something of a heavy, desperate hand. "We have to go."

When Maddie turned her vacant gaze to look at the realtor, she saw a hole in the young woman's face where her nose should have been.

Inside Terry Nolan's face, the roiling black clouds sped past at an unfathomable speed. Like time had sped up, leading them both towards some moment which would eclipse both of their lives as they had come to know them up until that afternoon.

"—going to call the police on my cell."

"Huh?" Maddie had no idea she was crying until Terry's shape beside her softened around the edges to running watercolors. "Huh?"

"There are squatters in the house. There are people inside. Living there. Down in the basement. I'm going to call the police after we've gotten a safe enough distance away."

"Take me home," Maddie pleaded, the tears coming faster now. "Please, just … *please* take me home."

"All right," Terry said, hugging her client closer. "It's all right. It's going to be all right. Come on."

IX. AFTER VISITING HOURS

Conor Crenshaw did not remember his father, did not know his face. But he felt he knew the man's voice once again. Finally. For a while following the attack, he had confused it with his own conscience. No more of that foolishness. And Conor was certain that was who slipped into his room at around three a.m., dragged the single foldout chair in the room back into the darkest of the dwelling's four corners, and took a seat in the obscurity of heavy shadow. The fingernail moon was high in the clouded sky. It cast a half-hearted murky band of light through the window of Conor's room, but it did not touch so much as a hair on his father's head. It was almost as if his father alienated the light, controlled it. Held it back like an unwanted friend or fearsome enemy.

The son envied the father's power over nature, real or perceived.

He also envied his father's speaking voice, a crisp and patient baritone that would have served Conor well had he the chance to employ it in the classroom. Conor's teaching career seemed as much an unreality as the marriage he'd shared with Madison and the house they'd mortgaged together years before. His memory book had edited itself mercilessly down to a few scarce pages, leaving thin and torn edges where whole chapters of his life had been ripped out. Chewed away. Conor no longer cared to mourn the things he'd lost, the memories forever lost to him following the beating at McCauley's. Granted, Conor's mother would have survived. She would not have been buried alive by Madison and the unknowing coroner who'd perceived a profoundly sluggish heartbeat for that of a death-state. If he'd never been attacked and his brain damaged, Conor would have gone on taking care of his mother and guiding The Nine further along in their *journey into the arms of The Father.* He could only hope they'd found their own way there.

The Nine.

Their minds were closed to him. He'd been able to contact The Cheerleader briefly yesterday, and it had been long enough for Conor to instruct her as to what should happen next. *You have to rescue The Mother. Mother Tilly has been buried, and you need to free her. Free her and then let her drink of all your blood. Then, you must protect her until The Father comes back. Can you do that?* The Cheerleader had assured him it would be carried out.

Then ... nothing.

The Bickby Clinic must have done something about their insect problem, for the gauze trap Conor had set up earlier yielded nothing more than a wolf spider. A small, baby one at that. Conor had foregone the single spider and reset the gauze trap under his bed. He held onto his optimism the insects would return. Maybe he would even ask his father if he could drive them into his room. Lead them into the trap with his talents, his power over nature and all it embodied.

Then, while working himself into an ever-tightening knot of blankets around his restless and tossing body, Conor was awakened by the sound of the foldable chair legs scraping along the linoleum floor of his room. Followed by the sound of his father filling the seat. Then, his distinctive voice. Sweetness tinged in assertion. A perfect balance. It's why Conor had not awoken from his surreal and confounding dreams with a start, but rather like a young boy rising to the sound of his mother's soft calls and the smell of breakfast sizzling on the stove.

I can't see you, Father, but I know *you're there.*

This is how it's been my entire life.

"And it's why I remain your faithful son and servant."

Conor climbed out of bed. He meant to join his father in the darkened corner. The fatherless child lingering inside him nearly brought the adult to weeping, but this was short-lived when the visitor to Conor's room resisted such a thing.

"..."

"But ... I'm not afraid of you. I want to see you. I've been waiting for this moment all my life. I want to know you. Why do you punish me?"

"..."

He sat there listening to his father. And Conor's failure to save his mother struck him like his father had crossed the room in a blur of motion to strangle him.

"I-I gave them *very* specific instructions. Why? How could they take it upon themselves to do that to her?" He stood and paced the room, mindful not to set foot within the dark corner where his father stared out at him, concealing himself. Conor ripped at his hair, bringing it up into thick spikes going every which way. He crammed his fists into his eye sockets. He would not cry in front of his father, even though the tears pricked at the corners of his eyes. No, Conor channeled the rage, calling it forth from beneath the layers of sedatives that had held his temper at bay from the moment they'd given him that first shot in the ass. He buoyed upward and embraced it, the hot blood in his body bubbling and rising to a boil. "We have to avenge her. Start over. Help me out of this place and I'll ... *we* will avenge Mother. We'll bleed them until they're nothing but nine white husks! I—"

"..."

It couldn't be true.

It couldn't be true.

He felt the strength suddenly leave his legs, and he fell forward, breaking his fall with his hands at the very last moment before his face smacked the floor. He drove himself up, his arms wobbly. He couldn't breathe. A stone wedged in his throat. The room spun around him like he'd stumbled onto a carousel. And Conor started to crawl towards the dark corner that hid his father from him.

"You? You told them to— to kill my, mother? Your *wife?* We—mother and me—we worked for years and years to make the way for you. She gave her blood to countless, *countless* worthy vessels. I brought them to her. On *your* orders. Christ, how it exhausted her afterward. Each time she allowed one of them to drink of her! This? This is how you *repay* her?" Conor's hands were claws scrabbling at the tile floor, drawing closer to the dark corner. To his father.

"..."

"How do you tell *me* to stay back? Your son? *Your loyal servant?*"

"..."

"I did not fail you! It wasn't my fault she buried Mother! I tried to convince her to leave Mother be. That she-she was fine. But Maddie ... she ... *you've got to understand!* I was powerless. The men at the bar! They stole my memories. They brought me low and I-I just couldn't remember what was important. What was always important! Our plan. I know I was weak. I could have fought them off. I could have *fought* ... *harder.* But there were five of the fuckers! What would you have had me do? *What?* And ..." Inches from the hem of ink black behind which his father hid, Conor stopped short. He could not bring himself to disobey. His father's anger was at a fever pitch. A boy should *never* disappoint his father. Not if that boy wanted his father to come back to him for good. To complete his broken family again. "I remember the plan. I remember. It all came rushing back to me. I ... holy Christ! ... I know what happened. I-I hit my head on the steering wheel on the way to school that day. It did something. Knocked some of the tumblers back into place. Dallas was going to kill all of us and, I don't know, it shook me to the core also. It jarred the memories loose, and they came rushing back. I haven't forgotten any of it since. And you, *you're* here because I made ready *the way* for your return. Please ... please ... forgive me—"

"..."

"..."

"A boy—he needs his father. All of them. They needed a father. I made ready the way! Don't be cruel—"

"..."

"No, *nonono*, you *can't!* You can't leave me again! Not *again!*"

"   ..."

"I—I—I ..."

"   ..."

"But, what good would it do? Why, why *me*?"

"   ..."

"I'm not questioning your word, it's just that I don't wanna—"

"   ..."

"It wasn't supposed to happen like this—"

"   ..."

Humphrey Quinn eased the door to Conor Crenshaw's room open enough to slip inside. He braced it with one hand so it wouldn't squeak and rouse Conor like it did most nights. It was close to four a.m. The wing and the last insomniac patient had shuffled off to bed in her pink bunny slippers only five minutes ago, having finally grown tired of the seemingly endless parade of infomercials on the television. The patient had begged Humphrey to guide her to her room, and it was because the teenage girl reminded him so much of his daughter, who he loved more than life, that Humphrey had decided to temporarily curtail his rounds by barely a minute so he could walk her back and help her into her bed. The moment the young girl's head hit the pillow she was snoring loudly. Humphrey had cracked her door an inch, then hurried back down the hallway to pick up where he left off.

Room 16.

Conor's dwelling.

"The Big Man," as Humphrey was known around Bickby Clinic, would never be the same after that night. What he found inside Conor's room when he crept inside with his clipboard and his pen, ready to check off the latest fifteen-minute inspection, would land The Big Man in the ER of Abington Hospital later on, having suffered a heart attack born of sheer terror.

Humphrey would tender his resignation at Bickby Clinic shortly after and would go on to work odd jobs and temp positions that failed to match his skillset or level of education.

Humphrey would come to develop a veritable smorgasbord of psychological disorders over time, many of which he'd seen in the very patients he looked after at Bickby and often pitied.

Depression. Anxiety. Post-Traumatic Stress Disorder.

He would go on to collect disability because a nasty, malignant case of agoraphobia would cripple him to the point he couldn't leave his home, let alone maintain a job.

He would also replay the events of that night over and over in an endless, soul-crushing loop that plagued his every waking hour. The one misstep he'd taken in walking the young female patient to her room because she reminded him of his daughter. Humphrey bludgeoned himself emotionally with that mistake and attributed what he found in Room 16, Conor's room, to his own carelessness. The cruel fact of the matter which would haunt Humphrey in his nightmares and stalk him during the daylight hours was he had only just checked on Conor Crenshaw fifteen minutes before that, and he'd found the poor man sleeping soundly.

Fifteen minutes.

Protocol for the overnight nursing staff dictated all patients were to be checked on every fifteen minutes. Without fail.

Without fail.

Conor Crenshaw, the way Humphrey had found him that night around 4:00 a.m., would imprint itself upon the inside of his eyelids from that moment forward. There was no escape from its gruesomeness. The harrowing, visceral culmination of a troubled young man's dark night of the soul for Humphrey to carry with him to an early grave. A death by Humphrey's own hand two years later. At the end of a noose. Humphrey's daughter would come to find him swinging in the garage, the rope groaning as it pendulumed to and fro.

"Oh Jesus-Jesus-*Jesus!*"

The dome light in the ceiling was blinking when Humphrey crossed the threshold, lunging towards the bed where Conor lay, but it fizzled and then winked out. The lowlight of the moon cast Conor's body in an ethereal glow, as if the young man's soul were slowly lifting off measure by measure. It was a dizzying array of atrocities that at first sickened Humphrey and then appalled him entirely. Conor's lower face was masked in blood, black in the darkened room, and it looked like some maddened cosmetologist had haplessly misapplied lipstick well beyond the boundaries of his lip line. His eyes stood open, and Humphrey discovered much to his own horror, they roved around and around, searching something out and failing over and over to make a discovery of it.

When Humphrey moved to grasp one of Conor's hands, to offer some meaningless word of consolation, he made a far worse discovery than the dying man's disconnected glances. Conor's wrists were ripped open. He'd done it with his teeth which were coated with the red runoff of his self-inflicted injuries. His sheets, once white, were a horror show of more slick black, like an oil slick had found him where he slept. His white t-shirt had turned a dark, glistening maroon.

Give him a kind word, you idiot! He's passing! Comfort him!

Swallowing his aversion to the terrible wound on Conor's wrists, Humphrey took the young man's hand in his larger, beefier one and leaned in close. He tried to meet Conor's roving eyes, but they continued their search for the unknown.

"It's going to be all right, my man," Humphrey said, his voice quavering under the weight of the blatant lie. "Stay with me. Help is coming!" Then, he swiveled his head towards the door, ashamed he had not thought of it sooner. "Maggie! Danielle! Help! Help! Code Blue! CODE-FUCKING-BLUE!"

The cries of the other residents in their own beds, asleep moments before, started with one and quickly built to a crescendo of moans and broken bits of prayer and laments to haunt the mind for years to come.

"Hold on, buddy." He patted Conor's hand.

Something skittered up his arm.

Humphrey saw the cockroach as it traced its precarious way up his forearm. "Shit!"

He straightened, his spine cracking in protest. Humphrey whipped his arm all about. But the cockroach had found its way under the short sleeve of his powder-blue scrub shirt.

Another tickle, this one radiating out from the center of his palm. He checked his hand.

Another, larger roach. A handful of silverfish. A wolf spider clinging to the webbing of his palm's lifeline as he sprang into awkward, childish motion trying to shake them off.

They clung to him.

He danced.

He writhed all about, trying in vain not to squeal in repulsion.

His eyes happened upon Conor while amid his stupid dance.

The door to Room Sixteen swung wide behind Humphrey, but he didn't hear either of the women enter, nor feel them when they tried to shove him out of their way to make room for the crash cart they'd wheeled inside.

All his senses had shut down except for that of sight.

Conor's ravaged, opened wrists were overflowing with insects. Bubbling over with carpenter ants. Stinkbugs. Spotted beetles. Moths that took flight and circled the heads of the three attendants. Earwigs. And all manner of spiders that clambered overtop of the rest as if they ruled them. Commanded them up and out to spill onto the blood-soaked bedsheets. Then to drop to the floor in numbers that produced endless *clickety-clackety* sounds.

It was then the Adult Stat Wing of Bickby Clinic exploded with screams of terror that shook the walls. The very foundations.

No one noticed the upended chair in the corner of Conor's room. Its legs were bent askew, facing different directions. Once a chair. Now a spiked weapon.

X. GHOSTS

Baldwin High School closed its doors the following day. Superintendent Mills ordered their flag out front to be flown at half-mast. It flailed against the pole like a choking victim assaulted by a stiff wind. The way Tony Stadt had put it to staff and faculty, "Come in and work if you must, but no one will blame you if you decide to stay home and hug your loved ones close." In another place and at some other time, the fact that the day off fell on a Friday may very well have excited Baldwin's student body. Many of them would have planned parties or social outings. Maybe a drive down to Wildwood for the long weekend.

Given the circumstances, it was as if a veritable shroud had been pulled up and over the entire town of Comstock considering the discoveries made the night before.

No one's celebrating, Mary Marguerite thought to herself. *This is a waking nightmare. Nine students missing. The parents left murdered in their homes.*

The thought of it, the implication was enough to speed Mary's heart to that of a jackhammer striking out at her ribcage with utter abandon.

Did they do it? Rise up and kill their own parents?

Does two and two make four, Mare?

She stood at the window inside her office, holding her lit cigarette outside. She made sure to blow the smoke from her Parliament directly out into the courtyard. She held her hand with the cigarette out the window, pulled it back in. Sucked on it. Craned her neck to angle her mouth as close to the opening as possible. Exhaled. Repeat. It did nothing for her nerves. The Xanax dissolving in her stomach failed her as well. She understood there was nothing she could do about her twitchiness, or the tears in her wide eyes skating down her cheeks seemingly without end. Relief had become as slippery to her as an eel between her shuddering fingers.

Mary flicked the cigarette out into the courtyard and cranked the window closed again. Next came the Glade spray, which she kept in the top drawer of one of the rusted, ancient file cabinets pushed back into the unlit portion of her office that doubled as a storage section for hard copy student backlogs and profiles. Mary sprayed the whole office with a generous mist of Fresh Linen scent and set it down on her desk. Lastly, she produced a Bic lighter from her purse and lit the Yankee Candle on her desk. In no time, her office smelled like a mixture of laundered sheets and cotton candy.

So many rituals, just to hide the smell of a cigarette. There's only four people in the building today. I could have just walked out to the parking lot.

But she knew why she'd chosen to hunker down in her office. The pregnant, funereal silence inside the hallways of Baldwin High School was too much for her to handle. On her way to her office, Mary felt like she was roaming the halls of a mortuary, rather than a public school. Standing there in her office, Mary's shoulders felt tight and weighted. Still, she decided her next cigarette break would happen outside where it belonged. Colleagues be damned!

It felt ridiculous, hiding the habit from them in such an elaborate way. Still, Mary was not entirely ready to commit to smoking again out in the open.

No weakness. I am not fucking WEAK!

Sure you are, Mare. And until you show a little resolve, our little girl isn't going to spend any more time with a weak mother *than she has to. Dig?*

Her estranged husband loved that tag word.

Dig?

Standing there in the center of her office, Mary felt unmoored. Adrift. Visions of Dallas Teller's mortal hemorrhaging from every orifice raked across the folds of her mind, snagging on it. She clutched the sides of her head and shut her eyes, as if the images in her mind could be closed off with a lowering of the eyelids. They remained, imprinted on the very insides of the lids in negative. She felt an anger rise within. Bordering on rage.

Her chest tightened and her pulse quickened. A familiar prelude to what Mary anticipated as a potential manic episode.

She had always taken great pains to keep her private life and personal afflictions just that. While she maintained strong friendships with many of her coworkers, Mary never dared reveal what she considered her darkest secret. A diagnosis of bipolar disorder at the age of twenty-five. A condition she'd managed to hold at bay with medications and weekly therapy sessions. The irony of a guidance counselor stricken by such a condition did not escape her. If anything, it plagued her with a lingering sense of inadequacy.

She felt like a fraud.

There were a couple of times she had nearly divulged a bit of her background to a coworker over drinks at the school's weekly Happy Hour gathering over at Shelly's Tavern, only to rein herself in at the last minute, to stuff that part of who she was back down into the dark recesses of her character where lack of light just might erase it over time.

She never told anyone at Baldwin how an especially frightening manic episode had cost her joint custody of her daughter, Jenny. An episode which had unfolded right in front of the little girl and terrified Jenny. Shortly after, the courts granted Doug Marguerite full custody of their daughter. As far as anyone at Baldwin High knew, Mary was a single mother balancing its rigors with that of a highly respected professional life. In fact, Mary was still tied up in court with

Dig?

her estranged husband over custody. And it was bankrupting her, as the motions of her lawyer had begun to number in the double digits.

You should call Jenny later tonight. You want to hear her voice. You need to hear her voice. Ask her if she can say Momma *for you, just like Dallas Teller told you she did in school yesterday.*

Mary had her doubts it had happened as he said. Jenny's autism had rendered the child a veritable mute for the first four years of her life. She had only recently begun to garner a vocabulary of small, simple words. At a painstaking pace, however.

"Trust, but verify," she said to herself.

Dallas Teller.

The troubled boy had made so many bold and unbelieve claims, Mary did not know where to start. The task was daunting at best. But according to Dallas, the clock was ticking down to something dreadful and monstrous, perpetrated by the new and changed Nine. The boy's words bled back into her brain pan.

Two to three per year. He was new at it. It took years for him and that bitch-whore mother of his to get it right. Lots of trial and error. And again … you don't believe me, there's got to be back files on students at Baldwin in your office going back eight years. Maybe more. Check me.

"Okay, Dallas," Mary said, shoving the top drawer closed and rolling out the one underneath it, *"trust but verify* it is."

Her lunch hour came and went in the blink of an eye, and Mary was far too consumed with her search and the stacks of folders piled high on her desk to notice her stomach was growling. Her secretary, Claire, had even popped her head in and tapped her watch, saying, "Saladworks?" Mary begged off as politely as she could manage without losing her drive of focus. She didn't hear Claire leave, and when she looked up again from the last of the manila folders amassed at her elbow, Mary only then realized she had lost an hour and a half.

they're busy dying right now, but they'll be back, and they'll be different

Mary stared at her computer screen. She'd opened a Word document and created a list of students dating back to Conor Crenshaw's first year at Baldwin. 2011. She was as surprised as she was relieved to discover Conor had not taught Driver's Ed for the first two years he was there. There was no Driver's Ed offered at Baldwin until Conor Crenshaw convinced the higher-ups to offer it as an elective. It would save parents money on having to pay for a Driving School for their teenagers. A strong selling point. Not to mention, Conor Crenshaw, the man he'd once been, was charismatic and handsome enough to charm even the coldest fish out of her panties if he wanted to.

2013.

Mary sifted through each student file for anyone who'd been enrolled in the Driver's Ed class, year by year. What she discovered was while the class did not boast high numbers of enrollment for each semester of the last six years, the attendance had held steady, somewhere between eight to twelve students. For each year, Mary compiled the students who were enrolled in Conor's elective and set their files aside, organizing them further into years of attendance. By the time Mary had gone through every file of every student to attend Baldwin in the last six years and separated out the students who'd taken Conor's class, she had to wheel back from her desk for a moment to let her eyes adjust to the list of forty-eight names she'd typed into the document.

Forty-eight victims?

She took a deep, ragged breath, then pulled herself back in toward her desk. *I can't believe I'm running a search here.*

She Googled the words "Obituary Search" and brought up a free site after some scrolling downward.

They're dying right now, but they'll be back, and they'll be different

"Okay," she said, and typed the first student's name on the list into the Search Pane. The first student from the Driver's Ed Class of 2013.

Stephanie Marks

Mary held her breath, waiting for the report …

Twenty minutes later, Baldwin's Head of Guidance burst into Principal Tony Stadt's office, bearing a stack of files against her chest, a printout dangling precariously from the top of said stack, and red eyes. Irritated eyes. But she'd finished her crying back in her office. Now, it had transitioned into another emotion entirely.

"How did this get past you?" she cried, slamming the items in her arms down onto his desk. "*All of you?*"

Tony Stadt spreads his arms out on either side like some oversized bird contemplating a way to break from the moment and fly away. In one hand, he held a Dixie cup of tepid coffee that sloshed over the lip and down his wrist. He'd only just rescued it from the heap of folders and papers his Guidance Counselor had nearly knocked into his lap. His dark eyebrows alternated quickly from surprise to an anger of his own. "What the *hell's* come over you, Mare?"

At first, Mary made as if to sit down in the wingback arranged before his desk. But she changed her mind in mid-motion, which made for an awkward backtrack. "No. I don't want to sit," she said, more to herself than to Stadt.

"You going to answer my question?"

"It's my understanding you came over here to Baldwin *with* Conor Crenshaw. You started out in the History Department here. Eight years ago. Am I right?"

"That's common knowledge, Mare—"

"*Don't* call me *Mare!*"

"What is going on, Mary?" Stadt asked, rising from his seat and crossing to the other side of his desk. "What is all this?"

You know he's not a bad guy, Mary! Just lay it all out for him. You'll see he had no idea.

Carefully, he laid a hand on her shoulder, tried to meet her gaze, which she kept turning away again and again. "You look like you've been … crying? Am I right?" Up close, she could see his eyes were bloodshot and sagging with fatigue like never before. The guy had probably been working round the clock with law enforcement, as well as his superiors and parents alike. This was an unprecedented tragedy for all involved, directly or by proxy. "We, we've all been trying to make sense of something that will *never* make sense. For as long as I live, I'll never ever understand how this all could have happened."

Mary sniffed, her shoulders rising and slumping as the rigidness in the tendons oozed out. She could breathe again. She'd held her breath the entire walk to Stadt's office without realizing it. She finally turned to him, nodded stiffly, and grabbed for the printout she'd paperclipped to the top folder of the stack. It was a stapled sheaf of papers thick enough to resemble a pamphlet. Mary flipped past the list of student names.

Eighteen of them.

"It's not that at all, Tony." She folded back the first page and held the second page out to Stadt. "Stephanie Marks," she said, tensely. The principal wore a blank expression as he gazed down at the page she'd opened to for him. "That's her Obituary. She—look, it says she *died suddenly.* That is code for either a suicide or fatal, unexpected illness. Six months after graduation. Graduated top five percent of her class in twenty fourteen. You see any mention of college there?"

Stadt scanned the obituary, nestled beside a graduation photo of the young red-haired girl in her cap and gown. "I remember Stephanie," he said, softly. When he looked up at Mary again, he looked like the young man he was, having shed the authoritative demeanor his position required of him. He looked like a dejected youth, if for a moment. "She was a good kid. The year I took this job, she was a Junior. I had her in class as a Sophomore. Helluva basketball player. Really tall. A good kid." Then, just like that, Stadt shed his boyish expression and the curtness and impatience of her boss returned. "Why are you showing me this?"

"Did you know?"

"Honestly, no. We only ever find out about the passing of alumnae if the parent or guardian makes us aware. Or a friend." His eyes adopted a far off, thousand-yard stare, and Stadt slipped into silence. Then, slowly, he continued. "No one let us know Stephanie died. You know if they had, we would have addressed it. So," he flipped to the page behind it, "what … *what* is this? I'd like an answer." When he read the next obituary, the boyish expression did not return. It angered the principal, but Mary knew it was because Stadt was not a man who liked being out of the loop. Not when it came to Baldwin and its students, past and present. "*John.* John *Stepp?* I, dammit, I'm waiting, Mary!" He flung the pages down on the desk and folded his arms across a barrel chest. He looked almost menacing in that moment. "I just, I'm waiting."

"You want to know what *this is*? Really?" Mary practically lunged for the file folder on top of the stack. She flipped it open and held it out to the principal, who somewhat begrudgingly accepted it from her. He did not look at it, though. Not until Mary started to elaborate. "Have a look at John Stepp's roster for his Senior Year."

Stadt gave it a glance, then raised his eyes to her. They were clouded by either anger or confusion. "Mary, do you understand what's been happening? Would you like me to break it down for you? What is wrong with you?"

"Driver's Ed. He took that class. Just like Stephanie Marks *her* Senior Year. And who was it that convinced you and the Studies Director to bring the class back as an elective for the first time in fifteen years?"

"Mary, *honestly,* we're all aware of how you feel about Conor Crenshaw. Your suspicions he was up to no good. And anyone not in the room that morning— you know the one I'm talking about—who *didn't* know how you really feel about the man, well, they came out of that meeting with their eyes wide open about the whole damn thing."

"Tony, you told me to explain myself, and I'm doing that."

"I think I've heard enough already, Mary," Stadt said, trying to hand her back the folder. "My God, Mary, what would you have me do?"

"DAMMIT, MATT, GET OVER YOURSELF AND LISTEN TO ME!"

"*Mary!*"

"Those files on your desk represent eighteen Baldwin students who walked these halls and graduated from this institution over the course of the last six years! Now, you check every one of their jackets and you will find *every single one of them* was enrolled in that bastard's Driver's Ed course their Senior Year! Want to know what else they've all got in common with one another?"

"Mary, *stop!*"

"Every one of them *died suddenly* after graduation. Within a couple months of graduation, to be exact!"

"STOP!" Stadt cried. He kneaded the bridge of his nose, shut his eyes. "Just slow down. Hit rewind. You're making me dizzy, you know?"

"All right."

"Just start again. Show me." He crossed back around to his seat and slumped down into it. "Come around."

Mary grabbed a handful of the folders and the printout. She skirted the side of the desk and spread it all open across the principal's blotter, emblazoned with the Baldwin High Wildcats logo in screaming black and blue. "If you cross-check all eighteen of these students over the last six years, you will not find any two that took the same Bio class. Uh, English. Math. Art. Anything. But every single one of them *did* enroll in Crenshaw's Driver's Ed course. Now, the guidance counselor before me was let go because parents started to complain how ineffective she had proven herself to be. I know this, Tony, because people talk, and that's the story I've heard time and time again regarding my predecessor. Their files also reveal every single one of these-these *children* met with her to discuss depressive symptoms. But there's no mention of any significant follow up. Not even a referral to a therapist or psychiatrist. For all we know, she sent them back to class with a kind word and a pat on the back. Nothing more."

"I'm not denying that was the reason we parted ways with Debbie Stone last year," Stadt explained. "And we did receive a few calls from parents stating their children were not sleeping for days at a time. That they asked their children if they'd spoken with Ms. Stone, and they all said she was … somewhat dismissive. We never should have hired her. I regret we kept her for as long as she did, but she was a *favor* hire to begin with, so it was sticky. She's best friends with the Superintendent's wife. She came highly recommended."

"Are you kidding me, Tony?"

"Her credentials checked out. She was a certified therapist, working on her Ph.D."

"From where, some bogus bullshit online university? Honest to God! This is malpractice! Do you have any idea what could happen to Baldwin should any of these parents decide to sue on the basis that we employed an ineffective, callous Guidance Counselor who virtually ignored very basic warning signs of mental health disorders?"

"It was handled," Stadt muttered, sighing. "And we were lucky enough to find you in a pinch."

"What do you mean *handled*?"

"All right," he said, scratching at the base of his skull. "Full disclosure."

"Oh no."

"I knew of *some of the students* who'd met with Ms. Stone, and they were young men and women with broken home lives. Fathers ran out. Or the dad passed away. Their mothers were too damned busy trying to hold a life together for their children by working two to three jobs. And the kids, you know? You *know* this sad story! They fall through the cracks. So do their symptoms of depression—"

"Wait," Mary said, bracing herself along the lip of his desk with hands tight as vises, "are you telling me these kids all grew up *without fathers*."

"Let me see your list and I'll try to tell you."

Mary laid the list of eighteen students before him. Principal Stadt glared down at the names. "Okay," he said, stabbing a finger down at one name. Then another. Another. So on. "Okay. Yes, I remember all these names. All from broken homes. Started out strong GPA-wise. Involved in clubs. Outgoing, despite their circumstances. Then … their Senior year. Their grades dropped significantly. And I, oh you can't be telling me this."

"How did you keep these parents off your back? How did they not sue the pants off all of you?"

"Okay, Mary! I don't care for your tone, so you might want to work that out real fast." Stadt's green eyes flashed up at her. "Second, we did what the superintendent of schools had been telling us to do when the calls came in about their dissatisfaction with Ms. Stone. We passed all of the students. Everyone you have listed here. And I am aware now, looking at this, how we could have been somewhat culpable in all their sad ends. We graduated every one of them when we should have held them back. Their grades were shit, to put it plainly. And from what I remember, they turned to drugs towards the end. They looked like zombies. Sleepless zombies."

"And you just handed them their diploma and sent them on their way."

"Watch it now, Mary."

"*You* watch it, *Tony!* You passed the buck, and you were more than happy to do it at the discretion of the superintendent. You wanted to wash your hands of the problem children, as you saw them. So, year after year, you graduated them out of Baldwin and out of your life. Never once giving any thought to what their future might hold. These abused, exploited children put in our care! At the mercy of a predator who you and your pals saw fit, for God knows whatever reason, to award a fucking *Educator of the Year* award, while all along, Conor Crenshaw was damaging Baldwin students." Helpless to her own destructive mania, Mary felt almost like a spectator to her own professional ruination. She could not stop the flow of unfiltered words from her mouth. "My God, Tony, you have no idea what you've turned a blind eye to. You have no idea what you let happen for the last six years!"

"Mary, I'm telling you right now, you're mistaken. You're out of line. And I'm in *no mood* for any of this!"

"Oh, so you'd turn me out and get rid of me just like you did with those eighteen troubled teens? How convenient for you! Sure you don't want to consult the superintendent first before you try to shut me up too?"

"Okay. All right. Mary. Listen. I *know* what's been happening behind the scenes with you."

"What are you talking about?"

"The custody battle for your daughter? Like you said, people talk."

"*Some* people rubberneck. *Other* people bullshit. That is being handled. I hope you're not implying that could be clouding my judgment, because—"

"I'm not implying it. What I'm going to come right out and recommend is you take some time off. Clearly, you're under an untenable amount of stress right now."

At that moment, Mary Marguerite knew she hated Tony Stadt on a personal level. It was suddenly much more challenging to conceal her contempt for him. "I'm right about this," she said, plainly. "Nearly every student Conor Crenshaw has encountered through that elective class of his has gone on to suffer depressive symptoms of some sort. One thing is for sure, the symptoms were serious enough they led to all eighteen of these young people taking their own lives or hitting the streets. God knows where *those* kids are now. Either way, you can't deny what is staring you right in the face. Conor Crenshaw screwed these kids up. And he's been doing it to his students, a handful of them each year, unchecked and while wearing the disguise of the devoted, selfless educator who has sacrificed so much of himself for his profession and his students. You've had a goddam cult leader teaching English here for the last eight years. A damn

Renfield

predator. Don't you see that? What about the tags all over the school? *Crenshaw's Children!* They're brainwashed. And like those eighteen students on that sheet in front of you, the nine missing students all have the very same things in common. Plummeting GPAs. Antisocial behavior. The appearance of insomnia disorder. And the same direct tie to Conor-fucking-Crenshaw! And now? They're gone too!"

"Where did you get all this from? Honest to God!"

She hesitated in telling him, then swallowed the lump in her throat and went all in. "I went to see Dallas Teller in lockup last night."

All the color washed out of Tony Stadt's face. He didn't blink, only stared glumly up at her like she was an apparition having only just made her presence known. "You what?"

"He filled in all the blanks for me. Answered all my questions. And I didn't believe him at first. Then, he died. Right there in front of me. Just ... bled out. In seconds. That's when I knew he'd told me too much and someone— some*thing*—saw fit to silence him once and for all."

"You saw him die? You were there?"

"I was."

"That is beyond unacceptable behavior."

"I needed *answers*! How did he choose the students to include on his Kill List? Did anyone ever think to ask him what the connection was? To try and believe him? He explained. He also told me the name that he'd crossed out at the bottom ... that was my name. He changed his mind at the last minute. He saw me as some kind of *innocent*. The rest were guilty and needed to be put down."

"Leave my office, Mary," Stadt said, his voice low and intoned. "Go home before you say anything more. You will be hearing from the board, and you will be given a hearing date. Because I'm going to recommend you be fired."

"What?"

"You've proven yourself a liability. You're insubordinate. Making wild accusations. You've become unhinged. We can't have that."

"I'll fight you," Mary said. "I'll expose you, Tony. You and your buddy, the superintendent of schools. *His* wife! All of you!"

Mary moved to scoop up the files she'd spilled across the principal's desk. Tony Stadt was faster, and he blocked her with his arm, sliding them closer to where he sat. "No, you don't, Mary. This is the property of Baldwin High School. You no longer have access to these confidential files, and I will see they are secured against you during your probationary period. You're not taking these."

"You sonofabitch! We both know you're going to get rid of all of this! I've spelled it all out for you. I showed you the paper trail for your own wrongdoing, and you're going to make it all disappear. That'll protect the superintendent. You. Even Conor Crenshaw."

"Get the hell out of my office!"

She backed off, held up her hands. Even laughed. This seemed to inflame and enrage the principal more than anything else she'd said up to that point. "Hey-hey-*my-my*. No need to lose your temper, Tony. Besides, I've got an even better reason for you to want to throw me out of the building and out of your office."

"What's that?" Stadt said through whitened and gritted teeth.

Edging towards the door, Mary fished inside her pocket and brought out a small black object and held it up for him. "It's all right on here. Scanned in. Ready for its close-up. And I'm gonna see to it everything sees the light of *fucking* day!"

Fingers already curled around the doorknob behind her, Mary put herself on the other side of the entryway. In her periphery, she saw Tony Stadt come out from behind his desk like a shot and lunge for her like a rabid animal.

XI. FALLOUT

There was no point in waiting until she drove home to unscrew the cap off the bottle of Merlot and take a deep swig from its mouth. She sat there in her Kia Forte with the engine running outside the Wine and Spirits Shoppe. The sweet and tart wine hit her bloodstream in minutes. She could only tilt her head back in submission to the moment, her radio turned up loud to the local rock station and a song she remembered adoring called "Fell on Black Days" by Soundgarden growling out of the speakers. She felt like a teenager, not just because the song dated back to her adolescent years, but because Mary couldn't help but peek out both the driver and passenger side windows for any police presence. This could be bad. Hell, everything could turn worse than it was in a blink.

Finally, Mary understood what life was. A series of events that turn from bad to worse over the course of seventy to eighty years, if you're lucky.

She set the bottle down on the passenger seat and grasped the steering wheel with both hands. A copse of trees across the street overhanging a small cemetery sparse with old and crumbling grave markers twitched with the jumping birds hidden inside the lush greenery like unseen hands up the back of a ventriloquist's dummy. As if suddenly alarmed by her attention, a fleet of finches burst from the treetops and slanted off due west.

The sudden and striking retreat of the birds hurt her heart. It also served to drag the reality of her circumstances back into the light, kicking and screaming. *I just lost my job.* Sure, she could and should appeal to the teacher's union, citing wrongful termination. Mary strained to remember the words she'd used against Tony Stadt, but they eluded her as the alcohol further diluted her bloodstream.

All of this, on the word of Dallas Teller? An unhinged, would-be school shooter?

A voice cut through the gathering mists of her memory. *A weak person walked into your boss's office earlier and blew up her life. That's always been you, Mare. You exploded your relationship with me too.*

"You can fuck *right* off, Doug," she droned, her head tilting and eyesight

250

softening. "Get out of my head … *dick*."

You want me out of your head, yet you call me every other day to give me updates about your life and your exploits. For someone you claim to hate more than anyone else, you sure do keep in consistent contact with me. You confide in me. Your deepest darkest thoughts and fears. Because you have no one else to turn to. Then you wonder why I'm in your head, Mare? I'm not as bad as you try to convince yourself. I'm your true north, whether you want to admit it or not.

"Fuck *off!*" Mary cried, bashing the steering wheel with the flats of her palms. "You stole my child from me!"

Then why do you call me? Why do you knowingly give me all the ammunition I need to keep you clear of our daughter until her eighteenth birthday? Huh?

"I—I …"

The wave of grief came crashing down on top of her, sinking her shoulders and collapsing her like a card table with a weak leg. It pressed her down into the upholstery of her seat. Her chest tightened, and she swore if she were to lift her blouse, she'd find a webwork of knotted vines wound round and round her upper body. Cinching tighter and tighter.

You gonna take your medicine, Mare?

"No," she gasped, and reached for the bottle of Merlot once more. She pulled long and hard on it. "I'm going to get to the bottom of this shit swamp."

You're not gonna get to the bottom of anything but that bottle in your hands. Then, you're going to wake up in your car either later tonight or tomorrow morning, and the consequences of your actions are going to beat you mercilessly into submission until you do what we both know you need to do.

"What's that? Doug? *Doug?*"

Aside from those Xanax pills, which you've been tripling up on for no good reason, you've been off meds for the last four days. Don't tell me you don't feel the world tipping a little more sideways every day. Every day you forego your medication. You've always had a problem with this. Self-medicating. Going on and off at a whim. Your brain is probably so baffled by the constant change in chemicals its eventually going to stage a mutiny against you. Then, where will you be? Take. Your. Meds. Take 'em. Enough to make up for the last four days.

"But that's unsafe."

So's skipping them for days at a time. Take 'em. Take. Your. Meds.

In her mind, Mary envisioned herself paddling against the strong current of what were ultimately her own thoughts delivered in the voice of her estranged husband. Yet, a gnawing part of her pressed the possibility Doug was, in fact, in her head and directing her. But, to his benefit or hers? *I am not my thoughts,* she reminded herself. *I am not my thoughts.*

I am not—

Mary lowered the music and scooped her purse into her lap from the passenger seat. Its contents clicked and hissed in her hands like a living thing, rather than a Dooney & Bourke handbag loaded with pill bottles and tissues and a change purse and a cell phone she'd forgotten all about. She fished her medicine bottles out of the bag. In a matter of moments, Mary held five antipsychotic pills and four anti-depressants in the palm of her mildly palsied palm. *I want to get off this carousel. I am not my thoughts. I need to downgrade them. Just … for a little while, so I can rest. Hit reset.*

She swallowed the handful of pills and washed them down with the red wine. Mary did not pry her lips off the mouth of the bottle until she had drunk it dry. Then she cranked her seat back and did not fight the slow-building heaviness lining her eyelids. Sadness stole over her that manufactured quick and fleeting images and scenarios that kicked her heart rate up. It was an anxious, shallow sleep she slipped in and out of. Mary thought of saying *fuck all* and driving out to where her estranged husband, Doug, lived with their daughter, Jenny. Of coaxing her into the car under the guise of taking her to Disneyworld or a carnival or to go see *Frozen* at the Cineplex. Then driving until she hit the southern border, augmenting the little bit of Spanish she'd retained from high school. Changing their names.

This series of musings gave way to something in stark, terrifying contrast.

Shifting in the increasingly uncomfortable driver's seat of her Kia Forte, Mary envisioned herself on the floor of an unfamiliar kitchen. She was prone at first on the tiles, then Mary lifted herself up onto her knees. The smell was that of decay, rotten eggs, and age-old meat left out for millennia. The floor was shaking. Rumbling. It felt as if it would give way beneath her at any moment. Mary saw what looked like a trail of mud beside her. It traced a grimy, brown path to a door a few feet away from her. A white wooden door. A pantry. Basement door, perhaps. The floor felt alive. It was trembling, as if frightened. Earthquake? She was in no rush to find her feet, and probably would have toppled over.

The room was spinning.

*Thur-rump-thur-rump-thur-*RUMP-THUR-RUMP-THURRUMP-THURRUMP*!*

Whatever was shaking the floor like a great seismic disturbance, it was closing the distance between itself and where Mary swayed atop her kneecaps. Then, it came crashing into the cramped, filthy kitchen, sounding more like a herd of buffalo than what it revealed itself to be.

The deer was crazed, bucking up and down like more of a rodeo horse than an animal of the forest. Mary rolled out of its unpredictably maniacal path of destruction as it came right at her. Its hooves punched imprints into the kitchen tiles. The rabid deer collided haphazardly with the walls, only to reset itself and tramp across the room where it turned the wooden chairs gathered around a simple wooden table to splintery lengths of kindling. The table went next, the deer lunging upward to stand atop the rickety piece of furniture. It collapsed beneath the animal, which seemed to spin the deer into something of a murderous rampage focused upon complete and utter destruction of all obstructions in its path. Mary dragged herself into a corner formed by the gas stove and the wall. She cowered there, screaming without sound. Dry and brittle hisses were all she could produce.

The deer wheeled on her, and that's when Mary felt her tenuous grasp on sanity slip.

Where the animal's eyes were, two bulbous black tumors protruded like large lumps of coal. Its whole body was spotted with these cancerous growths. There had to have been thirty in all amassed over its flesh from ears to tail. The Tumor Deer seemed to see her for the first time. Mary saw its nostrils flare like that of a human. The door she'd thought to be a pantry or a basement entrance flew open. The smell of rot increased tenfold. The Tumor Deer lunged at Mary, its hooves skittering madly across the dimpled tiles, its head lowered—

The scream that ripped Mary Marguerite away from the nightmare sounded so thoroughly alien she thought it was someone else in distress. She jerked awake to a painful crook in the back of her neck as the driver's side neck rest had worked into the rear of her skull. It was dark outside, and a parking lot streetlamp directly over her stationary vehicle cast a small circle of light down upon the windshield of her car. Mary reached for the luminescence like a child who has spied a cookie in the middle of the floor. Her breath was short. Labored. But Mary managed to gain her bearings, little by little.

Her panting became a soft, subtle respiration, and Mary cranked her seat back into its upright position. The radio provided further calm, Pink Floyd's "Mother" purring from the console like a lullaby. With the sound turned down and the horrid lyrics of the so-called lullaby indecipherable, Mary found it to be one of the most welcoming pieces of musical bliss she could have asked for in that moment.

"I'm fine," she told herself.

Whose fucking kitchen was that?

Her cell phone began to chirp inside her purse on the passenger seat.

Mary retrieved it, checked the Caller ID in the window.

You can't—you should't—ignore another one of her calls, Mary! You dragged her into this, after all.

"Maddie, hi," she said into the receiver. "I'm so sorry I didn't get back to you sooner."

"Listen, there's no time for that. I was pissed at you and now I'm not, because so much has happened since the coffee shop." From there, Maddie Crenshaw caught Mary Marguerite up, from her final visit with Conor to the disastrous, hallucinatory visit to Tilly Crenshaw's house of noxious odors. The words seemed to flow endlessly from Maddie like she'd been stopped up from telling anyone about these terrible events, and Mary guessed there was no one else she could have told without the listener questioning Maddie's sanity or grasp on reality. *This poor woman. She sounds about as desperate as I feel right now.*

"Oh, Maddie, I'm so sorry you had to go through all of this without a friend by your side."

"So that's what we are?"

"Well, unless you've got a group of girlfriends who would believe what you just told me. It would take a special breed of friend to take what you're saying at face value. But it just so happens, I believe every damned word of it. Couple days before this, I would have disconnected the call long before this."

"Have they found The Nine yet?"

"No word," Mary said. "But, their parents. They were all found dead in their homes."

"No," Maddie breathed. "Oh God, no."

"I am afraid so."

"Was it—did their own children.?"

"It's looking like it."

Silence on the other end.

"I had it out with Tony Stadt, and he fired me."

When Maddie answered, she sounded as dumbfounded by that as the murders. "Can he do that?"

"No, he can't," Mary said. "It would require a formal hearing to remove me from the position. But it's fine. If he hadn't fired me, I would have quit anyway." Mary explained what she discovered involving the cover-up at Baldwin that went all the way up the ladder to the superintendent of schools himself (and the *bastard's* wife, not to mention). There was no way for Mary to side-step explaining Conor's direct involvement in the situation, since it was Maddie's husband who'd abused the scores of students over the years and placed them in direct contact with danger and a monster who lived in the basement of his childhood home. Knowingly. Willingly. Like a drone. It was also equally difficult to withhold the malicious tone from her voice as she explained the fallout that transpired from Conor's and his mother's abuse of the Baldwin alumni going back six years. The residual mental trauma and PTSD that had driven them to either take their lives or simply to disappear altogether.

Of course, when Mary had finished and Maddie could be heard weeping on the other end of the line, she wished she'd tried harder to somehow offer a softer explanation to the wife of this monster. After all, she was innocent of all the horrendous liberties Conor Crenshaw had taken with his students, handing them over to his depraved mother for the sake of—

Am I really believing this?

Yes, Mary, it's time to accept the only plausible explanation.

creating a vampire coven.

Readying the way for Father. Isn't that what Dallas had said?

Conor's father. Long-lost.

I don't know. I can't accept this. I don't know that I can—

"Mary, you there?"

"Yes-yes, I'm sorry. To be honest, I'm a little impaired at the moment."

"Oh. I didn't want to say anything, but I thought you sounded like you've been drinking."

"Guilty as charged," Mary said. "And I'm going to take up smoking again, too. Full disclosure, my dear. No more secrets. I'm going to let it all hang out."

"So would you?"

"Would I *what?*"

Maddie sighed. "I need you to come to Conor's mother's house with me. I don't buy the police officer's story. I don't believe he *really* checked the house upstairs and down. And there is something dead inside that I have to get out of there myself, or that damn house of horrors is never going to sell."

"Why would the cop lie?" Mary asked, even though she could think of a million reasons why an officer would want to patronize a woman like Maddie. The woman sounded about as unhinged as Mary imagined she herself sounded. "What exactly did he say after he checked the house?"

"Well, I told him about the mud trail in the kitchen leading from the center of the floor to the basement door. He said the tile floor was spotless. The handprints all over the walls and the ceiling, I think I might have heard him chuckle on the other end of the phone when I told him about them. So, of course, he was quick to report he didn't find anything like *that* either." Maddie took a breath, pressed on. "Then, I asked him if he'd gone down the basement. I had said that was where the dead animal or whatever was probably rotting and causing the smell inside. This is where I'm certain I caught him bullshitting me outright."

"How so?"

"Well, he said not only did he check the basement, but the trapdoor underneath the throw rug in the middle of the basement floor. He said it's secured nice and tight with a padlock. He said if I wanted him to go down *there*, I'd have to hand over the key. But I don't have a key."

"No one ever gave you one after Tilly passed?"

"No," Maddie said, "because I have no idea what that cop is even talking about. He's making things up."

"I ... don't understand."

"He obviously never checked the basement. Because there isn't—nor has there *ever* been—any *trapdoor* under *any throw rug*."

Mary's stomach lurched, then it dropped what felt like twenty stories.

Don't do it, Mary. Stay out of it, Mary. You've got Jenny to think about. Jenny needs her mother, and she needs her alive! Don't you—

Yet, in the end, Mary felt as if she had no other choice in the matter. In a way, she felt the strangest notion of having always travelled along the very path of life that would lead her to this pivotal moment where she should, *she must*, not only say *Yes*, but take the lead in what came next. Not quite destiny. More of a duty.

You DO have a choice, you fucking fool! Don't be so dramatic.

Then why the pull on her conscience? The actual, physical sensation of something larger and grander than her or any other human being like her tugging at her limbs. Like when Jenny wanted to drag her into the mall arcade to throw some Skee-Ball. An unmistakable, undeniable insinuation. No choice.

"I'll go," Mary said. "But I'm going to need you to come pick me up. I'm in no condition to drive to you or to Tilly's."

XII. SPIARE

Matilda "Tilly" Crenshaw's house stood on one of Bucks County's many country veins, Big Top Road. Light was scarce at night along such routes. There were no streetlamps. Maddie's headlights revealed five feet at a time while the rest of the area's more rustic, rural stretch remained a veritable mystery enshrouded in the ink black of an early spring evening. In the passenger seat, the alcohol still altering her every thought, Mary contemplated what might happen if she were to suddenly throw open the door and roll on out.

Would I hit the ground or roll off into space? Where did the world go?

This sporadic, surreal line of thinking granted her an unsettling feeling she couldn't shake for the remainder of the ride.

Hauling herself up a little higher in the passenger seat, Mary broke the silence that had set in for a lengthy period of the ride. "You're sure there's no trapdoor in the basement?"

"I'm positive," Maddie answered, slightly annoyed. "Towards the end of Tilly's life, as I've said, I took over where Conor had left off with taking care of her. The woman was not decrepit. Understand that. She was only in her early sixties when she died, and the woman had no problem getting around. She spent a lot of time down the basement. And she was up and down those rickety wooden steps throughout the day, from what I gathered. I've been down there enough times to be able to say with certainty there's no throw rug and no fucking *trapdoor* hidden underneath either."

"Can I ask a question?" Mary knew to tread lightly.

"Go ahead."

"What if we get there and there is a trapdoor down the in basement? What then?"

"There won't be—"

"Maddie—"

"You're not hearing me—"

"I *am* hearing you, but I think we should mentally prepare ourselves for whatever we might find in that house. I-I'm just having a difficult time trying to reason out why the police officer would *make up* something like that. It's very random. Don't you agree with that, at least?"

"Mary, the house smelled like a thousand asses! You don't think he wanted to get the hell out of there as quickly as possible before he tossed his cookies all over the place? I think he's full of shit, but I'd also say I can't really blame him for wanting to get the hell out of there the moment he set foot inside. Hell, the realtor couldn't take it, and she had to run out the back door. She vomited all over the side flower bed. The only reason I could bear the smell better than her is I'm stuffed up with a cold. Even then, the smell was like nothing I've ever encountered before."

"Then what makes you think we'll fare any better once we get in there?"

Maddie didn't answer right away. She stared out the windshield, glibly. "I dunno. But we've got to try. If we can't, I'm just going to let them bulldoze the place and be done with it." She drew in a sharp breath and spun the wheel to the left, the car's tires crunching over the broken blacktop of a driveway. "We're here," she told Mary. "Check the glovebox."

The headlights swept across the face of the A-frame house at the top of a low hill. The ghost of black shutters against dirty white siding appeared, and then the night muted it once more as Maddie straightened the vehicle out and pulled slowly, warily, up the inclined drive. The sight of the Crenshaw house stole Mary's breath. It was a physiological response to her own anticipation for what they might find within, what sorts of answers to the remaining questions would be answered for better or worse. Not excitement, by any stretch. If anything, she'd failed to draw breath for a minute as the lights had splashed across the black, glittery windowpane sockets staring out the front of the house like the tumorous growths that served as the deer's eyes from her nightmare. Mary hadn't told Maddie about the Tumor Deer. No need to infect her with such a horrific vision to wrestle with when she laid her head down to sleep again.

The driveway terminated with a brick wall serving as the house's foundation and the north wall of the basement. Maddie put the car in park. She left it in idle, the headlights on. Neither of them was mentally prepared just yet for the terminal darkness that would swallow the house and the countryside in its terrible ambiguity once Maddie doused the lights.

"Glove box, Mary," Maddie repeated.

"Oh." She flipped the compartment open. Two white surgical masks dropped into her lap. "Where'd you get these?"

"Work," Maddie said. "I'm an RN. I don't know how much help they'll be, but better than going in there without an advantage, right?"

"Mm-hmm." Mary took one and handed the other to Maddie, who promptly strapped it on over her nose and mouth. After briefly considering it in her hands, turning it over and over like some inscrutable ancient artifact, Mary donned her mask as well.

When Maddie cranked her door open and stepped out, Mary watched the shape of the woman become reduced by the deep nightshade to nothing more than the white rectangle of her mask. It made for a disconcerting effect that stalled Mary from climbing out of the passenger side. But Maddie called to her from behind the car, and Mary finally snapped to, once and for all.

"Take your pick," Maddie told her, standing before the opened trunk of the Honda Civic. "I grabbed whatever I could find. Conor had a green thumb. These were all his."

A string of lyrics from an Ani DiFranco song, one of Mary's favorite singer-songwriters, traipsed across her mind, and she couldn't help but to give voice to them. "'Every tool is a weapon if you hold it just right.' *Right?*"

The trunk was packed with what looked like enough gardening tools to start a landscaping business, along with the standard items needed to maneuver a car jack and change a tire. Maddie had already selected the tire iron, which she held in her hands precariously, like it might do her damage inadvertently. There was a rusty garden trowel. An edging shovel. Steel-head rakes. An augur.

"Oh Jesus." Mary reached for the pale, elongated object mixed in among the other items. The irony was not lost on her as she held the wooden stake up into the pale cast of moonlight. A ratchet strap was still secured to the wood.

"We have a little birch tree on the side of the house that leans," Maddie said, watching Mary inspect the stake and work at tearing the strap away from the wood. "Conor has a bunch of these. He's been staking the tree to try and get it to stand up straight, to grow towards the light like it should."

She tested the sharpened edge of the implement with her finger. Not as pointed as she would have preferred, but it would do some damage. "What made you bring this? Just so I know where *you're* coming from. What are *you* expecting to find in there?"

"The same thing you are, Mary. You just haven't admitted it to yourself yet. I believe everything you told me. And I assume you believe what I've told you. The truth lies somewhere in the middle of all of this. Although, I wish you'd trust me when I say there's—"

"No trapdoor down the basement," Mary said, nodding. "I do. But if you're wrong, we're going to have to adapt pretty damn quickly to whatever the hell Tilly saw fit to hide away in a *basement* sub-level."

They stood there avoiding one other's gaze, straining to hide the naked fear standing inside their eyes from one another. A camp of bats skittered across the deepening night sky, and a loon answered from the woods a quarter mile out from the Crenshaw house's backyard as if they had disturbed it from an especially delicious dream. Maddie took care to shut the trunk with as little sound as possible. Then, she stepped back around to the driver's side and leaned inside.

"Ready?" she asked Mary, who had closed her door with the same attentiveness to stealth and then come around to stand in the glorious spray of the headlights.

"We couldn't have done this during the day?"

Not if you really want to know what the hell started all of this, what made someone like Dallas Teller get it into his head to gun down his classmates and his teacher one morning not so long ago!

Maddie laughed weakly and turned off the car.

The lights.

Then they were two floating white rectangles in the dark. The fingernail moon cast a weak glow, and their eyes did much of the heavy lifting when it came to adjusting to their surroundings. Gradually, things pulled into a soft focus consisting of blue and grey edged scenery. The moment the storm door swung inward, the putrid breath of death and decay gusted outward, striking both women in the face. Mary turned her head aside and crossed under the threshold, feeling her way along into the kitchen area of the Crenshaw house. Maddie followed suit, breathing exclusively from her mouth, and finding the stench somewhat more manageable this way.

The smell seemed to possess hands that grabbed out at them and teeth that bit into every bit of their flesh not covered by clothing. Once Mary's eyes adjusted to the kitchen, and the right-angled surfaces of her surroundings with glints of steel here and the ghost of white appliances announcing themselves there, she noticed what looked initially like a muddy trail running across the kitchen tiles.

My dream. I've been in this room before. In the dream.

Mary must have gasped loudly enough to stop Maddie in her tracks, for she stopped and turned around to her. Felt for her shoulder.

"You good?" Maddie inquired, her eyes crinkled with concern.

But Mary turned her head towards the adjoining long hallway that emptied into the foyer, now a black rectangle of inscrutability. Her muscles clenched, and she raised her stake without realizing it. Staring down the corridor and not hearing Maddie standing right in front of her, Mary waited for the Tumor Deer to burst through the darkness. To come charging at her with those terrible coal-stone eyes, kicking up its front legs and rearing forward like a bucking bronco as it lunged violently at her. Sweat spurted across her skin. Her arms shook with an overdose of adrenaline. *I think I hear it, standing just inside the black rectangle—*

Maddie squeezed her shoulder. "Hey," she hissed at Mary, mindful to keep it down. "What are you looking at? You see something?"

"No-no," Mary said, shaking her head emphatically. "It's nothing. I'm just a little overwhelmed."

Maddie studied her a bit longer before drawing her hand back and clutching her tire iron with both hands, wielding it like a batter up at the plate. She cocked her head towards a whitewashed wooden door a few feet behind her. The muddy trail did not appear to stop before the door. It continued beneath the bottom of the door itself. Mary shuddered at the implication.

Just as Maddie's hand slipped around the knob to the basement door, Mary came up right behind her and whispered in her ear.

"I need a cigarette," she said. "And it'll dull my sense of smell some."

"Good idea. I'll take one too."

"You smoke?"

"For six months. Away at college. And there's not a day I don't miss it."

Mary fished her pack of Parliaments out of her inside coat pocket, poked one into the corner of her mouth and handed another off to Maddie, who did the same. Mary lit them both up with a black Bic lighter from her pants pocket.

"Careful, Maddie. Take a small puff at first—"

But Maddie Crenshaw had gone too enthusiastically at her cigarette and pulled far more smoke down into her lungs for not having smoked in a long time.

"Oh shit."

Maddie's insides flared up as if she'd tried to deep-throat a hot poker. Her hand flew away from the doorknob and fell upon her hitching chest. Maddie had also forgotten she was just getting over a cold, something she'd mentioned to Mary not too long ago. The smoke set her back considerably, and when Maddie coughed, it was violent and jarring and brought up a mouthful of something vile lodged in her chest for weeks.

It had been ten years since her last Newport in the quad at Ballantine University—with the boyfriend who would break her heart and open the door to meeting Conor Crenshaw.

"Here," Mary said, moving up against the door to the basement, "why don't I take the lead until you catch your breath?"

This was all right with Maddie. She nodded without hesitation and fell in line behind Mary.

The putrid air was more concentrated just outside the basement entrance. There was no mistaking the fact its source lay on the other side of the door. *The policeman didn't see anything. He didn't even see the muddy tracks, and damned if that wasn't the first thing my eyes found in the dark. Maybe there won't be any throw rug. No trapdoor underneath. Maybe—*

Just as Mary's hand curled around the door, it pulled inward with brute force, knocking the stake from her hand and dragging her inside the darkened landing at the top of the stairs.

Just inside the basement.

On the other side of the door.

"*MARY!*"

She spun around just as the door slammed back into its jamb with a fractured, splintery sound like a shin bone splitting in half.

Mary fell upon the door, hammering it with closed fists and screaming in the pitch black.

At first, Maddie joined her in protest on the kitchen side of the door. Slapping at the suddenly immoveable door with the flats of her palms. She wailed, shouting the counselor's name through the wood separating them from one another.

Until Maddie's mantra was cleaved neatly in half, as if on purpose.

"Mar—"

Mary stopped deadand listened. "Maddie?"

Maddie's screaming turned to a tortuous shrieking that held until it broke in her throat. Then a splashing sound.

Sucking.

The basement made a sound like it had been holding its breath and then begun to slowly exhale in the silence. Precariously, Mary pressed her ear to the door and listened intently for some sign of life beyond the sickening slurps. She shut her eyes and tried to steady her hands as they bumped against the wood. The intention failed her. "Please," she said, imploring someone, anyone to put an end to what had so rapidly spun out beyond her control. "Please."

"Mare-*reee*?"

Maddie's tremulous, water-logged voice poured through the crack between the bottom of the door and the tiles. It was different from what it had been moments before. The pensive tone of regret had found its way into her voice. Hopelessness. The sound of a woman who has suddenly become unmoored from herself and everything she'd ever known to trust and to believe. Mary dropped to her knees, then strained to contort herself downward into an awkward arrangement whereby she could look through the opening. To catch a glimpse of Maddie Crenshaw. "Hey!" she called, her own voice made warbly by the onslaught of frightened tears. "Hey, can you hear me? Maddie?"

The unmistakable sound of a bare foot coming down repeatedly, swift and brutal as a jackhammer, shook the floor, and Mary's flank as well. Maddie managed one final trebly blurt of protest before the foot split something apart, the sound like a casaba melon striking the pavement after falling twelve stories.

"No-no-*no-nonononono!*"

Her throat raw and mouth a desert, Mary fell away from the door and settled roughly back onto her bottom. She sobbed, her shoulders hitching up and down as a stitch formed in her left side. Her thoughts were clouded and disconnected, and when Mary suddenly sensed the hard object stabbing into her thigh, she thought she had been bludgeoned in the dark. Her hands flew to the source of discomfort, and the realization of what her fingers felt. parted the swirling mists of her mind as it tried to shield her from any further trauma.

Cell phone. In her front jeans pocket.

"Oh God-oh God, *please be charged. Please have a signal. Dear GOD!*" The stitch in her side protested as she raised her core up just enough to angle and fish the cell out of the snug pocket of her jeans. An unconscious smile tugged at the corners of her mouth. It felt strange as it split her lips apart, detached from anything joyous and deriving from a base and animalistic place within.

Spiare

The word infiltrated her head and spun out in her mind, ricocheting off the contours of her skull and spiraling outward in endless waves of reverberation. It sounded breathy but accusatory. A language she could not place right off.

Spiare—spiare—spia miserabile.

"Shut up!" Mary cried out, dropping the cell and clapping her hands over her ears in a feeble attempt to silence the alien male voice pulsing between her palms. "Shut up!"

Spy, miserable spy

"Who are you, you sonofabitch! *Who are YOU?*"

A low, gloating laugh from the depths answered her, long and stretched to the very limits of sound itself.

Mary whimpered. Tears flooded her eyes. Frantically, she searched all around her on the cold, unforgiving floor of the basement landing for her cell phone. It had landed face-up, the screen glowing up at her. She snatched it up.

Its screensaver showed Mary's daughter, Jenny, beaming on a sunny morning in her best Easter dress and holding a basket full of plastic colorful eggs she'd hunted for bright and early that Sunday a year ago.

She traced the digital image with one trembling fingertip.

Jenny disappeared. The cell vibrated in Mary's hands. The screen turned black, white lettering flashing overtop of it:

000000000
Incoming Call

The last time Mary had gotten a call from such a strange number had been when she was still a college student and missed a couple payments on her Discover Card. Just the sight of the intentionally foreign and anonymous collection of numbers gave her a sour feeling as it summoned the memory of that difficult period in her life when a collection agency had hounded and harassed her relentlessly, hiding behind more phone numbers than she could have possibly blocked.

Mary, whoever the fuck it is, it's a living, breathing person who is outside this house and able to send help! Answer the goddam phone!

As she pressed the Call Accept button and started screaming into the phone, Mary realized, much to her surprise, she had somehow turned *nose-blind* to the stench of decay that walked the Crenshaw house like a living being with its skin peeling away and flesh sloughing off.

"*HELLO! WHOEVER THIS IS, I NEED HELP! I'M BEING HELD PRISONER IN A HOUSE ON.*" Mary strained to remember the name of the road they had turned onto, and when it suddenly flashed across her brainpan, she spat it out like an unsavory wad of gum. "*BIG TOP ROAD IN ENDSLEY, PENNSYLVANIA! THE, IT'S THE CRENSHAW HOUSE! MATILDA CRENSHAW'S HOUSE! I'M IN THE BASEMENT AND THEY LOCKED ME IN AND I-I DON'T KNOW WHAT THEY'RE GOING TO DO TO ME! PLEASE—*"

"MARY!"

"*SEND THE POLICE TO THE CRENSHAW HOUSE—*"

"MARY! STOP! IT'S—"

"THEY'RE GONNA KILL ME!"

'DOUG! DAMMIT, MARY! IT'S YOUR HUSBAND! IT'S DOUG!"

"Doug!" Mary gasped, squeezing the phone so tight it clicked. "Doug! Oh-God-you've-got-to-help-me-thank-God—"

"Mary—"

"Big-Top-Road—"

"Jenny's missing, Mary!"

"What?"

"Jenny is missing!"

A flicker of motion at the bottom of the wooden staircase snagged Mary's attention, and this gave way to what sounded like the grinding of ancient hasps against one another. The mouth of what looked at first like the yawning maw of a dragon with fire glowing in the base of its gullet opened in the darkness below. Another quick flurry of movement near enough to the amber, fiery glow of the opening, backlit the thing for but a moment. Mary gasped, bit her lower lip. The thing was not moving around in an upright position, but rather in a spidery, all-fours skittering, with a loose-fitting black fabric flapping in its wake as it folded itself back into the darkness beyond the reach of the opening in the basement floor.

Oh Christ, there it is! The motherfucking trapdoor—

"MARY! DAMMIT, MARY, DID YOU HEAR WHAT I SAID?"

Your daughter! Your love! Doug just said she's—

"Missing? Are you sure?"

She heard Doug draw a sharp breath. "That's what I just said!"

"Oh, Doug, you've got to help me!"

"Oh, *stop* it! Just *stop!* You've gone off your meds again, haven't you? Why do you keep doing this to yourself? Don't you see what's happening? *This* is why I can't share custody with you!"

"No-Doug—"

'Mary, just tell me where Jenny is. I won't call the police. I'll just come and get her, and we can keep this from getting any more out of control than it already is. We'll get you into a hospital—"

"You-you think that *I* took Jenny?"

"Mary, I didn't hear any struggle and the front door was wide open. Jenny didn't scream or anything. I put her to bed, and then I went to check on her before I hit the sack, like I always do, and her room was empty. Now, whoever came in and coaxed her out *knew her* and *had a key* to the house. So, Mary, forget this nonsense about being held *prisoner.* You've taken my child from me—"

"You sonofabitch, you took her away from *me!* How's it feel!?"

"So you *did* take her?"

"How dare you! Of course I didn't take Jenny! And you're wasting time accusing me when I most certainly do *not* have her!"

"Then I have to hang up and call the police."

"*No, don't hang up, Doug! Please, don't hang up! I'm telling you the truth! I'm locked inside a basement, and I think they're going to kill me!*"

"Wait-wait-wait-*Jesus Christ!* Who is *they*? Where are you?"

"Big Top!"

"Big Top?"

"Big Top *Road!* The Crenshaw house!"

"What about a house number? You got that?"

"I-I-I dunno. I didn't pay attention!"

Spiare … your children … they await you

"OhmyGod-*ohmyGod-he* took Jenny!"

"Who? *Who, goddammit!*"

"I think-I think she's here!"

"You *think?* Mary, goddammit, did you—how long have you been off your meds *this time?*"

The cocktail of medications Mary had been on for the last five years of her life were as cumbersome with their side effects as they were ineffective when her borderline personality disorder and bipolar manic episodes were strong enough to override and resist any dose, no matter how heightened the milligrams. Yes, she'd tried to wean herself off the more numbing, debilitating medications.

I took them! I took them all! I remember! At the Wine and Spirits Shoppe! I took more than I'm supposed to times three!

Whether or not she'd been trying to overdose by chasing it with an entire bottle of Merlot, Mary could neither face nor admit to herself in that moment.

"I'm taking everything! This is not in my head! I am not paranoid, damn you! Send the police!"

"Okay-okay-*okay, just-just don't hurt her,*" Doug pleaded. "Just hold this inside your mind and don't let go of it, no matter what the *voices* tell you to do. Are you listening to me?"

The skin of her forehead felt ten times too small, stretched across her skull like ill-fitting hosiery. The glowing, amber opening in the basement floor flared, and red shot through it like the stitches of a bloodshot eyeball. Mary crammed herself up against the wall. A splinter from the rough and unsanded wood planks dug into the small of her back. The pain was something, and then it was of little consequence. Then it was nothing to concern herself with. The sensation reminded her of the beating heart in her chest and the life that held on. The brain that functioned despite its flawed, smoking circuitry. Eyes that showed her true and tangible evidence of a sub-level to the basement. Real. Real. Real. This was no paranoid withdrawal symptom.

"I'm going," she said into the phone, her voice airy and wistful. "I think Jenny's down in the hole."

"DOWN IN A HOLE? MARY, I SWEAR TO GOD I WILL KILL YOU IF YOU HURT HER, YOU SICK, CRAZY BITCH—"

"I'll save her, Doug. I'll bring her up and out of the hole."

"WHAT HOLE? DON'T DO THIS! MARY, PLEASE, I AM BEGGING YOU—"

"I'm going to bring her up and out, Doug. I'm her mother and—"

Doug disconnected the call. When she realized she was talking to dead air, Mary cast the phone over the side of the stairwell railing and into the abyss. With her eyes and full attention fastened to the flickering, fiery square appearing to float, to levitate in the pitch of the basement, Mary stood and ascended the wooden stairwell until her sneakers touched down on invisible cement. *I'll bring her out of the hole, and they'll give her back to me. And Doug, he'll wish he never tried to cut me out of her life.*

Mary strode towards the opening.

She stooped and stared down into the opening. The sub-level.

Come and see ... Counselor

The burnished light that lit her way to the opening guttered and went out. What little orientation it provided for Mary vanished, and she felt suddenly lost at sea, floundering in the black for some spatial sense. Stress sweat squirted across her skin, and her joints stiffened as true, primal fear of the dark seized her by the throat and the mind, echoing back to her Stone Age ancestors and their terror of the unknown. The urge to run back up the stairs shook her legs. That would require some sense of where the stairwell was in relation to where she now stood. She would have heard the door to the kitchen if it had opened again. There had been no such sound, that of possibility and choice. Safety.

There was only the hole before her, now a pit. Mary thought of trying to recover her cell. But the thought of clambering around on her hands and knees, feeling around blindly for what was probably a broken phone, seemed futile.

A real *mother would have already jumped down into the pit.*

This is why she's better off with Doug.

"Jenny!" she called, clambering down onto her knees and swinging her left leg blindly over the lip of the door in the floor. "I'm coming, baby! Mommy's coming!"

"Mommy! Mommy! *Mommy! Mommm-eeeee—*"

"*JENNY!*" Mary screamed, the desperate and mournful cries calling goosebumps across her arms. She swung her other leg over the lip. "Mommy's coming," she said to herself, as if she needed reminding. Nosing around the side of the pit with the tip of her Converse sneaker, Mary found what felt like a plank of wood protruding. She tested it by applying a small bit of her weight onto it. The plank held and bolstered her confidence enough to plant her other foot beside its brother. The fatalistic side of her anticipated the wood ledge giving way, dropping her into the ambiguous mouth of the sub-level. She even heard her bones snapping, her back breaking when she hit the ground below. She descended the series of wood planks leading into the earth. Mary looked down and caught a glimpse of both the depth of the hole and the surface of the ground below. It looked like stonework, bearded in moss and glazed with damp. Sunken some twelve or so feet down.

Man-made? By who? For whom?

The answer confounded and frightened her so much she shoved it aside and nosed the wall with the tip of her Converse for the next plank below. She stretched her leg, gathered enough purchase to plant it along the lower step.

That's when she heard the squawk of a rusted wheel as it turned in the lowlight below.

Mary screamed. Her foot slid off the lip of the plank, and she felt the pull of gravity as it sucked her down into the pit.

Bracing for a crippling impact with the stonework below, Mary's whole body clenched. When she landed on her side and realized she had not fallen nearly as far as she anticipated, only about four feet, her muscles oozed with relief. The surge of adrenaline left her feeling woozy as she lay there on the cold stone. She hadn't injured herself. Her right thigh, the one she'd come down on, smarted and protested as she pulled herself up the side of the cold, tacky stone wall, but it relented and faded once Mary managed to put all her weight on it.

A passageway lay before her, lit by flaming sconces set into the masonry and casting a warm, benign glow that strained the eyes. A cold and cruel wind whipped about her where she stood and funneled its way down the wide corridor, calling the flames along the walls into a sort of guttering, psychopathic dance that threw wild shadows across the stonework.

"Jenny?" Mary called, her voice quavering.

"*Mom-meee!*"

"Jenny!"

"*Come die with me! Mom-mee!*"

Jenny called to her mother in a sprightly, sing-song voice as if she were riding a seesaw for the first time and wanted Mary to watch her. The little girl's words betrayed her tone, perverted it. They stabbed a frozen shard of ice into Mary's heart as it flubbed along.

"*It won't be so scary if we do it together, Mom-meee.*"

"Oh God, JENNY! WHERE ARE YOU!"

Spiare, if you're going to come, then come all the way

"If you hurt her, I will fucking end you! Do you hear me?"

Coarse, ragged male laughter rang off the stone walls.

The sound of a rusted, squeaky wheel crooned behind her. Mary spun around to find a broken-down wheelchair. One wheel had come off its spoke, and the chair canted severely to the right as if it were sinking into the cobblestone floor. Mary remembered Maddie had mentioned how Conor had bought a wheelchair for Tilly. Had the woman's blood disease proven that debilitating, or was it something else that exhausted Tilly to the point she would need such a thing to move around? *Like an exchange of her own supernaturally charged blood with that of a series of impaired teenagers?*

Clearly, the wheelchair had been ill-used or overused. Tilly had needed it after all, despite what Conor had told Maddie. A dark, oily stain was set into the leathery fabric of its seat. It did not carry a gleam. The stain was not new.

This offered Mary some small comfort, knowing someone had not just come up out of the wheelchair and now hunkered somewhere inside the ambiguity of sub-level shadow.

Another gust of wind startled her, seeming to seize her around the throat with icicle hands that squeezed before breaking apart and funneling back down the cold corridor. Once more, the sconce flames guttered.

Where is it coming from? Is it even wind?

Someone gasped near her, as if they'd heard her thought in *their* head and seen fit to judge it.

Mary wheeled around in its direction and found nothing but the stone wall, which upon closer inspection, revealed a grimy but nevertheless wet texture splashed across it.

And a series of small, simple etchings in the stone. The look of it, its prehistoric and primal quality, hinted at something her mind could not reconcile itself to. Cave ancestors? Predating the birth of Christ? Mohammad? Moses? Abraham? *No, no, this is a basement. I'm standing inside a hidden passageway, yes, but I'm still well within the boundaries of a modern dwelling.*

Are you certain?

"*Mom-meeee! Come die with me!*"

Disorientation pressed upon the folds of her brain. The feeling was paralyzing, and Mary's sudden, crippling sense of having become disconnected from her *here and now* felt how she imagined an astronaut marooned in space must feel. Drifting in the deep, endless dark of nothingness.

"They're just kids, you piece of shit!" Mary cried, calling upon what could very well be the last of her brazenness. "Please! *Please, damn you ...*"

Come all the way

It was no longer a sticking point, that of allowing the disembodied male voice to lead her along like a well-trained animal. Mary crept along, at first holding close to the wall on her right-hand side until the tacky brown substance covering the elaborate stonework grabbed at her clothing and caught her up. She felt like a fly in ointment and quickly moved to the center of the corridor, feeling more exposed than before.

An alcove revealed itself to her along her right-hand side, centered between two glowing sconces. A black, arched wrought-iron gate closed off its interior, fitted snugly beneath the arched threshold of granite framing the entrance in an elaborate design that harkened all the way back to the medieval coldness of the catacombs. Mary approached the gate and linked her fingers in its ornate design. The iron was cold and uninviting to her hands, and she recoiled after a moment lest she pull back digits red and stinging with frostbite.

The short and narrow annex within bottlenecked into a crypt of sorts. A lone white candle, barely burned down and bearing strange, alien insignia, stood atop a gold stand set against the center of the rear wall. A certain square recession in that rear wall hinted at a window, or the surreal ghost of one. *A window underground? A lovely view of the worms and maggots.* Mary's gaze plummeted towards the floor, drawn by a quick, scurrilous, and almost imagined movement along the floor.

That same antagonizing wind sliced at the nape of her neck and froze her vocal cords for a moment.

Otherwise, what Mary saw set into the cement floor of the crypt's deeper interior would have elicited a scream the likes of which she would have never thought herself capable of.

She withdrew her hands from the iron gratings of the crypt gate, recoiling from what she saw within.

It swung inward.

The rats racing to and fro across the floor sped her heart up. They ranged from small and squirrelly to old, black, and grease-grizzled like the elders of the vermin tribe. One of the more aged stopped cold and sniffed at the air, its ink-spot eyes seeming to size her up from afar before it darted into a crevice out of sight.

The lot of them skirted the partially buried body protruding from the ground as if it had been brought up and out of his or her own grave. Expelled, like a sinner vomited out of hallowed ground.

If Mary was going to come, it was time to *come all the way* ...

She slipped inside the crypt. Like the phantom buzzing of a cell phone along one's thigh, she felt a strange current conduct itself through the thin sole of her black Converse and emanate up her ankle. Not a shooting pain. More a curious pleasure that seemed to keep her moving forward through the frigid time and space of the antechamber into the crypt proper. She no longer felt in control of her actions, and her thoughts seemed to multiply and layer themselves with every forward step.

Mary crossed into the crypt proper.

A mere three feet from the front white rubber nub of her sneakers, the body half-submerged in the rectangular opening in the cement stirred. Shuddered.

Warily, Mary hunkered down onto her haunches beside the figure. A thin layering of silt and dirt coated the body before her.

"Oh my God," she said, eyes wide and horrified. "Michael. Oh God."

Michael Malone, one of the Nine, murmured and shuddered. Fissures opened in the caked dirt molded to his body. His mouth opened wide as if he were yawning. The grime that appeared to have sealed his lips shut dropped down his throat, coated the picket-sharpened teeth lining his gums. Michael gagged, his head forced upward in spasm, then his teeth snapped shut like a bear trap. The sound startled Mary, who had gone still beside him. She had been silently studying him, the terror quietly mounting within as her poor brain strained itself to make some sense of what she was seeing. The fractures in the dirt mold widened and collapsed down the sides of his head, his torso. Legs. The teen had become unsheathed from whatever membranous cocoon of earth he'd been nesting in. He wore jeans and a black t-shirt with yellow lettering across the chest that read *West Point Academy*.

Yet, it looked like Michael Malone had been lying there for ages, forgotten and dismissed over centuries, rather than missing mere days.

Oh dear God, Michael. Michael Malone. You were the boy everyone believed would be skipping college after Baldwin in favor of the Army. Michael Malone. The tall, athletic-looking boy with a square jaw and mop of blond hair who wore an American flag backpack and stood the straightest during the Pledge of Allegiance every blessed morning. What did ... he ... do to you?

His hands were folded over his heart. They held even when Michael's chest hitched as he struggled to breathe.

"The dirt! Oh, shit! Okay!"

Mary sprang into motion. She leaned over him and reached for his face. She would pry his lips apart and somehow dig the dirt out of his mouth. She would clear his airway.

Michael Malone's eyes flashed open. His pupils were whited out, edged in black and yellow, stitched in red bloodshot. His mouth opened once more and let loose with a scream. But it was not merely Michael's scream, but a cacophony of seemingly countless cries combined with his mannish outburst. Mary heard female screams intermingled with his, as well as an assortment of other male voices that had not deepened like Michael's did when he was a Freshman.

The scream held for an eternity, long after the teen's breath would have run out or lungs given way. Mary scrambled away from him, crab-walking gracelessly until she had crammed herself up against the far wall.

Michael Malone whipped his head to face her, his inhuman gaze charting her every move. Mary noted hunger in that gaze. Carnivorous longing.

Grasping for words where there seemed to be none, Mary said the first thing that sprang to mind. "You are Michael Malone! You're going to be a service member! You're going to be a soldier! *Please, Michael! Remember!*"

The crypt was neither a place of memory nor silence in that moment.

The teen's prolonged, tormented scream gave way to a series of quick, breathy shrieks. Nonsensical words dribbled from his lips, unfathomable and incoherent.

Then Mary heard the others out in the corridor. Girls. Boys. Gasping. Letting loose those same bursts of screams mixed with strange, incomprehensible words and phrases that tore out of them like a string of angry profanities.

The Nine. They're all down here.

And they're suffering.

"They're dead or dying," Mary said, barely believing her own admission. "Changing over."

I'm too late.

"*Mom-meeee! It's starting!*"

Jenny.

Come all the way

"I'm coming, you bastard!" Mary cried, hauling herself back onto her feet and hot footing it out of the crypt. The sudden frenzy of motion was grounded in maternal instinct. "I'm coming for all of them. Then I'm coming for *you*!"

The horrific reality of her surroundings set in as something to be accepted as a new *normal* or truth. There are dark corners boasting even darker lurkers and longer, leaner shadows.

We all know nothing. Until we know more than we ever wanted to.

The high school Junior, Tara Neeley, lay half-submerged in the ground just as Mary had found Michael Malone. Her hands grabbed and fingers closed around something hovering above her only the teen girl could see. Tara Neely, in the pea-colored cardigan and Nirvana t-shirt peeking out from under the V of the sweater's center hems. Mary had always suspected the girl to be an old soul. Mary rarely saw Tara without a Moleskine notebook clasped to her chest and a pen clipped to it in the event (which occurred frequently) the girl needed to commit her innermost thoughts to its pages. A flash of memory came upon Mary, that of Conor bragging to the guidance counselor in passing about how Tara Neeley was a budding novelist who would one day grace the New York Times Bestseller list. Like some proud papa, Conor was beaming.

All the while, the English teacher had been remaking the young girl into the screaming, twitching form stretched out inside a crypt under his mother's house of horrors. Over the course of months. Under the guise of the trusted educator and all-around beloved *nice guy*.

The girl coughed violently, her head jerking upward. Blood ringed her lips. Tara Neeley let loose with one final hack and sprayed a cloud of crimson into the dancing dust motes of musty air above her head.

"Tara," Mary gasped, her hands squeezed into fists. "Oh, Tara. Honey. I-I—"

"*Mom-meee,*" Jenny called from further down the corridor. The little girl's previous tone of urgency had diminished considerably. Now, Jenny Marguerite sounded as if she were using the last of her breath to accuse her mother of one final abandonment.

"Jenny!" Mary cried, exiting the second crypt on sneakers that seemed barely to touch the ground. "Keep talking to me! Call to Mama! I'll follow the sound of your voice!"

When Mary emerged once more in the corridor, she found the sconces on the walls had all gone out. The gates to Michael's and Tara's crypts swung shut, as did the others all the way down. Iron latches slammed home in one nerve-jangling noise that sounded like a grand death knell. The entire crypt had slipped into utter blackness, the candles inside the tombs having snuffed out as well. She could not see her hands in front of her face. Her eyes could not adjust to the darkness quickly enough.

Mary knew she had to move.

"Jenny!"

A teenage male voice moaned in the abyss.

The heart-wrenching sound of a girl choking, gagging, glanced off every stone of the corridor, driving Mary further down into the pit of her own despair.

"Jenny! *Please, dear God! Jenny!*"

Mary heard the wheelchair's rusted shriek behind her.

Something nudged at the backs of her ankles. She could not bite back her scream. She lunged forward, away from the hard and unyielding object that touched her legs.

The chair's footrests.

Then, the male voice that had, up until that moment, confined itself to Mary's mind bloomed in the stygian blackness of the crypt.

"Behold your children, Mother. The forgotten. Fatherless children, no more. Bear witness to their becoming. Comfort them, for they will comfort you when *your* time is upon *you*."

"Give me my daughter or, so help me, I will hunt you to the ends of the motherfucking Earth!"

Laughter sounded, all at once close enough for the man to be at her elbow and further down the corridor in the same instant. It was patronizing, yet patient. Doting, like a parent with an endless capacity for *waiting*. "Your Jennifer does not wish to be saved, Mary. In fact, if anything, her wish was for her new family to save her from you. But she will return to you when you have accepted her new brothers and sisters as your own. When you have consented to being a Mother to these poor, poor, discounted children. Jennifer will join you in the Red. You will see her again in the great *down below*. Do you understand?"

Mary's body shook like a tuning fork. She could have sworn it produced some audible note of resonance. "Where is she? *Where are you?!* Jenny, I will follow the sound of your voice!"

Jenny's breathy voice, frail and weakened, whispered in the black. "Afraid of the dark."

The sound of her daughter's voice seemed both near and far in the same instant, as if the rules of amplitude and impression did not apply in the Crenshaw crypt. Still, Mary had to try. She turned in the direction of what she could only deduce was the sound of Jenny's soft voice. It was strange. Mary had somehow gotten herself turned around from how she'd been standing a moment before, facing the opened, extending corridor before her. But Mary stuck out her arm in the darkness, roughly the seven o'clock position, and pressed forward.

The male voice produced a deep humming sound in the base of his chest. It broke off and he spoke. "Your daughter is afraid of the dark. I do not want her afraid. Not now."

The sconces along the walls relit, splashing Mary's shadow across the wall. The candles within the crypts on either side had also rekindled.

Mary saw she'd been walking back towards the makeshift ladder leading back up into the basement. She turned around to face the mouth of the crypt's corridor once more and nearly ran headlong into the two of them spread out along the cold stonework.

The man held the limp body of Jennifer Marguerite in his arms.

I know you.

I. Know. You.

It was Doug, her estranged husband.

But it *wasn't*, at the same time. This man looked like Doug if he'd spent a long, hard decade on the streets or become addicted to crystal meth. The voice was a far cry from the one Mary had only just heard on the other end of her cell phone what seemed now like ages ago. Yet, Mary thought it could quite possibly *pass* for her ex's voice if he kept vaping like a lunatic for the next twenty years straight. *This Doug* had long, poker-straight black hair that oil had tamped down to his skull so severely the pale skull shone through the strands. He looked decrepit and threadbare.

You wear the face you deserve, Doug!

This Doug was bare-chested, his pallid skin accordioned along the slats of his ribcage and pulled taut across the divot of his breastbone. He looked like a disassembled kite stuffed into a bag made of human hide. The Doug From Before had been toned to perfection from head to toe, an avid gym goer and strict vegetarian who supplemented his iron deficiency with One-A-Day tablets. The Doug From Before had olive skin that never knew a blemish or imperfection, the blessings for a man of both Cuban and French descent.

This Doug's face was creased with red eyes that glowed in the sunken sockets bright as blood moons. His pants were mangy black chinos. His knobby knees poked out from the splits in the fabric. His feet were scaly and covered in sores.

This Doug beseeched Mary with his unblinking, red-sun eyes. He spoke to her no longer in the doting, patient tone he'd been using. "*He* made me bring her here," *This Doug* said, a croak placing a vile period at the end of the sentence. "*He* said you would know what to do. That you've ... always known what to do."

"You're not The Father then?"

"Naw," *This Doug* managed, before swiping his hand across his mouth to stifle a gag. "Just a *Familiar*. An *instrument*. To draw The Mother here and to empower her."

"Empower me?"

"The Mother. Their Mother." *This Doug* swept his bony arm wide.

Mary had no idea what he'd just done was an invitation to *them* until each of The Nine came shambling from their individual crypts. They inched along with backs stooped, clothing dusted in the dirt of their temporary and half-hearted graves. Fattened maggots wriggled along their arms, wiggled up their torsos. To their mouths. Then, into their opened maws for The Nine teenagers to chew and swallow with the picket-sharpened teeth lining their black gums. They lurched towards Mary and *This Doug* and Jenny like humbled worshippers to some lost ritual and sacred art. Their eyes were blacked out and unblinking as rodents in the nightshade. Disclosing nothing of emotion or a residue of humanity.

Husks.

Walking fleshy bags of blood with great white shark teeth, crooked and razor and menacing, that made it impossible for the lot of them to even close their mouths. Consequently, their lips had peeled back, further completing the ghastliness of The Nine's transformation. As they drew closer, crowding around the three of them like some dark adoration, Mary became fully aware of what had become of The Nine.

Black holes flared in the middle of their faces where their noses had once been. A single thin rib of cartilage ran down the center of the opening, and it quivered with every breath the teens drew in and blew out.

Made in the image of The Father.

Not This Doug.

"Mary," *This Doug* implored from the floor before her, "He drained our Jenny to the point of death. I tried to stop him. I failed her. I failed you. Mary, you know what to do. You have to. It's already in your mind. I can see it there. It's tickling the back of your brain, but you're fighting its temptation. You can't. Do what you know needs to be done. What you've been wanting to do. Follow the thread of thought all the way to its end."

It was true.

The bastard was practically baring his throat for her. Daring her to do what that impulse willed her to do. What she'd fantasized about more often than she would ever admit, to herself or anyone else. She imagined women like her as legion. Separated. Stripped of their parental rights. Brought low.

Every time he'd belittled her.

Every court date that ended with her alternating between crying in her car and battering its steering wheel in a blackout rage that left her breathless and helpless.

Every night she'd tried to call Jenny so she could tell her *goodnight*, only to have Doug tell her with a hint of gloating he'd already put her down for the night. Better luck next time.

Every time Doug had hidden her medicine so she would go into withdrawal, for her to find them later under the bed or the kitchen table or inside the folds of the sofa like some sadistic, staged egg hunt. Mary always knew she hadn't simply lost or *misplaced* them.

Couldn't have!

Doug had just wanted to build his case for taking Jenny away from her, as well as his own case for divorce. *She's unfit, your honor! I can't do anything for her, and oh, how I tried-tried-tried-*

Unfit

It felt like she'd stuck her thumbs into a jaw of fruit preserves.

The screams jolted Mary from her reverie as violently as a sturdy, strong hand at her shoulder.

She did not pull back or withdraw her thumbs from *This Doug's* upturned eyes, not even when she realized what she had done. It felt as if a thin veil, membranous and translucent, had drawn itself up between her and the man on the cold cobblestones before her. The man who let her daughter's limp body slip from his lap when Mary had dug her thumbs into his eyes. There could be no hope for the veil to lift itself, to turn aside. The ethereal quality of a dream does not withdraw to show the dreamer they are merely dreaming. No, the obscurity and the question are meant to linger.

A nightmare? Like the terrible, haunting nightmares I've been suffering for the last few weeks.

Regardless, Mary did not withdraw.

Instead, she relished the insufferable shrieks of *This Doug* as she burrowed deeper into his ocular cavities with the tips of her thumbs, searching for a stopping point. Bone? Cartilage? The brain? *This Doug* flopped about like a fish on a line. Mary did not (would not) release him. She had ensnared him. Hooked him. Like never before.

Besides, this was the plan?

Isn't that what he said?

This Doug? My Doug?

Whoever he is?

Doesn't matter!

Mary scooped his ruined eyeballs out of the sockets and watched them drip down his cheeks. The red, bundled nerves held onto them, having burst from his eye sockets like exotic red roots.

Why this made Mary laugh to herself, she could not be sure.

You've come along, but that is not the end of the line, come all the way

This Doug looked up at her. "Th-th-thank y-you." He slumped over. His face was a mask of smeared blood. His body shuddered; legs kicked out in a final death throe that spilled Jennifer Marguerite down onto the cold cobblestones of the vault's corridor.

Staring down at her hands, gory with blood and bits of nerve, Mary felt like she was looking upon someone else's hands. Not hers. She had always experienced trepidation when it came to so much as killing a spider in her house. Yet, she could blind her husband in such a savage way. The remorse touched her conscience, a quick fingertip at the base of her skull before she stuffed it down out of a need to be practical.

There was Jenny.

Drained.

Dead

Mary took a knee beside her daughter's still, prone body. She slipped her hands ever so gently underneath Jenny's body and scooped her up into her arms. The last time she'd felt so helpless in terms of caring for her daughter had been when Jenny was only a couple months old and developed a fever of 103. She and Doug had worked together, trading off on wiping down Jenny's whole body with a warm, damp cloth to try and bring the temperature down.

It didn't work. Nothing they had tried at home seemed to lower the fever so much as a decimal. Ultimately, the young couple drove Jenny to the hospital, but the sense they had failed to care for their child and save her themselves hit home for Doug and Mary in that they could only shield their daughter so much.

This time I won't fail, my sweet baby girl!

In that moment, there was only her child in her arms. The crypt now seemed to breathe like a giant calcified lung. The thing that had once been a seventeen-year-old Honor Roll student named Delaney Lindberg stooped to shove the seizing body of *This Doug* out of the way. His tongue lolled out of the side of his bloody mouth, and he managed a strange, incomprehensible string of words that might have been a protest before going still along the cold, gory stones. The Nine crept ever closer, crowding around Mary and Jenny. Then, unnoticed by the mother who stared vacantly down at her limp child, The Nine enclosed them in a close-knit circle. They murmured and tittered. They locked arms.

Tara Neeley, the shortest and most petite of The Nine, with black hair cut into a pixie style, leaned in. Her rank breath burst across the nape of Mary's neck.

"Mother," she said, "do you see now?"

Pete Mason, a young teen who had once harbored aspirations to join the electrician's union like his father and *his* father before him, touched the Guidance Counselor's shoulder. Mary did not so much as blink at the undead teenager's finger's cold clasp. "Tilly is gone. She was our Mother and she's gone. You must take her place. Please, we need you. And you've been there. For every one of us. Now, it matters the most."

Valerie Parent, the blonde cheerleader whose hair had turned to a mop of rigid, tufted straw that once fell down her back and now stood out in all directions, smoothed Mary's hair along the crown of her skull. "Tilly made us. But she has been wasted. And The Father, he is in love with you now. The Father loves his family. And he longs to come home to us. But he can't until his family is whole. Complete."

The Father loves me?

Steve Teague, a quiet and unusually pious Senior who had been giving serious consideration to entering the seminary before Conor Crenshaw sank his claws into him, clacked his picket-fence teeth together. "A father is nothing without his family. He is vulnerable. Weakened. But with his family? His coven? His army? There is nothing The Father cannot do. No one beyond his reach."

Tara Neeley squeezed Mary's shoulder. "Do you understand?"

"Just tell me how to save my baby," Mary begged in a dry, brittle voice. "What do I do?"

The sound of countless rows of teeth clacking together in a mad, cacophony of excitement and anticipation.

"Do you understand?" Delaney Lindberg pressed, ever so slightly.

"I understand! I do! Just *please* tell me how to save my Jenny! I'll do anything you want! I'll be anyone you want me to be! But she's innocent! *Please tell me how to help her!"*

Pete Mason withdrew his hand and hunkered down beside Mary, who had taken to absently rocking Jenny in her arms. Valerie Parent, the undead debutante, came around the other side. The circle of Nine began to hum, like a closed circuit conducting the Devil's electricity, with their arms linked and black, sunken eyes shut. Vicious teeth clacking in unison.

Rhythmic.

Hypnotic.

"This way," Pete Mason said, as he drew Mary's arm, the one not securing her daughter's head, into his pale, vein-shot hand. Mary offered a weakened resistance in response, then submitted. Pete Mason drew Mary's hand to Jenny's mouth, pressed her wrist down into Jenny's mouth until the little girl's lips parted. "Call to her."

"What?"

"Say her name."

Mary hesitated, her mind unravelling the longer she gazed at Pete Mason's unblinking doll's eyes and chittering teeth behind fattened red lips. If she hadn't torn her eyes away, Mary was certain her nerve would have shattered and her mind would have ruptured. She looked down at her daughter. "Jenny," she uttered. "Jenny."

"Louder."

"Jenny!"

She felt the teeth break the skin of her wrist. Jenny's blue eyes flashed open, wide and shocked at the sound of her name. Mary winced. Her mouth formed a perfect O, and while she wished to turn away, she could not. Whenever Mary had her blood drawn at school for the Blood Drives, she had never been able to watch the bag fill up beside her. A clear aversion. Until now. Mary watched with a rigid, alien fascination as her daughter drank from her ripped vein. The pull on her arm was cosmic in its sensation. Unlike anything Mary had ever experienced. Not unlike the pull of Jenny on Mary's nipples when she'd breastfed.

Swooning, Mary asked, "N-now what?"

"Don't be afraid," Delaney Lindberg said, her tone prayerful and otherworldly.

Then, The Nine fell upon Mary and Jenny with their gnashing, terrible teeth and rancid breath and grunting—

—warm and wet—legs kicked out and arms pushed down over and over. Buoyed upward—rose in the black liquid by slow and excruciating degrees. The circle of light shimmered above with a heartbreaking brilliance—heartbreaking only because it loomed above lovely. It beckoned yet seemed to retreat with every upward surge—limbs turned to rubber—breath burned like a torch wedged in a windpipe. Arms kicked out— breaststroke. *The circle of light suddenly appeared to dive, to meet her, no longer in retreat—* froggy kicks—fanned the water back behind her. The light was within arms-reach—*up* and out—

276

—the fire crisping her lungs surged upward through her chest. When it forced her lips open wide, Mary expected a blaze of light to burst from her mouth like some mythical dragon. Instead, a thick liquid dribbled down her chin, and the absence of pressure behind her breastbone made her wheeze, then cough violently. They drew her up off the hard surface she had been leaning against with her back. It was a flu-like expulsion. A great jerking of the limbs and fierce tightening of the neck muscles.

It was dark where she was, but by no means pitch as it had been down in the tombs.

She tried to speak her daughter's name, but her tongue and teeth would not oblige. Her lips were stuck together, the syrup she'd expelled from her mouth having worked on them like an adhesive.

All around her, Mary heard the low, groveling whimpers of things suffering. Wasting. Dying. Sounds shifting about. Crawling. Like sandpaper grazing a wood surface in twitchy, rhythmical bytes. The floor shuddered and shook, carrying the vibrations of their every movement, desperate and graceless, as they dragged themselves about in the lowlight. Mary felt as if she'd woken inside a room full of alligators.

That's when Mary became aware of the searing pain that seemed to encapsulate her. Every inch stung and itched like she'd stumbled blindly upon a beehive and stirred their wrath.

When she tried to engage her right arm, Mary found it immoveable.

Otherwise engaged.

Calmly and quietly, a naked man who looked like he'd painted himself in black diseased sap from head to toe hunkered beside her with Mary's wrist up to his mouth. Her mind tuned in to the subtle sensation of his mouth as it siphoned blood from her arm. His head was shorn, his body starved and angular as a contortionist. His eyes glowed red in the darkness, producing their own luminescence, which backlit his long, horse-like face. The hole where his nose was supposed to be. Sunken and sallow cheeks. He looked at Mary as if she ought to pay him no mind. Nothing she could do to stop him. Every lap of the thing's tongue against her exposed veins activated the many, many unseen wounds streamlining nearly every inch of her flesh.

The Dark Sap Man withdrew his teeth from her wrist. The sensation was madly erotic, like a lover withholding pleasure for one teasing moment. The Dark Sap Man turned his head and spat out the mouthful of her blood onto the floor, like a cowboy reeling off a brown line of tobacco into a spittoon. When he returned his burning red gaze to her, Mary felt her chest tighten. Her bowels loosen.

The hatred.

It paralyzed her, and at the same time, Mary felt the strangest and strongest compulsion to free her flesh of the dirty, rumpled clothing clinging to her and soaked clean through with sweat. The countless points of pain bisecting her body from head to toe cried out as one for their freedom. For the air to hit them head on. For Mary to tear her clothes off. To let the wounds breathe in the cold air that gusted about the cramped, low-lit room littered with unseen things scraping themselves along the floor.

The Dark Sap Man repeated his suck-and-spit ritual over and over until a puddle of Mary's vital life's blood ran black and glistening across the warped floorboards of the room.

Finally, Mary managed to find her voice, small and shrunken, at the bottom of her being. "Please stop."

The Dark Sap Man blinked vacantly at her, paused in his seemingly automatic motion.

They regarded one another for what seemed like a lifetime.

She could not withdraw her arm. She could not move. Her brain barked commands to her arms and legs, but the line of communication had become severed somewhere along the line.

This is what it's like to be stuck in a spider web, wound round and round in sticky silk while a fat garden spider slowly devours you.

"Please—"

A voice exploded inside her skull, an auditory migraine that shut her eyes and pushed the wind out of her. It flattened her back against the wall with such force, her angel wings screamed.

What kind of mother? What kind of mother poisons her own children?

"What-what are you doing?"

She screamed from her toes when The Dark Sap Man suddenly moved his dark, elongated face and bloody fangs within an inch of hers.

He snapped his teeth together, viciously. It made a sound like a femur snapping in two.

Your blood is toxic. You knew it to be toxic. Your addiction? Your weakness? You murdered our children. Tell me!

"I-I don't understand—"

Tell me! Because I cannot discern it! I've been trying, but the chemicals are elusive to me.

"Where is my daughter? Where's Jenny?"

Dead! Dead! Like the rest! What drugs are these in your bloodstream? What is your addiction? Confess yourself! Cleanse your soul!

"Can't be!" she cried. "You're *lying!* Lying bastard!"

Mary grabbed for the thing, her tremulous claws clamping down onto his black and sinewy arms. The Dark Sap Man slipped her in an instant, and his hands curled around her throat just as quickly. His grip and the closeness of his malevolent, demonic gaze shut out all other things in her midst. The slithering sounds of the things along the wood floor. The things she knew to be The Nine. The teenagers. Dying as they climbed haphazardly over one another like a mound of serpents seeking their own individual succor or relief. White fireworks exploded before her eyes, dappling her vision of the monster before her. Her killer. The Father.

The Father.

Yes. Oh, yes.

His red eyes screamed at her in unison with the voice that attacked her brain like a siege.

You weak bitch! You weak, drug-addicted whore! An unfit mother!

It was no longer The Dark Sap Man with his hands around her throat, closing her windpipe, but Doug Marguerite. His eyes swelled within their sockets, and a smile touched his lips as he shook her in his grasp. He spat in her face, and his voice had escaped the confines of her mind to come roaring out of his mouth like a tempest. He called her a *weak whore.* "Murderous *mother!*" The meager moonlight pouring into the room softened with every second Mary's brain screamed for oxygen. The shadows stirred all about. Splashes of blue and gray twitched along the ground like running watercolors. And Doug's red eyes finally blinked, just when it seemed they were incapable of such a human reflex. "*You pill-head! What is your pill,* PILL HEAD?"

My meds. The Wine and Spirits parking lot.

Chemicals.

Killed the children.

Toxic blood.

The Dark Sap Man's fingers loosened just enough as a look of sheer confoundedness swept across his pitch face. A shadow ran across his red eyes.

Mary sucked in a breath.

She grabbed for his forearms. Coarse, tufted hair covered The Dark Sap Man's arms, and Mary dug her fingers into the thick follicles.

Measure for measure, she pushed back against The Dark Sap Man's resistance.

The muscles and tendons of her arms jumped and rippled as she strained desperately to gain some impossible upper hand.

Puttana! Spiare!

"Fuck *you!*"

His lips peeled back to reveal two fearsome rows of triangular, shark-like teeth stained in blood cast in black by the moonlight. He lunged for her. Mary braced herself for the attack upon her throat, the pop and burst of those razor teeth as they punctured her carotid artery. But The Dark Sap Man's rank, burning breath bloomed against her right ear instead. The Dark Sap Man's words raised the hackles on the back of her neck at first. Injected fire into her veins. Called adrenaline into every muscle, flooding them with a primal rage. Then, before Mary Marguerite could fully process what he'd said to her, The Dark Sap Man's message, delivered in an oddly deep and calm baritone, lulled her into a sleep as bottomless as a coma.

Later, she'd awaken with one word on her lips and stamped upon her brain.

Maledizione.

Curse.

XIII. ACTIVE

Mary was terrified to open her eyes. Her legs felt as if they were bound. Made immobile. Her mind's eye showed her what she would find should she dare to look. Tangled arms wound around the lower half of her body, cinched tight as a hundred sailor knots. Hands grasping along her thighs and squeezing her knees together, struggling for a firmer purchase upon her body. She heard their moaning lament, animalistic and inhuman. The Nine. They clung to her. They meant to drag her along, to feed her to The Father for what she had done. Her whole body howled with pain.

Blindly, she swatted at her legs. Her breath stuck in her throat.

"Please, God, help me!"

Mary shot up from the bed, and where she expected to find The Nine clinging to her legs, she discovered her legs were tethered in crème-colored linen sheets. They had come untucked from the corners of her queen-sized bed and bundled together, wound round and round her lower limbs. The clear and present evidence of a dream so distressing, she had tossed and turned with a violence Mary had not experienced since she was small. Her feverish mind sought refuge, no matter how imaginary.

She snatched up the digital clock from her bedside table.

5:47 a.m.

Casting her eyes all about the bedroom, Mary scanned every inky corner and crevice of her surroundings for the slightest of stirrings. She listened for the smallest gasp, the faintest intake of air. The silence had a weight to it, like that which precedes thunderclaps. She shivered. The bedroom was colder than normal. Mary had lost her coat along the way, somewhere between Tilly's house of horrors and her little rancher on Sycamore Lane twenty miles east. It wasn't on the floor beside her bed. She thought she remembered having violently clawed it off her body at some point like it was causing her physical pain.

An unreliable memory.

Everything about her bedroom remained unchanged. The oversized clock on the wall across the bed she'd bought for a song and dance at an antique shop in New Hope. The waist-high bookshelf weighted down with all her first-edition Margaret Atwoods. The black rectangle of the bathroom entryway loomed ominous and stoic as a dark wood casket standing on end inside the recessed archway to her left. Her flat screen was still on, its screen blank and twitchy.

A dream?

The sheers resting over the window to her right slowly ballooned and billowed outward like a lung filling with air. Mary jerked as the vaguely familiar sensation of cold, bodiless hands found their way around her throat. With an unsettling but gentle ease, the chill played about her neck, toying with her. Little love bites. The sheers fattened without a sound, expanding like the belly of a glutton. She listened for the sound of the wind pouring through what had to be an opened window behind them.

There was nothing.

Her mind was suddenly awash in another, far more lucid and overwhelming memory.

A string of words, hot and stinking, in her ear.

The sheers began to dance, a herky-jerky motion, mimicking the movements of something or someone concealed beneath them.

"*Maledizione,*" she said, her voice unfamiliar and seemingly displaced from their source.

Curse.

The words of The Father. To send her on her way.

His words bled into her brain pan, a thick and intoxicating fluid that consumed her all at once. Before Mary knew it, she had come off the bed and lunged at the sheers. They collapsed in her hands. The sudden motion enraged the full-body pain and anguish she had mistakenly thought a figment of her nightmare. Every inch of her flesh flared with a furious discontent.

Mary crossed the room in five wide strides and switched on the dome light above her bed.

Instantly, her body wailed in dissent from head to toe.

Mary caught sight of herself in the standing wall mirror to her left.

She never would have believed it, if not for her reflection.

A small, black hole along the nape of her neck, about the size of a silver dollar.

Gaping.

What looked like tiny white pebbles ringing the hole like a—

"Nononononono-*nononononoNO!*"

Mary yanked her shirt up over her head and flung it down. She unzipped her pants and wriggled feverishly out of them. Panties too.

Standing there naked before the mirror, Mary felt her world go sideways and her brain slip into its own self-preserving mode of denial.

The opening in her throat numbered one of what were fifty or so that encircled her body. The randomness of their symmetry and the closeness of their proximity to one another had transformed Mary's flesh into something of a beehive. Only the hives were, in fact, mouths lined with tiny, needle-fine teeth. They screamed. Gasped. Hacked. Muttered unintelligible things, lips twisting and contorting and pouting. Joined in a sonorous cacophony for the damned. Before Mary realized, she started gouging her fingers into the mouths. She pulled fiercely at them, seeking to somehow tear them free of her flesh. They responded with bites that called blood onto her fingertips and quickly turned her palms tacky with red the more she strained to loosen them from her chest. Her sides. Her navel. Inner thighs. Buttocks. Everywhere her fingers grabbed, she found a set of small, deadly incisors and felt the stinging pinch of their bite before she wrenched her hand away.

The protective denial of her mind compelled Mary to squeeze her eyes shut. To vanquish the mirror's image by the only means possible.

Self-imposed blindness.

Her knees turned to rubber, buckled, and she fell forward, barely bracing herself from crashing into the looking glass before her.

Behind her, the sheers billowed outward once more.

A tall, dark figure walked behind them, the black bulb of his head ballooning it ever further until it dropped down behind him.

"Your children may not forgive you," he said in a familiar, mildly water-logged voice that transported Mary's mind back to that low-lit room in Tilly's House of Horrors. The Dark Sap Man. Father. "Nevertheless, they will always be with you. A mother must never lose sight of her obligations. They will remind you when it is required."

"I AM NOT THEIR MOTHER!"

"Well …"

Mary's vision was drenched in the red of rage. She heard her heart in her head, thrumming like a bass drum. With palsied hands, she suddenly grabbed the sides of the mirror before her and drove it back against the wall with such unabashed force the glass shattered in its frame. The sound rang in her ears like a morning bell. Long, lethal shards clattered to the rug. In the chaos of the moment, she did not realize the burning mouths embedded in her flesh had disappeared until she snatched up a piece of the mirror and pain did not slow her body. No, adrenaline had taken the wheel of her intention and she snapped to her feet. Mary spun around and charged at The Dark Sap Man with the shard upraised.

"MARY! STOP!"

Doug Marguerite caught Mary's wrist in mid-air.

Behind her, Mary heard the hysterical screams of a little girl.

"NOOOOOO!"

XIV. BROKEN

"I dunno," Doug Marguerite told the officer with the patchy salt-and-pepper goatee that hid a series of descending jowls. "I honestly dunno. I haven't spoken to her in over a week."

The officer, whose name (Broderick) was engraved in a small gold pin pinned to his right breast, nodded stiffly. His Oakley sunglasses winked at Doug when Officer Broderick turned his gaze upward to stare unflinchingly at the burgeoning sun of a curiously warm March morning. "Take your time, sir."

Everywhere Doug turned, he saw the ghostly mirage of his estranged wife standing before him with what had been a long shard of mirror glass upraised to bludgeon him. A thousand-yard stare set deep into her heavily bloodshot eyes as she looked through him. Beyond him. Mouth wrinkled into a painful grimace. *My God, the things she said to me. Mary is gone. She's fucking just* gone. He blinked his eyes, remembered he held a rapidly cooling cup of coffee in his hands, snuck a sip, and tried to regain some focus on his surroundings.

The altercation had taken place out on the sprawling front lawn of the Colonial home he'd once shared with Mary. A major selling point of the property had been its spacious front and back yards, with the quality of its school district running a close second in terms of importance. Retired couples outnumbered the thirtysomething, first-time home buyers in a four-to-one ratio, but the two generations blended nice as pie. Doug remembered how Mary enjoyed mowing the lawn, much to his surprise and relief. Dressed in a pair of Daisy-Duke denim cutoffs and one of her many concert t-shirts, her flip-flops kicking up clumps of clippings behind her as she trudged along happily behind their Lawn Boy. Yet another mirage borne of Doug's greatly frazzled mind. He wondered if he stood there long enough, with little to no meaningful explanation to supply the investigating officer before him, just how many scenes from his life past with Mary would come back to haunt him.

He could not help but imagine they would feel like separate indictments. *I've been a shit to her.*

283

Mary had shown up at the house just as Doug was pouring milk over Jenny Marguerite's Honey Nut Cheerios. The little girl was dressed for her day at Comington Pre-K, an outfit she'd picked out herself that included a glitzy, sequined tutu and star-shaped sunglasses.

Then, the dull *splat* sounds of flat palms slapping at the outer front door.

The storm door was open, and the glass door beyond revealed the early-morning caller, backlit in the strange concoction of colors born of the minutes connecting night to day.

Jenny had waved to her mother when she saw her.

But Mary didn't wave back.

Come to think of it, I don't think Mary so much as acknowledged her own daughter the entire time. It was like she had no idea Jenny was there, watching her own mother unravel—

"Mr. Marguerite," Officer Broderick patted Doug's bath robed shoulder, "you still with me?"

"Oh yeah." Doug had become mildly preoccupied with the appearance of his front lawn. It was a gray, shaggy mat that looked like it would never, *could* never, come back from its own death. Not even a series of warm April showers or humid heat rays could return it to its former glory. At least, that was how Doug saw things. He had no idea why the thought traipsed across his mind and then took hold of his consciousness while the investigating officer was in the process of questioning him. *I don't feel in control. Strange.* "I'm sorry, Officer. It's just, I'm trying to process."

"Mr. Marguerite, let me be frank with you. And this advice comes from running point on a little north of three-hundred-fifty assault cases. There's just no point in trying to make sense of things when you're dealing with a traumatic experience. The mind is a miracle machine, but it'll never be up to the monumental task of just *bouncing* back, of reconciling itself to something like attempted murder. I say, let yourself live with it for a bit. Breathe, of course." Officer Broderick gave Doug's shoulder a small squeeze. "Don't forget to breathe. Looks like you're holding your breath. You with me?"

"Yes," Doug answered. "They all saw it."

"Who? The neighbors?"

Doug nodded, casting a furtive glance in the direction of the older man and woman who had decided, much to his horror, to take *rubbernecking* to the next level by having their coffee together out on their enclosed front porch. They watched with rapt, unashamed eyes while the events slowly wound down beyond the rapid red and white spray of the four police cars' dome lights parked haphazardly out in front of the Marguerite residence. Mr. and Mrs. Grayson. He, a retired car salesman. She, a retired manicurist. They'd had Doug and Mary both over for dinner on three occasions. They'd laughed together. Finished off bottles of Pinot Grigio while playing Wii Sports on into the wee hours of night. How Doug wanted to lunge across his lawn, to throw the remains of his coffee and the mug at the screened in porch where they hunkered like rats in pajamas. *Get an eyeful, you miserable pricks? Some fucking friends—*"Mr. Marguerite, why don't

284

we step inside where it's warm."

The hint of an edge had crept into Officer Broderick's voice.

Too many ghosts on the front lawn. Too many eyes all around. Good idea.

Doug agreed, and they moved inside. Just inside, a female officer sat with a visibly shaken, weeping little girl with blonde pigtails and her favorite sunglasses crumpled into her face as she nuzzled into her comforter. Officer Broderick and the female officer exchanged a communicative glance. She whispered something into Jenny's ear, who sniffled loudly and ripped her sunglasses off her face. Jenny turned her red, sodden blue eyes to Doug. "Daddy too?"

The female officer, a pretty black woman with big, wide-set brown eyes, rubbed the little girl's shoulders. "Very soon. He'll be along. Promise."

Jenny stiffened.

Doug took a step into the living room where they were. "Honey," he said, "I'm just going to talk to the police a little while longer. Then we'll have our own talk. It's going to be all right. It's over now."

Fog shifted behind the little girl's gaze. Then, Jenny slowly lowered her little Keds down onto the hardwood floor and allowed the female officer to lead her deeper into the house, most likely to the playroom adjacent to Doug's cramped study. Officer Broderick took a seat where his colleague had been warming the sofa cushion a moment ago. Doug lowered himself down into the loveseat nearby. He set his cold coffee down on the wrought-iron end table beside him, switched on the Tiffany lamp resting there. The warming sun outside had yet to fully breach the bay window of the living room.

Officer Broderick started in; a compact computer tablet balanced across his lap. "Let's go back to the last time you spoke to Mary. Tell me about what was said."

"Well, we had our usual *disagreement* about her meds. I want you to understand something. I care about Mary. And I would always ask her if she was taking her meds regularly. That she wasn't self-medicating. It got her hackles up every time, but I wouldn't stop trying. If she ever wanted to have a normal schedule seeing our daughter like it was before, this was non-negotiable."

"And what is Mary's official diagnosis?"

"She's been to a number of doctors since she was twenty-five," Doug continued. "They all tend to lean heavily towards bipolar one. It's been a struggle for her ever since she was a teen, but she managed to really hold it at bay for a little over a decade. Regular therapy visits. Sticking to her meds. Then, there just came this sudden resistance one day. To anything chemical as a means of helping her. She wanted to get better holistically. Spiritually. And Mary's stubborn. What I always reminded her of was that it had been *while* she was on her meds that we met. That she received both her bachelor's and master's. She had even started on her Doctorate studies, but I don't know what happened with that. Another sore subject. Not to mention, she had Jenny."

"What does Mary do for a living?"

"She's a Guidance Counselor at Baldwin High School. In Comstock Township."

"Mm," Officer Broderick mused, "I know it. My cousin's son went there. A track star." He thought for a moment, fingers poised over the virtual keyboard of his tablet. "Baldwin had a spot of trouble a little while back, right? An active shooter?"

"Yes," Doug sighed, "and it really affected Mary. She called me that night. She was … slurring her words. Obviously drinking. I yelled at her because she's not supposed to mix alcohol with her pills. Mary said she had decided she was going to take a *hiatus* from her meds, and only take her Xanax as needed. Her biggest gripe about her medicine was they made her foggy. Mary said she needed to be sharp as a tack if she was going to help the students through what had happened that day with the shooter. The kids were scared. Do you want to know what *frustrating* is? Trying to convince a bipolar person their medicine has been helping them and the *fog* they're feeling is the *tranquility* their brain needs to function normally. They see it as a negative side-effect. But that's what the medicine is *supposed to do*. Slow down the spiraling thoughts and the paranoia. The delusions. Slow them down just enough that the person has enough time when they crop up to, I dunno, properly evaluate them? To judge them as useful and truthful, or unreal and harmful. I begged her to stop drinking and to get back on her meds. And that was when she said the strangest thing. The first of many."

"What's that?"

"She said she had to go because there was a deer walking across her back lawn … and it frightened her. 'It's a monster, Doug!' she said. 'Can you come and shoo it away? It's standing there, staring at me.' I live twenty miles away, and I was just putting Jenny to bed. Plus, I wasn't going to get into the habit of running to her every time she asked me to. I told her it would go away, and she said it had been standing there in the yard for hours. The same spot. Staring at her. And that it looked like a monster."

"*'Monster Deer'*," Officer Broderick repeated, entering it into his Word document. "All right, and at that point, you must have sensed she was set on a bad path."

"Yes, and it's a path I'd come to know well. In the last three years or so, I've seen her experience episodes and heal, only to jump off her meds again when the mood struck."

"Is that part of the reason you and Mary are separated?"

"It is. But I couldn't bring myself to file for divorce. I knew she'd do something drastic if I were to take that step. I kept that off the table, even though I've been seeing someone. And believe me, my concern for Mary has put a strain on this new relationship. Mary, she doesn't know about Cheryl. She can never know."

"How long ago was this call?"

"Mm, two and a half months ago, I wanna say?"

"All right," Officer Broderick nodded, scratching at his goatee. "Walk me the rest of the way. From then to this morning."

"Mary went back on her meds, mostly because she knew I wouldn't let her call to talk to Jenny if that didn't happen stat. Things kind of fell back into some semblance of normalcy. A month in this way. She said she had been having nightmares. Almost every night. I asked her what they were about. She said she dreamt the shooter, that kid Dallas Teller, made it all the way into the school and she was giving chase. He didn't turn his gun on her, just kept running. At one point, he shouted something over his shoulder at her. 'Help me kill them!' Something like 'You have to help me kill them! They need a Mother! They'll make you!' Something like that, I dunno. Just a bad dream. She even managed to explain it away with me on the phone. The therapist in her kicked in, and she translated it to mean she was feeling guilty because she felt, subconsciously, she wasn't doing enough to help those kids. The ones who had the misfortune of showing up on Dallas Teller's Kill List. I thought that was the end of it for her, and she even told me not to worry. But I don't think I've ever stopped worrying about Mary."

Silence.

Drawing his wide shoulders upward again from their slump, Doug straightened in his seat and a drew a deep breath. "I think things started to really go sideways when she told me she suspected the students from that Kill List were following her home from school each day. And she started talking about how she thought one of the English teachers at Baldwin had established some kind of underground cult with those very same kids. That this was all somehow connected to that shooter, Dallas Teller. That he had all the answers and his motives for wanting to kill those kids may have been justified somehow? I couldn't believe my ears when she said this. So, of course, I asked her the magic question. 'You taking your meds?' She flew into a rage. Cursed me out. Said it was none of my business. That she wasn't crazy. I threatened her with Jenny again. Not being allowed to have any contact with her until Mary got back on her pills. And, . dammit, *why* didn't I just go over there and see? *Why?* It must have been pride. I don't know. I should have done something. The things she started saying to me."

"What did she say that alarmed you?"

"Mary said, *Christ*, she said The Tumor Deer wasn't in her backyard anymore. That it was in her dreams now. And it told her she was going to be a mother again." Doug looked past the officer, on into the dining room where a model airplane he had built with Jenny the night before was drying on a page of newspaper atop the table. "I thought she was trying to tell me she was pregnant. I mean, *expecting*? But there'd never been any mention of her seeing someone on her end. Still, I never mentioned my girlfriend. Who's to say she wasn't? And that she wasn't pregnant? Isn't? Will you run a test? Just to be sure?"

"We will," Officer Broderick said, gruffly. He shifted in his seat and studied his tablet. "What else can you tell me?"

"The next time I heard from her, Mary was highly delusional. Extremely manic. She called me in tears, but it sounded almost like she was laughing and crying at the same time. Like her mind couldn't decide whether to be happy or sad. Mary went to visit the shooter."

"Wait, *what?*" Officer Broderick broke in. "The shooter? You mean, the Teller kid?"

Doug nodded, stiffly. "Yes. She, um, Jesus, the things she claims he told her. I feel foolish even repeating them."

"Don't. It's important."

"The kid asked her to come. He said Mary was the only one who would believe him. He told her all kinds of crazy shit, excuse my language. That the kids on his list *were* part of this English teacher's *vampire cult*, and they tried to, I dunno, enlist him as well, but he figured out what they were doing and decided to take matters into his own hands. Apparently, the kids had something planned he just couldn't let them carry out. They were … operating beyond what that English teacher had guided them through. They were listening to this-this *head vampire* they called The Father." There, Doug chewed his tongue, perhaps to stop it from talking so he could get his bearings. "Mary said the kid told her that this *cult* or *coven* or—I don't remember what word she used—they had their sights set on her."

"For what reason?"

"Well, it fits with what she told me about her dream. About being, you know. Mary said they were looking to make her the *Mother. The Mother. The Queen.*"

Officer Broderick smirked, then reddened when it was obvious he'd shown his skepticism so overtly. He cleared his throat, looked at Doug, and folded his hands over the tablet as if he'd given up keeping anymore meticulous notes. "I'm assuming you asked her if she was still foregoing her meds?"

"You better believe it, I did. And she lied. I know she did. I mean, how the hell could she have been fully medicated and still talk about these things with such conviction? Like she accepted it all at face value."

"Maybe because it involved her being a *mother* to other children? Maybe in her mind, it was like a second chance to get it right where she had come up short with Jenny. You said you weren't letting her talk to Jenny on the phone. Now, I'm no shrink, but it's possible she fully embraced this delusional thinking and maybe even fabricated a good bit of it because she wanted children, by any means."

"She told me the shooter, the Teller kid? He hemorrhaged right there in front of her at the prison. Just bled out. From all his orifices, she said."

"Yeah," Officer Broderick said. "I read about that in the paper too. Man, oh man." He drummed his fingers along the glass of the tablet, blew out a breath, and glanced across the room at nothing. "Mm … vampires, huh? I gotta say, that's a new one for me. Just when I thought I heard it all."

"Yes, well, the last thing she said to me before this morning was that she was going to *verify Teller's story,* and if it led where she thought it would, then she was going to confront the guilty parties. She said … she said it will probably cost her her job, but if it's all true, she will have saved the kids and the ones that came before them.'"

"Save them? From this *cult?*"

"Yes," Doug said, in a small voice. "I should have called you guys right then and there. Hell, long before that."

"Well now, I don't know we would have been able to do a whole hell of a lot for her other than to pick her up and three-oh-two her at the local psych unit. Standard operating procedure. Although, it doesn't sound like she was making any kind of threat against you or anyone else. Not bodily, anyhow. They would have had to let her out if testing showed she was not a threat to herself or to anyone else." Officer Broderick winced, grabbed at his goatee, smoothed it down like some modern-day Freud, and touched a finger to the tablet screen. It lit up in his lap. "That brings us to this morning. Go ahead."

Doug blurted, "Could I grab an aspirin and some water real fast before we start with that?"

"Go ahead." Officer Broderick became engrossed in his tablet, fingers ticking against the glass as he typed or revised his report.

Quietly, Doug rose and shuffled into the kitchen in his night slippers. The nook still smelled of his daughter's untouched Cheerios. Motes of dust danced in the air, and a blazing band of sunlight poured through the bay window set above the kitchen table. A glass of orange juice he'd poured for his daughter to go with her morning cereal rested on the mat at her place, the pulpy liquid now warm and less desirable than it had been before Mary came to call. Muscle memory drove Doug's movements as he located the bottle of ibuprofen in the cabinet above the stove, shook two into his hand, poured a glass of tap water, and washed them to the back of his throat. They stuck there, and he gagged on the tiny brown tablets before they finally dislodged and slid down his throat.

What to say?

I'm not innocent, and I've been telling a one-sided story so far. Every word of it is true. That's not what I'm thinking about. But I've been lying by omission, and it's the reason my head is throbbing like a sonofabitch right now. When she used to have her episodes, I was the one who whipped out my cell phone to film her while she unraveled before my eyes. My lawyer advised me to do that. It would bolster my case in the event Mary tried to challenge sole custody. It made me sick and I took no pleasure in doing it. That doesn't get me off the hook. Not in any of this. I'm culpable. I know how that sounds. I know how it seems. The fact is, I should have helped her long before this, instead of turning her out like I did. It's just like Officer Broderick said. Mary never posed any kind of threat to me or to our daughter. I tortured her in my own way. And it doesn't matter whether her stories are true, although a part of me knows Mary was medicated when these things happened. A part of me can't help but believe it all happened as she described it.

You wanna know why? I'll tell you, Doug.

289

Because you know she wanted joint custody back more than anything, and she wouldn't have let herself go off her meds. She knew what was at stake. Mary wanted to be a mother to her child again, and I should have helped her to stay strong. To overcome her illness.

What kind of husband am I?

What kind of man am I?

"The kind who has decided at the eleventh fucking hour to believe in his wife," he muttered to himself, then swallowed the rest of the water down. "The kind of husband who recognized the lucidity in his wife's eyes this morning." *The clarity, once I'd wrested the glass out of her hands and pinned her down in the grass of what was once our front yard.* It had been like a switch was thrown within her, and he'd seen it. The fog and the spiderwebs crowding her mind, muting her impulse control to such a degree she would try to stab her husband. It was like a great God-like hand had swept them away, like clearing the brambles of a thicket to expose the smooth soil beneath. *My God, I know how it sounds, but when I had her down in the grass, and I looked in her eyes, the woman I'd married and loved for as long as I can remember was staring up at me with pleading eyes of resolve. What had she said in that moment?*

Mary had wept, and she'd apologized. Not just for the early morning call and the glass shard that lay a few feet away from her stayed hand, but for all the times she'd been weak and lost sight of her duties as a mother and a wife. As the matriarch of their household. And he'd wept with her. He'd lifted her up into his arms, and he'd held her quivering body in his own. She shook like a leaf against his nightclothes. She'd also felt to him as if she hadn't eaten in months. *Literally*, a leaf in his embrace.

And she'd begged him to let her go.

To let her leave in her car, a white Optima he was sure was not her vehicle, pulled halfway up onto the front lawn, the windshield wipers whipping back and forth in a frenzy and largely at odds with the clear morning.

Mary had said, "I'm awake, Doug. And I've got to finish this. I've got to clean up this mess."

I almost didn't let her up. I nearly kept her pinned, until she swore a solemn oath to me in the dewy, damp grass that no one would come to harm. That she only meant to put things right.

"Mr. Marguerite?" Officer Broderick called to him from the living room.

"Yeah, be right there. Sorry."

So do I tell the officer I let her go? Let her drive off with this strong will and irrepressible sense of purpose shining in her eyes for the first time in a long time? Do I tell Broderick that I waited twenty minutes before I placed a call to 911, so Mary would have a head-start getting where she meant to get to? Because I believed her, and I believed in her?

Not on your life. *Christ be with me, not on your life.*

So, Doug padded back into the living room, and he lowered himself back down into the love seat. A strange sense of calm washed over him. His mouth was wet, tongue damp as opposed to the strip of sandpaper it had been up until then. They started again, and Doug told an alternate tale of what had transpired on the front lawn of his house at roughly seven-thirty that morning. Sure, the neighbors had seen a good bit of what transpired, but Doug could only pray they had missed the initial slash of the mirror shard before he'd gotten her down and splayed in the grass. He was certain they'd only come out to have a looksee once he'd already gotten the shard free of her grip. Eyewitness testimony is for shit most of the time, and Doug trusted this notion. He had to.

Just to be sure, he asked, "Will you be interviewing any of the neighbors?"

"I don't think that'll be necessary, unless of course, there's more to this than what you can remember."

"No," Doug said, "that's all there is. I just hope you can get to her and ... save her from herself. She's not a *bad* person. This isn't her fault."

Another smirk from Officer Broderick, one he did not even try to conceal. "If you say so." He paused, then asked, "And you have no idea where she might have run off to after here?"

It felt good, the fact Doug did not have to lie when he said, "No idea."

He did not. But he hoped Mary was on the way to whatever healing reckoning she needed to be at peace with herself.

Finally.

XV. A MOTHER'S SACRIFICE

The sun was a strange miracle that had burned the dew off the waving green fields surrounding The Crenshaw House. Still, the structure looked to be something of a repellant to the natural light when Mary Marguerite pulled up the long drive and put Maddie Crenshaw's white Optima into park. Its gray clapboards and dirty white trim appeared to pout despite an otherwise bright and blooming morning. Its windows disclosed little of life, their black panes shut and recalcitrant to the day. For all intents and purposes, the house looked like a great sulking monolith, but Mary knew it did not stand empty as any passerby would have falsely predicted. They stirred, and Mary felt the blight and the suffering of their existence. Much of what Mary had experienced in the last twelve hours confounded her as much as it defied truth and logic. But when she climbed out of the driver's seat and stood there staring up at the side of the house, let her mind's eye wander along the hatch work of mortar holding the brick face in place, the stinging that had tortured and ravaged her entire body before returned. The mouths, some gaping while others clicked their teeth together in admonishment or distress, hatched from the nape of her neck downward to the tautness of her hamstrings.

It was all Mary could do not to slap and claw at them as they laid siege to her torso. She turned to walk to the trunk of the vehicle, and they sent up such a gut-wrenching scream of pain and resistance, Mary had to brace herself against the side of the Optima. It was impossible to know whether it was a sound locked inside her mind or something the birds in the trees an acre out would have trembled by. Her legs buckled, and she clung to the antennae on the roof of the car. It bent in her hands but held her upright. She stifled the powerful urge to vomit, bile burning its way halfway up and down her throat. *You know why I'm here, and you know there's no other way. Let me do it! Please, let me help you all.*

The pain lessened, holding on as more of a series of pinches here and there. Manageable.

292

Averting her eyes from the quarter-sized black maws encircling her arms at the risk of losing her nerve altogether, Mary moved to the rear of the car and pressed the button on the key fob that released the trunk. The hatch clicked and slowly yawned open wide. Inside, two red gasoline containers sat nestled against the right rear wheel hub. The interior of the Optima smelled strongly of petrol. Its undercarriage had also rattled and banged the entire drive, and Mary imagined she'd torn something loose when she'd reversed the car back down off Doug's front lawn, then bumped it further down off the steep curb. It was okay. Mary's plans did not extend beyond the property. *Last stop. Have your tickets ready to be punched.* She leaned in and brought out the first can. It was filled to the brim, and some of it splashed up and out of its long nozzle to splash a rainbow stain onto the cracked blacktop of the driveway. Then, she took the other canister out of the trunk and slammed the trunk shut again. The cashier at the Sunoco had sold her the two canisters without a second thought, because there was nothing to prompt any other response. The madness was gone from her eyes. She did not look like a woman who'd just tried to cut up her estranged husband with a shard of broken mirror. No, Mary looked like a woman who'd had a long night, her t-shirt wrinkled and mussed, and jeans stained in some black substance anyone would have taken for oil. She looked like a woman whose car had broken down a mile down the road, and she had played on that scenario by parking the Optima a little way out of view of the cashier's window.

The teenager behind the register had reminded her in an instant she was a beautiful woman, the way his gaze found her breasts while he rang her up for the gas and the containers, and the way she felt his eyes on her ass as she exited the little booth, barely concealing the strain the weight of the containers in both hands put on her shoulder joints. Randomly, Mary thought of the last time a man, or a male of any age, had looked at her that way, and her memory failed her. *Has it really been that long? Or have I just been blind to it all this time, and now I'm awake to more than I imagined.*

Still, today is not the day.

Far from it.

Doug had told her he would wait to call the police to the house, leaving her time to do *whatever it was she desperately needed to accomplish*. He hadn't wanted to call at all, but the neighbors being the Nosy-Nellies she remembered them to be had left him with no choice. She'd flipped off the older couple as she left. Mary knew they'd always thought her *queer* in the way of people and company. Never liked them. Never would, now.

She knew she had a small window by which to finish this.

On her way up the walk that ran parallel to the front bay window and dead garden boasting little more than upturned earth and an orchid that had crumbled into itself while its black stake stood tall beside the ruined plant, Mary was suddenly aware of an absence inside her fractured mind. A vacuous hole where the night before an all-encompassing baritone drone had mocked her and manipulated her and ultimately sent her to kill Doug when it saw it had lost and ceded so much control back to her. The Dark Sap Man had told her Doug was his *familiar* and had taken the place of Conor Crenshaw when the teacher died. The Dark Sap Man had told her Doug had craved immortality and had agreed to sacrifice their daughter, Jenny, for the cause of controlling Mary so she would step into the role of Queen Mother of The Nine. Queen Wife to The Father.

And Mary, whose mind was already poisoned against Doug after months upon months of being at odds with him, accepted the lie as neat as you please. She'd also driven to his house with intent of cutting his throat.

But Jenny was there. Unharmed. In tears at the sight of her mother brandishing the shard at her father.

That's when Mary had felt the full extent of The Father's last, parting manipulation of her. His *consolation prize* after having lost The Nine to Mary's blood, poisoned unknowingly with a handful of antipsychotics and the Xanax she'd been popping. He'd whispered it in her ear, sending her on a direct murder path to Doug's front door.

"Stop," Mary told herself, stopping before the front door to the house. She set the canisters down and tested the entry. It groaned open like an old man climbing out of a recliner after days of languishing there. "Just stop. You're awake. Jenny was never in any danger. Doug never called you last night. And *you failed, you sonofabitch!* You hear me? What happened to you? Where'd you go, you bastard!"

Nothing.

The Dark Sap Man, if he still hunkered within the walls of the Crenshaw house, had gone silent and still.

It unnerved her, his absence.

She hated him for that as well.

Gathering up the gas containers, Mary stepped up into the darkened foyer of the little, isolated rancher.

"Hello?"

Oh dear God, is that Maddie Crenshaw?

"Is somebody there?"

The voice was faint but recognizable. Mary set down the gas cans and navigated the living room through to the kitchen, following the sound of Maddie's weakened call. She sounded breathless, like someone had their hands around her throat at that very moment, allowing just enough intake of air for the downed woman to put out her distress signal. To offer her false hope. She wheeled round the wall separating one room from the next and slowed only for a moment when her eyes snagged on the framed oil painting of The Crenshaw Family hanging askew beside the threshold. A moment was enough to call the hairs on Mary's arms to stand on end, and for the hackles to rise the back of her neck.

Conor Crenshaw sat on Matilda Crenshaw's lap. For such a small child, his posture appeared painfully erect, as if his mother controlled him with a hand up the back of his shirt. There was a vacuousness deep-set into the boy's dark eyes, and he looked vaguely catatonic. Matilda smiled thinly, the sparest of makeup dusted across her cheeks and smeared across her liver-like lips. Not a pretty woman. Matronly and imposing, at least when it came to her son. The tall, dark, and gaunt-looking man standing behind them could have been any waifish-looking and overworked tax accountant in a sleek black suit. The place where The Father's head had been was burned through, the hole's edge crisp and blackened. Mary would never know the man on sight other than the figure he presented to her in the waking nightmare her life had become. That of the Dark Sap Man.

She hurried around the corner, seeking to put distance between herself and the painting as rapidly as possible. The kitchen was dark, the air, weighted and murky. Maddie Crenshaw lay sprawled up against the dirty white door leading down into the basement. The last thing Mary had heard (*thought* she had heard) was a struggle between the woman and some unseen force that stomped its feet against the kitchen tiles before crushing Maddie's skull with one final crashing down. Mary swore she'd heard it.

Then again, I swore Doug called me while I was locked inside the basement. I swore he told me Jenny had been taken. Another ruse by a desperate entity. To bend the truth to his will.

Either way, Maddie Crenshaw jerked and twitched as she lay pulled into a tight fetal position. Signs of life.

"Mary?" Maddie begged.

Mary rushed to her side and hunkered down beside her. "I'm here, darling. We've got to get you out of here."

"Y-you … abandoned me."

"I thought he killed you. But I was going to come back for you, regardless. The Father … he deceived me."

"The … *Father?*"

"Conor's long-lost patriarch. Come back from the Boot after all this time."

"Conor's father died … when he was a little boy."

"They ever find a body?"

Maddie's silence answered the question. She shuddered, pulled her legs further into the crook of her ribs. She cried out. "He's—he's gone. But he bound me. I'm locked in this position. Can't get up."

"Of course, he's gone," Mary said, and curled her arms around Maddie's bent knees. "An absentee father, through and through. But that's good for us. You've got to concentrate while I pull on your legs. I'm going to help you to extend them."

"Nonononono-I tried that! Don't-don't-*don't!*"

"What do you mean?"

"I-I-I mean I tried to move out of this position and I felt my bones breaking."

"Oh God."

"There's someone upstairs," Maddie said, baring her teeth against the pain just Mary's slight touch had elicited from the fragile bones and tendons. "People. People upstairs. All night. I've had to listen to them. Crawling around. I hear them above my head. Suffering."

"I know," Mary said. "Conor's students. The Nine. They're poisoned. They're dying." Her mind had become awash in a flurry of ideas for helping Maddie to her feet. All promised to end in failure. Maddie would end up in traction, her back snapped like a tree branch under a heavy boot. *But he's gone. How can he still wield such a hold on her? There's got to be a way to shatter the spell!*

Yet, residue of The Father's presence remained. In the death room upstairs. *And my flesh.*

The mouths.

"Not yet," Mary muttered. "I'm coming to that."

"What?" Maddie asked, her voice tremulous.

"Nothing, honey. Listen. I think there might be a way to, I dunno, to *weaken* The Father's hold on you."

"H-how?"

Mary did not want to say it out loud. She knew Maddie would not approve. Hell, Mary felt sick just considering such a thing, but it added up in her mind. It was perfect cause-and-effect, as she saw it. If it wasn't, Mary would hold the knowledge of what she was about to do inside until her dying day. Maddie would never know, and if it worked to free her of the invisible shackles that held her painfully in place, then—

No. I can't say it's necessary. I can't even think it!

There was only action.

The preconceived notion of it made Mary want to kill herself.

"Lie still," she told Maddie. "I'll be right back. Then, we're going to get you out of here. One way or another." *Oh no, oh fuck!* "Oh Maddie, do you know what happened to the stake I brought in last night?"

Maddie's nostrils flared, and a deep crease formed between her eyes. "The stake?"

"Yes, where is it? I need it!"

"For what?"

I can't—

Mary stood and paced around the room, searching the grimy tiles for the item. "I dropped it. Did you see it? Is it in here?"

"What are you going to do, Mary?"

"Maddie, *please just tell me where the hell it is!*"

"Oh no, you can't do that! *I don't want you to do that!*"

"I have to try! I have to move you!"

"Why? Why do you have to move me?"

"There!"

The wooden stake lay under the kitchen table, a pale bone gleaming in the terrible lowlight. Mary crawled underneath and seized it like a good dog. She could not bring herself to look at Maddie, so she exited the kitchen with the woman begging and admonishing Mary in her wake, a shrill serpent of tears and pleadings that trailed her all the way to the front door, where she grabbed up one of the gas canisters and made her precarious way up the stairs.

Maddie's laments rang out, a living thing that walked the rooms of the Crenshaw house in a broken studder of words.

"they're children! somebody's babies! Can't—can't—murder!"

All the doors along the second-floor hallway were closed to her, but one. It lay at the end of the corridor to her right, a trail of something black and bubbling leading up to the room itself. The smell suggested long-rotting carrion having been dragged along the flattened, beige rug. Mary stooped to examine it, thought of touching it, and then begged off. The bubbles popped and heaved, breathing or swelling. One of the two. Both? It was best to keep moving, her motivation already was sagging within at the sight of the respiring substance on the floor before her. She dared not tread in it and was forced to bow her legs out on either side of the trail. The sides of her black Converse grazing against the paneling, she took awkward, widened strides down the hall.

The room was quiet and unsettling, the gaping door a black rectangle disclosing nothing of its contents. It was impossible *they* would have somehow crawled their way out of the Crenshaw house. Mary imagined having pulled up out front and finding the wasted, dying teens scattered across the dead front lawn like dormant, starving alligators. But Maddie would have heard them. According to her, the dying vampires above her head had carried on with their slow and agonizing death throes for much of the night.

A groan, gravelly but decidedly female, flared inside the room. It began as a low rumbling and climbed to a trebly whine that lifted at the end, as if the being were asking a question of Mary. It made Mary's hands tremble and her heart thrum loudly between her ears.

As Mary came upon the opened door, one rough-hewn moan blossomed into a terrifying barrage of male and female moans, lifting at the end of their lamentations. Questioning Mary in the same incoherent, primal tone that frightened her to the very marrow.

Stalled outside the door, the stake banging against her side absently and the gas can pulling on her shoulder, Mary thought she understood one of them. An audible needle in the haystack.

"aaaaaa … thuurrrrrrr?"

Sounds like Father? *They're calling to him. He abandoned them.*

Father. I know it. That's what they're saying

Then, she heard the belabored *M* sound from one of them.

Oh God. Dear God.

Mother.

They're calling to me.

Questioning me.

It was time to go to them.

The smell of rotten cabbage wafted up with her first step beneath the threshold. Somehow, the room had contained the crippling odor, holding onto it for release at her approach. Mary felt the quick bilge of vomit gather in her mouth. It doubled her over, and she spilled the acidic contents of her stomach all over the floor before her. When the floor moved, her upchuck having splashed across the back of one of them, Mary shrieked. The one she'd gotten sick all over grabbed for her leg, locked its thin, sinewy, pale fingers around her ankle. Strong as a shackle. Still, Mary tried to shake the limb free. White, bloodshot eyes shone in the darkness at her feet. "*Maaaaaaaaaaaa th-th-thurrrrrrrrrrr?*" Its face had shrunken into itself and blackened to such a degree the mouth within its ruin looked like a decaying eggplant splitting open.

Suddenly, what looked like a thousand eyes surfaced in the darkness within. Dreadful beacons to lead her to her own demise. To suffer alongside her *children*.

Voices clambering over one another in a mad cacophony. Mouths pitched to the ceiling and opened to expel the whining question. Now an eternal doom on their lips.

"*Maaaaaa th-th-th-thurrrrrrrrrr—*"

"STOP IT!" Mary screamed.

The hand around her ankle disappeared. The blood flowed once more into her foot.

They did not cease. Could not stop.

Things shifted in the murk.

Where is the goddam light in here?

Mary fumbled along the wall beside her for a light switch. Her fingers clumsily clawed at a fixture, and she flipped the switch up.

Nothing. Her eyes had begun to adjust, much to her dismay.

The faint outline of a window across the cramped space revealed a pan that had been almost completely covered over.

Just as soon as the previous claw had left her ankle, two pairs more took its place and seized Mary. Pulled her further into the room.

The gas can slipped from her grasp as she struggled to bat and swat and strike at the seemingly disembodied hands. The strong, pungent odor of petrol filled the room. The gas emptied out, the nozzle producing a *glopping* sound as the fuel saturated first the floorboards and then the things skittering about along top of them.

The mess of bodies obstructed her forward motion. They felt like logs dumped haphazardly about, thumping against her shin as the disembodied hands yanked her deeper within. Mary felt her mind turning inside out. Incapable of a rational thought she could seize upon. It was white noise inside her skull. Broken neurons. Shattered receptors. The white eyes and mewling mouths of the blackened, compressed eggplant faces seemed to swallow her up. Her memory must have tried to grant her some quick, fleeting reprieve from the horrors surrounding her, for Mary did not come to realize she'd come all the way in and the door to the room had shut until her internal recorder started running again.

Something sighed behind her.

Hot, rank breath bloomed against the side of her neck.

"*Maaaaahr ... greeeeeeeeet?*"

If not for the blonde ponytail erupting out of the top of her shrunken head, Mary would not have recognized Delaney Lindberg, once on her way to being Valedictorian of her graduating class and now counted amongst the undead. The line of spare light coming through the window cast a thin, ethereal white strip across the center of her face. Delaney stared at her with a squashed, blackened face that looked like someone had walloped her where her nose had once been with a strong and true sledgehammer swing. Her white eyes were unblinking beams holding Mary in their tractor beam of terror. *And she said my name. Marguerite.*

She can still remember?

"Delaney?" Mary asked in a tremulous voice.

The thing that had been Delaney Lindberg fell silent. Went still.

White staring eyes

Then, without warning, the teen girl let out a wild, haranguing scream like a banshee that did not break and seemed to carry on forever.

I'm losing my mind. Losing my mind. Losing my mind.

Mary witnessed a blur of motion, then felt the hands around her throat now. Throat and ankles.

Wrapped in a fog of disorientation, Mary raised the stake.

Teeth grazed the nape of her neck, tenderizing the supple flesh.

Mary brought the stake around behind the girl, gripped it at its furthest end, and drove it home between Delaney Lindberg's angel wings.

Then, it was Mary's turn to scream. This set off a chain reaction of nerve-jangling cries from the things slithering about on the floorboards.

The young girl slashed a deep gouge down Mary's face, scrabbling for some purchase as she folded over with the stake jutting out of her back. Before Mary knew what she was doing, she dove and wrapped her hands around the stake. Hyperventilating, she pulled at it, trying to free it. "I'm sorry-I'm sorry-I'm sorry-I'm sorry!" The thing that had once been Delaney Lindberg gurgled and spat black blood out that flew back in her face as Mary worked at trying to remove the implement of death from between the narrow slats of her ribcage where it had become lodged.

Hands slid up underneath her shirt. They slipped around her midsection. The long talons that had shot out of the fingernails raked her breasts.

By degrees, the coven of the abandoned brought Mary down lower and lower until they had formed a veritable webwork of undead teenagers overtop of her straining, struggling form.

One of them tried to pin her right arm back. Mary swung her elbow blindly in the dark and felt it connect brutally with something thick and immoveable.

In that instant, she fished her hand down into her jeans pocket.

Found the Bic lighter just as the mouths formed once more within her flesh and began snapping their jaws, not in defense of their bearer, but in the sheer delight of having been reunited with their physical beings.

The children began to cackle in unison, like a room full of smartass students.

XVI. BURN

Maddie Crenshaw listened to the stomping above her head and felt her heart sink. What she was hearing was the sound of the coven overpowering Mary, her last hope of ever regaining the use of her arms and legs again. Visions of some cannibalistic orgy both surprised and horrified her in the same instant, and she fought to vanquish them from her frantic stream of consciousness. But everything she'd ever known or learned of things to fear in the world returned to roost within her fractured mind. To torment her as she lay there on the filthy, stinking tiles of her dead mother-in-law's home on a hill. Maddie had nothing to occupy herself or to aid in shutting out the nightmarish sounds of defeat raining down on the floorboards overhead, and there was only the will to stuff down the terrors that seized her by the brain stem and flooded her brain pan like a swampy soup.

When her thoughts turned to memories of Tilly Crenshaw, Maddie fought harder than ever. Her mind had taken control of itself and rendered her a helpless, hapless prisoner locked within the confines of her own dark imagination. She had no idea the mere thought of the old, scheming, and decrepit woman who'd raised her son up to be a monster who preys on trusting children would conjure Tilly Crenshaw before Maddie's very eyes until the woman was standing over her.

Stooping over Maddie. Head tilted slightly, like the *Vampire Maker* was making a study of Maddie's incapacitation. Her helplessness. Her submission to darker things of the earth.

"You *fucking bitch!*" Maddie cried, and spit in Tilly's face. The saliva came back down, landing cruelly along her left cheek. "They didn't bury you deep enough!"

"You know, He gave both of us the screws." A wry, shockingly regretful smile spread the old woman's wrinkled lips apart.

Breathlessly, Maddie strained to try and raise herself up in some way. The rare, putrid stench of sulfur coming off the old woman was all-consuming, but

Maddie could not let that stop her. She would not surrender this moment by which she could curse the woman who'd laid ruin to her life and sought to leave her a dead cripple inside a House of Horrors. *This can't be how it ends!*

Upstairs, the sound of a teenage girl screaming stopped Maddie cold. She'd been rustling about like a paraplegic.

Tilly's low-lit face floating above Maddie shook from side to side. Soft flames of irony and remorse flickered behind the old woman's cataracted eyeballs. In a craggy voice, she said, "He left you here to rot. And he left me to starve under six feet of dirt. I did everything he asked me to do. I turned all those kids for him. One after t'other. It left me weak. Used-up. Like a pair of saggy tits once baby after baby had sucked em' drier than *dry*. He let you bury me alive. And then? *Then,* the sonofabitch tries to trade me out for another *Queen Mother.* Younger. Prettier. Desperate for a family of her own." Tilly sucked her cracked, twisted teeth with a thin sliver of tongue. "My husband— a cruel, *cruel* sonofabitch. And he won't stop. This ain't the end of him. But it is for us. You wanna know why?"

"Fucking pig! Fuck you!"

Tilly prattled on, as if she hadn't heard. "Because all that matters to The Father is preservation of the species. Conservation of the Red. And a never-ending supply of blood. You? Me? My baby, Conor? Did you know his own father sent those men to the bar to attack him? His own *father!?*" Fury locked the old woman up, her mouth a rictus line. She gasped. "We were all nothing more'n steppingstones to help The Father get to the other side. Where His utopia lies. Rivers of blood. Bodies piled to the sky. And a family to feed with. Younger. Stronger. So … you might wanna turn that hatred and your potty mouth aside because you always thought you were better'n me. Look at you now! Look at *us!* We. Are. The. Same. *Suckers.*"

The sheer force Maddie exerted and channeled into her right arm as she swung it upward at the old woman's face brought her full off the tiles. Tilly Crenshaw vanished into the ether just as quickly as she'd materialized. Still, Maddie wasn't expecting the follow-through of her own arm. The limb had been dead and useless, curled up into her belly a moment before. Something had happened upstairs. Mary had been right. *That means she had to kill one of the children! For me! So I could be free?* It was freedom, a bittersweet release. Maddie feared trying to engage her legs. The last time she'd actually tried to extend them away from her belly, the pain that shot up her spine had been exquisite, and she'd blacked out from it. Maddie knew she had to try, and she did.

Both legs unfolded across the filthy, stinking tiles.

Tears of joy leapt from Maddie's eyes and wet her cheeks as she grabbed for the doorknob of the basement door and hauled herself up into what was, at first, an unsteady, drunken standstill.

As she rounded the corner into the short hallway that led into the downstairs foyer, Maddie smelled the smoke. She heard the raucous cries of torment and smelled the burning and disintegration of flesh as noxious flames claimed every scrap within reach of its lapping tongues. She thought she'd smelled gasoline in the air. But the evidence of immolation ravaging the things in the room above the kitchen could not be denied. *Oh no, Mary! What has she done?*

Maddie moved around the crooked banister. She called up the flight of steps in a weakened voice. "*Mary! Mary! I'm coming! Just hold on!*" Smoke descended the stairwell in a roiling, boiling cloud. The entire upstairs landing had become obscured by the thick fumes that walked across, to and fro, like a dream of frantic souls. Maddie held fast to the rickety railing and ascended the stairs. Her lungs started burning like she'd deepthroated a burning lance, and she had no choice but to clap a hand over her nose and mouth while balancing herself precariously as she moved slowly up the risers. One by one. Her airways constricted with every upward step, and Maddie's eyes watered over. Her cheeks stung. *Just a little bit further. You can't leave her. You can't!*

The smoke cloud enveloped her, unfurling all around her. Closing her in. Panic pressed at her temples, and her heart threw itself repeatedly at the slats of her ribcage like a caged bird.

Can't. Leave. Her.

Two steps below the landing, Maddie caught sight of the room at the end of the hallway to her right. Angry amber flames filled the doorway, dancing psychopathically along the threshold like a beast contained but soon to breach its confines.

"OH, DEAR GOD!"

In between the drifts of smoke laying a serpentine trail down the hall, Maddie caught sight of movement on the ground. Twitching. Eyes set aflame and mouths opened only to expel the fire crowding up against broiling lips. Burning heads with flesh falling away from black bone. Flaming hands and skeletal arms grabbing haplessly for the ceiling, which looked more like a torched parchment than whitewashed surface.

There was little time to mourn Mary Marguerite. Maddie could only acknowledge it in that instant before the will to escape and to survive the conflagration took center stage and turned her about face. She fled gracelessly back down the stairwell, taking them two at a time and nearly twisting her ankle in the process. Her Reeboks came down hard on the linoleum of the foyer floor.

Lunging for the front door, which stood wide open into a painfully ironic sunshine that fell upon the grassy plains beyond, Maddie had the woman's name on her lips. Like a prayer she knew by heart. *Mary-Mary-Mary-oh-Mary-*

Bounding down off the porch, Maddie Crenshaw nearly tread on the downed deer lying on its side just outside.

The animal was covered in big black growths that looked like either sores or tumors. Some of them had split open, and a black, viscous liquid poured out of them. It's middle rose and fell, hitching occasionally. Maddie side-stepped the deer, backed away from it. The deer stiffly moved its neck, angled its head around. Its eyes seized upon Maddie. Found her widened eyes.

Her hand clamped over her mouth, Maddie stared in disbelief at the animal lying a little ways from her on the cement walkway.

"I'm … I'm sorry," she said, spare adrenaline still jumping in her muscles and spinning her thoughts into an incomprehensible jumble. "I-I can't help you. I have to— I have to go. I'm so *sorry*."

A voice bloomed inside her mind, opening like a flower long wilted.

So soon?

"I can't—*can't stay.*"

Stay with me. Stay with me. Stay with me.

An upstairs window blew out. Then another.

Stay.

Before Maddie knew what she was doing, she lowered herself down in the grass. She lay down all the way, facing the deer as she lounged. Sleep beckoned to her like a long-lost lover, and she felt her eyelids gaining weight. "I could- I swear I could just die. Right here. Just stop living. There's nothing left for me."

Take me into the woods. It's just a little way over there. We can die together.

"I'm weak. I'm so weak."

Drag me. It's only a little way over there.

"Why?"

The deer shuddered. Its little tail lifted and fell.

Death is only a chapter in your book. If you choose it.

"What are you?"

The forest. All will be revealed. Madison.

Maddie Crenshaw felt fatigue like a palpable force pressing her down into the grass, but she fought, and she rose. She stood, swaying like a topsail in the wind that had kicked up across the fields. She started for the deer. In a dream, she watched herself from high above. Watched herself take The Tumor Deer by its front legs and start to drag it towards the dense, confounding perimeter of the forest fifty paces north of the Crenshaw House of Horrors.

December 15th, 2019-April 3, 2020
Bensalem, Pennsylvania

ABOUT THE AUTHOR

Peter Molnar is an author, singer-songwriter, musician, educator, and editor. His short stories have appeared in "City Slab: Urban Tales of the Grotesque", "Necrotic Shorts", Hydrophobia: A Charity Anthology to Benefit Hurricane Harvey Victims, and the upcoming Tenebrous Tales Anthology. His blog, "As the Shadow Stirs", is a mashup of music, movies, horror, and superheroes and can be found on his home web page. *Broken Birds* is his debut novel. He lives and works in Southeastern Pennsylvania with his wife, daughter, and two cats. Visit Peter at the following sites:

www.petermolnarauthor.com
www.facebook.petermolnarauthor.com
www.PMolnarAuthor/twitter
www.instagram.com/pmolnar423